In Love with George Eliot

In Love
with
George
Eliot

A NOVEL

KATHY
O'SHAUGHNESSY

SCRIBE
Melbourne • London

Scribe Publications
2 John St, Clerkenwell, London, WC1N 2ES, United Kingdom
18–20 Edward St, Brunswick, Victoria 3056, Australia

Published by Scribe in 2019
Reprinted 2019

Typeset in Garamond Premier by the publishers.

Printed and bound in the UK by CPI Group (UK) Ltd, Croydon
CR0 4YY

Scribe Publications is committed to the sustainable use of natural
resources and the use of paper products made responsibly from those
resources.

9781912854042 (UK edition)
9781925849103 (Australian edition)
9781925693843 (e-book)

Catalogue records for this book are available from the National
Library of Australia and the British Library.

scribepublications.co.uk
scribepublications.com.au

For William,
Patrick, Tom, and Beatrice

What shall I be without my Father? It will seem as if a part of my moral nature were gone. I had a horrid vision of myself last night becoming earthly sensual and devilish for want of that purifying restraining influence.

Marian Evans, *Letters*, 1, 284

I say, Philo! how is it that most people's lives somehow don't seem to come to much?

Edith Simcox, *Episodes in the Lives of Men, Women and Lovers*

Prologue

Prologue

1

The train had shuddered to a halt. Clatter of doors opening and shutting, noise echoing in the huge vault of Euston station, a smell of oil-flavoured steam and soot. A last door opens, and a woman neither young nor old, slightly round-shouldered, descends to the platform. She looks round, possibly she is short-sighted; a tall man walks towards her. Everything about his stride and the way he greets her suggests a contrasting certainty and vigour.

A minute later, they are in a hansom. 'I have looked forward to this,' says John Chapman, as it jolts along. 'With you at my side, it will be the best of its kind.'

The pale and plain-faced woman, who's been looking down as if preoccupied, while her left hand surreptitiously sets her collar straight, murmurs, 'Kind of you to say so.'

He gives easy voice to his emotion, she thinks, in the way of the beautiful. Another country. But still — the proximity to him — they are sitting opposite each other, and the cab is so small their knees are practically touching. And she is aware, each time she encounters his glance, of him looking at her, with the keenest interest. Yes, this is why we live, she thinks, with a sort of joyous sigh, an inner trembling and sensation of release. Suddenly she is smiling, as she sees the sights, hears the cries, the thundering rattle of wheels, the indescribably varied din of the city. Then they are turning in to the Strand, where the newspapers have their offices, lit all night. This is the path, she knows, from the City to the nexus of power, Parliament. They draw to a halt at No. 142.

The year is 1851, the day is January 8. London is the capital of the empire, a centre not just of power, but of ideas: education, women's rights, positivism, atheism, evolution, workhouses, prostitution, to name a few.

Marian Evans is shown to her room, down a long corridor, overlooking the Thames. The window is small; the room is small too. In the diminutive grate is a fire, giving little heat. Sitting on the bed, the excitement of the journey is fading, her naturally depressive tendency is asserting itself. So, this is the beginning. She is come from Coventry to make her way in London. John Chapman is hoping to be the next publisher and editor of the *Westminster Review*, but he has not bought it yet. She will help him, but her exact role is unclear.

Marian's spirits revive later in the day when tea is taken in the drawing room. She has washed her hands and face, tidied her hair. Her reflection — one look is enough.

She is seated, as the newcomer, nearest to the fire. It's a biting cold January afternoon, already dark outside. The oil and gas lamps have been lit, and on sideboards and small tables there are more lamps than she would have thought possible in one room. Mrs Chapman is fourteen years older than Mr Chapman, and it is rumoured that he married her for her money; there are rumours, too, that she might help finance the *Westminster Review*. They have three children. Mrs Chapman says, without even the appearance of sincerity, that she's privileged to have Marian to stay. 'Thank you ma'am,' replies Marian, her own mood peculiarly restoring as she registers Mrs Chapman's sourness.

The door opens, and Miss Tilley, the governess who also helps with housekeeping, enters the room. She didn't know tea was being taken, she says, as she seats herself. Mrs Chapman doesn't glance in Miss Tilley's direction. Marian is now a spectator. The two women form a contrast. Susanna Chapman has a tiny cap perched on the top of her large chignon. Her face resembles a floury milk-pudding, mouth downturning, and she blinks constantly. Miss Tilley is wearing a snug-fitting bodice, tight-waisted above a flowing maroon skirt. Her front ringlets sit as if glued to her forehead above her small, strangely perfect — like a cat's — nose.

Mrs Chapman [looking straight ahead of her]: Did you speak to Mr Hodgson and Mr Janis?

Miss Tilley [also looking straight ahead of her]: I did.

Mrs Chapman: And Cook?

Miss Tilley: She is clear about supper plans.

Now Chapman speaks. 'Great heavens — my dear Miss Evans,' — he briskly exits the room, returning with the *Westminster Review*, which he gives to Marian. 'It bears the first piece by your hand.'

Impossible to suppress the bright wave of pride and pleasure filling her. She is aware of two pairs of female eyes watching her.

'It is a long book, surely,' — Mrs Chapman.

Miss Tilley, regarding her, finally bursts out with: 'What is it, Miss Evans?'

'I wrote a review of Mackay's book, *The Progress of the Intellect*.'

'It is a long book, I am sure.'

'It is an anti-Christian book?' asks the governess.

'That would be a simplification,' says Marian, in her musical, low, cultivated voice. She hesitates before adding: 'I tried to argue that if we cannot still learn from earlier ways of thought, our way forward must be the more circumscribed.'

Total silence has fallen. Miss Tilley and Mrs Chapman are staring at her.

'Quite so,' puts in John Chapman, quickly. 'Miss Evans argues that erudition on its own can be mere sterility.'

'Not exactly,' smiles Marian. (Either he hasn't been listening, or he has the fuzziest of intellects.) 'I said — I think I said — there is always a place for erudition and knowledge of the past, but alone they won't suffice. But this is very dry matter for the present company,' — introducing a note of humility, she bows her head.

'You're right, as ever, Miss Evans — Miss Evans here has such remarkable clarity of outlook, and compass — I am not fearful, with her support, of failing with the *Review*. I can say that quite confidently. Eh, Mrs Chapman? Good news, my dear, eh?'

'Doubtless,' said Mrs Chapman, looking ahead of her now, one eyebrow slanting in a wild new direction.

Marian is murmuring about flattery when Miss Tilley gets up from her seat, scarlet-faced, and leaves the room.

Chapman soon takes Marian with him to Hunt's to rent a piano for her — eastwards, to the City. On the way, he asks what she thinks of the romantic scenes in Eliza Linton's novel, *Realities*, which he, as London's most radical publisher, has promised to print. 'I have doubts about the moral tone of certain scenes of intimacy. Do you concur?'

'Most certainly.'

'In my view, such passages are intended to excite nothing less than the sensual nature of the reader.'

Marian wants to see his face in the gloom of the cab as he says these words. She just manages to catch his expression of solemnity.

They enter the piano shop. 'Your choice,' he says, turning to look, from his height, with fearful Byronic intensity, into her eyes, as they stand in the back room with its low ceiling, its array of uprights and grands, wood gleaming in the scattered pools of light. There is the smell of beeswax.

'This is too kind,' she says in an undertone, choosing the small Blüthner for its sweetness of tone, and because the keys are not resistant, which will make it easier to play.

Later that day five men take it up to Marian's room. Alone, Marian begins playing Mozart's Mass in D minor. Soon the door opens, as she secretly expected it might; Chapman, tall, hair tousled, with a troubled, fascinated look on his face, moves to sit on the chair. Now Marian plays with special feeling. To have Chapman close by, that dynamic, extraordinarily handsome presence — he is listening to the music, and to the expression she is putting into the music. She is exhibiting her sensibility, of which she has no doubt.

In the following days he comes often to listen to her play, spending long hours alone with Marian in her room.

A week later a grand piano is delivered to the drawing room. Duets and singing can now take place there, in public. 'And I hope very much,' says Mrs Susanna Chapman, 'that you, Miss Evans, will play for us also.'

The message is clear.

Three days later, walking in St James's Park, Chapman murmurs to Marian: 'It is a privilege having you in the house, with your — mind — learning — so close to hand. Your knowledge of German —'

His hand steals into hers.

'I can teach you, if you like.'

'Could you? Could you really?'

The next day, Chapman spends two hours studying German with Marian in her room (she has translated the radical German text, *Das Leben Jesu* by Strauss, into English). Three days after that Elisabeth Tilley, the governess, declares she wants to learn German, too.

* * *

'Yes ... it's true ... it's true ... Elis — Miss Tilley — is my mistress — God forgive me. But mentally — you understand — it's a desert — To be in your company — feel the effects — your understanding — humour — incomparable ...' — his voice trails off as his mouth finds her mouth.

He's kissing her; the smell of tobacco — his hands are beginning to move, over, in, under.

'Wait —' she says, gently pushing him away, and catching her breath. She bends her head to listen intently.

'They're out!' he says, desperately. 'What's the matter?'

'The servants —'

She has an idea that Alice, who had been looking at her coldly at breakfast today and the day before, is reporting to either Mrs Chapman or Miss Tilley.

They are breathing heavily. Marian has a pleasant feeling of her neck and cheeks being flushed, of life being underway.

'You don't understand,' he says, in an urgent undertone. 'My soul is in a state of deprivation — to be able to talk, to be understood, as you understand me; to talk about more than the mundane — is like being given food when you are hungry.'

He is passionate, and his conviction feels sincere. In fact, she feels a spark of pity for him. He has the dynamism of a dog kept on a too-constraining leash; a sort of pent-up vigour and hunger. He is the publisher of radical books in

London: the downstairs floor of the house is dedicated to this enterprise; he hosts weekly literary parties. Like Marian, he hasn't been to university, he has educated himself — and his ambition, to create a forum for new ideas, is all of a piece with his personal dynamism. But each time they talk, she is aware of his effortful formulations, that then lead him into an intellectual tangle. Whereas she, by marshalling her mind, as with a scalpel, can simply cut these interfering threads, and the thought, the important thought, can be seen. She knows this, he knows this.

He is pulling her to him.

'Dear Mr Chapman,' she whispers.

'John. John.'

'Dear — John,' — the stairs creak; they break away.

He stands close against the wall; they wait in the darkness. Before he leaves the room, where they have spent fifteen minutes kissing, he takes her wrist. 'It was the right decision — *Realities* — it was right not to publish it,' he says, hoarse with a combination of excitement at his new bond with this lodger who will also be his helpmate, and fear of the two other reigning women in the house. 'I hope you agree —'

★ ★ ★

On January 18, it is the servants' day off. By ten in the morning, Mrs Chapman and the children have left for Brighton. By two-thirty, Miss Tilley has gone to visit her sister in Greenwich. The house is strangely silent. Marian is in her room, aware of the silence as of another person. She can hear the clock ticking. Footsteps, a knock on the door, and Chapman enters. 'I can be with you now,' is all he says, drawing off his gloves, putting his coat on the chair, but his look tells her everything. He loves her. He has been suffering from the mental chasm that exists between himself and the other, hopelessly uneducated women of the house. He draws the curtain, they kiss, he draws her to the bed, they kiss more, move down —

2

John Chapman kept Pepys-like diaries, detailing his hopes, his humiliating sense of failure, his confused sexual relations with women. At his death they disappeared. But in 1913, in Nottingham, they turned up on a small book stall. From there they made their way to Yale, and now the first volume is on temporary loan to the British Library, which is where I sit, with my colleague, Ann.

There's a slight awkwardness as we sit there. A growing damp patch has appeared on Ann's chest, on my right — where her left nipple is, to be precise — and I am shifting my eyes to try to stop noticing it.

Ann Leavitt is my new colleague at QEC, Queen Elizabeth College. She has just joined the literature department, along with her husband, Hans Meyerschwitz. He is the one we actually wanted, but he wasn't going to come unless she came too. It can be tricky being the lesser half of a spousal hire, but it must be a good move for them; they live in Finsbury Park, and previously were commuting outside London.

I don't know Ann well, but I'd like to. I'm moving to Finsbury Park myself; we're organising the conference on Eliot together this summer; and we're both writing books about her. Ann's book is a critique of Eliot's feminism, which sounds quite political. Mine is a novel, but a novel based on fact — biography, letters, diaries.

Still, there are certain things we can never quite know.

Chapman uses his diary, for instance, to record his private life. He notes with a small number each time he has sex with Miss Tilley (whom he calls *E*.

in his diary), and with a cross when Miss Tilley is menstruating. And Marian, too, finds her way into this coded account, when Chapman writes *M. P.M.* on January 18, and *M. A.M.* on January 19 — both of which references were later erased.

'It's likely she slept with him, but it's not certain,' concludes Ann, with a sigh.

I agree. Saying I won't be a moment, I slide the diary gently to my part of the desk, and start photographing pages with my phone.

'Kate — why are you doing that?' whispers Ann, with an uncertain smile.

I murmur the word 'evidence'. I haven't yet told Ann I'm writing a novel.

★ ★ ★

By five o'clock, Ann has left. Alone, I freely weigh the diary in my hand, and feel a kind of exultation in being alone with it, too. I want to tell Marian's story as accurately as possible, and just now this diary seems to take me into the past, as if it has magical properties. Chapman's words, the faded ink, the crossings out and cut pages, the dusty, old-paper smell of it bring me to a bona fide glimpse of George Eliot, or Marian Evans, as the story unfolds of Chapman and the three women, all rivals for his affection. The words tell of the high, riding feelings of attraction, jealousy, indecision, possessiveness, fear that played themselves out at No.142 Strand in that spring of 1851.

In fact the overall impression given by the diary is of four puppets pulled in different directions by their desires and dreams, all negotiated within those walls; with Chapman the cause of the scenario, victim and hero of it, and secret director of it, too.

On February 18, Chapman writes that wife and mistress (*S.* and *E.*), previously rivals, are now plotting together, comparing notes *on the subject of my intimacy with Marian (M.),* and have concluded

that we are completely in love with each other. E. being intensely jealous herself said all she could to cause S. to look from the same point of view, which a little incident (her finding me with my hand in M.'s) had quite prepared her for.

So Marian had been caught holding Chapman's hand in her bedroom.

Over the next month, Marian became so unpopular with the other women, she had to leave. Chapman took her to the station. Before she boarded the train, *she pressed me for some intimation of the state of my feelings. — I told her that I felt great affection for her, but that I loved E. and S. also, though each in a different way. At this avowal she burst into tears.*

There it is: George Eliot's first London adventure — disastrous.

As I read the diary in the yellow library light, I can imagine how it felt — the balloon popping. Marian sobbing; aghast at herself for weeping in public, yet relieved at venting the tension that has been mounting all these weeks. All her ideas of a future life with Chapman have collapsed. The dance is revealed to have been only a dance, antics that belong in a farce. Her hazy dreams of a grand future in London feel further away than ever.

3

Marian returned to Chapman's house six months after she was booted out, to help launch the *Westminster Review*. This time, Chapman didn't visit her room. She went on to fall in love again, eventually with George Henry Lewes. And it was this relationship, the main relationship of her life, that tipped her into the scandal for which she was first famous.

Lewes was called the ugliest man in London, and when she first met him, Marian didn't like him much — but then she often didn't like people on first meeting. One day, she went to see a production of Shakespeare's *Merry Wives* in Lewes' company. The production was bad, but with Lewes joking and mimicking all the way, it became hilariously bad. Marian began to laugh and find him charming.

George Lewes was writing for the *Westminster Review*, and he quite often dropped by to chat with this unusually clever, thoughtful woman. Marian knew by hearsay of his situation: that his wife Agnes had for years been having an affair with his best friend, Thornton Hunt. Recently Agnes had had children by Hunt, too, and Lewes now lived separately from her. As Marian began to see more of him, he began to confide in her about his unhappiness. She found him a serious thinker, and kind, too. He even let his wife's illegitimate children by his best friend have his own name, so they wouldn't be stigmatised.

Marian moved out of No. 142 Strand and took lodgings, so she could see Lewes in private. They fell deeper in love. They wanted to marry — but because he'd let Agnes' children by Hunt bear his name, he had 'condoned' the adultery, and was legally unable to obtain a divorce.

And now Marian is in a dilemma. The custom in Victorian England is to have affairs discreetly, but Marian wants to be open. They're both atheist, they wrestle with the problem. Finally, they decide — they'll do it, she will live openly with this married man. They'll live together in Europe, then England.

It's a momentous step. If she goes ahead, Marian will no longer be received socially. Women will fear to visit her. No one will bother to understand the facts as they are, see the situation 'in the round'. She is so secretive about her intention she doesn't even tell her long-time confidantes, Sara and Cara.

In front of me is Marian's diary. I turn the pages until I get to July 1854. There it is, in her own words, the summer evening when she changes her life. She describes taking a hansom cab in London to St Katherine's Wharf; boarding the steamer, The Ravensbourne; waiting in terror for George Lewes — until at last she sees 'G's' *welcome face* over the porter's shoulder. They spend the whole night on deck. They are both astonished at what they've done; there will be no going back — word will spread quickly. But as the night goes on, they begin to lose their fear. They are moving down the silent river. They too have become quiet, elation has taken them over.

The sunset was lovely, writes Marian, *but still lovelier the dawn as we were passing up the Scheldt between 2 and 3 in the morning. The crescent moon, the stars, the first faint blush of the dawn, reflected in the glassy river, the dark mass of clouds on the horizon, which sent forth flashes of lightning, and the graceful forms of the boats and sailing vessels painted in jet black on the reddish gold of the sky and water, made an unforgettable picture. Then the sun rose and lighted up the sleepy shores of Belgium with their fringe of long grass, their rows of poplars, their church spires and farm buildings.*

They had left England behind.

Reaction was not slow to come.

Now I can only pray, against hope, that he may prove constant to her; otherwise she is <u>utterly</u> lost, wrote John Chapman.

From George Combe, the famous phrenologist, a friend of Marian's:

I should like to know whether there is insanity in Miss Evans' family; for her conduct, with her brain, seems to me like morbid mental aberration … an educated woman who, in the face of the world, volunteers to live as a wife, with a man who already has a living wife and children, appears to me to pursue a course and to set an example calculated only to degrade herself and her sex, if she be sane. — If you receive her into your family circle, while present appearances are unexplained, pray consider whether you will do justice to your own female domestic circle, and how other ladies may feel about going into a circle which makes no distinction between those who act thus, and those who preserve their honour unspotted?

The artist, the sculptor Thomas Woolner, also had damning words:

By the way — have you heard of a — of two blackguard literary fellows, Lewes and Thornton Hunt? They seem to have used wives on the ancient Briton practice of having them in common: now blackguard Lewes has bolted with a — and is living in Germany with her. I believe it dangerous to write facts of anyone nowadays so I will not any further lift the mantle and display the filthy contaminations of these hideous satyrs and smirking moralists — these workers in the Agepemone — these Mormonites in another name — stinkpots of humanity.

No one was going to get the story right. Carlyle saw it as Lewes finally abandoning his family. No one, in fact, would get the story right for decades.

•

Part One

1857

1

It was the middle of the night on Jersey. Thoughts distinct from dreams were penetrating Marian's mind; finally she was awake. Now she could hear the sea, the fir tree branches too. She was awake and it wasn't even light.

This happened night after night. Each time words were weaving in her mind: *My dear Isaac, you will be delighted to know that I have a husband.*

Or:

Dearest Brother,

Knowing your affectionate heart, I feel certain that you will rejoice that at last I have found a harbour for myself — or, to put it more plainly — I am married, and have been so for the past three years.

The dawn had begun to glimmer at the sides of the window as the sea became louder, as if the wind and water were rising in company with the light. George was beside her. George and the sea, his breathing, the exhalation of breath and surf. As a child, there was no sea, only a pond at the bottom of the giant's hill. They would race down it, she and her brother Isaac, Isaac's jacket whipping outwards side to side as he went ahead, the magic boy ahead of her. It was natural and right that he was ahead of her. But one day, her own legs were more encompassing, her stride was extending, and she began to gain on him, until seconds later she passed him. He arrived dark and panting, saying his leg hurt, he had let her win.

At supper, she had passed Isaac her apple turnover under the table. But he, giving her an odd, crooked smile, gave it back to her.

'Well done, Rabbit,' he said, carelessly, that night, from his bed, when he settled his head on the pillow.

His words had cost him. Even now the memory moved her, and with it sleep finally came.

Lewes and Marian had arrived on Jersey three days earlier, having taken the boat from Plymouth. When they docked the weather was white, drizzly, and cold, but then they took the omnibus to the west side, where, dismounting, they looked around in disbelief. The mist had cleared. The sea was a brilliant blue, the air warm. Inland there were green hill slopes, thick with cream-flowering orchards, and in the town of Gorey they found Rosa Cottage tucked away, up from the harbour.

'Thirteen shillings with board — not bad!' Lewes had whispered to Marian, as the landlady, a slight woman, with her daughter in tow, showed them where they would be.

They signed in at the register as Mr and Mrs Lewes.

'Choice!' was Lewes' verdict, once they were left alone.

The lodgings consisted of three adjoining rooms at the top of the house. They had walked around, exclaiming at the nooks they could inhabit — Marian at once had her eye on the small table in front of the bedroom window.

The following day they began their routine. After breakfast Lewes headed out to the beach with traps and muslin nets, to find marine specimens for his work. Marian stayed in the bedroom, with her notebook and pen at the small table. She had to push thoughts of her brother Isaac out of her mind; she must write. She had started 'Janet's Repentance', and it was going slowly. She mulled, sketched, wrote, mulled again — but now — the glittering light at the window and the blowy island air seemed to ask her to come outside.

She'd go for a quick walk, that was all —

But at the foot of the stairs, the little girl was waiting for her. 'Will you come with me?' she asked, with the directness of look and tone peculiar to children. Marian followed her, remembering she was called Janie, with her tight-drawn hair and single plait, to see the goldfish, trapped in its glass bowl, swimming round and enlarging through the water as it swam near; then on to a cupboard in the wall. First she was shown a startling dress in red chiffon, which looked large for Janie and small for her mother; then a long white wedding dress, turning yellow at the edges. Janie leant back against the wall, looked up at her. 'Was your dress like that?'

'Like what, my dear?' asked Marian.

'Like ma's,' said the little girl gravely.

Marian hesitated.

'Not entirely,' she said. She knew she was smiling an odd, proud smile. Turning, she saw the landlady in the doorway. Marian found herself blushing, as Janie was scolded for disturbing her.

An hour later, on the beach, she reported this conversation to Lewes. He listened as he attended to his selected jars, his longish hair falling in front of his face.

'She is as *sweet*,' said Lewes, referring to their landlady, giving the jar a firm circular push into the damp sand on each emphatic syllable, 'as — apple — pie. Nonsense.'

'I saw it.'

'We're not in London, we're not even in England,' said Lewes, in precise accents. 'We are on the eastern side of Jersey island.'

Reluctantly she smiled.

The following day it was the same routine. This time Marian stayed at the desk, she wrote. But before the hour was out, a pain was flicking at her neck, cresting in her temple. She moved onto the bed, taking the pages onto her knee. As she read through what she had written, her stomach did a curling, sinking movement: finally she tossed the pages in the air, heard them fall with a dry fluttering noise on to the floor. She closed her eyes.

'I could laugh as well as cry, when I read what I've written,' she said to Lewes, when he returned, with the outdoors on him. The first thing he did was open the curtains.

'Well, I've read it, and it's only the freshest thing I've set eyes on for a long time,' said Lewes, giving her a kiss on the forehead. 'You remember what Blackwood said.'

Marian nodded, then gave a feeble laugh. 'You have faith in me.'

'For good reason,' he said absently. He had a jar in his hand, full of murky, salty, sandy water, into which he was now gazing. 'Polly — I found the most fascinating little creature today: a mollusc with two bodies. That renegade Huxley will eat his words when this is published!'

'He will, George,' said Marian, taking his hand. Privately she thought he was too obsessed with Thomas Huxley, who'd once dismissed Lewes as a 'mere book scientist'.

But the next day her concentration was poor again, and reading what she'd written, she slapped the pages face down on the table. Outside the kid-goat was following her, but she shut the gate, began to walk fast up the hill. And once she was walking, she thought again about Isaac, Fanny, Chrissey, her siblings. She wanted to tell them about George. It had been three years now. Their life in Coventry was so remote from the world of London letters that no rumour of her situation had even reached them. They still sent letters to Marian Evans; they still thought she lived alone.

There was abundant soft May air; up to the right, the cream-flowered orchards.

After climbing some more, she began to descend towards the sea, then realised she was walking towards the beach where George was. Was that him? No. Then — surely that was him, that figure kneeling. No hat, foolish. She watched him, unseen, from a distance. Strange, the landscape: the line of the horizon splitting sky from sea, sea rimming into darkness. What was it he had said? 'The freshest work he had read for a long time.'

But he probably read her work, she thought gloomily, with an idealising eye.

The following day, she mustered her determination. No matter if it was bad. She wrote. She wrote.

By the end of the morning, grim faced, she was again lying on the bed. She had fallen into a slow, head-aching doze.

Some time later she heard George's footsteps. Thud, thud, a springy repeated thud on the stairs, evidently bounding up two at a time. The door swung open.

'Her fame's beginning already!' he said, radiantly. He was waving a letter in his hand.

'Whoever "she" may be,' said Marian, weakly, but with a smile beginning in spite of herself.

She sat up and began to read.

She didn't recognise the handwriting.

Sir,

Will you consider it impertinent in a brother author and old reviewer to address a few lines of earnest sympathy and admiration to you, excited by the purity of your style, originality of your thoughts, and absence of all vulgar seeking for effect in those 'Scenes of Clerical Life' now appearing in Blackwood? *If I mistake not much, your muse of invention is no hackneyed one, and your style is too peculiar to allow of your being confounded with any of the already well-known writers of the day. Your great and characteristic charm is, to my mind, Nature. Will you always remain equally natural, preserve the true independence which seems to mark a real supremacy of intellect? Pardon this word of greeting from one whom you may never see or know, and believe me your earnest admirer,*

Archer Gurney

'Well!' she said, looking round the room. It was as if she had drunk some pleasant tonic water. She was feeling different. The walls looked a better colour. George had his arm round her shoulder, was calling her darling and kissing her cheek. They laughed, he kissed her again, she exclaimed. A minute later, though, he'd stepped back. Arms folded, he was regarding her with a new, quizzical, shrewd expression.

'Ocular proof, eh, Polly?'

'Yes. Yes, indeed.'

'This man Gurney writing out of the blue. Are you convinced?'

'I am, George,' she said, her voice sounding small and a little odd. The tears had come to her eyes. Her chest was expanding and feeling deliciously light. And the headache — it was vanishing fast.

'And now,' he continued, smiling sternly, 'do you remember the people at the club Blackwood told me about? The man who blubbed like a baby at Milly's death? And Thackeray himself, eyes sparkling with tears?'

It was true. She'd learn to trust herself. She was capable. More than capable.

Lewes went next door to begin his dissecting. Marian picked up the manuscript of 'Janet's Repentance', and began to re-read. As she read, an unconscious smile was shaping her mouth.

... they had that sort of friendly contempt for each other which is always conducive to a good understanding between professional men; and when any new surgeon attempted, in an ill-advised hour, to settle himself in the town, it was strikingly demonstrated how slight and trivial are theoretic differences compared with the broad basis of common human feeling. There was the most perfect unanimity between Pratt and Pilgrim in the determination to drive away the obvious and too probably unqualified intruder as soon as possible ...

For the next two days, she was aware of being happy as if it were a physical state: she had energy as she walked up the hills; looking at the sea, the glitter of the sun on the water bulged into melted silver in her vision. Back in the cottage, Lewes, who had been in his 'workroom', put his head round the door. 'Progress?' he asked.

'I am writing to Isaac,' she replied, without looking up.

My dear Brother, she wrote, and she knew a steady, confident feeling of strength in herself, as she continued:

You will be surprized, I dare say, but I hope not sorry, to learn that I have changed my name, and have someone to take care of me in the world. The event is not at all a sudden one, though it may appear sudden in its announcement to you. My husband has been known to me for several years, and I am well acquainted with his mind and character. He is occupied entirely with scientific and learned pursuits, is several years older than myself, and has three boys, two of whom are at school in Switzerland and one in England.

The same day, she wrote to her sister, Chrissey, and her half-sister, Fanny, informing them also. Usually Lewes posted letters; this time Marian walked there alone at the end of that day, and, lightly kissing each envelope, stood still a moment — before dropping them one by one ceremoniously into the postal box.

2

The weeks went by. It was Lewes who went to pick up the letters. Each time he returned, Marian's eyes were on him, but there was nothing from her family. Sometimes in the day, walking up the hill alone, the solitude became oppressive. It had lasted now for three years, even since going with Lewes to the continent.

They had stayed on the continent for nine months, and, returning to England, she had been reclusive. She, the illegal Mrs Lewes, certainly didn't go 'in' to society. She saw George, and more George. But they had each other and their work. And for over a year now, with George intent on becoming a marine biologist, they had been travelling to coastal spots — to Ilfracombe, Tenby, the Scilly Isles and now Jersey.

But she missed women, and talking to women; especially her old friends from Coventry, Sara Hennell and Cara Bray, whom she hadn't seen these last years.

On the other hand, there was Barbara.

Looking at the sea, she was reminded of the shore a year earlier, where she had walked with Barbara Leigh Smith, in Tenby, a small town in Wales. She and Lewes had been staying there, and a woman, no less, Barbara, had come to stay with her. And had changed from being an acquaintance to a great friend.

It was Barbara herself who suggested the visit. Marian wouldn't have dared. She could remember the day of Barbara's arrival, standing by the White Lion Inn, waiting for the coach to arrive. Looking and looking down the road, unable to stop staring at the bend — empty. 'Four in the after,' the man had said. The clock struck four, there was no coach; each time she heard a noise, she was hopeful, then disappointed; finally, after half past, there it was, hoving into view, dirt spraying from the wheels, clattering to a halt. The door opened, an elderly gentleman and woman came down, ginger fashion, then two young serving-women. Then — nobody. Marian had drawn her breath in sharply.

But then shoes and a skirt were descending from the coach, followed by gold-reddish hair, and Marian sprang to her feet. 'Barbara!' she said. They embraced each other, laughing. Barbara's bags were carried by an older man with a weathered face; while her easel, paints, canvases — Barbara was a painter — were brought along by a great ruddy-faced boy, as they made their way to the Coburg Hotel, where Barbara was to stay.

Marian couldn't suppress her smile as they walked through the town. Barbara had come to visit her — travelled a long way, too.

⋆ ⋆ ⋆

The first chance of private talk with Barbara only came the following afternoon. The two women had walked past the harbour: black tug-boats, dark stony shingle, smell of tar mixed with sharp creosote. There was no sun. The road wound down to the shingle; they walked in step, silently.

Marian had wished the scene looked better for her friend, she knew Barbara was not in good spirits.

'It has not been easy,' confessed Barbara.

'I can imagine!' said Marian.

Gladness and sympathy were filling Marian. It was inexpressibly soothing, after the last three years, to hear the confiding tone of a woman friend again.

'I know you understand,' said Barbara now, in a very low tone; almost, Marian had to lean sideways to catch her friend's voice.

Marian knew Barbara was still deeply upset about John Chapman, with whom she had had an intense affair. *I shall say nothing of sorrows and renunciations,* she had said tactfully, in her last letter to Barbara, about the latter's impending visit; *but I understand and feel what you must have to do and bear.*

Yes — I hope we shall know each other better.

They had walked on, past a fisherman dragging his boat out to sea. The gulls were crying; soon they had walked so far that the quaint houses of Tenby, including the steeple, were out of sight. They sat down on a smooth rock that seemed to form a natural seat, the wild horizon open before them.

'I understand his attractions,' said Marian, feelingly, after a moment. 'He is so charming to women. Now — no — I can't see him as I did! But I remember. I do indeed,' — and she took Barbara's hand, pressing her fingers so that Barbara would feel her sympathy.

Barbara hesitated. Then, mournfully, but half smiling: 'He has tried in every possible way to bring us together.'

Reaching inside her pocket, she passed a letter to Marian, who instantly recognised Chapman's handwriting. *Sex,* she read, *is certainly not a barrier to the most perfect intercourse of the soul. On the contrary, it ensures the fullest intercourse of all and reveals depths in our being which without it are never fathomed ...*

'He is insistent,' murmured Marian.

'He says my health would benefit — and that we could have a child. Do you,' said Barbara suddenly, 'think you will have children?'

Marian said it was unlikely. 'George has three children of his own, and supports Mr Hunt's, too. But even if it were not for that —'

She was thinking of her sister Chrissey in Warwickshire, widowed, alone with six children. Staying with her, she had been woken by the baby's cries in the next room — the sound urgent, unspeakably rasping in the pitch darkness. She had drawn the blanket over her head.

'But how —'

'We are very careful,' said Marian, with a faint smile. 'George is scientifically minded.'

Barbara let the topic drop, and they sat in silence.

Marian was glad the conversation stopped, but deeply pleased that Barbara had broached this intimate terrain. It was a sign of Barbara's affection for her, and it made her hopeful. She glanced at her friend, admiring the statuesque slope and grace of her shoulders and bust, the way her thick, long beautiful hair was held in a single tortoise-shell clasp. Tonight, Barbara and George would start to become friends, though she was sure George had impressed Barbara the previous evening — he had told the funniest anecdote about Mr Tugwell, the fisherman who'd helped him, and Marian had basked in his wit, good humour, and, behind the light façade, his integrity. But then she remembered Barbara going silent. Perhaps she'd been upset by the contrast between their happiness, and her loss of Chapman.

She must soothe her.

Marian took a breath and said, 'Your letter to me, when I first returned to London, was noble. Barbara, you will find someone to love you, who's worthy of you. We human creatures are vulnerable, and breaking any attachment is painful.'

They were both moved. She saw gratitude in Barbara's face. It was a moment of power for Marian, of restoration.

'I understand the attractions of John Chapman,' went on Marian. 'Unlike Mr Lewes, he is a Byron to look at! And at least he has in his own way loved you properly. With me —! I was too ugly for him.'

Weakly, Barbara was demurring.

Marian laughed. 'When we visited Kenilworth Castle together, he told me how important beauty was to him. I could not fail to mistake his meaning.'

And she turned modest, amused eyes on her friend, who clucked and shook her head as if she did not understand what Marian was saying. But Marian knew she did.

'And because I have money,' admitted Barbara, 'I think he had ideas about my helping the *Review*.'

'I bet he did!'

The *Westminster Review* was always verging on bankruptcy. Marian frowned. Chapman had a distinct opportunistic streak. Barbara was wealthy.

Suddenly her arm was seized, Barbara turning to her with tears in her eyes, and hot red cheeks.

'But I have to tell you, because the thought still torments me ... he suggested we do as you and Mr Lewes! And it still torments me — surely we could! He said to me, "They are perfectly happy." And I keep thinking, he might be right.'

The sun had begun fitfully to shine, the scene in front of them became intermittently illumined with colour.

'My dear Barbara,' murmured Marian, and she pressed her friend's hand again. But even as she spoke, she was mulling what she was seeing. It always struck her as an intriguing spectacle — the helplessness of the rational mind in the grip of strong emotion. It would be a disastrous move for Barbara to live openly with Chapman, who would not be faithful for one week. But Barbara knew this.

'It is not an easy step,' said Marion carefully.

Her words were like a key. If Barbara chose to recognise the implications, she could do so. The filtered sunshine meanwhile had irradiated the water. Marian was struck by the greenish waves — a picture beautiful and unreal in its tints.

'But you are happy!' cried Barbara.

'I am. But you see too how happy it makes me that you have come,' — Marian broke off, and changed the subject. She didn't like to talk about what she had given up.

* * *

The following day, Barbara set up her easel, her paints, her sketchbook on the beach, while Marian read. Later, they went walking along the coast to find St Catherine's Cave. At low tide, the beach was glorious — stretching seemingly for miles, the long smooth sand extending sheer and outwards, on and on, so that the sea seemed at a great distance.

'You are very sure of the way,' commented Barbara as they walked, following the coast round.

'I came here thirteen years ago,' admitted Marian. 'I remember it well.'

They could now see the cave, rising like an ancient structure out of the rock, surrounded by grand, strange-shaped pillars of stone. Inside the cave, the air was suddenly cold, and the new atmosphere made Marian instinctively lower her voice. 'It's surprising how dark it gets,' said Marian, as they picked their way carefully over the wet slippery rocks, avoiding the little gleaming pools.

'... gets ... gets ...gets ...' they heard.

'An echo!' said Barbara.

'... o ...o ... o ...'

They played with their voices, exclaiming and hearing the sounds come back. When they emerged, they blinked in the light. It was a relief to be back in the sun, everything coloured a mellow, golden hue; there was the shushing sound of the surf again, and the warm air was welcoming after the queer damp of the cave. They walked quickly, as the tide was starting to come in.

'Who did you come with, when you came here all that time ago?' asked Barbara curiously, once they were nearer to the harbour, and could stroll at a more leisurely pace.

'The Brays. Charles Bray, Cara Bray, and Sara Hennell.'

As they walked on, Marian was remembering how she had shared a room with Sara Hennell, in the house they lodged in, not far from Bridge Street. They had had to share a bed; laughing in the morning about their hair, unbrushed and wild-looking.

Barbara linked arms with her. 'It must be a comfort,' said Barbara, 'to have such old friends. Especially in the last few years,' she added, meaningfully.

'It is', said Marian. 'Although,' — she broke off.

'Although what?' said Barbara, turning to her with a smile.

Marian shrugged as they walked.

'Tell me Marian,' she said, suddenly serious. 'Were they not your true friends?'

Marian hesitated. She did not feel like talking about Cara and Sara now.

⋆ ⋆ ⋆

Each morning in Tenby, Marian watched Barbara: how she set out her paints and easel; the way she rolled back her sleeves with an intent, imperious gesture. Marian tried to read Beaumarchais, but she found herself repeatedly distracted. It was the way her friend glanced out and then looked steadily at the lines she was drawing — Marian scented happiness.

Barbara had begun sketching, within two days she was painting.

'My dear Barbara,' said Marian softly, in wonder, on the third day, 'already you have made something.'

A landscape had rapidly formed in front of her eyes. Silently, Marian took her seat on the rug again, picked up her book, but after a few minutes she was drawn once more to look at her friend. Again and again, Marian admired the skill with which she held the brush, diluted paint, the way she would let it half dry and then use her finger to achieve an effect; the deliberateness with which she worked to realise what she saw in front of her, and in her mind.

And a certain disconsolate feeling settled on Marian. What was it that she, Marian, had done? True, she had translated two difficult texts from the German into English. She had edited the *Westminster Review*, and her own essays for it were more than fine. She said to herself she had no reason to feel dissatisfied.

After a time Barbara came to sit with her.

'Tell me about your painting,' said Marian, intently. She knew Barbara had been taught by Ruskin.

* * *

On the last night, after supper, they sat by the fire. They discussed Barbara's beautiful pencil sketch of the annelid that she had done for Lewes: the millipede of the sea, Lewes called it. After stoking up the fire, and adding a log, Lewes pointed to his own cross-section diagram: the main heart and the five offspring. The curious creature had five tiny hearts in addition to a main heart!

'Not possible,' protested Marian.

'It's true, Polly,' said Lewes, puffing contentedly on his cigar. 'They're astonishing creatures. This has been a fruitful day for me. Thomas Huxley — look out!'

'It has been fruitful for me, too,' said Barbara.

'You are an artist,' said Marian with sudden gravity. She was tired. And Barbara — there was a certain complacency about her, she felt.

The three sat silently. The fireside was crackling a little, making a comforting noise. Outside it had begun, in the way of changeable coastal weather, to rain and it sounded rhythmically on the pane.

'Do you know,' said Lewes, turning to Barbara, 'I keep telling Polly to try her hand at fiction. I read a capital story she wrote when she was a girl.'

'George,' sighed Marian. To Barbara: 'He is an optimist. I hope you have noted that about his character.'

'Oh I have!' laughed Barbara.

'Polly, start tomorrow!' urged Lewes, genial and completely unabashed. To Barbara, he inclined his head in Marian's direction and said, sotto voce: 'She had a dream, and it was as good as Coleridge's.'

'You never know,' said Marian. Her tone was even.

An hour later, the two women were alone. Marian had poured them both two small glasses of brandy. She was thinking she would miss Barbara, leaving the next day.

Barbara said it had been a pleasure to get to know George, who was not debauched, as his reputation suggested.

'No he is not,' agreed Marian, steadily. 'I am glad you can see him for who he is.'

'And your brother, Isaac? He must be so glad of your happiness!'

Marian cleared her throat. 'Isaac? My entire family are in ignorance. They know nothing about Lewes.'

Smiling, she leant forward. 'It doesn't concern me — it really doesn't! I can't let it.'

Then, in a more stately tone: 'George and I were separately very taken with Feuerbach's views, even before we met. "Love is God himself," Feuerbach says — meaning that marriage is the free bond of love. I think of our relationship as sacred.'

She had drawn herself up, she realised then, to sit very straight. She glanced at Barbara, but Barbara had dropped her eyes. Something outside her vision: as usual, she couldn't catch it.

3

Marian knew that she had made a good friend in Barbara. And now here in Jersey, ten months later, when she walked with Lewes on the beaches, she was reminded of the walks on the Tenby shore. Marian and Lewes often walked to Grouville Bay, where they could see the castle of Mont Orgueil, silhouetted on the rocky promontory. Some days they wandered down the small narrow twisting streets to the harbour with its fishing boats, tug-boats, brightly coloured sailing boats. At low tide they walked on the sand, now washed clean, but often it was so wet they would start to laugh as their feet began to get stuck.

Marian finished the first section of 'Janet's Repentance', which she sent off to John Blackwood, publisher. Glory of glory, she'd done it. To celebrate, they took their favourite inland route along the Queen's Farm Valley. Meadow and pasture lay between two high slopes of trees and ferns. For part of this walk, they stayed in contented silence: Marian absorbing the views each way, the different greens and browns in the May light. Better still, a letter had come from her sister Fanny, with no suspicious questions, auguring well for her brother Isaac and sister Chrissey.

The summer weather had arrived — in the shade of the Castle, they lay down with a bottle of wine on a rug, read *Sense and Sensibility* aloud, taking it in turns. Marian liked to lie on her back, looking at the white clouds as they slowly passed, while George's expressive voice sounded in her ears. They were both struck by the near-savage liveliness with which Austen lampooned the mercenary values of society.

'It's almost caricature,' said Marian. 'The satirical parts, I mean.'

'But she keeps just this side of realism,' said George quickly.

George was the most percipient critic, thought Marian. How lucky she was to have him at her side. Here, she had everything she needed. Their landlords were a good couple, decent, honest, kind (she'd long ago forgotten all her suspicions of Mrs Aymes). As for the white kid-goat, he was comic and endearing, with his human-sounding bleat, his responsiveness to a pat on the head, his warm nose and soft lips — she had taken to feeding him bits of apple in the afternoon. In the last week, she had risen at six-thirty with the brilliant morning light — on clear days she could see France from the window — and worked without strain through till two o'clock.

The night before, he'd read it, and said she'd managed a 'tricky' subject 'superbly'. And it *was* a tricky subject, she thought, the eponymous Janet being married to a wife-beating alcoholic, called Dempster.

It was good in Jersey. She could enjoy the air, no curious critical eyes were watching. But one day, returning to the sitting-room, still feeling the exhilarating wind and sun on her cheeks from outside, her eyes adjusting to the relative darkness of the parlour, she saw a letter on the table. It was addressed to her, but the handwriting made her stop — and then walk to it more quickly to pick it up. Not family, but familiar. In the light of the window, she saw the script more clearly. Black ink, meticulously small. Opening it, the name at the bottom made her heart beat faster. *Vincent Holbeche, Esquire.* Her family's solicitor in Warwickshire.

Dear Mrs Lewes,

I have had an interview with your Brother in consequence of your letter to him announcing your marriage. He is so much hurt at your not having previously made some communication to him as to your intention and prospects that he cannot make up his mind to write, feeling that he could not do so in a Brotherly Spirit. Your Brother and Sister are naturally anxious to obtain some information regarding your altered state. Permit me to ask when and where you were married and what is the occupation of Mr Lewes.

She sat down on the sofa. George came in; he was telling her about creatures, holding up the jar for her to look at. 'You're not listening,' she heard him say. Then he was taking the letter from her hand. Lewes burst into a diatribe about narrowness and ignorance. Marian tried to ignore what he was saying, to concentrate instead on what she knew: Isaac teaching her to ride, or blowing warm air on her hands to warm them, that freezing day by the pond. And then there was Chrissey — she had faith in Chrissey.

She wrote back to Mr Holbeche, saying that Lewes was a well-known writer, and they both regarded their marriage as a sacred bond, even though it wasn't legal.

Letters arrived from her siblings — Isaac, Fanny, and her favourite, Chrissey. They all broke off contact with her. At supper, the second night, she was quiet. Later, reading Hawthorne's *The Scarlet Letter*, Marian put the book suddenly down, excused herself, and went early to bed.

★ ★ ★

The days were spent quietly. Each time she thought of her family, she knew a cold and queasy sensation, a light trembling in her stomach; she shifted her thoughts back to work. She was glad when a letter arrived from the Scottish publisher John Blackwood, about 'Janet's Repentance':

It is exceedingly clever and some of the hits and descriptions of character are first rate, but I should have liked a pleasanter picture. Surely the colours are rather harsh for a sketch of English County Town life only 25 years ago.

'Harsh indeed,' said Marian, her lip curling.

The first scene especially I think you should shorten. It is rather a staggerer in an opening scene of a Story of Clerical Life. *Dempster is rather too barefaced a brute and I am sorry that the poor wife's sufferings should have driven her to so unsentimental a resource as beer. I feel certain that I am right in advising you to SOFTEN your picture as much as you can.*

'Soften it!' she said, derisively, before passing the letter to Lewes.

'He's thinking of the god fearing public,' said Lewes, jokily. He did like to keep her spirits up. Also, Blackwood was his publisher too, he didn't want him too lambasted by Polly.

'I have no illusions at all about the public,' said Marian. The cold sharpness of her tone made Lewes look up.

Without looking at George, she sat down to write her reply.

Everything, she said in the letter, that she had written in 'Janet's Repentance' was already softened from the fact, so far as it was permitted to soften and yet remain essentially true. The real town was more vicious than Milby; the real Dempster was far more disgusting than hers; the real Janet, alas!, had a far sadder end than hers.

Let him know the truth.

'Polly! You've gone through the paper!' cried Lewes.

It was true: she had pressed so hard with the nib, it had broken through.

In the early evening she went for a walk down to the beach. It had been a breezy, sunny day, but now the wind had died down and the sea was peaceful, glassy, the light was golden. There were scarcely waves. The surf came in with a quiet shushing noise. She sat in the usual place and waited for her own feelings to quieten.

What would it be like, no contact with her family?

How fitting, being on an island.

As if reflecting her thought, the bowl of the horizon so perfectly still, the deep ultramarine of the sea below the golden colourless sky, paling and paling; the line between sea and sky dark, dividing the two.

4

Monday afternoon, I'm locked out of my new flat. I sit on the steps, think what to do. I have no idea where a second set of keys is. I check pockets and bag a last time.

I can ring the bell of the downstairs flat; but the man who lives there, Dale, carried my flatpack up the day before. I ring the bell all the same. Dale answers. 'Ah, Kate,' he says. 'What can I do for you?' Dale has reddish hair, is Northern Irish, is an actor and a dog-walker. He doesn't have keys for the top flat.

An emergency locksmith fits a new lock at chronic expense. The flat is more or less empty except for five packing cases.

It's January, cold and soon it will be dark. But the light comes a little later, I notice. I'm in my own place at last.

* * *

'You don't think you've come too soon?' says my sister.

I've been living for a year in Tooting with Sal and her family, while lawyers sort the money out. Furniture is in storage until building and painting are done. She suggests doing a packing case a day. As she is leaving, she says slowly, 'You know, I saw Rob. I saw them both, actually.'

She pauses, then adds, with a strange anxious look, 'She's not that bad.'

'Right. Okay. Well —' I go to open the door for her. We stand there without speaking.

'Well, bye!' I say. She gives me a kiss on the cheek. 'Speak tomorrow,' I add, as I shut the door.

A minute later there's a knock.

'Look —'

'It's fine,' I say hurriedly. 'I'm serious. Now —'

Sal's expression makes me stop talking. Now we're both silent. Then she says, steadily, 'I — don't — like them, you know. I really don't. I don't know what I was talking about. Do you believe me?'

She's laughing a bit. We hug.

★ ★ ★

It's night. The flat is solitary but I walk around; I'm restless and half excited being in my own place in London. I open the window to the unfamiliar street sounds. There's a pub at the end of the road. Mainly there's silence.

I am woken before dawn by the dogs barking below.

★ ★ ★

I'm getting used to the journey from Finsbury Park to Bloomsbury, where QEC is. I like Bloomsbury, with its trees and soiled air and dilapidated buildings. Pleasant and shambling, it feels like a part of London that's been left to itself, developers haven't quite got there. But just now there are ructions.

Hans Meyerschwitz, our new departmental star, whose specialty is 'Personal Writing in the 19th Century', is throwing his weight around. He has vetoed a man called Jo Devlin from speaking at the Eliot conference — Jo Devlin works in the same field at Queen Mary's College. There's a known history between Hans and Jo Devlin: they both competed for the job that Devlin has now, a year before.

I go to see the chair of our department, Marcus, who inhabits a large office with recessed lights. He is usually very busy, but when I come in he's lolling in his chair. 'Hey, Kate, sit down.'

I explain that I'm scheduled to teach a class with Hans next term, on personal writing, and I'd rather not. Marcus asks why.

'His veto of Jo Devlin,' I say.

Before Marcus can object, I add: 'No one can do that! Did he bring it up with you?'

Marcus says it's timetabled now, he doesn't want to mess Hans around. 'It's just a weekly class.'

★ ★ ★

Not long after that, in Finsbury Park, in the corner shop near my flat, I recognise Hans Meyerschwitz at the end of the aisle. He's buying milk. He is easy to recognise because of his height: tall, with straw-coloured hair, Aryan colouring. I look at him again — I like the scarf he's wearing, hard to say why. He's talking in an easy way to the Iranian man at the counter.

'Hans?'

He says hello; then — 'What are you doing here?' — smiling.

'I live here. Just moved in. In Osborne Road.'

'Since when?'

'Since — a week ago.'

'How's it going?'

I say there's building to do and painting.

'Ah so.' Hans is German, and his voice is slightly accented. He goes on to say, in a voice of perfect indifference, that he is looking forward to teaching our class next term. We are doing a class on Victorian letters and diaries, starting in April.

That night, I'm woken by the dogs downstairs, the yelping coming through the darkness. I check my phone: 5.02.

1859

5

On a cold, clear afternoon, Marian and Lewes did the long walk from Richmond to Wandsworth, to see the new house again. On the way back they fell into a happy silence, the darkening afternoon sky flushed with faint pink as they passed through Richmond Park. Lewes had just published his *Physiology of Common Life*; Marian had high hopes for *Adam Bede*. It was her first novel.

They were still quiet when they reached home. The prospect of the move was elating: Holly Lodge, the new house, was sturdy and solid, with larger rooms, and they would now have a study each. Yet the unfamiliarity of those strange streets in Wandsworth made them thoughtful. They would no longer see the brown-green river Thames with the boats going slowly along, or Richmond Green, or the handsome white-painted houses of Maids of Honour Row. They didn't know anyone in Wandsworth. Barbara had recently got married, and gone to live in Algiers with her French doctor husband.

The new house was unfurnished. On a foggy, freezing January afternoon they went in to London to buy rugs, glass, a dining table and chairs; a bed and linen; a set of blue and white china, a silver tea caddy. Back home in Richmond, they were exhausted. 'Way of the world, Polly,' said Lewes with a rueful laugh, patting her on the knee. She was silent. They'd run into a couple Lewes knew, on St Andrew's Hill, and the woman had cut her — literally looked through her as if she were a ghost. She could still see the superior, cold rictus on that woman's face.

That night she dreamed she was back in Griff House, her childhood home in Warwickshire. She was outside. She could hear the gentle roaring noise made by the leaves of the beech tree, wildly rustling, but she couldn't work out if the sound were loud or soft. Then she was standing on the threshold, then going inside; she knew exactly where she was going, to the bedroom on the second floor that was Isaac's. As she was mounting the stairs, she had a gathering fear that he would have gone, until she was running, pushing the door open, only to find the room empty, silent. She went into room after room, looking for Isaac, but also Chrissey and Fanny. At this point, she woke up.

She had had no contact with her family for two years.

She was a pariah, she said to herself drily. After Christmas, Lewes had gone to Vernon Hill to see his old friend Arthur Helps, while she stayed at home.

She'd watched him from the doorway as he walked down the road — his quick step, the way his small suitcase swung jauntily as he walked. She spent four days alone, correcting the first proofs of *Adam Bede*, reading Horace. On the fourth morning, perhaps because she had talked to no one for so many hours, the silence became a noise, a high sustained splitting sound in her ear. She walked around the sitting room, regarded herself in the mirror. 'I am ugly, and I am mad,' she said aloud. Then she put her coat on, walked to Richmond Park. Alone on the bench, she cried.

On return Lewes was in good spirits. His voice was deep and nasal because he had a cold, but he was full of stories about the charades they had played.

She listened to him in silence. He had been carousing, she was in hiding.

But hadn't she always liked hiding places? As a child, in Griff House, she liked to hide upstairs in the first-floor corridor, at the top of the linen cupboard. It smelled of lavender mixed with soap, and the dense, sharper smell of raw cut wood — her father had built the cupboard himself. It was like a hiding place, living here in Richmond with Lewes. He could freely visit, but she could not.

Adam Bede was shortly to be published. And she would still be hiding in the most important way of all, behind the name of George Eliot.

6

Marian surveyed the parlour of Holly Lodge. That morning they'd tried the new sofa in the bay window and against the wall, but nothing quite worked. Aloud, she said it was a square, charmless sort of room.

'I know what you mean,' admitted Lewes. 'But we've got some fine almond cakes.'

'Is that the shirt you'll be wearing, George?' asked Marian, lightly.

'Is anything wrong with it?'

'No — no.'

Marian had asked Caroline to make sure the fire was properly lit, to wear a clean apron. On the dot of four the guests arrived. Marian shot Maria Congreve a swift glance under her lids: yes, she remembered her from years ago, when they were both living in Coventry. Maria was a girl then, very slender; now she was a married woman. As for Richard Congreve, she instantly registered the dark-brown tweed jacket that suggested the university man, and his upright bearing. He'd taught at Oxford, Marian remembered. Lewes, of course, was not a university man. While Mr Congreve sat stiffly, Lewes, by contrast, rather short, his wide sunken cheeks narrowing to a chin of unusually small width, was moving around the room quickly, clapping his hands, saying he was delighted they'd come, he'd see about the tea. Glancing sideways at the guests, Marian wished he'd moderate his enthusiasm a little. And Lewes' shirt — had he chosen it on purpose? The collar, in its blowsy, scalloped way, resembled — ruffles — like something an actor in an Elizabethan play might wear. She was forgetting. He had at one time been an actor.

'I hear you're a follower of Comte,' said Lewes then. He addressed his remark bluntly to Richard Congreve. It sounded like a challenge.

'A follower,' echoed Richard Congreve.

'My dear,' murmured Marian. 'I'm sure Mr Congreve is the first and finest exponent of that illustrious movement.'

Mr Congreve inclined his head graciously.

'Of course he is,' said Lewes.

Caroline brought in the tray, but it was Lewes, making a great show of it, who poured the tea, holding the pot high, like an affected waiter.

Mr Congreve's eyebrows rose.

Quickly, Marian looked away at Maria Congreve, who had her hands clasped in front of her, and seemed to be regarding the floor. The kind gentle expression of those dark eyes. Also, Maria was glancing at *her*, with evident interest.

Lewes was handing Maria a cup, and doing an absurd little bow, like a lackey. She looked back at Maria. Was he deliberately riling her? Or mocking Richard Congreve? And Marian couldn't stop glancing at Mr Congreve's face, the play of irony on his dreadfully fine features — straight nose, fine sculpted mouth, too perfect, like a Greek statue. She managed a forced smile in his direction.

'Thank you,' said Maria.

'And you, m'sieur?' quipped Lewes, to Richard Congreve.

Yes, Lewes was pushing it.

'Thank you,' said Mr Congreve briefly, clearing his throat. Then his face seemed to unbend. 'I have an idea that, regarding Auguste Comte, you're no longer the admirer that you were. But I remember, Mr Lewes, that you once wrote admirably on Positivism for the *Leader* — the same piece was in your book, *Comte's Philosophy of the Sciences*. I read it a few years ago. I liked it.'

Lewes thanked him. The atmosphere seemed to soften.

In the next moment Maria spoke for the first time, in a voice that was only just audible. 'Is that Icarus?' she said. She was glancing at the silver tea caddy, the one they had bought in the Strand. On the side of the caddy was a raised figure of a boy with wings, so delicately done that tiny drips of wax were visible, intricately figured at the base of the wings. The boy was flying into the arms of a hot sun, a ball of fire, with rays emanating from the ball, in the shape of little pear-shaped tears.

'It is,' said Marian smiling. 'How observant of you.'

Did Mrs Congreve remember her?

Richard Congreve cleared his throat, before saying, 'I rather agreed with Pater, who prefers Dryden's translation of *Metamorphoses* above Pope's.'

Then, softly, and with an unexpectedly playful smile, he began to declaim:

> *When now the Boy, whose childish Thoughts aspire*
> *To loftier Aims, and make him ramble high'r,*
> *Grown wild, and wanton, more embolden'd flies*
> *Far from his Guide, and soars among the Skies.*
> *The soft'ning Wax, that felt a nearer Sun,*
> *Dissolv'd apace, and soon began to run.*

'I couldn't agree more,' said Lewes, gulping down his tea. 'The Dryden's better!'

'*Tabuerant cerae: nudos quatit ille lacertos,*' murmured Marian. They are people like us, she thought, happily.

'Do you think, Mr Congreve,' asked Marian, 'that it's a tale of hubris? Or just ordinary human folly?'

As they discussed this, it seemed to Marian that Maria's dark eyes had become larger, darker still, and that she was smoothing her hair away from her forehead, as if to enable her to see Marian better.

'Mrs Lewes,' said Mr Congreve now, turning in his chair to face her. His face wore a look of concern. 'I greatly enjoyed your pieces in the *Westminster Review*. I would be very sorry if you were no longer writing. Are you?'

Marian hesitated. 'Not at present.'

'— Regrettable,' said Mr Congreve, with a look of gravity.

Soon the atmosphere lightened again. Lewes, Marian was relieved to note, was expressing his recent disillusionment with Auguste Comte and Positivism, in such a way that would not offend Mr Congreve.

★ ★ ★

In a letter to his wife, Congreve wrote: *I like what I see of her. It is rather unfortunate that they are so inseparable.*

In his journal, Lewes noted that Congreve had no respect for men of specialities, like himself; clearly, he'd been infected by his hero, Auguste Comte, in this way.

7

The Congreves quickly invited them to supper at their house; they soon began to meet regularly. And when Maria Congreve wrote suggesting a walk, Marian replied at once, accepting.

They met at Wandsworth Common, strolling first around the lake, commenting on the newly planted oak saplings so regimentally spaced. 'It's an alien look for nature,' said Marian. But on the right was a pussy willow whose buds were showing, in spite of the morning cold, and the new, lemon-coloured light of the year was invigorating. A flock of geese were crying as they flew over the lake, the raucous cries echoed across the water.

'I must tell you,' said Maria Congreve, smiling shyly, 'that I always remember the first time I met you. In Coventry.'

Marian asked her to tell her about it.

'Well, your father was very ill, and of course, my father was his doctor.'

'I remember! Dr Bury.'

'I was coming towards your house, and I heard the piano through the open window. The playing was so musical, I couldn't help feeling surprised. Beethoven, I think.'

'Very probably. I love to play. Though,' said Marian, turning her eyes on her younger companion, 'I was always in a predicament when it came to playing.'

'Predicament?' said the younger woman.

'I could make music with my fingers,' explained Marian, as they walked round past the poplars, bending in the sunny cold breeze, 'and when I played I was admired. Now you will laugh at me, but I loved that admiration so much, I came to feel that playing was a sin.'

'But it wasn't,' said Maria Congreve, with a kindly smile Marian appreciated.

'Perhaps not,' agreed Marian. 'But I had discovered I was moved not just by the music, but by the fact that I was moving other people. It was a sort of double experience.'

'I think I understand,' said Maria, evidently intrigued.

'I became self-conscious. I had discovered a kind of ecstasy — a very dubious kind,' went on Marian, smiling, 'and of course, I was greedy for the admiration! Before playing, all I could think about was the prospect of being admired. I say this to you in confidence,' she added, in a murmur.

Instinctively, correctly, Marian guessed that her friend would not be alienated by this confession, but drawn to her for her honesty. 'Yes,' Marian went on, pensively. 'Strange that the act of moving the audience actually heightened my own musical sensations. And yet, I see it as a good thing, to play for people.'

'Indeed!'

They walked in silence. Then Maria Congreve turned to her. 'Are you often self-critical?', she asked, timidly.

'I am. I can't work out if it's a bad or a good thing,' said Marian. She didn't want to admit to her new friend just how prone to self-examination she was: to the point of sickness, she sometimes thought.

The sun shone, and there was beginning to be some warmth in the air. Maria Congreve was wearing a scarf of brown merino wool, and her hair in ringlets: Mr Congreve, in spite of his Positivist intellectual interests, had a handsome face that matched his well-tailored jackets, and probably liked to have a pretty wife. And why not? What could be more natural — that link between the senses and the emotions? Why would beauty not please, and help along those developing feelings?

She had a momentary return of her old melancholy. To change the subject she said. 'Seeing you now reminds me of Cara and Sara. Cara Bray, and Sara Hennell. My dearest, oldest friends. Whom I never see,' she added, with a melancholy laugh.

'But of course. I know them too, as you must know.'

They walked on.

'As I was saying, I heard your piano playing that time, and then inside — so many books! I didn't expect to see so much culture. You quickly divined that I wanted to learn German, which I've never forgotten.'

At the suggestion that she had mattered already to this younger woman, Marian looked away towards the pond. She was almost ashamed of the relief and happiness she felt. She had missed female intimacy, in which personal experience could be talked about honestly.

And yet — how honest was she being with Maria? Not at all! Her novel *Adam Bede* had just been published, on the first day of February. She was already working on a new book, about a mill, and a sister and brother, Maggie and Tom. None of this had she told Maria Congreve.

Each day she waited at home for Lewes to come back, to hear the news about *Adam Bede*. Lewes went in to London, to editorial offices, clubs, drinking houses — he would catch the word as to how it was being received, and he would bring back the newspapers too. So far, no word at all. She had woken twice in the night. She struggled now to go back to the conversation.

'And did you — did you get on well with the German?' asked Marian.

'Not as well as I would like. But I remember,' said Maria, darting her a conspiratorial smile, 'your famous argument with your father about religion!'

Marian's step slowed. Maria, she saw, was perceiving her as a rebel — a romantic, defiant figure.

In Coventry, when she was nineteen years old, Marian had publicly renounced her faith, refusing to go to church with her father, which had caused a scandal. Her father had threatened to eject her from his house. They compromised: Marian would attend church with him, but think her own thoughts.

These days she saw it differently: that earlier self seemed full of egotism and selfishness.

They walked on to the great expanse of grass. 'I often have disliked this Common,' said Marian, changing the subject. 'But today, walking with you, I find it charming.'

'My father,' volunteered her friend then, 'always said that you must be a good person, because of the way you nursed your father.'

Marian smiled, but with a certain tightness. Maria had to be referring to her stained reputation. They began leaving the Common, walking South towards the new shops. Maria Congreve said, in a low voice: 'It mortifies me, that you, of all people — have been cut off from your very own family. And, my dear Mrs Lewes, both Mr Congreve and I feel for you. To us, it seems so extraordinarily wrong that your family should have cut you off. And the imbalance, between you and Mr Lewes. That he should be able to go out and visit as usual, while you,' — and she broke off.

'It would be natural,' she resumed, 'if you were to feel no love for your brother Isaac in the circumstances, who has so unjustly stopped communication. It would be natural,' she went on, in a glowing tone, 'to hate him!'

Marian gave an incredulous laugh: 'Hate him? Oh — that's impossible.'

Marian experienced the familiar inward shudder. It was as if she were able to turn herself inside out, and emerge re-made, though she caught her face in the mottled mirror of the engraving shop — her smile half-twisted, animal, as if with glittering effort. Her voice was guttural, proud, harsh: 'My dear friend, narrowness, a want of knowledge, habits of feeling; I hold them in compassionate view.'

She caught her difficult smile again in the glass.

She proceeded breathlessly: 'Ruskin opens the mind, read Ruskin, my dear Maria. This is how life is lived. Through feeling. I hold nothing against my brother.'

The moment between them, as they stood there in the street, these two women, was intensely awkward; Marian noticed that Maria Congreve was twisting her foot this way and that like a child — as if she were wishing to run away.

Marian had a sorrowful sensation, inside herself, like rain. She had told too much, pushed them into a closeness for which they weren't ready. And then, as if the world and she were forming a brief unity, drops of water sounded on the pavement, small repeated pattering sounds, and the pavement was staining with the drops. Rain was falling; her friend, Marian saw, had no protection. Silently, she held out her parasol, and Maria Congreve, as if it were strangely incumbent on her to obey, stepped closer and they stood together in the falling rain under the parasol.

Soon after that, they parted.

Back home, Marian secreted herself in the bedroom, and went over carefully what she had said. Maria Congreve had mentioned Isaac, but why had she, Marian, mentioned Ruskin? Maria Congreve had no idea that she was writing, no idea what she was talking about, no idea that she was waiting constantly to hear about *Adam Bede*.

When Lewes came to see her, to ask her how the walk had been, he found her in bed with a headache.

8

At Marian's request, Blackwood had sent copies of *Adam Bede* to Charles Dickens, Thackeray, Froude, Owen Jones, Charles Kingsley, Richard Owen, and Mrs Carlyle. She was, she admitted to herself, aiming high. Reports from Blackwood trickled through: a cabinet maker had commented how real the scenes in the carpenter's workshop were. Good, good, but he was a cabinet maker. In her time at the *Westminster Review*, she had become acquainted with distinguished men and women.

After weeks of waiting, a letter arrived whose handwriting Marian recognised: Mrs Carlyle. With fluttering fingers, she tore it open:

Dear Sir,

I must again offer you my heartiest thanks. Since I received your Scenes of Clerical Life *nothing has fallen from the skies to me so welcome as* Adam Bede, *all to myself, 'from the Author'.*

Oh yes! It was as good as going into the country for one's health, the reading of that Book was! — Like a visit to Scotland minus the fatigues of the long journey, and the grief of seeing friends grown old, and Places that knew me knowing me no more! In truth, it is a beautiful and most human Book! Every Dog in it, not to say every man woman and Child in it, is brought home to one's 'business and bosom,' an individual fellow-creature! I found myself in charity with the whole human race when I laid it down.

In the darkened hallway, Marian peered to read the last three sentences again.

'George! George!'

She found him in the drawing room, and gave it to him. 'She's a percipient woman, I must say!' he said, when he finished.

Marian murmured: 'I found myself in charity with the whole human race when I laid it down.'

She might have achieved what she wanted.

'A masterwork, eh?' said Lewes, beaming.

'George — please.'

Five days later, she heard the familiar sound of George's key in the lock. He came in with the mysterious but brimming air of a Father Christmas, silently handing her *The Athenaeum* journal. The reviewer declared *Adam Bede* a work of true genius. They hugged, laughed, Marian cried a little, then left the room, reappearing in her coat.

'Where are you going?'

Marian was going to walk, she left quickly, she wanted to walk alone. She did not want to go to the flat Common. She would make for the wilder, hillier Richmond Park, which she knew better and preferred.

It took longer to get there. By the time she reached it, the temperature had dropped. Walking made the blood turn round her system, but in any case she had an uncontrollable tingling in her limbs. The word Genius had been pronounced, everything was opening, opening wonderfully: how arrestingly beautiful the bare black trees were in their shapely clustered gathering on the hill; how good, sharp, fresh, the air smelled here in the park, away from the streets. She could smell burning leaves, she didn't know where from.

How extraordinary, that her innermost yearning was bearing fruit — actually coming true. So they did see her fineness, her quality. And now, only now, she could admit she wasn't entirely surprised. The previous month she had read again the great scene where Hetty confesses to the preacher Dinah. The emotion had risen in her own throat, the tears pricked at her eyes; it's good, she had thought, better than good; life as life, awkward, breathing, particular. Everything working in concert, plot, character, the live tissue of feeling.

Was anybody else doing what she was doing? she asked herself — she could admit this now — as she began striding up the low hill. Her realism struck deeper than Dickens' and Thackeray's. Dickens, a master dramatist, was also the master of caricature, for good and ill. Weren't both a little *crude* beside her? Then there was Trollope. Storyteller of the first order, excellent dilemmas, human, yes, so inventive, true, yes; but some of his women! With exceptions, such as Glencora, they tended to be ciphers, stretching out the plot and providing the rote pleasures of romantic fiction. A subtlety, a psychic dimension, a reality missing.

Her odd life, she thought, had worked to her advantage. She knew working people from her childhood life in Warwickshire, cultured people also. She knew the delicate indices of class, from the obvious to the scarcely perceptible; the way voices were decoded: hadn't she carefully moulded hers on successive teachers', and then Sara Hennell's? She once had a Midlands accent. She knew her comprehensive social canvas.

And then, in her ostracised life, lonely now, so aware of being held in disrepute — writing had offered her the freedom to speak, which felt beautiful. In passages outside the drama she, the anonymous Marian Evans, had spoken directly to the reader.

In real life she spoke to so few people.

In the distance deer appeared, beside a clutch of trees, as still as if caught in a painting. It began to rain, the deer disappeared in an equally dream-like instant, she took shelter under two great elms. The rain grew heavier, percussive on the leaves, a thick constant drumming sound, enclosing her as in a house of sound. When it stopped, she drew her coat round her shoulders, and hesitantly emerged. Already the dark sky was splitting open to show floating gaps of blue; in the west, the clouds had broken to allow a weak low sun to shine across the park. The green glass glistened with an irradiated, unnatural brightness. Surveying the scene, she knew a luxurious pleasure in the beauty and her own sense of solitude and power, which felt a little dangerous. What was that danger?

A wind began to rise, clouds broke once more, and then came the roll of bells. There in the distance, distinctly silhouetted in the mellowing light, was the dome of St Paul's.

★ ★ ★

Good reviews kept coming, the book was selling; everyone, according to Lewes, was talking about *Adam Bede* and its mystery author. The mystery author continues a mystery, said Marian, sourly, to herself. This morning, she had raised herself out of bed when it was still dark, lighting the oil lamp, to take up her pen.

She was working on the Mill book, about Tom and Maggie, brother and sister. For the third day running, she set the pen down after less than ten minutes. Four days earlier she had opened a letter from her sister Chrissey. An initial burst of joy had given way to sickening bouts of sadness. Chrissey had been ill with consumption for the last eighteen months and didn't expect to live long. Chrissey expressed regret at cutting off contact with her. Marian had clenched and unclenched her hands. Because of Isaac's influence, almost certainly, suggestible, good-natured Chrissey had fallen into line; which meant that Marian had been unable to offer help to her. The thought of Chrissey in bed, impoverished, widowed, and the five children — they used to be six, but little Katie had died — made Marian rise abruptly from her chair and pace round the room.

Nor could she visit the dying Chrissey: a letter came from her daughter, saying that a visit might be too much for her mother. Each time the post came she dreaded further news.

As for the praise that was heaped on *Adam Bede*: 'I am like a deaf person,' she wrote to John Blackwood, 'to whom someone has just shouted that the company round him have been paying him compliments for the last half hour.' The praise was aimed at George Eliot, but who was that?

'What are you laughing at?' asked Lewes.

Marian was laughing until she sounded hysterical; Lewes was patting her on the back, pausing only when she grew calmer. Now she had tears in her eyes.

'My dear,' said Lewes thoughtfully. 'In two weeks' time, Herbert Spencer will be in London. Let's invite him to lunch. Here you are, with this *succès d'estime* on your hands, and we can't tell anyone, let alone celebrate! But Spencer knows. We'll have him round.'

9

A fortnight passed, and the day of Spencer's visit arrived. After discussing the lunch menu with Caroline, Marian hurried out of the house. She had arranged to spend the morning with Maria Congreve in Kew.

The two women had decided to visit the Palm Building together. It was still early in the day, but as soon as they walked in, Marian was hit by the strangely hot, exotic air, she could feel the palpable moisture, too; and what plants! Great, green, monstrous tropical plants rising to the ceiling, putting out their thick rubbery leaves like creatures with tentacles, in the warm smokily damp air, in this miraculous building of glass and iron, with its vast high arches. Marian's hand crept to her hair: yes, it was damp: probably forming unbecoming frizzy tendrils. Maria Congreve did not seem to notice. Surreptitiously, Marian wiped her brow. They sat on the bench. For a minute Marian could hardly speak — the damp, febrile, warm atmosphere made her lightheaded. Outside the English spring had yet to acquire warmth; inside, it was tropical summer: all around, the densely sweet, heavy smell of white-yellow jasmine.

'I was very happy at what you said, the other day, about Mr Lewes,' said Marian, thoughtfully; beginning their conversation as she often did, by picking up the threads of a former one. They were now accustomed to speak frankly of personal matters. 'Because of his free-thinking views, he is often misperceived. But no one could be more   true, loyal, devout.'

Marian spoke with intense earnestness.

'Devout?' said Maria Congreve, with a crease of puzzlement.

'Oh!' said Marian, laughing, and colouring a little. 'I don't mean religious. I don't know why I said that. I really just meant, devoted.'

'He is devoted to you, and I like him very much,' said Maria Congreve.

Marian was annoyed at her slip of the tongue. It implied that Lewes was in some way not just her husband, but a worshipper at her shrine; and for some reason she was blushing.

'He is a good man', said Marian, in an attempt to regain her equilibrium. 'I couldn't have been happy but for him. There is so much I would never have attempted!'

Maria Congreve coughed. 'I have meant to ask,' she said, with a suddenly timorous, embarrassed smile, 'about your writing. I know you translated two most extraordinarily difficult texts from the German. And of course, I read you in the *Westminster Review*! The range and depth of your pieces struck me. And I wondered how you are spending your time these days, now that you are no longer writing for the *Review*.'

'Ah — well,' said Marian, clearing her throat, 'it is always hard to describe how one is spending time.'

What mendacity! But the younger Maria had her eyes fastened on her, in that nearly worshipful way, and was nodding as if she had spoken something oracular.

'I know just what you mean. Time goes past each day, and you do not know where the day has gone.'

Marian bent her head to examine her fingernails. 'How is Mr Congreve? Is his cold better?' she enquired, politely.

'Oh, he is fine,' said Maria Congreve, almost impatiently, as if something beautiful had been spoiled by the mention of her husband. 'As a matter of fact, Mr Congreve is worried that — that — by — uniting with Mr Lewes — you have forfeited your writing. He has expressed pity for you. He says this is what happens in almost all marriages and unions, that a woman becomes submerged, like a rock within the sea, and is no longer visible. I hope the fact that you do not write any more is not connected to the world's misperception of your bond with Mr Lewes.'

'The world does misperceive it. But it is a sacred bond,' said Marian, gravely.

She had got used to saying this phrase.

'It is!' agreed Maria Congreve. 'I have never seen two people so truly in sympathy with each other. And the very fact that you have been willing to bear the pain of public disapproval, bears witness —'

'— to the strength of the bond,' put in Marian. They looked at each other in the same mutual instant; Marian struck by Maria Congreve's beauty. Yes, she was beautiful. The light flush caused by the warm tropical moist atmosphere made her skin translucent, the colour in her cheeks fluctuating; and the sheer beauty of her eyebrows, those perfect arches, compelled Marian, and everything else went from her mind.

But Maria Congreve was obviously determined to pursue the matter of what she was doing with her time, and repeated her question.

'I have —' began Marian '— plans,' she finished, lamely.

'Do you have anything specific in mind?' asked her newly acquired friend, who was more than ever seeming like a protégé, the eyes so willing to drink in wisdom, with their soft brown eager glow.

'Ah — not at this moment,' said Marian.

Marian opened and shut her reticule, opened it, clipped it shut for a second time. It would be so pleasant to confide in Maria. Tell Maria her hopes, what she felt about writing, expand on the potential moral power of fiction, and as for the splendid reviews — why, she could quote great chunks of them, word for word! 'I —' she began, and then paused.

'Life has been ... good to me,' Marian went on slowly, enigmatically.

'Has it?' asked Maria, staring at her, as if hypnotised by the truly unfathomable aspect of her statement.

'It has,' said Marian, in the same slow, painful way.

A work of true genius.

The next second, her sister Chrissey's words came to mind.

My object in writing to you was to tell you how very sorry I have been that I ceased to write and neglected one who under all circumstances was kind to me and mine.

Chrissey had died nine days earlier.

They began the long walk home; Marian no longer talking, just hurrying forward to be home in time for lunch and Spencer's visit. Her spirits had abruptly sunk, her mouth tasted bitter. Chrissey had been ill for eighteen months. While her work was acclaimed, her sister had lost her life — at this thought, she walked even more quickly. 'Wait!' Maria Congreve was saying, laughing. Marian made herself slow her step. She had told Maria about Chrissey's illness, but not yet of her death. She'd tell her soon. She tried to concentrate now on what Maria Congreve was saying. Chrissey's words came again.

... who under all circumstances was kind to me and mine.

Each time she thought of Chrissey's generous, honest words, at the end of her life, she swallowed and set her mouth. As they walked by the river, the high trees, with the new pale leaves, formed a long bower; Marian kept glancing at the gleaming darkness of the water below, slow, snake-like: an oppressive sight. Grief, and lies. She was suddenly tempted to be open with Maria.

But you could ruin everything, said a voice at the back of her mind.

Aloud she said: 'I do believe everyone perceives the world differently, Maria; that we all look through an individually shaped prism. But I also believe that where truth is struck, the reader, or —' hastily '— the viewer, if it is a picture, will respond. That person will feel the spark of truth; and the smaller sympathy can enlarge.'

They stopped walking, on the river bank, by the tall reeds. What on earth had she been saying? She had a tipsy, dizzying moment, as if she'd peered down a precipice and lost her balance. She had let her mind unfurl as it would with Lewes. 'My dear Maria, I am sorry for boring you,' she murmured, patting Maria's hand.

'Boring me! On the contrary,' said Maria: and for a strange moment, Marian had the notion that Maria might be about to kiss her.

10

Marian returned just in time for lunch with Herbert Spencer. At the sight of him, her spirits began to revive.

She had met him through the Brays seven years earlier, at the exhibition at the Crystal Palace, where she'd been immediately struck by his conversation: a polymath, Herbert Spencer combined several disciplines in his work — philosophy, biology, anthropology, sociology, and liberal political theory. The friendship developed through the autumn. At evenings in the Strand at Chapman's, while she played the piano, they sang together; she remembered the time his jacket thrillingly kept brushing her shoulders, while she played Schubert's 'An die Musik', and warbled along above his tenor vibrato. There was a period when they saw each other every second day; visiting Chiswick or Kew, discussing pieces for the *Westminster Review*, which she was editing.

Spencer had been highly intrigued by Marian. In his characteristic style, he wrote to his friend Edward Lott about her, as *the translatress of Strauss, and the most admirable woman, mentally, I ever met. We have been for some time past on very intimate terms. I am very frequently at Chapman's, and the greatness of her intellect conjoined with her womanly qualities and manner, generally keep me by her side most of the evening.*

Marian's feelings had as usual become strong. In the summer, she boldly rented two rooms in a cottage in Broadstairs on the Kent coast. Spencer visited, they went for walks by the peaceful summer sea; over supper, on the second night, he placed his palm over her hand. The loosening, the warming that had kindled inside her, that he could take this step — as if by magic, they both rose from their chairs, he took her hand, drew her to the sink, and they kissed.

As abruptly as he had put his knuckle into the small of her back, to draw her further into the kiss — he had then disengaged himself, gently pushing her away; to her everlasting humiliation, he had given a strange little chuckle; said good-night; and gone with an insouciant air, up the stairs, to sleep in the other bedroom.

Well! The friendship had survived, and it was Spencer who had introduced her to George. And after she had begun living scandalously with George, he had visited them just at the time she had started writing *Clerical Scenes*, she had confided to him that she had begun writing fiction. He was the one other person in the world who knew, apart from Blackwood and Lewes.

Perhaps it had been a mistake to confide in him — some months before, irritatingly, it seemed he had let John Chapman prise the secret out of him. Still, it was pleasant to anticipate being with an old friend, in front of whom there was no need to dissemble.

★ ★ ★

Just after the clock chimed one, the philosopher arrived, with his keen eyes, strong, beak-like nose, and the forehead that seemed to declare him an intellectual before he'd even opened his mouth — a great expanse, made all the more so by his receding hair, which still curled, dark, under his ears. Lewes wrung his hand in greeting, Marian was able to forget Chrissey and lies, Lewes said that in his honour they were having beef for lunch, and were going to drink a bottle of Chateauneuf du Pape. Spencer, meanwhile, was surveying the room, going to the window, looking out, scanning the road; then they clinked glasses, sat down, Spencer hitching up his trousers as he did so.

'Congratulations to the author,' he said, raising his glass in Marian's direction. 'I hear it's a success. So this is the new abode!' he continued, changing the subject at once. 'Well, the ceilings are a reasonable height. How many rooms?'

'Rooms? We've got the whole house!' said Lewes.

'The whole house. Really.'

'You must realise,' pleaded Marian, smiling, 'that this is an unusual treat for us. Up until now we have been working side by side, in the same room, driving each other mad with the sound of our scratchy pens! At last, we can each work in solitude.'

'I imagine it's an agreeable contrast. Because, if I remember rightly, the amenities have not always been so forthcoming. I seem to remember you eating bread and dripping for lunch!'

They laughed. It was true — until recently, they'd been very badly off.

Marian asked how Spencer was, but Spencer, sniffing his glass, and sipping it carefully, briefly holding it up to the light with a suspicious air, seemed disinclined to talk about himself. When Lewes went to speak to Caroline about the beef (he favoured, he said, the French method of cooking it), Marian and Spencer were left alone. Marian regarded her old friend. On his last visit, at the end of January, his mood had been forthcoming: today he seemed more withdrawn. She leaned forward.

'My dear Spencer, I was re-reading you only last week, and was very impressed with your writing on ritual, its fundamental importance, as preceding those more developed constraints such as law.'

For the first time since his arrival, his eyes acquired some warmth.

'Thank you — thank you.'

He considered, and then said: 'I think I said that the modifications of behaviour that we call "manners" and "good behaviour" precede those modifications wrought by law and religion.'

'Yes, indeed,' said Marian.

Ah, she was remembering.

'The great advantage of studying primitive societies,' Spencer was saying, warming to his theme, 'is that we see human rituals laid bare. But even in a society such as ours, primitive rituals persist. When I entered your house not thirty minutes ago, Lewes and I extended our arms, and shook each other by the hand. Why? We could as well extend our legs and rub knees. We think the handshake civilised, but the relationship to older ritual is very visible, to my way of thinking. We thereby announce that we are friends, not enemies. We will not murder each other. Just as a man in a railway carriage might offer his newspaper to a stranger when he has finished with it: he too is saying, we will not kill each other, though we are strangers.'

It was a relief to see her old friend animated at last. But what a lecturer he was — interested and happy in his own thoughts, above everything else! He turned to her.

'It doesn't surprise me that those passages interest you,' he said, eying her with a suddenly malicious, gleaming smile. 'You were always an observer of social ritual — not just in others, but in yourself.'

Marian looked questioningly at him.

'Ah, you don't remember!' he said, laughing. 'You said to me, one day, that you suffered from a double consciousness. That you were constantly aware of whatever you were saying, as you were saying it. That you listened to yourself in a critical way. You were, in your own words, split in two. When you told me that, I pitied you from the bottom of my heart.'

Marian smiled thinly.

She did recognise what he described, and remembered confiding in him, too. Foolish. Fortunately, lunch was ready. Spencer seemed more cheerful now, attacking his meal with good humour, while she felt damped down. He up, she down, like a seesaw. She must recover herself.

They had a good lunch of roast beef, cabbage with cream, potatoes; for once, Caroline had excelled herself. They drank and moved on to a second bottle at Lewes' suggestion, though Spencer at first demurred. Caroline had put coal on the fire in the parlour; they retired there after lunch. Once again Lewes said what a pleasure it was to see Spencer.

'And,' said Lewes, indicating the lunch, the room, 'if we live like this, it's all down to Polly. What a success, eh, Spencer? The sales of *Adam Bede* … I still find it hard to believe!'

'It is really very good news,' murmured Marian.

'I congratulate you both,' said Spencer, earnestly.

'But no saying anything, eh, Spencer? I know you say that Chapman wheedled it out of you —'

'He did.'

'— but that has been a nuisance for us, as you can imagine. He's written to Polly making all sorts of insinuating hints, which we've had to deny. Because Marian feels strongly, as do I, that we need to keep the incognito.'

Marian sat forward intently, to hear what Spencer had to say. She half hoped he would disagree.

'No doubt about that. No doubt whatsoever,' said Spencer, with an expression of the utmost gravity. 'If the authorship of the book were to become known, it would be impossible to vouch for its continued success.'

'You think so?' said Marian.

'I do, I'm afraid.'

He had folded his arms, in the manner of an inexorable judge. Lewes shrugged, found his cigars, offered Spencer one, but Spencer declined, saying he never smoked, he was convinced it was injurious to the heart. 'Fine,' said Lewes carelessly, taking one for himself and lighting it.

Marian looked restlessly at the clock. She wondered when Spencer would leave.

Abruptly Spencer said: 'I may have exaggerated. Please don't take it to heart, Miss Evans —'

'Mrs Lewes, not Miss Evans!' said Lewes. 'You have no idea the problems we have — half of Polly's old friends keep addressing her as Miss Evans, and if the Captain and his wife were to hear of this, life could become very difficult. The landlord,' he added.

Spencer apologised. Puffing on his cigar, Lewes waved a hand to indicate he was mollified. 'Yes, my dear fellow,' went on Lewes. 'The success of *Adam Bede* is unprecedented. Mudies has had to increase the supply of the book. Nearly all of the first edition — eighteen hundred copies! — have been sold. And even though the type's been distributed, it's just been re-set for a second edition! Yes — the whole of London talking about it.'

'I have heard talk about it, too,' admitted Spencer. 'Very admiring talk.'

'Like —?' said Lewes. He looked like a parent keen to hear more about his favourite child.

Spencer cleared his throat, then said: 'I've heard many tributes, as you can well imagine. At the same time, it must be said, the book has its detractors.'

Marian and Lewes looked at him.

'I would be a liar if I didn't mention it,' went on Spencer, with a sanctimonious air.

'But being the good friend that you are,' said Lewes, smiling, 'you're not going to repeat those edifying remarks.'

'But of course you are.'

The words came clear, spoken by Marian. She was sitting suddenly very upright, pale-faced, staring at Spencer.

'No, I hesitate to elaborate —'

'Then don't,' snapped Lewes.

Marian said, 'You'd better tell me.'

'My dear Mrs Lewes, as I say, your book has many admirers, but also its detractors. I shall not name names —'

'Then don't speak at all,' interrupted Lewes again, red in the face, holding himself straight.

'I shall not name names,' proceeded Spencer, smoothly, 'but as I say, there are some who feel that the subject of infanticide is intrinsically tactless. And also that your treatment of it is questionable — in danger of arousing quite the wrong sort of attitude in the public at large. Now, I must at once say — this is, of course, not my feeling. I myself am, as I always have been, an admirer of your writing, whether for the *Westminster Review* or otherwise.'

'The *Westminster Review* be damned!' shouted Lewes. 'Polly, take no notice,' he added, scowling, in a deliberately audible aside.

The two men's eyes met, and Spencer lowered his. Now there was a ritual, thought Marian, mechanically. Soon afterwards, Spencer left.

'Good riddance!' burst out Lewes, once the door had shut. 'I would be happy never to see him again.'

'And I,' confessed Marian.

'He's jealous, that's the truth of it. He can't stand your success. He may even baulk at mine; after all, *Physiology*'s been selling well too. Where are you going?'

Marian was going to bed, saying she had a headache.

Upstairs, Marian's thoughts were running hard. Spencer's petty smallness of heart, and it was with this creature that she'd been in love! Lewes was right, he was jealous. Was this what she had to look forward to? Was this how people would respond when they knew?

When Lewes came in to the bedroom. the curtains were drawn, the room was in deep shadow. It was March; outside, the spring blackbirds were twitting. He sat on the bed and without saying anything held her hand.

'I know what you're thinking,' said Lewes.

And she, lying there, knew what *he* was thinking. That it was like an illness, she was so sensitive to put-downs. It didn't matter that *The Atheneaum* talked of genius, that Owen Jones was praising this book to the skies, that public demand had outstripped supply: a few words from an envious old friend and she lost her way. They sat in silence in the darkened room.

'It was a mistake to have confided in him,' she said eventually. 'I don't even know if he'll keep it a secret.'

'Very likely not.'

★ ★ ★

By early evening she was back in the wing-back armchair she liked. Lewes grimaced when he saw her shawl. It usually indicated a certain mood.

To cheer her, he suggested she read aloud her story to him. For the last few weeks, with Chrissey dying, she had put her Mill book to one side. There was too much of her own family life in it for comfort just now. Instead she'd begun working on a story — the Veil, it was called, or rather 'The Lifted Veil'.

'Really?' she said, and she turned her beautiful grey-blue eyes on him, as if emerging from a dream.

'*Really.*'

They liked to read aloud in the small sitting room. Lewes asked Caroline to stoke up the fire and make scrambled eggs, then poured out two brandies, the inevitable prelude to a reading of her work. The evening would work as the antidote to Spencer. When the fire was burning nicely, and Caroline had lit the oil lamps — lighting also helped her mood, he noticed — Lewes sat himself expectantly in the wing-back chair opposite hers.

'Did I tell you it's a Gothic tale? A Gothic tale of an *outré* kind?'

'Not in so many words.'

Holding her manuscript in front of her, she began speaking in the tone that never failed to charm him — still the most musical, low, pleasing voice he had ever heard. He listened carefully: the hero, Latimer, is rejected by his family because of his poetic, shudderingly sensitive nature. But how odd! In an unusual departure from realism, Marian had created a hero not merely sensitive, but supernaturally gifted — able to see with magical clarity into other people. He hears their thoughts, experiences their feelings. The essential gap that shuts off one person's consciousness from another's, is missing.

At the end Lewes was silent. Then he asked her to read again the paragraph, early on, where Latimer summed up his supernatural abilities.

Marian leafed back through her pages; as she read, her colour rose:

I saw the souls of those who were in a close relation to me ... as if thrust asunder by a microscopic vision, that showed all the intermediate frivolities, all the suppressed egoism, all the struggling chaos of puerilities, meanness, vague capricious memories, and indolent make-shift thoughts, from which human words and deeds emerge like leaflets covering a fermenting heap.

Lewes had shut his eyes while she spoke.

'What a vision! It's really worthy of Bosch. This calls for a cigar,' he added, feeling in his pocket for one. Then he squatted down by the fire, held it out to the flame, puffed, so that the end of it glowed; then resumed his seat.

'It is a little sour,' she admitted; but it seemed to George that her eyelids lowered just then.

'It sounds like our Friend,' said Lewes.

'The Not-Friend.'

Marian said she felt lighter for working on it. 'It is an odd, reflexive tale,' she added, enigmatically.

Soon after that, Marian went walking alone on the Common. She found it conducive to thinking, both of the brother and sister book, to which she had returned; but also of her strange story. She was reaching the end of the walk when the word 'morbidity' came to her. Was she — 'morbid'? Was she — different from other people, with her too-volatile feelings? She could remember the hall in Coventry, being escorted out by her aunt, sobbing. She had had a fit of hysteria because no one had asked her to dance. No one would love her, not with her nose, her chin, her long face.

Was she still 'morbid'? She had noticed Lewes' attempts to stop Spencer from voicing criticisms of *Adam Bede* the other day. She was reminded of the time in Jersey, before she met Blackwood in person. She had come across a letter by Lewes to Blackwood, as yet unsent, on the table.

Entre nous, *let me hint that unless you have any* serious *objection to make to Eliot's stories,* don't *make any. He is so easily discouraged, so diffident of himself, that not being prompted by necessity to write, he will close the series in the belief that his writing is not relished. I laugh at him for his diffidence and tell him it's a proof he is not an author. But he has passed the middle of life without writing at all, and will easily be made to give it up. Don't allude to this hint of mine. He wouldn't like my interfering.*

The ease with which George diagnosed her! The freedom with which he explained her to Blackwood! She didn't know whether to be irritated, or amused.

11

Ann and I keep meaning to meet to talk about the George Eliot conference, and finally do so at the small Greek restaurant off Queen Square. After lukewarm kebabs, hers without meat, we move outside so she can vape. It's a mild night for early February, but still quite cold, so we put our coats back on. At least they have a heat lamp above. I explain we should have a list of speakers soon, but first we have to grab the star — ! — so I've asked Hans to be keynote speaker. I say this with a pleasant expression, although I'm still irritated at his veto. I assume she'll smile back, at this reference to her husband, but she pulls at her vape, exhales, saying thoughtfully, 'But he's a man.'

'Is that a problem?'

'It's a conference on George Eliot. The name George Eliot says it all.'

At the end of this sentence, her upper lip twitches involuntarily.

'You feel it's repeating the problem.'

'Absolutely,' she says, another spark of anger in her eyes.

Ann takes her coat off, and in the strong lighting I am struck by her dress. Everything about it is carefully calculated. It's vintage, of white smock-cotton, with baggy pockets, edging in the style of lace, above Dr Martens boots, dark tights. The Victorian look is compounded by her hair, which is long and straight. She is watching me carefully out of her small but pretty eyes. She has the skin of an English rose: pale, so that fluctuations of colour are as visible as blood behind glass.

I explain. I have no leeway here. The Chair is keen for Hans be the keynote speaker, he is a big name, this conference is supposed to attract the paying public, not just students and academics. We are holding it in the great hall, we need to fill it.

I don't add that the last conference I organised had been a failure, with scanty attendance, the two best speakers cancelling just before; and that when I raised this conference with Marcus he looked at me over his spectacles, and said with a friendly smile, 'But make it work this time.'

I don't refer, either, to the email I received this morning from him.

Be reassured — I'm already talking to management about the promotion. But let's have a five-star conference first.

Marcus

I reach for my glass of Domestica. I am going to be drinking a lot of Domestica in the next few months. When you put on a conference with someone, you're thrown together, you get to know how willing the other one is, how selfish or unselfish, efficient or sloppy, flexible or rigid. I try to change the subject. 'What about you,' I ask, 'will you speak on a topic related to your book?'

'Still thinking about it.'

Books. Our books on George Eliot are the elephants in the room. We still haven't discussed them.

* * *

Over the next weeks, the temperature changes between us. We exchange neutral emails to do with themes and matters like the goodie bag (when people are paying £40 for an event, they quite like a bag with a pen and a pad, a map, a list of events, tangible return for money). And then a fortnight later, after an inaugural dinner, Ann suggests a drink and we end up at midnight in the Doubletree Bar on Southampton Row. Cheesy orange lighting, over-varnished tables, brown-orange-green carpet, drinks at tourist prices. 'I'll get these,' says Ann. As I sit in my plush velour chair, I hear her grilling the barman about kahlua. Does he know how to make Black Russians? *Properly?* Black Russians. She doesn't ask me if I want one; she comes back with two wicked black drinks, and plonks mine on the table. 'You'll enjoy this,' she says, with perfect certainty, drawing another chair up, to put her feet on it. After she's drunk what looks like all of it in one go, she lets her head flip right back, runs her hands luxuriously through her hair, and says, 'That feels ver-ry good.'

I feel, in some mysterious way, that she has gone beyond me; as if I am standing dustily on the shore. I follow her then, drink mine fast too. I don't know how much alcohol is in it, I think it's a double or triple, but I feel my head reel and suddenly I am feeling good, extraordinarily good, and outright happy. All worries dissolve. Ann has her head resting back in the chair, and now, without lifting it in the slightest, simply turning her neck, so her face is towards me, she smiles a slow, unabashedly drunken smile. Then she is frowning as she is smiling. 'I realise I don't know anything about you. Do you live with someone?'

I shake my head.

'Divorced,' I say. I add, for good measure, 'You could pay me money and I wouldn't go back to a "relationship"!' — doing air quotes with my fingers.

'Good for you!' she laughs. There is a mood of sisterly solidarity in the air.

I am lightheaded the next day at work; I feel tired, but as if my head has been hoovered out and cleaned. I see her at a staff meeting. Our eyes meet, her smile a coded reference to the night before.

Only now do we talk about our books on Eliot. 'A novel!' she says, her eyebrows shooting up. She admits she is surprised. Hers is a critique, a revisionary critique, she says, of Eliot from a political, feminist viewpoint. She rather dislikes Eliot, in fact. 'Lewes is my favourite,' she admits. 'You know he was into Free Love?'

12

In early April, Marian heard from her old Coventry friend Sara Hennell.

I want to ask you if you have read Adam Bede *or the* Scenes of Clerical Life, *and whether you know that the author is Mr Liggins,* wrote Sara.

'George!' Marian called out, from the breakfast table.

He shouted from the bathroom, saying he would be there in a minute. Marian continued to read. The letter was fascinating. Sara was talking about the man called Liggins, who was currently rumoured to be the mystery author of *Adam Bede.*

More, Sara was giving her an account of a group of parsons actually approaching this man Liggins in the local town, *washing his slop-basin at a pump.*

(Well. That wasn't very dignified.)

He has no servant, went on Sara, *and does everything for himself, but he inspired them with a reverence that would have made any impertinent question impossible. The son of a baker, of no mark at all in his town, so it is possible you may not have heard of him, but he calls himself 'George Eliot'. They say he gets no profit out of 'Adam Bede', and gives it freely to Blackwood, which is a shame.*

(Giving it away to Blackwood! Why would any author do that?)

We have not read him yet, went on Sara, *but the extracts are irresistible.*

Irresistible. Sara thought they were irresistible.

'George!' she called out, louder, in high good humour.

George arrived, and they laughed over the letter together. Since Spencer's visit, they both feared their malicious old friend might further leak her identity;

and though Marian had the occasional yearning to come out and declare herself, as soon as the idea of exposure began to seem imminent or real, it was enough to wake her up at night — and last week had done so. Just in time, Liggins, that bragging imposter, was coming to the rescue. He was, they agreed, the perfect smokescreen.

Marian wrote back to Sara, saying gaily that she hadn't read *Adam Bede*, but would do soon, as Lewes had liked it a lot. Straight after that, she copied out Sara's letter to send to Blackwood — he'd be amused at the idea of this strange fellow Liggins declaring himself the author, boasting he didn't take any payment for it!

But the following day, Marian re-read Sara's letter again.

She'd lied to Sara freely, even with relish. In fact, she'd been lying to her for some time. *Do not guess at authorship — it is a bad speculation,* she had written reprovingly to her, seven months before, when Sara asked what she was doing. Her old friends were clearly curious at the lack of journalism. Charles Bray — married to Cara Bray, who had been the third great friend, along with Cara and Sara — had written also, suggesting jocularly that she might be writing a novel; she wrote back asking, also jocular, when his *poem* was going to come out. *Seriously, I wish you would not set false rumours, or any other rumours, afloat about me. They are injurious. Several people have spoken to me of a supposed novel I was going to bring out. Such things are damaging to me.*

The four of them had not been together in one room since the day she left England for the continent with Lewes.

Rosehill had been the start. Rosehill was one of the big houses in Coventry, where people of note met — writers, thinkers; Marian had heard gossip about their progressive ways, conversations, and social connections. Now, as she sat in the high-ceilinged sitting room — it was nearly dark outside, and Lewes was still not back — she thought back to the first time she ever visited. She had changed her blouse three times before. *I am going I hope today,* she wrote with dry lofti-ness, and portentousness, to her teacher-friend Maria Lewis, *to effect a breach in the thick wall of indifference behind which the denizens of Coventry seem inclined to entrench themselves, but I fear I shall fail.*

How stiff she was.

Two hours later, in the early afternoon, she had arrived at the gate, and there was the house itself, at a small distance, and it made her stop. The size of it — and the beauty of it too. Yes, it looked beautiful in the mellow sun, white, low, two-storeyed, terrifyingly gracious; with its small spreading trees on either side. Coming closer, the doorway had two columns, a portico showing two urns.

The maid had shown her in, she'd walked into the drawing room. A man with abundant dark hair rose abruptly from an armchair. A look of open, frank good-natured tolerance — a little dogged, and a little hopeless, yet warm. Her own nervousness began to recede. And the two women — the sisters Cara and Sara — seemed to be looking at her kindly. Soon she had an even better sensation: when she talked, their interest was stirred. She herself was entranced by them, particularly by Sara's voice: there, Marian, with her quick ear, detected all kinds of subtle modulations of vowels and phrasing, intimating a new hinterland of culture, different to anything she had yet heard. Sara had been, she later learned, friend and governess in the Bonham Carter family in London.

Now Marian went to the bedroom, and returned to where she was sitting, Sara's letter on her lap. She had in her palm the brooch, cool and heavy, a garnet set in blackened silver, gift from Sara. She still had it. Yes, they'd been generous. How many hours she had spent with them, how she had quickly learned to share both affection and ideas. She had lost her bumpkin-ness. Shutting her eyes, Marian could see the garden at Rosehill, the bearskin under the acacia tree on which they talked in the afternoons, the wood pigeon making his curious muffled, rootling, repetitive sound in the chimney, a soothing sound she liked. The sheer elation of being in this new kind of company: her initial conviction that pleasure like this wasn't possible, couldn't be — to sit in the warm shade, Charles Bray, shirtsleeves rolled up, waistcoat open in louche fashion, bringing glasses of wine (against Cara's protests), to 'help the talk along'. Florid-faced Charles spitting (the more intense the talk, the more he spat) with reformist zeal. Education, contraception, labour relations, atheism, literature, phrenology (Charles' passion), Free Love. Anything. They talked, all four of them. She was twenty-one. Her own views about religion had already been shifting.

They had cracked her provincial shell open and let in the light. She had learned the priceless freedom to think as she chose.

There was a wisp of dry hay or grass still threaded through the top of the brooch, that she plucked out now, and held out in the light; yes, there it was: and then she did remember it, the afternoon of the brooch, when they had pronounced themselves sisters. Cara and Sara were sisters, but she had been invited to join, a guest sister, as the brooch was pinned to her blouse.

'I owe them a great deal,' admitted Marian to herself, sitting there. She leant over to stoke the fire, which was flickering low, though outside the wind was still up. It was through Sara she'd acquired her first task of translating Strauss' *Das Leben Jesu*; in fact, thinking about it now, everything had followed from meeting them: London, the *Westminster Review* — her translation her calling card — and George. For more than a decade, she had been treated as family. They had taken her with them on holiday: to Tenby, Geneva. They wrote to her constantly, as she wrote to them; her life was their concern. For years, Marian poured out her deepest fears, about being ugly and unloveable, how her fate was to be alone, as she repeatedly fell in love and was rebuffed.

And then she had met Lewes. At this point she had become more private. Lewes' reputation was bad — the debauched man with the weird marital history, who believed in Free Love: and not only was he married, he couldn't divorce. When she considered living openly with Lewes, she discussed it with Charles Bray and John Chapman, but not with Cara and Sara. She said to herself: for their sake, I will not involve them, they are women.

And deep in herself she was dreaming of *Villette*, which she had recently read: Charlotte Brontë's heady brew of passionate love, unmoored from England; the town of Labassecoeur as odd as a region of the unconscious.

On her last visit to Rosehill, late June, just before leaving England, there was one afternoon, talking in the garden, sitting as usual under the acacia tree, on the soft bearskin (she liked to lie on her side on it, knees curled up, propping her cheek up on her elbow), when mid-sentence, Marian stopped speaking. She had looked at the two dear women, a little as she imagined Crusoe, from the boat, regarding the island he was leaving forever. And had a sharp fear inside her chest

— that she was going away, making this momentous change in her life, without saying a word to either of them. And then those sensations changed quick as the weather. Leaving her with an impression of the day's heat, Cara wearing lace at her throat, her sleeves unpeeled on the warm day to the elbow; Cara's arms, Marian had seen for the first time, having freckles.

Before going, Marian packed up belongings to return to Sara: a print by Titian, Sara's *Hebrew Grammar* and *Apocryphal Gospels*. She had told them simply that she was going abroad. *I shall soon send you a good bye, for I am preparing to go to 'Labassecour':*

Dear Friends — all three

I have only time to say good bye and God bless you. Poste Restante, Weimar for the next six weeks, and afterwards Berlin.

Ever your loving and grateful,

Marian

Three months later, in a letter to Charles in which she described fully her resolve to stay openly with Lewes as his nominal wife, she mentioned Cara and Sara. *I am ignorant how far Cara and Sara may be acquainted with the state of things, and how they may feel towards me. I am quite prepared to accept the consequences of a step which I have deliberately taken and to accept them without irritation or bitterness. The most painful consequence will, I know, be loss of friends. If I do not write therefore, understand that it is because I desire not to obtrude myself.*

Having posted the letter in the leafy streets of Weimar — the leaves had begun to fall, it was a wet, October day — she made her way with a new sensation of lightness to the rosily lit Kuchenladen, bought a rare treat for that night's dessert — strüdel — before returning to 62A Kaufgasse, the room she had rented with George. The thought of Cara and Sara had been nagging at her since she had left England. Yet how liberating the time had been! Everywhere they were accepted without question. Researching and writing his biography of Goethe, Lewes knew writers and musicians, and their circle had rapidly expanded. Soon they had become great friends with Liszt, and his astonishingly ugly mistress, the Princess von-Sayn Wittgenstein — the ease with which these

Europeans accepted the less conventional relationship! It was like drinking good wine.

But all this time Cara and Sara had existed at the side of her mind, as a sort of weight. To think of them had been like putting on old clothes, that were too familiar. And her dreams! She had a dream of a newborn cuckoo in the nest. The strangest dream. She was the cuckoo, and yet she devoured it, which made no sense at all; and then she flew; none of it made sense.

Shortly after writing to Charles, a letter had arrived from Sara. With a slight sense of being captive, she stared at the familiar handwriting on the envelope. At the same time, with awful clarity, she recalled the years, the many years, of her woeful, intimate, outpourings to Sara, addressing her playfully as *Cara Sposa*, and *Beloved Achates*, to tell her yet again, laced with apologies for doing so, about her unhappiness, her illnesses, her fears, her loneliness. Abruptly she put the letter down. Instead she went out to walk — to the green at the end of Weimar, a place without borders or fences, a park that blurred into the surrounding nature, in a beguilingly unEnglish way.

She opened the letter in the evening.

Not to obtrude yourself, Sara expostulated, *when if you ever thought our friendship good for anything, you must know how we have been longing to hear from you!* Sara went on to say: *So much for my own feelings of your treatment of us, a trifling subject indeed compared with that of your change of life — but on that I hardly dare to enter.*

Marian frowned, put the letter on the table. That night over supper she said, vivaciously, 'My dear George, she completely misunderstands me! She is failing to see the central situation. I did not want to compromise either Sara or Cara.'

George agreed.

'Yes indeed. I did not want to compel either to associate with me! George, are you listening? If I had taken them into my confidence, they would have been less free to choose.'

'You tell her that, then!' said George, but he seemed more interested in scraping off the last bit of meat from the mangy, half-starved pheasant they had bought cut-price for their landlady to cook.

She would reply to Sara the next day.

Three days passed before she took up her pen.

My dear Sara

The mode in which you and Cara have interpreted both my words and my silence makes me dread lest in writing more I should only give rise to fresh misconceptions. I am so deeply conscious of having had neither the feeling nor the want of feeling which you impute to me that I am quite unable to read into my words, quoted by you, the sense which you put upon them.

She read through what she had written and approved. She was aware, too, of a sense of indignation stirring slowly in herself. With more spirit she continued:

When you say that I do not care about Cara's or your opinion and friendship it seems much the same to me as if you said that I didn't care to eat when I was hungry or to drink when I was thirsty. One of two things: either I am a creature without affection, on whom the memories of years have no hold, or you, Cara and Mr Bray are the most cherished friends I have in the world.

Good. Good.

It is simply self-contradictory to say that a person can be indifferent about her dearest friends; yet this is what you substantially say, when you accuse me of 'boasting with what serenity I can give you up', of 'speaking proudly' etc.

She drew in her breath. Goodness, the roar outside — she got up to look out of the dirty window. So dirty she could hardly see. She could just make out the Michaelmas fair going on below: small, primitive-looking crooked stalls, in this dear town of Weimar, that seemed two hundred years behind England. She sat down and continued.

There is now no longer any secrecy to be preserved about Mr. Lewes' affairs or mine, and whatever I have written to Mr Bray, I have written to you. I wish to speak simply and to act simply but I think it can hardly be unintelligible to you that I shrink from writing elaborately about private feelings and circumstances.

There. It was her right to be private. She had a trembling sensation inside herself, like the tremor of rage.

Cara, you and my own sister are the three women who are tied to my heart by a cord which can never be broken and which really pulls me continually. My love for you rests on a past which no future can reverse, and offensive as the words seem to have been to you, I must repeat, that I can feel no bitterness towards you, however you may act towards me.

But when she showed the letter to George, he merely laughed. 'Fine!' he said, picking up the *Leader*. The Brays and Sara Hennell, he seemed to be saying, were her affair.

After that, Sara had accepted the new terms between them. They both wrote to her. 'It's good we are friends again,' said Marian to herself, now, in the empty drawing-room. But how strange that Sara was reading *Adam Bede* without realising it was her.

Back in the old days of Rosehill, she used to talk a great deal about the question of faith, and also about writing, with Sara. Even now Sara was still sending her odd portions of the book she was writing, called *Thoughts in Aid of Faith*, asking for her advice.

Marian had read bits of it, and passed some of it to Lewes.

'Awfully mediocre,' sighed Lewes, puffing on his cigar, after he'd read ten pages.

'It really is!' agreed Marian. 'I think it's worse than her previous one. But I'll have to write to her as truthfully as I can. It won't be helpful otherwise.'

'You do as you think fit,' said Lewes, twinkling.

Marian coloured. Wheels within wheels: here she was, sending her old friend criticisms of her work, with commendable truthfulness; and all the while she was lying to the same friend about what she was doing. Lewes, with his usual tolerant good nature, saw it all.

13

The week after Sara's letter about Liggins arrived, the Congreves came to supper. Before they dined, Lewes opened a promisingly dusty bottle of Pouilly-Fumé 1847; within ten minutes, alcohol was running through their bloodstreams; and even Maria Congreve's pale skin was becoming duskily flushed, her smile brimming. Talk soon turned to the new Scottish National Gallery, which had opened towards the end of last month.

Sitting in his chair, Richard Congreve, legs crossed, thumbs in his waistcoat, said: 'It's a fine building — very handsome indeed. Designed by —'

'Playfair, wasn't it?' put in Lewes, quickly.

'Precisely,' said Congreve, inclining his head in the way he did. 'In fact, I had the privilege of attending the opening, in Edinburgh. It's chiefly a re-housing of the old Scottish Academy works, of course.'

'Did you go to Edinburgh too,?' asked Marian, turning to Maria Congreve.

Maria explained that she'd been too busy preparing for their trip at the end of the month. In fact, she had news. They were taking her younger sister Emily to the Continent for five months.

'Five months! You're away for five months!' echoed Marian.

Marian was silent. It came to her, as the plates were being cleared away, that she didn't really like Wandsworth.

'I will miss you,' she said to Maria, at dessert. She spoke so that no one else could hear.

'I feel the same,' replied Maria, in a tender, low voice. 'I remember what we talked about on our last walk, and always will do. I am glad that I have your permission.'

They were both silent for a moment, each thoughtful.

'So,' said Marian humorously, but still in a quiet voice, putting her hand on the younger woman's arm, 'you will tell me that you love me? So that I can be happy?'

After supper, Lewes put a decanter of port on the table, with a flourish. 'Ten years old,' he announced, with satisfaction. 'I'd be interested to know how you rate it.'

Mr Congreve sipped it, with a look of great attention.

'Excellent,' he pronounced. 'Excellent. Which reminds me, talking of excellent, have you by any chance read *Adam Bede*?'

He went on to say that they might well be tired of the subject, as it had been talked up to death, but he had rarely read a finer book. In fact, from something they'd said, he had the impression they *hadn't* read it.

'It is,' announced Richard Congreve, folding his arms, 'true to nature in an unprecedented fashion.'

'Really,' said Lewes.

'Most definitely. But what I find astonishing,' went on Richard Congreve, 'is the way this fellow Liggins is doubted! Why?'

The clock ticked in the silence. Lewes seemed to be concentrating on the decanter as he poured himself another glass. 'People have different ideas,' he said casually. 'There's some dispute about his claim, as I take it.'

'I don't think there is, actually,' said Congreve, quickly, with warmth. Marian could hear that this was not the first time Congreve had discussed this — he had the air of someone returning to a favourite topical debate. 'I don't know if you saw the letter in *The Times* today? It just about clarifies it.'

Marian took care not to glance at Lewes. They had both pored over the letter this morning, Marian speaking more and more loudly, cheeks reddening with anger. In the space of minutes, Liggins no longer seemed a helpful smokescreen, but an infuriating imposter. They had drafted an immediate peremptory reply to be sent to the editor.

Mr Congreve was glancing inquisitively at them — perhaps their expressions struck him. He went on, briskly, 'The letter's from a fellow by the name of Anders, who says Joseph Liggins, of Nuneaton, wrote the book; and he says that if anyone doubts Liggins is the author, they just have to ask someone in the neighbourhood! Apparently the connections are very obvious. The characters in the book are just like those in real life. Everyone local recognises them.'

A gross simplification of the creative process, thought Marian, irritably. In actual fact, the beginning was minute observation, but imagination did the rest.

'Right-oh,' said Lewes. He was drumming his fingers restively on the small table, looking round the room with a vacant expression.

'And someone suggested a woman wrote it! I don't think so, I don't think so,' said Richard Congreve, in a complacent tone. 'You only have to read the first chapter to see that the author is a man, with a clear moral horizon, as at home in a carpenter's workshop as I was in an Oxford college. My guess is that this Mystery Author is a clergyman who's good at carpentry.'

Marian said: 'Perhaps Mr Congreve wants some more port.'

Lewes said: 'Yes. How about it?'

Richard Congreve assented, and Lewes filled his glass.

★ ★ ★

Marian had gone to the kitchen, ostensibly to speak to the new servant, Martha, who'd arrived the week before. Martha said, in her thick west country voice, that everything was fine. Through the steamed-up window, Marian could just make out the dark backs of the houses at the end of the garden. Blocking out so much sky.

Marian missed the countryside, the lanes, dishevelled, sweet, dirty, winding, the open free prospects. Away from this talk, gossip, posturing, lies.

The tenacity of this man Liggins.

Good that Mr Congreve liked the book.

As she walked back to the front room, she wondered about declaring herself. If she could overcome fear —

* * *

Richard Congreve, one leg crossed over the other, hands deep in his pockets, was saying, 'Superb vintage, by the way, Lewes,' nodding in the direction of his glass.

'You like it?'

'Superb. But as I say — the most extraordinary reviews. The *Westminster Review* gave it twenty-seven pages. Twenty-seven pages! And there was a magnificent piece in *The Times* yesterday. Ah,' — and with a nimble movement he'd risen, having evidently spotted the newspaper on the sideboard, the same one that Lewes had brought home the day before. 'Well, here we are!' exclaimed Congreve. 'You've got it! Hmm — wait — three whole columns — "first-rate novel, and its author takes rank at once among the masters of the art". I urge this book on both of you,' he finished, in a tone approaching severity.

His face was severe, too. That was the thing with Richard Congreve, thought Marian. He looked at ease, but was stiff, tricky, formal underneath.

She sent George an affectionate glance.

'... wonderful ... wonderful ...' Richard was continuing, about his new discovery.

'Unprecedented, I think you said?' said Lewes, with a casual air.

'I did.'

'In — what way?'

'Oh!' said Congreve, promptly. 'The artistry of the whole thing. The work of a master. A complete master.'

He spoke quickly, almost dismissively.

'It shows such human understanding,' said Maria, in her quiet voice. 'I liked the author's approach to life.'

Richard laughed indulgently, and shook his head. 'A hazy generalisation, my dear. The thing is a superb make-believe.'

After supper, the two couples divided up: Lewes talking to Maria about

Lucerne, while Richard and Marian sat side by side on the chaise longue. Abruptly, Richard swung round to face her. Face distorted by pity, a dark cleft showing between his brows. In a low, rapid voice: 'My dear Mrs Lewes, I have talked about this with Mrs Congreve, but I wanted to say this personally to you before we travelled. When I used to read you in the *Westminster Review*, I was impressed — exceedingly. I did not feel that your mind travelled in narrow grooves. And,' — now he lowered his voice further — 'I am distressed that since your — marriage — I have seen no pieces by you. A voice has gone —'

She made a face that might pass for gratitude; saw him flick Lewes a suspicious look.

Later that night, once the Congreves had gone, Marian reached for *Adam Bede*. Lewes had pursued Maria Congreve about liking the author's 'approach to life', and when pressed, she had mentioned the Rector Irwine, his 'reluctance to judge'.

Marian was curious to see precisely what had stirred her young friend, and she eagerly turned the pages until she reached the passage where the reader meets the Rector Irwine, playing chess with his mother. The Rector, explains the author, is sometimes criticised by the local methodists, as being too lax. He has no zealous preference for the Bible over poetry; he's partial to enjoying life; thinks *the custom of baptism more important than its doctrine*; is decidedly not an *earnest* man; fonder of church history than divinity. Has no very lofty aims, no theological enthusiasms. Feels no serious alarm about the souls of his parishioners, in fact.

On the other hand, the narrator says (and how pleasurable it had been for Marian to write this defence):

I must plead, for I have an affectionate partiality towards the Rector's memory, that he was not vindictive — and some philanthropists have been so; that he was not intolerant — and there is a rumour that some zealous theologians have not been altogether free from that blemish; that although he would probably have declined to give his body to be burned in any public cause, and was far from bestowing all his goods to feed the poor, he had that charity which has sometimes been lacking to very illustrious virtue — he was tender to other men's failings, and unwilling to impute evil.

She was satisfied. Although Maria Congreve hadn't recognised her in the book, she had, unknown to herself, pinpointed a precise example of Marian's philosophy of tolerance and compassion. Here, in short, was her argument against the world.

14

Towards the end of April, the Congreves left for their five-month stay on the Continent. Some days later, Lewes found Marian reading a letter, expression rapt.

'What have you got there?'

She had a letter from Mrs Congreve — that's all.

'Well, it may be *that's all*, but you look remarkably like the cat with the cream.'

When Marian went to walk Rough on the Common — the Congreves' dog — Lewes noticed she had pocketed the letter. He guessed she was taking it with her to read again on her favourite bench.

He had noticed that after Marian met up with Maria Congreve, her mood was improved, even until the next day. He had noted, too, the adoring looks Maria Congreve sent Marian. All, he thought, to the good.

★ ★ ★

The red-bound book of *Letters* edited by Gordon Haight is in my dusty hand, I'm sitting on the floor in my dusty flat. I want to read again that letter from Maria Congreve that meant so much to Marian. I flick through the years until I reach May 1859. Up floats Maria Congreve's gentle voice, writing to Marian from Dieppe:

I slept about a dozen times I should think, and woke once with a full persuasion that I was coming to call upon you in the afternoon. You must have a very strong influence over me. I usually wake so entirely mistress of the situation, but you do make such a difference to me in my rising up and lying down and in all my ways — now I actually know you, and that you will let me love you and even give me some love too.

I usually wake so entirely mistress of the situation — but no longer. Maria Congreve has been disturbed by Marian. Deeply, but perhaps joyously. Marian makes a difference to her in her *rising up and lying down and in all her ways.* This is a love letter of sorts. Perhaps not sexual, but passionate and involved. Marian has a powerful, bewitching presence.

Since that one time I saw you years ago very frequently I have thought of you and often said to myself that if you were living still near Coventry I would have gone to you and told you my troubles and difficulties, and I never felt that towards any one else except of course Richard. Sometime I should like to talk over my difficulties, past though they are, with you. I should never be afraid of your misunderstanding them or me. I have such a perfect confidence in you.

And suddenly I remember. I did too — have such perfect confidence in her.

It was in my teens, my first boyfriend had left me. Nothing made me feel better. My brother fed me hashish from a water-pipe, which didn't help at all. I went to stay with an older male friend at Cambridge. That seemed a glamorous idea, until, sitting cross-legged as we rolled joints, he confided that his ex-girlfriend had 'made love like a whore'. Everything seemed darker and chillier still. But on the floor in my sleeping bag I pulled out George Eliot, *Middlemarch*. And it was she, and only she, who comforted me. Her voice told me that she knew what it was to suffer and go wrong. And I'm sure Maria Congreve was comforted, too, when she talked to her; just as I suspect *Adam Bede*, with the author's fame spreading like wildfire, was enchanting and comforting readers by the thousand. I'm thinking, that voice couldn't have come from the male sphere of life: could it have been brewed by female friendship?

* * *

I receive a text from Ann one night, asking if she can come round. She appears, and in ten minutes she is drinking tea and whisky, alternately, on my sofa. She has her legs tucked under her like a girl. She has had a row with Hans. 'Do you row a lot?' I ask politely.

'Yes.'

Then she adds, simply, 'He's fabulously selfish.'

Sipping her tea, I can see she isn't seeing me. She is seeing tall, lanky Hans, German, with his straw-coloured hair, his slightly Aryan chalk-and-poppies complexion. Hans, who wears a tracksuit at work, and trainers. The clothes that seem a mark of freedom, I can't say why. She ticks his faults off on her fingers. He doesn't give the kids a tenth of the thought she does. He is doing a new seminar, today has announced he won't be taking Ben to karate for three weeks. The ironic thing is, he is furious with *her*. Do I mind if she has some more whisky?

Preferably in a small shot glass?

She goes on talking, in her picturesque tweed suit with its long skirt. The problem is, the department. She's so behind in it! She feels this constant pressure, her breathing is shallow.

'Do you think I'm behind?' — anxiously.

'What do you mean, behind?' I say.

She's stuck as a lecturer. She never gets promoted. She's published one book, but that was ten years ago. But maybe if she gets on with this book —

'— exactly!' I say. 'Get that published and then see.'

She is thoughtful, half frowning as she looks at her whisky, holding it this way and that in the light.

'What about you?' she says suddenly. 'You were married, weren't you?'

There is an insistent glow about her small eyes as she says this. And I realise something then — Ann possesses, like an aura, a slight yet constant atmosphere of drama about her.

'What about me,' I repeat. I say I am happy. Sort of.

I end up confiding in her. I was married to a lawyer, a 'kindly' lawyer. Maybe we both worked too hard. To sum it up: he left me for his assistant, who I really liked.

Ann says, 'Grim,' and for some reason we laugh.

'On the other hand,' she says, 'marriages aren't always a piece of cake. I seem to have lost all interest in mine.'

'Right.'

That's quite a statement, I think.

She tells me more about herself. She was brought up by her father, who was subtly dominating. Her views were his until she went to university.

Just before she leaves, she asks me if I will read two chapters of her book. I say, fine.

15

During May, George would often return in the mornings holding the newspaper, his moustache looking especially drooping as he set the paper down on the table. Usually this meant he was about to show Marian another letter either about Liggins, or the supposed originals, in Warwickshire. They would discuss it after supper, and agree once again that the authorship must remain a secret. 'We don't want to kill the goose that's laying the golden egg,' warned Lewes, a trifle tactlessly.

'True, true.'

The sales were tremendous. So was the book's reputation. 'Still, I find myself rather minding about Liggins!' added Marian, with a laugh. The laugh sounded forced.

By now, as soon as she saw the name Liggins in a newspaper, she'd flush and turn the page. All these people believing in Liggins! What could she do?

A letter from Barbara in Algiers set her thinking. Barbara wrote to say that she had read *Adam Bede* extracts in an obscure Algerian newspaper. *The passages instantly made me internally exclaim, that is written by Marian Evans, there is her great big head and heart and her wise wide views ... it is an opinion which fire cannot melt out of me, I would die in it at the stake!*

Marian coloured with pleasure as she read her friend's words. The book's fame had reached as far as Algiers! More, Barbara had found her in the writing, as no one else had — not Maria Congreve, and certainly not her old Coventry friends, Charles, Cara, and Sara. Barbara went on to list what especially pleased her.

1st. That a woman should write a wise and humorous book which should take a place by Thackeray. 2nd. That YOU, that you, whom they spit at, should do it! I am so enchanted so glad with the good and bad of me! both glad — angel and devil both triumph!

Marian wrote back immediately:

God bless you, dearest Barbara, for your love and sympathy. You are the first friend who has given any symptom of knowing me — the first heart that has recognised me in a book which has come from my heart of hearts. But keep the secret solemnly till I give you leave to tell it. You have sense enough to know how important the incognito has been, and we are anxious to keep it up a few months longer.

Re-reading the letter, Marian frowned — Barbara's language was a fraction displeasing. *You whom they spit at* — she quickly shifted her gaze. And then Barbara's tone, in its wild, tribally female gleefulness ... She was counted a heroine by friends who actively promoted the position of women, Bessie Parkes and Barbara, for having flouted convention so openly, the same friends who wilfully insisted on introducing her as 'Miss Evans' instead of 'Mrs Lewes', no matter how often she asked them not to. Still, she admired what they did: Bessie Parkes, whom she had first met at Rosehill with the Brays, edited the progressive *English Woman's Journal*, while Barbara generously used her private income to provide most of its funding. In fact, Bessie Parkes, when taking the journal over, had consulted Marian, as a more experienced editor.

Marian had replied crisply to Bessie:

It is a doctrine of Mr Lewes', which I think recommends itself to one's reason, that every new or renovated periodical should have a speciality — do something not yet done, fill up a gap, and so give people a motive for taking it. But I do not at all like the specialité *that consists in the inscription 'conducted by Women', and I am very glad you are going to do away with it. For my own taste, I should say, the more business you can get into the journal — the more statements of philanthropic movements and social facts, and the less literature, the better. Not because I like philanthropy and hate literature, but because I want to know about philanthropy and don't care for second-rate literature.*

Art and politics, Marian felt, were uneasy bedfellows.

16

Barbara's letter set her off on a new train of thought. Barbara was now the fifth person who knew the secret. As Marian walked Rough over Wandsworth Common, she said to herself that she would give a lot to kill the Liggins rumour — and stopped walking in surprise. Was she really ready to announce herself and take that risk? After all, she'd talked it to death with George, and John Blackwood's recent letter had stated, *KEEP YOUR SECRET*, in capital letters, which was typical, and disheartening.

But what about Barbara? Surely the ideal person to talk it over with: a sympathetic interlocutor, interested in the best way, and disinterested too. At the same time, returning Rough to the Congreves' housekeeper, admiring the trees in their fresh May leaf, she found herself questioning Barbara's reliability. Might Barbara be taken up with radical zeal on her behalf, to the exclusion of more careful thought? Still, when a letter announced Barbara's return to London, Marian suggested they meet.

Marian took the train from Putney to Charing Cross, then a hackney carriage to Princes Street, Barbara having persuaded her to come to the offices of the *English Woman's Journal* near Cavendish Square. The two friends embraced each other, with Barbara murmuring congratulatory exclamations about *Adam Bede* in her ear. 'I'm so glad you're here, Marian! I must show you round. Follow me!' She was duly taken into the *Journal*'s office, Barbara opening the door with a grand flourish, and a mock-bow, laughing — evidently she was very proud of the premises. The room was book-lined, with a fireplace and several chairs, and a large desk, behind which a woman in a riding jacket was seated. Marian's eyes narrowed: she recognised her as a journalist she'd previously encountered, Matilda Hayes. At the same time, Marian couldn't stop looking at the way she was smoking — the wrist so theatrically, oddly flung back.

'Bessie's co-editor, Max Hayes,' Barbara was saying. 'Marian Evans.'

'Mrs Lewes,' corrected Marian, glancing irritably at her old friend. 'I think we met some years ago.'

The three women chatted, before Marian followed Barbara out. As she followed Barbara's flowing, attractive, deep-russet skirts down the corridor, she mused on her friend's look of pride as she was introduced, as if she, Marian, were a trophy-figure for women now; and of course she had registered the automatic look of respect on 'Max' Hayes' face. She was, she thought drily, a legend.

She could remember Max Hayes submitting a number of poorly written, poorly thought-out pieces to her for the *Westminster Review*, which Marian had rejected, urging Chapman to reject them also, saying they were full of 'feminine ranting of the worst kind'. It didn't bode well for the *English Woman's Journal*, she thought now, that she was co-editing alongside Bessie.

The premises at Princes Street consisted of the editorial office, as well as a large room emulating a gentleman's club, where women could read in comfort and quiet. They went into this room now. There were low tables, two plump armchairs upholstered in red twill, the wallpaper a discreet but pleasing pattern, a grey background with a twisting flower motif. After Barbara had shut the door, Marian explained why she wanted Barbara's counsel.

'I have a lot to tell you,' said Barbara, at once, meaningfully. 'The other night, I visited Mr and Mrs Owen Jones. As soon as I walked in the room, they attacked me as knowing all about you! They're convinced you're the mystery author of *Adam Bede*.'

Slowly, Marian sat down.

'Anyhow,' went on Barbara, 'I denied it and demanded to know their evidence. Mr Spencer, I'm afraid, seems to have been a source, with all sorts of leading remarks about knowing the authoress.'

'That doesn't surprise me.'

Edward Pigott, another friend, had apparently commented on the change in their style of living. And Owen Jones had seen the way Lewes' eyes lit up at any mention of her books.

'Quite likely,' admitted Marian.

But then Mrs Owen Jones had spoken. She had said that Marian, in her circumstances, was right to keep it secret.

'My dear Marian,' said Barbara, passionately, 'what she said made me so angry. She said that the book couldn't have succeeded if it had been known to be yours. Every newspaper critic would have written against it. And she also thinks that when it is known to be yours, it will be seen differently.'

Barbara had stood up; framed by the long curtains at the windows, with her statuesque figure and her glorious reddish-golden hair, gesticulating, she reminded Marian of an indignant goddess.

'Apparently,' concluded Barbara, 'all the literary men are now certain it's you! But they're not saying so in public, because they think it won't help your position if you're known to be the author. I suppose that's at least generous.'

The words were so awful that they were momentarily unintelligible.

'They thought you would do the book more harm, than the book do you good, in public opinion —'

'Yes, I understand,' said Marian, unable to keep the agitation out of her voice. She wanted Barbara to stop talking. Barbara offered to bring her water. While she sipped it Barbara regarded her with concern.

'I've said too much.'

Which way shall I go? Marian was thinking.

Barbara was walking restively around the room. 'What cowards people are! No — Marian — I won't be quiet. I actually tried to make Mrs Jones say she would like to know you, given that she thinks so highly of your book, but I swear, she looked afraid! I mean it, Marian. The purest fear in her eyes, I saw it!'

Barbara's voice was shaking now with emotion.

'Here is this book,' continued Barbara, breathless, 'everyone in London — England — talking about it — but this woman still wouldn't call on you even if she knew you were George Eliot! — I told her about *my* visits,' added Barbara, proudly.

'You didn't have to say that.'

'I didn't do it for you. I am interested for myself, to see how much people can see — how much freedom they have. Oh Marian, Marian, what cowards people are!'

* * *

Marian walked back down Regent Street. Some crows were gathered in the gutter, excitedly picking at a carcass. The carcass was a trampled bird. An acrid smell had risen; she held her handkerchief to her nose. The handkerchief had been given to her by Chrissey, with an embroidered apple in the corner.

As the train to Putney rumbled along — she preferred the walk from Putney station to Holly Lodge — she saw Barbara in her mind's eye. She felt, she thought gloomily, as confused as ever. She mused on her friend. Barbara meant so well; yet it had been excruciating to listen to her.

Most important was the information Barbara had given her.

A few days later, at the breakfast table, Lewes passed her a letter from Blackwood. Blackwood, it turned out, was forwarding 'for their interest' a letter sent to him by the editor of *The Times*. It concerned the mystery author.

The books, *Adam Bede* and *Clerical Scenes*, it said, were written by a lady who lived with Mr Lewes, 'a very clever woman'.

17

'All we like sheep —' the chorus sang, staccato; and the strings replied in steps, backwards one, forward two.

'All we — like — sheep —' they repeated, with greater intensity. Marian was sitting beside George in Crystal Palace, and more than 2,700 singers were assembled. In front of them was the silhouette of Sir Michael Costa, baton raised. The sound loud and streaming from all directions, filling the iron and crystal vault. To look upwards made her dizzy. Funny to think Owen Jones had designed this strange light-filled edifice: always so modest and unassuming.

Moving into the dominant key.

Isaiah 53:6.

How well Handel conjured a trite, brittle, obedient sound for those unthinking sheep. How well she knew those sheep — cheap judgements following well-trodden grooves. The atmosphere darkened, the tone broadened and grew grave.

'And the Lord hath laid on Him the iniquity of us all,' sang the choir.

On a close, oppressively humid afternoon, Marian and George had come to the Handel Festival to hear the Messiah, with Clara Novello singing. The performance would finish at five o'clock; they were meeting the Brays later: Charles, Cara, and Sara Hennell. At this thought, Marian's left foot, under her skirt, began nervously beating time.

What would she say? For nearly three years now she had not been honest with them. At times she had deliberately deceived them.

'Thy rebuke hath broken His heart,' the tenor was singing.

It was difficult to let the music absorb her entirely: thoughts kept interfering. She looked over and around the audience, more vast than the choir: a sea of heads, endless, everywhere she looked.

The plan was to have supper at the Brays' lodgings afterwards. Lewes had the address in his pocket. Sir Michael Costa's baton raised, silhouetted in front of them: audience holding its breath — and then a sound started.

On the roof: a light, light pattering everywhere, in seconds becoming hundreds and thousands of tiny pattering noises, all over the vast glass and iron roof. Rain.

Sir Michael's baton moved, the violins struck up: 'I know that my redeemer liveth.'

A song of belief, she thought nostalgically.

After, the rain was pouring so hard, it was difficult to see; the rain had swollen the gutters; walking among the crowds along the kerb in the wet, trying to hail a cab, was difficult; only after twenty minutes did they find a free one, climbing up and in, relieved to be out of the wet. Marian's woollen stockings were damp through, the bonnet on her lap squashed and dripping. She moved the hat onto the floor. 'I hope he knows where he's going,' she said.

It was still light. From the swaying hansom, through the thick rain, Lewes was peering out at the unfamiliar Sydenham streets, with the small new houses. Marian sat forward in the seat. She saw the high trees, the thick wet green summer leaves.

Was this the right thing to do? It surely had to be. She'd struggled through to this position, and she now must stick to it. Word was getting out, she wanted to tell her old friends the truth, before they heard it from someone else.

The cabbie was shouting above, they were slowing. They had arrived in Norden Grove. The rain was still thundering down: they made a dash for the door.

* * *

The three women were together, a circle of linked arms: Marian, Cara Bray, and Sara Hennell. Lavender — it was Cara, it was Cara's old delicate smell, mixed with the smell of wet wool. They hugged, laughing, crying out, her head was now on Cara's shoulder.

But Cara had grey hair now — the sight had shocked her.

They broke apart, sat in chairs. Cara was glancing repeatedly at Marian, with keen, puzzled interest, as if she couldn't stop looking, a smile of unconscious delight beginning to show. Her small shoulders looking strangely quaint and frail.

Sara was smiling boldly, broadly. 'Here we all are, here we all are!' She was holding out a large envelope to Marian.

'For you!' said Sara. 'Oh Marian, you have no idea. Your counsel has been so helpful to me.'

It was five years since they had all been in the same room.

'My goodness,' exclaimed Charles Bray, grinning. 'It does my heart good to see you all together.'

'It's a great pleasure to see you,' said Cara in her gentle voice. Cara was looking at her steadily, as if to commit her to memory.

Something painful about Cara's kind face.

Marian realised her hands were holding paper. The envelope. Ah, Sara's book.

Sara looking at her, brimming, expectant.

'Thank you,' said Marian, automatically.

'My dear Marian,' said Sara, excitedly, 'you at least know how hard I've worked! But here it is. And,' — she leaned forward, earnestly, lowering her voice — 'I may have a publisher interested. George Manwaring.'

Marian was too full — she was about to burst. She glanced at Lewes, who was sitting outside the gathering entirely. He gave a meaningful nod.

'Dear friends,' said Marian, unsteadily, 'I have something to tell you.'

Perhaps it was her tone, but there was silence straight away. 'I have   I am,' — she gasped. But she couldn't help it: tears were coming down, then strangely loud, noisy sobs.

'Marian.' Through her tears she heard the voice of Cara.

'I can't,' — she gasped, weeping.

Lewes saw the sisters go and put their arms round her.

'Oh listen my dears,' he said, rising from his seat now. 'She's just trying to tell you that she's an author. She's the author of *Adam Bede*.'

No sound now except for the low sobs of Marian. The Brays and Sara had seemed to turn, for a moment, into statues.

★ ★ ★

Lewes and Charles Bray were drunk. 'I'm enormously gratified,' Charles was saying. 'This confirms all my convictions about Marian. I knew she was capable of greatness. From the moment she appeared at Rosehill.'

'And you were right, old man!' said Lewes, lighting his cigar. All Lewes' dislike of Charles, with his absurd devotion to phrenology, had vanished.

'She's remarkable,' went on Lewes, complacently.

'I think the girls are a little shocked,' went on Charles, his speech slurring ('shogged').

The three women were sitting in a huddled group at the other end of the room: Marian on the sofa; Sara and Cara in armchairs, drawn very close.

'My dear fellow,' whispered Charles then, leaning towards Lewes with his plump lips and cheeks, 'I'm afraid Sara's going to want her pound of flesh. Her book, you know —'

Close up, Charles looked quite a sensualist, thought Lewes. He remembered rumours about a mistress and a child, possibly even something about a sister of Cara's and Sara's, who Charles was in love with, living at Rosehill. Perhaps even something about *Marian* and Charles. Was that possible?

'Pound of flesh?'

With Charles' face and breath so close, the word 'flesh' seemed appropriate.

'I have a feeling,' said Charles Bray, in a loud whisper, 'that she wants to discuss her book.'

★ ★ ★

'It's a great relief to me,' said Marian, as she leant forward to take a hand from each sister in hers, 'to have disburdened myself. It's been a weight — here,' she added, thumping her chest.

Sara still looked white-faced, shaking her head, saying, 'I just can't believe it. I can't believe that it's you.'

'It must seem strange, my dear Sara,' said Marian, with an awkward laugh.

'It is very strange,' said Cara, quietly. 'Strange but wonderful.'

After another pause, Sara burst out again: 'In a hundred years, I would never have guessed — after all the speculation — the mention of Liggins —'

'It is something of a shock,' agreed Cara.

'But you must have had some idea!'

Cara and Sara both shook their heads.

'My dear Marian, the change in your fortunes, your giftedness, your fame ... it's a plot worthy of a novel!' joked Cara, in her quiet voice.

'To have written *Adam Bede*!' said Sara. Her eyes looked bewildered. Or terrified. Staring, anyway.

Then Sara said, with an oddly troubled look: 'So ... are you working on another book?'

'Yes.' Marian was reluctant, but she felt it might be insulting not to elaborate. 'It is,' she went on slowly, 'about a brother and a sister.'

There. That would do. How hungrily were their eyes fixed on her now.

'Does it — how long did it take you then ... to write *Adam Bede*?' asked Sara, with the same hungry look of interest.

Marian said the writing took her thirteen months.

'But you, Sara,' said Marian quickly, 'you've nearly done your book! That is something to be proud of.'

'Doubtless,' said Sara, with a wry look.

Marian shifted in her seat.

'Do you remember the day you gave me that brooch?' Marian said suddenly. And now her voice was easier. 'And I was christened your sister? I found it when we were packing to move! It took me back so vividly.'

'I do!' said Cara, who seemed perhaps the least agitated of the three. 'We played charades after supper. You were staying at Rosehill.'

'But how have you managed it?' Charles Bray was asking, at the other end of the room, waving his cigar in the air. 'How on earth have you managed to keep the secret so well?'

'No thanks to Herbert Spencer!' said Lewes at once, almost surprising himself with his own vitriol. 'He's been a treacherous brute. But we can trust you, I hope.'

'Of course you can. But I'm still baffled how you managed to keep the secret — what a strain — what a burden!'

'Secrets and debts: that's our life,' joked Lewes.

'Debts?'

'Oh, we have to pay a lot of debts,' said Lewes. 'Not our debts, I can tell you! No. Dear Agnes's,' he finished sardonically.

Charles looked intrigued.

'Thornton Hunt won't pay 'em, so I do. Or rather, we do.'

'That's infamous!' cried Charles.

'True, true.' Lewes never could be bothered to rise to too much indignation, although he was intermittently irritated and occasionally furious at both Agnes and Hunt. For the most part he just did what needed to be done.

Marian had turned to him.

'I was just saying,' said Lewes, 'how treacherous Mr Spencer has been.'

The men moved their chairs closer to the women.

Marian agreed.

Lewes went on to say that Spencer had been jealous, malicious, unable to be generous, and, contrary to the rules of friendship, had been leaking news about the book — like a rusty old tap. A rusty old tap.

'It's indeed true,' said Marian, frowning.

'I must say,' said Charles, 'I didn't realise you were both saddled with Agnes' debts. That seems beyond the pale!'

'Is that true?' asked Cara, innocently.

'Oh my goodness, yes!' said Lewes. 'Agnes sits there, doing just about nothing, while we toil away, helping her support the children fathered by Mr Hunt. Mr Hunt is infinitely feckless.'

'I'm afraid her moral nature is quite limited,' sighed Marian. 'To speak honestly, she's both selfish and lazy.'

There was a chorus of agreement. Then Lewes, consulting his watch, said it was getting late, they'd better leave.

'I'm sure you are very busy', said Cara, rising to her feet at once, in her soft voice.

'It's been wonderful to see you — hear your news,' stammered Sara, also rising to her feet.

'We don't have to go yet,' said Marian.

It was sad, somehow — the two women standing up as if she were a grand stranger.

'Then stay a bit!' said Charles, so loudly it was as if he were shouting. 'Here we are, for the first time in years!'

Marian asked them all to come and dine with them the next day — and that way, they'd have a chance to discuss Sara's work.

The following evening the Brays came to Holly Lodge. Lewes, with his usual theatrical gestures, led them around the house. Marian saw the way they looked at the new furnishings, commenting on the number of rooms. She remembered again that because of Charles' business failing, they had had to leave gracious, large Rosehill, and move into a small cottage.

After supper, Sara, Lewes, and Marian went to the top of the house, where Marian's study was, to discuss the book.

'This is where you work,' Sara said, as they entered, peering around with the most intense look of curiosity. This room had not been included in the earlier tour. In the armchair, with an expectant look, Sara's dark hair was drawn back, leaving her broad forehead exposed. She wore a large white lace collar under her dress of dark dimity.

Lewes and Marian began by praising her — the portions they'd read showed evidence of hard work; then Lewes began listing their criticisms. Marian let George do the talking. But slowly Sara's reaction began to irritate her. Instead of seeming receptive and possibly grateful for the remarks, which, in truth, could help her, Sara's chin grew more and more set; two red spots appeared in her cheeks. Marian eventually interrupted Lewes, saying impatiently, 'My dear Sara, the arguments are really so weak, they need complete re-working! The book simply doesn't stand up at the moment.'

'It's not an improvement on your last, I'm afraid,' added Lewes.

Charles took Sara home before she wanted to leave. Though Marian didn't like to admit it, it was a relief when the door shut, and the old friends had gone.

'Well, I'm glad that's over,' said Lewes. 'What a business.'

A letter arrived from Charles:

My dear Marian,

I am sorry we did not get another look at you — but to find you famous and my convictions confirmed, produced a more agreeable internal confloption than the four and twenty fiddlers all in a row. We had Sara in strong stericks all the way home, because she had missed her final chance of explanation and advice from you.

By now, Marian was more bothered by the evening with her old friends than she liked to say. That morning she put down her manuscript, collected Rough from the Congreves' housekeeper — Rough making agreeably wild yelps of enthusiasm at her appearance — and went for a walk on Wandsworth Common, gathering twigs, which she proceeded to throw from the comfort of a bench; Rough, she could see, already eagerly anticipating the familiar game.

It was a gloomy, overcast June day. Sitting there, she was able to lose sight of the expanse of green grass and the distant plane and horse chestnut trees, as she re-lived their meeting with the Brays, the tumultuous embrace, Sara entering, and yes, Sara bearing her manuscript as a special gift — mixed up, in her memory, oddly, with an image of a biblical offering, that included a kneeling woman. But then had come Marian's revelation, and Sara's face.

And now, like a thief, like a novelist, she entered into Sara's feelings. There was the great shifting of fortune between them, the great adjustment, that often must happen in the course of life between friends. Leading to a cruel new self-assessment, in relation to Marian's success. The same Marian who had dreaded her first visit to Rosehill. Such sophistication Cara and Sara had. Yet now she, Marian, was the more adjusted to London; she had even, when she walked in, had the very queer, fleeting sense of beholding three — could she say it to herself? — provincial people.

Marian reflected, with a sigh, that Sara didn't have the discipline or capacity to write a good philosophical book. Why had she attacked her? She recalled her own excited urge to break Sara's defences down, break down that mutinous thrust of the chin, below the red-spotted defiant cheeks, while Lewes had delivered his criticisms. The urge had taken her over, as for Sara's good. But how fragile such shells of willed unreality are, how painful when they break open.

Sara had strong stericks, Charles had written.

Dear Sara,

There is always an after-sadness belonging to brief and interrupted intercourse between friends — the sadness of feeling that the blundering efforts we have made towards mutual understanding have only made a new veil between us — still more the sadness of feeling that some pain may have been given which separation makes a permanent memory. We are quite unable to represent ourselves truly — why should we complain that our friends see a false image?

I say this, because I am feeling painfully this morning that instead of helping you when you brought before me a matter so deeply interesting to you, I have only blundered, and that I have blundered, as most of us do, from too much egoism and too little sympathy. If I am too imperfect to do and feel the right thing at the right moment, I am not without the slower sympathy that becomes all the stronger from a sense of previous mistake.

Dear Sara, believe that I shall think of you and your work much, and that my ear and heart are more open for the future because I feel I have not done what a better spirit would have made me do in the past.

She posted the letter at noon, at the red pillar box recently installed at the bottom of the street. Returning to her desk, she felt cleansed, rather like after going to church in Nuneaton as a child. Relieved, she even found herself wondering about incorporating such painful sensations as she had just experienced in a future fiction.

But waking up the following morning, she remembered more. Those remarks about Agnes ... why had she said them? Probably, she admitted to herself, to remind the Brays of her own rectitude, in spite of her scandalous situation, by invoking Agnes' faults as a contrast. Ah, how faulty she was.

'What's this glum face for?' asked Lewes, munching his toast during breakfast, and eying her.

'Nothing. Well — I was just remembering what we said about Agnes and Spencer,' she admitted, colouring.

'Marian, leave it alone! You don't have to be perfect. Though of course you are,' he added, with a twinkle. 'Frankly, they deserve it.'

Again, she didn't work. Instead she took pen to notepaper.

Dear Friend, she wrote to Charles.

Pardon me for troubling you with a few words just to say that I am uneasy at having listened with apparent acquiescence to statements about poor Agnes which a little quiet reflection has convinced me are mingled with falsehood — I fear of a base sort. And I am also angry with myself for having spoken of her faults — quite uselessly — to you and Cara. All such talk is futile. And I always hate myself after such attempts to vindicate one person at the expense of another. Justice is never secured in that way — perhaps not in any other.

Also, may I make a suggestion — not to regard the last thing Mr Lewes told you about Herbert Spencer ...

There. The weight began to roll off. Somehow that phrase — *Justice is never secured in that way — perhaps not in any other* — in its momentary achieved wisdom, reassured her. Giving voice to formulations about human nature, she felt as usual better — an image came to her mind, then, of the bleached white sheets being ironed in her childhood.

Now she could resume her work.

A letter came from Sara:

Dear Marian,

I have been fancying you, as ten years ago, still interested in what we then conversed together upon. I see now that I have lost the only reader in whom I felt confident in having secure sympathy with the subject — that she has floated beyond me in another sphere, and I remain gazing at the glory into which she has departed, wistfully and very lonely.

How for ever remote we should have felt if you had made a pretense of being quite unchanged from your former self, and tried to converse as of former times!

Marian read the letter twice, with close attention. *Floated beyond me in another sphere* was touching as well as gratifying, referring to the extraordinary scale of Marian's achievement; but then she knew a stirring of discomfort. If she had *made a pretense of being quite unchanged from her former self* ... how had she changed? Had she been — condescending? Was she too comfortable now in her secret position of achievement? Was she letting it tilt her perception of the world and people? Surely not. And if she had been, a little, wouldn't her letter to Sara have put paid to that idea? She pushed the doubt out of her mind.

A few days later, a letter came in the post, again in Sara's handwriting. Another one! Slowly she opened the envelope, pulled out the small sheet of paper.

Dear Friend, when all thy greatness suddenly
Burst out, and thou wert other than I thought,
At first I wept — for Marian, whom I sought,
Now, passed beyond herself, seemed lost to me.

A poem. By Sara.

The sonnet gave her a strange little pain.

Human happiness is never without its alloy, murmured Marian to herself. She began to feel better.

* * *

In July, a glorious summer day, Lewes and Marian crossed the Channel, glassy and smooth. In Paris, they found themselves in a room with gold and white wallpaper, a small desk with cunningly fitted drawers, a bed with the smoothest whitest sheets, in the Hotel du Danube. They were on their way to Switzerland. The main reason for the trip was so that Lewes could see his sons at Hofwyl: Charles, the eldest; Thornton ('Thornie'); and Bertie, the youngest. Lewes had finally persuaded Marian to come with him. She wasn't going to meet the boys on this occasion — she had still not met them — but she would have a holiday with George.

She was glad she came. Although sales were extraordinary — 5,000 copies in two weeks! — the rumours had reached a pitch of unpleasantness, even though the truth was also coming out: they had begun revealing her authorship to certain people, including Dickens, who could be counted on to spread the word as benignly as possible. But a piece in *The Atheneaum* had left a sour taste in Marian's mouth. It suggested the whole identity of Liggins had been fabricated by Marian herself, on purpose to arouse interest in the book. The worst sentence referred to her as *a rather strong-minded lady, blessed with abundance of showy sentiment and a profusion of pious words, but kept for sale rather than for use.*

The insinuation that she was an immoral woman given to mouthing moral sentiments was just the kind she feared most.

But how lovely to be walking in the Tuileries, then spending time in the cavernous Louvre, in the pleasantly still silence, looking at the Poussins, Rubens, and Claude-Lorrains; driving through the elegant Boulevards and the Champs-Élysées. In fact, the moment she left English soil, Marian's spirits improved. As the train rattled comfortably along to Strasbourg, great swathes of fields, dotted with short-shadowed haystacks flashed by, and she found herself smiling as she imagined her reunion with Maria, whom they would be meeting in Lucerne. The prospect was particularly pleasant after the bittersweet reunion with Cara and Sara. Having been out of England since April, the Congreves would not have heard the rumour about herself as author, and at the last moment she'd hurriedly packed a copy of *Clerical Scenes* to inscribe and give to them. She couldn't help imagining their reaction when she told them the truth — she could just envisage their amazed, admiring faces. Maria Congreve had a habit when she listened to Marian, of keeping her mouth slightly open, irresistibly reminding Marian of a young bird waiting to be fed.

In Lucerne, they went by cab, which stopped outside a long impressive many-tiered hotel directly overlooking the lake. Looking up, Marian saw the sign: Hotel Schweizerhof. 'George!' she said in astonishment.

'Nothing but the best,' he replied, with a grin. He had kept it as a surprise.

Marian got out, stood back to survey it: a consummately stylish, neo-classical façade, that just now was catching the afternoon sun on its upper flank, turning it into gold. The air was warm but fresh from the water and the nearby pine trees. 'Designed by Berri,' murmured Lewes.

They followed the porter who was deferentially loading their bags — still rather shabby, Marian noted with a slight twinge of nostalgia — towards the lobby.

The suite with its parquet floor and Persian rugs overlooked the lake. What luxury! As soon as they were unpacked Marian drew an armchair up to the window, to sit and contemplate the lake, mirroring the sky, ringed by mountains. The Congreves would be arriving in two days. While Lewes went off to see his three boys, Marian enjoyed the solitude for a few days. She had the view, the soft feather-filled pillows, the attentive service, and by the time Lewes returned, she was well-rested and recovered from the journey.

The following day the Congreves arrived at the Schweizerhof hotel for tea. Admitted by the uniformed hotel attendant, Maria Congreve came in with quick steps, smiling; suddenly stood stock-still, turning pale.

'How lovely to see you,' said Marian, and she went towards her and embraced her. But Maria Congreve was stiff in her arms. Marian stepped back awkwardly. She wondered if she had offended her. They took their seats in silence.

'How have you been spending your days?' asked Marian.

'We have enjoyed ourselves,' said Maria, in a subdued voice, looking at the floor.

Marian's next question met with a similar response. Marian looked across at Lewes, but he was in animated conversation with Richard. Now she could not think of what to say.

Talk became more and more stilted, until finally, when Marian looked at Maria in open bewilderment, and Maria didn't meet her gaze, with a stifled cry Marian rose up, and rushed out of the room.

Some forty minutes later, Marian returned composed, but with red eyes.

'Ladies,' Lewes said, 'I suggest you go for a row on the lake. It's the common practice here.'

Ten minutes later Maria Congreve and Marian were indeed stepping into a small rowing boat, which a Swiss boy, who looked about fourteen, proceeded to drag noisily off the gravel shore, into the buoyant water. Suddenly there was silence, except for the odd very gentle, occasional slap of water on the boat. The water was smooth, gleaming — extraordinarily calm.

Maria Congreve had reached out gravely to take the oars, saying, 'Shall I begin? I have had a bit of practise,' — and they rowed outwards.

Now here they were, lifted suddenly by the occasional low-rising swell, buoyed, moving through water out into this vast lake under the sky. There was no sound except for the plash of oars. Marian's mind couldn't help turning to her Mill book. She had planned to end it with a flood — must recall this peculiar sensation of being afloat, water's unpredictability.

'Will you have supper at the hotel?' Maria Congreve was asking her. Her tone sounded timid.

'I imagine so.'

Marian was silent. Then the old friendly feeling stirred, and she glanced at Maria's face. But how strange! Maria was looking straight back at her, and she could at once see, the softness in her friend's eyes was back.

'I think we've gone far enough,' Maria Congreve said, in her gentle voice.

They could now just let the boat go where it wanted. There was no wind. Delightfully, the boat simply bobbed. The sun was making the water sheer and shining and brilliant all around them, the air warm.

Marian couldn't resist talking about the strange atmosphere when Maria Congreve had arrived. At the mention of this, the other's face seemed to pale, then redden. 'It meant too much to me,' said Maria Congreve, in a low voice, looking downwards at the oars, 'to see you again.'

On seeing Marian, she had had palpitations, she said; so powerfully — that in order to achieve calm, she had had to avoid looking at Marian, or letting any expression at all enter her voice or face.

From the end of the boat, Marian reached out to touch and hold fast Maria Congreve's hand. All was well.

By the time they returned to the suite at the Schweizerhof, the men were sitting sprawled comfortably at the table by the window — at least Lewes was sprawled, Richard Congreve seated in a more upright fashion. They were dining on smoked sausage and cheese, followed by lemon tea with apple cake. Lewes looked up as the door opened.

The women came in, he noted, with a quite different air from before. Both were flushed from sun and water. They sat on the sofa beside each other, Marian made a humorous remark under her breath to the delightfully demure Mrs Congreve, who now laughed, a low gurgle. Thank goodness. He had noted before how Maria Congreve looked at Marian in a rather reverential way: that was to be encouraged. To his amusement, he saw Richard glance repeatedly in their direction, with a look of perplexed, not altogether pleased curiosity in his face.

Now would be a good time, calculated Lewes. As soon as he could catch Marian's eye, he indicated the book on the shelf.

Marian rose to the occasion. At the end of five minutes, Mr and Mrs Congreve knew that they were in the presence of the author everyone was talking about in England, George Eliot.

'Well I'll be blowed!' said Richard Congreve, looking in astonishment at Marian. His expression did not change for some minutes. 'I don't believe it!' he kept saying.

'Well, you better had,' said Lewes, complacently, lighting his cigar, and stretching out his legs. Not only did he love Marian, not only had she brought happiness into his life, it was very pleasant being her custodian; he couldn't help but feel that her emerging genius reflected agreeably on him. And even he was amazed at the book's fame: when he had met up with his boys, he had said to them (without having mentioned anything, ever, about Marian writing) that he had brought them a present. 'Is it *Adam Bede*?', they had chorused excitedly — simply because the book was a universal talking point, even in Switzerland!

Suddenly, Richard Congreve gave a hearty laugh, and advanced towards Marian. 'My dear Mrs Lewes, I blame myself for the most appalling blindness! There was I, thinking you had lost your way — that the brilliant writer of the *Review* was buried in domesticity! I feel an idiot — a veritable *dummkopf*.'

Lewes began to like Mr Congreve properly, for the first time.

Smiling all over, Marian embraced him, and apologised for misleading them.

Maria had risen with a tearful wide-eyed staring smile, saying that now she understood, understood everything — and the two women clasped each other; and stayed that way.

Richard, having sat down again, began to drum his fingers on the small table beside him, every now and then turning to regard the women who remained in each other's arms.

'I say!' he said, testily.

'Don't worry,' said Lewes, with a wave of his cigar, sanguinely. 'It's an excellent thing.'

Richard muttered something. Lewes thought he caught the words 'damned' and 'pandarus'; but perhaps he imagined it.

They ended up dining together in the suite, Richard's humour recovered. The table was set by the windows, where they had a grand view of the water in the setting sun: through the window they could see, above the tops of the trees, the vast Lake Lucerne glimmering in the paling, rosy light, below the uneven line of the distant mountains. After the main course, which featured a variety of Wurst, Richard stood up. This was the kind of view, he said, that made one think about a higher power. Many people no longer believed in God, and were searching for another system, another kind of spirituality.

'I would like to quote,' he said then, 'a few lines written by an old teacher of mine at Rugby school, Mr Matthew Arnold:'

> *Wandering between two worlds, one dead*
> *The other powerless to be born,*
> *With nowhere yet to rest my head*
> *Like these, on earth I wait forlorn.*

Red-faced with drink, hair unruly, cresting at the top of his head, he raised his glass.

'A toast,' he said, 'to the incomparable author among us, whose work,' — and here his tone dropped, became more serious — 'may, alongside the writings of Auguste Comte, yet help provide that home.'

Part Two

1869

Lewes called and asked us to come and see his wife, saying that she never made calls herself but was always at home on Sunday afternoons. She is an object of great interest and great curiosity to society here. She is not received in general society, and the women who visit her are either so émancipée as not to mind what the world says about them, or have no social position to maintain. Lewes dines out a good deal, and some of the men with whom he dines go without their wives to his house on Sundays. No one whom I have heard speak, speaks in other than terms of respect of Mrs Lewes, but the common feeling is that it will not do for society to condone so flagrant a breach as hers of a convention and a sentiment (to use no stronger terms) on which morality greatly relies for support. I suspect society is right in this: at least since I have been here I have heard of one sad case in which a poor weak woman defended her own wretched course, which had destroyed her own happiness and that of other persons also, by the example of Mrs Lewes. I do not believe that many people think that Mrs Lewes violated her own moral sense, or is other than a good woman in her present life, but they think her example pernicious, and that she cut herself off by her own act from the society of the women who feel themselves responsible for the tone of social morals in England.

Charles Eliot Norton, 1869

May I unceasingly aspire to unclothe all around me of its conventional, human, temporary dress, to look at it in its essence and in its relation to eternity ...

Marian Evans, *Diary*, I, 70

1

In the rainy, gusty spring, Marian and Lewes travelled through Europe, along the Rhône and by the Riviera, and down to Naples. By April, they reached Rome, the Hotel Minerva, and the first good weather of their holiday.

And so it was in the late Roman spring, on a hot, sunny April day in the Pamphili gardens, with clear blue skies, that Lewes ran into a beautiful, recently married young woman, Elizabeth Bullock, walking with her mother.

The new light of the year, that strong spring light, was streaming over the umbrella pines on the surrounding hill, when Lewes and Elizabeth Bullock greeted each other with the pleasure and surprise people feel when they meet by chance in a foreign place. The day felt lucky, new green everywhere. Elizabeth Bullock reminded Lewes she had once come to the Priory to show Marian her poems. Anna Cross, her mother, came forward to be kissed and gallantly greeted.

It was entirely as a result of this chance meeting that the same Mrs Anna Cross paid the Leweses a visit at the Minerva Hotel in Rome. Mrs Cross did not come alone, however; she brought with her a tall young man, with dark hair and a reddish beard, one of her sons.

After the visitors left, Marian remarked to Lewes how much she had warmed to both mother and son. The son, particularly, stayed in her mind: his fine features including a broad, high brow; his air, that had seemed at once quiet and good-natured; he had been silent, but when an outing was mooted, he had at once volunteered to go downstairs and find a hansom cab in the street.

'They seemed charming,' said Marian, aloud, earnestly.

'The family is delightful,' pronounced Lewes. 'I met the whole crew in Weybridge that time.'

Marian did not say so, but while she had been talking to Mrs Anna Cross — whose keen interest in books, William Gladstone, and the Irish problem had impressed her — she had noted the stance of the twenty-nine-year-old son, sitting with his right hand in his pocket, in a gentlemanly way, wearing a jacket of what looked like the best cream-coloured linen. But she had also noted that while he was talking to Lewes, every now and then he had glanced in her direction, with a certain hunger in the eye. His presence was modest — charmingly so; expressive of a contented nature, yet some undefined eagerness to help. Yes, she had taken to both mother and son.

The son's name was John Walter Cross.

★ ★ ★

And this was the start of the closest friendship with an entire family the Leweses would have. Though as history might privately relate, the family member who became the most intimate friend of all, John Cross, had been reluctant to pay that call in Rome in the first place. He had protested strongly in the high-ceilinged, newly painted rooms of the handsome apartment his mother, the splendid matriarch Mrs Anna Cross, had rented in the fashionable district of Rome, in the hours leading up to that significant visit.

2

All through the duskily sunny and too-hot morning, there had been discussion of the suggested visit to the famous author and her husband or lover (a certain cloud of confusion persisted here), George Henry Lewes. Johnny's mother, Anna the Elder, though she did not like to be called that, said Johnny would accompany her.

'If you refuse, I shall simply insist,' she had laughed, then rang the bell, at which the Italian serving girl appeared, with her yellow skin and cap the wrong way round. Anna Cross said, in a slow kind voice: '*Spremuta di limone, per favore — con molto acqua e zucchero. Zucchero.*'

'Mother,' said Johnny (but how hot he was in this Roman climate; though it was at least not the wet heat of New York; but the smell from the street, on opening the window, had been vegetative, rotten, so that he had shut it smartly). 'I do refuse. I'll just sit there dumbly and talk about rolling stocks, bears and bulls. My guess is, folk like her and, for that matter, Lewes, would rather be alone, and private. In fact, that is exactly what they said to you.'

'You are considerate to a fault,' laughed his mother. 'And what is this word, "folks"? You've been in America too long.'

'Take Zibbie instead.'

It was true Elizabeth, or Zibbie as she was called, had now met them twice. But his mother said that Zibbie must lie down, and he could see the sense of this. Zibbie was pregnant, and she had not only been sick this morning, her feet had suddenly swollen tremendously, her toes like roses and so strangely large.

His mother cleared her throat, and at that moment Johnny knew he had lost the battle. It was that little guttural noise: it always preceded a statement of a decisive kind, but also, it undid him — too close, too fleshly, somehow, altogether too much of the body. At the same time she moved her chair nearer. 'Johnny,' she said, smiling. Her tone was dulcet now, her eyes fixed on him. 'Zibbie said we would call. Zibbie is in bed, and we must go regardless. Make no mistake: this is not about fame, which is what you fear, if I guess right; they are the best company in the world. She is delightful, he is delightful. Why do you look so hesitant?'

'So I will speak news about the Stock Exchange.'

'You will speak about whatever you feel like speaking about. I want you to come.'

After a brief pause, Johnny kissed her hand.

★ ★ ★

At four o'clock precisely, having walked in the heat, which in the advancing hours had become more fetid, thick, with a snake-like undertow of effluvia, just detectable; in the strong yellow light, they walked along the Via dei Santi Apostoli, taking the way close to the Spanish Steps; then began climbing the Via del Piè di Marmo, at which the air became dry and salty and much improved. Johnny was regretting his choice of cravat: too close, sticking unpleasantly around his neck. (He was fastidious about washing, especially since living in New York.) There it was, in the bend of the street, with a pleasant awning extended around the entrance: the Hotel Minerva. Inside the lobby, it was by no means unimpressive, with two great ferns in high imposing urns, and the air was thankfully cooler and very shaded. The man at the desk, who shouted for the *signora* to come, had no teeth at all, Johnny saw. No — he had a single tooth, in the bottom of his mouth. At the sight of this aged, virtually toothless mouth, Johnny shut his own lips tightly. It's a bad omen, he thought to himself. He turned, in the shadowed lobby, to look at the ferns, which rose and bent forwards towards him with their great fronds. He was reminded of a gaping mouth. He attempted to quiet himself. Now they were following the *signora* upstairs, following her vast behind in its floral dress, and Johnny saw quite clearly the patches of sweat in the centre of her back, and spreading beneath her armpits, and the repulsion and the dread grew.

The *signora* indicated the door. His mother knocked. There was no reply. After a minute, Anna Cross knocked again. Again there was no reply. Johnny listened intently. And now he could not stand it. 'Mother, we should go.'

When the door opened, and in Johnny's memory, though he would not like to exaggerate, the door opened in every sense, as the dark landing was suddenly flooded by the light of the room, a man, who instantly reminded him of a monkey — he looked at once so spry, so energised, with a face whose jaw was exceptionally narrow below an upper lip protruding in a forward and, yes, monkey-like, way — was saying: 'My dear — my dears — how lovely to see you: Come in — come in — Polly — look — look who's here — Mrs Cross!'

And he indicated, seated on a couch of ochre velvet, a woman. Dressed in dark clothing, she was diminutive, with a large head. She was looking downwards; and then she quickly raised her head, in an almost imperious motion, and Johnny had a light, fleeting shock. This was George Eliot, or Mrs Lewes, or Polly — all of them. Hadn't he been reading George Eliot, hadn't she just been speaking to him in the most direct voice of understanding he had yet encountered in his life, in the book called *Adam Bede*, and now here she was — and he knew only the shocking sting of disappointment. The face was not pretty. The hair artificially smooth in look, above a large, long nose, and then, perhaps most surprising of all, the large chin. All atop a body that looked quite small.

But Johnny knew himself to be a relatively handsome man, and the famous author's ugliness gave him courage. He stepped forward, they were introduced. 'My son,' Anna was saying. 'Just come from New York, where he has been a banker in our family business; thankfully, he will now be nearer, with an office in London. He is just twenty-nine.'

'Mother,' laughed Johnny. Did she need to give such a potted summary of him? He put out his hand, and Lewes shook it; and now the great authoress had risen, and he was kissing her hand, though his fear came briefly upon him again, and for a moment he did not know where to put his eyes. 'So you're Johnny,' she was saying, with a most peculiar leap into informality; and still with his earlier shyness, because he was nothing, absolutely nothing, he hesitated before lifting up his head, though again what held him back he couldn't say. But then he did look up, and the eyes were looking at him and seeing entirely his shyness; had comprehended all of him, this he knew in less than a second; and did not judge him, simply understood. The eyes were greyish and quite luminous, and they were regarding him with a tender warmth, almost, it seemed, before the fact.

And now he found his voice.

'It's an honour to meet you. I'm sure Mother has said, our entire family has been enslaved by your books. I finished *Adam Bede* less than a fortnight ago, and before that, *The Mill on the Floss*. The wrong way round, I take it. But I was never more moved in my life. I can also add, the whole of New York is talking about you, and them.'

And in the next instant, in the uncanny way of things, he knew he had said the right thing. How had he known not to be shy with praise? Partly, he wanted to tell it true. Also, he had, as by magic, divined in her look, not just tender warmth, but some supplicating need, that called for an answer.

The authoress' eyes were following him attentively and his words had drawn a smile.

The eyes were not at all ugly, he was dimly realising, not at all, quite the opposite.

'And how are you liking Rome, Johnny Cross?' she asked; and her voice seemed very musical, pleasing to the ear.

She had sat back down on the ochre velvet seat, and was now patting the low stool that was beside her chair, inviting him to sit beside her. He did so. Except that, being a tall fellow, with great long legs, his knees stuck up rather. Which Mrs Lewes, as he later learned she liked to be called, at once observed. 'Is that comfortable for you?' she said, with a worried expression.

'It's delightful', said Johnny. He had found himself, his own best prompt humorous and kind self. He could tell she liked it, him.

He now attempted to convey to her his impressions of Rome: the confusion of images, their splendour, and the confusion of ages, ancient and, to use the new term, Renaissance —

No sooner was that word out of his mouth than Lewes, from the other side of the room, sprang to his feet, saying, 'Someone has been reading Burckhardt, no?' with a thoroughly joyous expression on his face.

'Not me,' confessed Johnny, with a smile. 'I wish, though.'

He was honest, he was modest. He did not have to try. This was how he was. Yes, he had the instant sense that his nature was grasped, understood by Mrs Lewes, and approved of.

'Our dear friend Mr Spencer has been talking about it,' said Anna the Elder, Johnny's mother.

'Ah, Herbert Spencer. Well, if Mr Spencer will acknowledge the originator as Jacob Burckhardt, he's doing excellently! Very unlike him! Forgive this joke, Mr Cross,' said Lewes, whose face underwent sixteen expressions, it seemed to Johnny, in the space of a minute, and now he was bending forward towards Johnny, one eyebrow imploringly raised. 'If Mr Spencer has his way, he is the only thinker on planet earth, and owes nothing to anyone else. But you know — even as I say this,' — and now Johnny saw, most endearingly, a woebegone, self-reproachful smile light up Lewes' features — 'I owe Mr Spencer a great debt! A great, wonderful debt! Before my life was to join with Polly's, when I was effectively reborn, I was for a time at risk from despair you know; despair was drawing me down, and the person who gave me a new lease of life, and all because of his talk, which was extraordinarily stimulating, was Mr Spencer. The very same. Now — toast. A toast to the maligned Mr Spencer! Polly — what are we drinking? We haven't even offered our guests anything to drink!'

'We must remedy that at once,' murmured Polly, or Mrs Lewes.

They drank white wine, and small candied-almond pastries were brought in.

The day was quickly forming itself to last in Johnny's memory; he was moved by the unprecedented candour of Lewes, the way he talked about his life, and by the sympathy between the couple, readable in the glances that went back and forth. Johnny had even forgotten the heat, the sweatiness of his undergarments — he did set store by hygiene and order, but a most charming disorder was here beginning to rule the day. For, just as they were now toasting the absent Mr Spencer, Mrs Lewes, who had been momentarily rapt, or lost, in thought, her gaze locked on to the floor, said, 'Tell me, is it the eighteenth of April today?'

(Again, Johnny was moved; curiously so. Such vagueness, such confusion, in so great a genius! She didn't even know what day it was.)

'It is the eighteenth of April, the year of our lord 1869,' said Johnny, with a promptness, a verve, that he knew would please.

'George. It is your birthday. I am sure of it.'

Mr Lewes confirmed that this was the case! And at once, he began to sing, and though Johnny did not know much about opera, he thought he recognised Rossini; at the same time, as he was singing, Mr Lewes, adeptly opening a second bottle of wine, crowed: 'Well done Polly! She's got a better memory than me, infinitely better. Do you know, it's Polly who remembers my own children's birthdays? A better *Mutter* never existed.'

'George is exaggerating,' said Mrs Lewes in a soft voice, but she had a look of tranquil happiness on her face as she spoke.

The afternoon ended in great spirits, as Mr Lewes, as if fulfilling in some mysterious way Johnny's perception of him, rushed outside of the hotel, having spotted something from the balcony, and returned with an organ grinder, an accordion, and a veritable monkey, and the actual monkey and the music entranced them all, particularly Mrs Lewes, who found its gestures so uncannily human, irresistibly comic, and laughed until she had tears in her eyes.

Johnny gazed at her. He had not expected this much laughter, this much humour. But then, he reflected, there was much humorous observation in her books.

Towards seven o'clock, when the heat had begun to die down, the light had grown more mellow and gold and the shadows of evening had appeared, they said goodbye. Mr Lewes had ordered a carriage for them, asking it to come *presto, prestissimo*. Mrs Lewes had taken his hand. 'You will come and see us in England, won't you? Don't be a stranger. And then in England you can tell us why you are come back to our native country. You must have interesting reasons.'

All said in a calm tone, the warmth of which was, Johnny said to himself, splendid.

Returning to their hotel, mounting the badly lit stairway, Johnny had a sense of life returning to its usual rhythm, and that rhythm felt a little ordinary, in contrast to where they had just been.

'What a strange man! What a strange woman!' he kept saying to himself.

Back home, in the shared sitting room, Zibbie was red-faced and fretful, still complaining about the heat, and showing again her feet so rosy and splayed and fearfully enlarged. 'Will you touch my stomach?' she begged, piteously, with one eye a-slant. For she knew he did not want to, and he knew that she knew that. Zibbie had for many years teased him about what she called the mystery of the feminine moon-tide; his clever older sister had always plucked out his weakness. But there was no clever, merry teasing in her face now. He had been out, she had stayed here, her eyes uneasy, looking down, up, everywhere. The room was hot. He didn't like to see her fear, and so he did as she asked, though it was an effort, laid his hand gently on her stomach.

'Press,' she instructed him.

Was she teasing?

'Zibbie, it will be all right. I know it will, and I do not know why you are so frightened.'

Through the chiffon of her dress, he felt the heat of her belly-skin, and the tautness of her stomach. Quickly, he lifted his hand away. He hadn't liked touching it. Then he took her hand and said again that she would be all right.

She said she was glad he was here. He could hear their mother asking the servants about *cena*, dinner. Then Zibbie asked how he had enjoyed it.

'I enjoyed it, more than I would have thought possible.'

'Is she not extraordinary?'

'She is extraordinary.'

'Did they ask you why you were moving to London?' said Zibbie, with a sly, good-natured smile.

Johnny said, 'Not in so many words.'

Because Mrs Lewes had touched gently on the subject, that was the queer thing, as if she had divined pushing matters in his life, and her divination had been correct. He had formed a rash engagement, from which he had lately escaped.

Zibbie said now, 'You're glad about Miss Jay.'

'Why,' he said, 'that is true. I gave them the slip. The family.'

'A narrow escape,' said Zibbie, and now the elder-sister teasing smile was back. 'With my help and Mother's. So you met *Her*. You know she liked my poems? She did. She really did.'

Johnny pressed his sister's hand. He looked only at her hand, as he had seen, when she mentioned her poems, tears fill those eyes. Of course he knew that. Mrs Lewes' encouragement had long been a part of family mythology since Zibbie had, a year ago, visited Mrs Lewes to present her with a copy of her published poems. Then Zibbie whispered: 'Was the talk good?'

'It was,' he agreed gravely. 'The best.'

'And now, what do you think of Miss Jay?'

The spirit of mischief was rekindled in Zibbie's eyes, along with an exultant smile. He smelled then the most delicious smell, suddenly, through the window: was it onions, or tomatoes, or something softer, more mysterious, like saffron?

'Don't ask me,' murmured Johnny.

Why was it that women, at least his sisters, and his mother, penetrated him so easily? It was nearly occult. Miss Jay, to whom he had been engaged, was no longer his fiancée, and all had fallen beautifully into place. Freedom, that most precious asset, was his again. Whether he had acquired it through his own agency was another matter. It was, he had to admit to himself, with his mother and Zibbie's encouragement, that, in the face of virtual pursuit from Miss Jay's family, who had followed him to Europe, he had finally made the almost impertinent suggestion that the engagement should be of a four-year-duration, conveying a message of no muddied kind. At the end of that period, he had written, each party could proceed if still inclined to do so; in a reasonably kind and gentleman-like way, he had made his wishes clear.

But yes, Miss Jay, as they had been coming home in the carriage, had most inopportunely come up in his mind, and the image had been of her giggling, there was no other word for it, over the servant's pronunciation, as this had been in New York, and the servant had been from the South; he had remembered the moment, he had flinched somewhat, as the giggling seemed both ignorant and unkind. Also, on their own, talk had not been forthcoming. He had been unable to envisage their married life together, it had remained blank as a calm sea in the early morning.

He crossed himself. It was a nervous tic, though — he was not even religious!

'What are you doing?' said sharp-eyed Zibby, smiling up at him, her cheeks too rosy, breath coming fast.

3

The Cross family lived in Weybridge, in an expansive pretty house in docile rolling grounds that were equipped with a tennis court. The family was extensive. Anna Cross was the widowed mother of boys Johnny, Willie and James (who lived in America), and girls Emily, Eleanor, Florence, Mary, Anna and Zibbie. A month after leaving Rome, Johnny was due to accompany his mother to call on the Leweses at the Priory to drop by a German translation of *Adam Bede* they had stumbled on, with engravings that were, both son and mother agreed, exquisite. They would be calling because on Sunday the Leweses were known to receive visitors. That Sunday morning, Johnny had entered his mother's bedroom to take his usual seat in the armchair beside her bed, where he would take his coffee. (His father, when alive, had done the same.) When Johnny entered this morning the breakfast tray was untouched, his mother was lying with a flannel covering the eyes. She had a headache, it turned out. Johnny said they would go the following Sunday. At this, Mrs Cross took the flannel off her face, and slowly rose to a sitting position. Her smile was tender.

'My dear Johnny — they were so hospitable to us in Rome, I would not want us to be slow in this instance.'

'But Mother. I would rather go when you are better.'

Anna's expression did not falter. An arm emerged from her shawl and she put a hand on his hand. 'My dear,' she said earnestly, with that same pained smile, 'you will not fail me.'

Johnny was silent before saying, in rather a blurting tone, that sounded even to his ears a jarring note in the Sunday morning sunny silence, 'Mama, I will feel hopelessly presumptuous. I would rather we went the following Sunday.'

Mother prevailed.

Early afternoon Johnny Cross arrived. He stared at the gate, tall, pillars on either side. Two bells. He pulled the one on the right. It rang with surprising volume. Then there was silence, only wind whispering in those high trees. A curiously situated house, he thought. In London, yet not in London. He seemed to see country beyond the house, immediately so, to right and left. Big space between this house and the next.

He was ushered into a room, the sitting room. He expected to encounter a social scene, a crowd, perhaps, of people standing and sitting and talking, but instead the room was silent and scantily occupied. The first person he saw was Mrs Lewes, sitting with her eyes unnaturally wide, staring, it seemed to him. There were only three other people — guests, he worked out immediately — stationary on chairs: two women, and a youngish man with a rather formidable jaw and heavy-lidded eyes. But Johnny started when he registered the object of everyone's gaze — the body on the floor. The body was evidently a very young man: face strangely both whitish and dark in different places, moving or squirming as if with pain, still, and then twitching, the knees curling in the direction of the chest. Johnny averted his eyes. He regretted having come.

He greeted Mrs Lewes and her face showed no expression at all.

'Mr Cross. We met in Rome. My mother, Mrs William Cross, sends her greetings.'

The features dissolved and warmed. She took his hand between her two hands, of course she remembered him.

A second later she was again *la pietà*.

The boy on the floor moved, then lay still, eyelids fluttering, sweat shining on nose and cheeks, then came a gasp, then silence, eyes fluttering shut.

The four visitors sat awkwardly, before introductions were made.

The woman who was called Mrs Norton rose. 'My dear Mrs Lewes, we are intruding. We must leave you. Unless I could do something to help?'

Silence. The atmosphere tinged, as with a dubious perfume, with uncertainty. Mrs Lewes said a faint thank you, but nothing else.

'I, too, would like to assist if I could,' said the man with the heavy-lidded eyes, Mr James. His voice was mellifluous: Johnny couldn't elucidate further, but he felt that the voice emerged as if it had come through tunnels of thought. It emerged — wrought. 'I would be deeply gratified, if it were not too much trouble, if you could — ah — explain these most piteous sounds.'

In her low, musical tone Mrs Lewes explained that Thornie was Mr Lewes' second son, who had just returned from Africa. He was in terrible pain, they didn't yet understand it. He needed help, but today was Sunday. Mr Lewes had gone out to try to find morphine. They had also sent a note to Dr James Paget.

'But my dear Mr Cross, I am pleased that you have brought yourself to the Priory,' she said, automatically, turning to Johnny.

He couldn't help smiling, in spite of the dreadful situation — he had a sensation he had been singled out.

'I thought,' she added gently, 'that we might not see you again after our lucky meeting in Rome.'

She did remember him.

Before Johnny could speak, Mr James cleared his throat, shifted in his seat, and said, 'You have been in Rome? I would find it most — ah — edifying, if you could render your impressions to us, in the meanest shape or form, as it occurs to you. I am, Madam, I must say at once, your most ardent admirer. *Felix Holt* has a place near to my heart. I study it. But perhaps I have spoken precipitately.'

'You study it?' asked Mrs Lewes, eying this guest, with what looked like genuine curiosity.

'I — too — write,' said Mr James, with a modest air, inclining his head. 'I am your apprentice. Your dramatic structures, ma'am, your deep understanding —'

He seemed lost for words.

'May I be allowed to know,' said Mrs Lewes, with infinite graciousness, and she was *la pietà* no longer, 'what it is you have written?'

(Thankfully the boy on the floor was now motionless, eyes shut. Perhaps he was sleeping.)

Mr James raised his eyes to look at Mrs Lewes. Johnny was interested in his eyes. He was looking at Mrs Lewes, yet his eyes were veiled. He coughed. 'Nothing, uh, that would be likely to have attracted your attention, not least because your attention is, I imagine, filled so richly in the first instance. I cannot conceive that my small offerings could have entered those precincts, as it were,' he added with a modest, yet hovering, inscrutable half smile. 'I have written as yet only short stories, and what I would call — ah — journalism.'

The man was American, like the women, but his voice was tinged unusually with an English accent simultaneously, which shaped and changed the vowels.

'I am sorry to say I have not read your stories. I am sure it is my loss,' said Mrs Lewes politely, and she inclined her head, with an incipient sympathy, which, noted Johnny, stopped short of being presumptuously too much.

'Mrs Lewes,' said the man called Mr Henry James. 'Although I have enumerated my — ah — novice works to you, I cannot fail to register that there is a crisis on hand. Would you not let me go in search of this Dr Paget whom you mentioned? I am full of compassion for your situation. I could endeavour to find him.'

Mrs Lewes accepted gratefully. The ladies rose to leave. In an inspired moment, Johnny resolved his sensation of awkwardness by offering to aid Mr James in his search. The offer was accepted. As he was leaving, Johnny remembered. He reached into his briefcase, pressed the copy of *Adam Bede* in its German translation into Mrs Lewes' hand, saying that his mother, and he, hoped she would enjoy the engraved illustrations. Of the translation, he had no such expectation. She was, as everyone knew, expert in the German language, and would doubtless find many infelicities.

Johnny Cross and Henry James walked across Regent's Park together, Johnny regulating his naturally athletic stride to keep time with the more measured step of Mr James. They found a hansom in Park Crescent. They were on their way. It was a breezy, sunny May day; there was an odour in the hansom — stale pipe tobacco; the motion was jerky. Johnny sat in one corner; Henry James in the other. Henry James did not speak. He had hardly spoken when they were walking: he had worn a look of the most intense preoccupation.

However, now that they were in the cab together, Johnny broke the silence by saying to him that he had heard of his writings in relation to, possibly, American journals.

'Very kind of you to say so,' said Henry James, hardly looking up. Then he seemed to wake up, and spoke with sudden affability: 'I find myself absorbed, my dear Mr Cross, by the lady whom I have for the first time in my life encountered in the flesh: Mrs Lewes, to be exact. I do not exaggerate when I say that I have worn, metaphorically speaking, *Felix Holt* here,' — he dabbed with his hand emphatically at the left part of his chest, his heart — 'since I first read it, when it penetrated into the depths, the very depths. She goes in, if you follow me,' he said, turning his eyes onto Johnny. His eyes with their heavy lids, and inscrutable gaze.

'I think I follow you,' said Johnny, trying his best.

'Her art, is what I mean: the broad, wide-ranging, deep picture of us.' He cleared his throat. 'Having read her, I find it indescribably moving to meet the person in life.'

'Ah,' said Johnny.

'I do,' murmured Mr James, almost to himself; so that briefly Johnny felt Mr James had forgotten his existence.

'A moving incident … a stirring incident … to see her deal with the most extreme yet ordinary crisis, the younger relative in pain, the white-faced boy. Just as it is moving,' he went on, without a pause, 'to see her ugliness. Her magnificent ugliness.'

Johnny did not immediately speak. He had a sensation that some sort of blasphemy had been uttered.

He stared at the imperturbable face on the other side of the hansom, swaying lightly to and fro with the cab's movement, the eyes half shut, the slight smile. He felt it incumbent on him, strangely, to protest.

'Really —!'

At once Mr James' eyes were on him, with an ironic and sceptical smile. It was as if Mr James sensed his own light sensation of shock, and was now enjoying himself as he proceeded.

'That delicious hideousness!' went on Mr James, with enthusiasm, looking amusedly, yet compellingly, at Johnny. 'That low forehead! The dull grey eyes. The vast pendulous nose. The huge mouth. The chin! On and on, as to infinity. Those ill-shaped teeth; the rather small body — she is a feat of ugliness.'

'Oh I say!'

'You do not find her so?' enquired his new friend, politely.

'Not, ah … as you describe,' said Johnny, with equal politeness, but he did not look at Mr James.

'Interesting,' said Mr James, but it seemed to Johnny that he discerned a smile behind the other man's beard.

'And yet, and yet,' said Henry James, proceeding thoughtfully, 'she has a beauty also.'

For the second time Johnny was lost for words.

'A … beauty,' he echoed, half frowning. He was mistily attempting to follow James' thought. 'You — you — think that also?'

'I do,' said Mr James, firmly. 'There is a deep charm in that soft, rich voice. The sense, too, that one is approaching a hinterland behind that soft voice. A vast hinterland, rich with thought and experience, and the golden thread of erudition. She is able to name, if you follow me. She has a multitude of examples, you might say, of those facets of experience — and where it has not been named,' he finished, 'she will still go. Stop me if I go on too long.'

'Not at all,' said Johnny Cross, politely.

The hansom cab did a violent turn round Trafalgar Square, and for a moment the two men were rocked, each flung into the respective corners; then the cab achieved a steady rhythm once more, Johnny coughed as he smoothed his jacket, centring himself once more on the seat.

Now Mr James turned to Johnny with a smile. 'Yes, behold me literally in love with this great horse-faced bluestocking! The understanding —' Mr James sighed. 'The understanding, that surpasses the average person's, as an ocean eclipses a pond: today I glimpsed it. And a vast tenderness, too. No, a beautiful tenderness.'

'Right-oh!' said Johnny.

Johnny looked out of the window after that. His companion was indeed strange, he thought. Yet he couldn't resist glancing at the stocky man on the other side of the carriage, who produced words and ideas so effortlessly. Still, Johnny had a faint sensation of relief when they finally knocked on Dr Paget's door, and as soon as the maid heard the name Mrs Lewes, they were shown in — but Dr Paget was not at home, it was only Mrs Paget who greeted them and heard their story, and said she would notify the doctor as soon as he was home. Henry James and Johnny said their goodbyes. Johnny made his way to the station.

Waiting for the train to Weybridge, Johnny sat on the platform, in the sunny smoky air. What a strange morning. That poor boy. Mrs Lewes, and then Henry James, the heavy eyelids, the veiled look, the faintly prim-looking mouth that seemed to harbour a possible smile in that well-trimmed dark beard. What was it he said? *Magnificently ugly. Deliciously hideous.*

Johnny went back to the moment in Rome when he had beheld Mrs Lewes for the first time, sitting in the shadowed part of the room. He had had to control his features which had dropped at the sight of her. The idea that the smallish woman on the far side of the room, with the strangely large head and — and — his thoughts tailed off.

But no, he could not instantly put her together with *Adam Bede* and *The Mill on the Floss*. The beauty of feeling he had found there.

'Behold me literally in love ...' Mr James had said.

* * *

At Weybridge station the florist was open, and he bought an especially large bunch of peonies, pink and white, for his mother.

The next moment he frowned. The word 'hideous' had swum back into his mind. It was ... a kind of blasphemy! He had a sore, affronted sensation.

Had Mr James been laughing at him?

4

Marian sat regarding Thornie as he slept. He was at least peaceful now — had been dosed with morphia, and was surely exhausted, too. Sometimes she could see George in his face.

Only two weeks ago they had been in Rome. She could remember all the preparations for the journey home, but it seemed a very long time ago. Then there was the travel itself. For some reason she kept remembering the Munich station in the cool half-light of the breaking dawn, silent and deserted, a little disturbing. There, they had taken the train to Strasbourg; after which, roaring through the night-time countryside, they had travelled to Paris.

Lewes had rested his head on her shoulder, the gas light burning only faintly, bathing the room in a queer sallow colour, the train carriage smelling of heated metal. Sometimes he rocked forward, but Marian would steady him.

Hurtling through northern France in the darkness, with Lewes asleep, knowing she was nearly home, Marian had at last had her mind to herself.

She had a low, simmering instinct that she hadn't yet used her powers as a writer fully — had hopes of returning to the strengths displayed in *Adam Bede* and *The Mill on the Floss*, yet on a larger canvas, everything deeper, broader. Lifting the blind in the carriage window, she could see blackness, occasionally shapes in the distance, what looked like the far line of the horizon under the night sky. Some minutes later, she could make out a hilltown in the night. Just visible! This was how the new novel was, she thought: projecting dimly, fantastically in her mind.

Within twenty-four hours, the hansom cab reached Regents Park, The Priory, and servants Amelia and Grace were letting them in. They were home. The house looked swept and tidy: two piles of post visible, a new cloth of maroon velvet on the hallway table. With dazed, tired eyes, warmth beginning to seep through her, Marian couldn't see enough of the familiar hallway and stairs. Ben the bull terrier was jumping up in a frenzy of joy. In the dining room, they had leek soup, Welsh rarebit, and a refreshing glass of red wine. 'Eh, Ma'am, you've had a journey, you have!' Amelia kept saying, then returning to ask if there was anything else they wanted: it was pleasant to see Amelia's wide, pale, pudgy face again, with the monk-like fringe, unable to stop smiling as she collected the plates. Afterwards they sat, just George and herself, in the drawing room. There was a fire burning. Even Marian's chilled feet began to be warm. It was good to see the long room again, she had forgotten how pretty the flower-tracing wallpaper patterned in gold and green was; how comfortable the wingback chairs, with the low table linking them. Just perceptible, along with the smell of the burning wood, was the medicinal, reassuring smell of beeswax. Amelia or her sister Grace had polished the furniture for their return. The sense of relief deprived her of speech for some minutes. They were back.

The next morning she woke early — she could see cracks of light either side of the heavy curtains, spilling gold. Downstairs, one of the servants was up already: the sound of running water, low bang of the pots. She found Amelia on her knees, sweeping the kitchen stove with a brush.

Amelia said Marian had looked 'done in' when she arrived last night.

'I am fine,' said Marian, smiling, suppressing a sensation of impatience. 'I wanted to ask if you would be so kind as to bring up coffee to my study.'

'Done in,' Marian repeated under her breath, making a face, as she climbed the stairs. Reaching her study door, she paused. In the early morning, the house was silent, except for the steady ticking of the tall clock downstairs. And, distantly, birds.

She turned the door handle, stepped in, seated herself — her breathing steadied. Here she was, the familiar garden below, at her desk. She drew from her travelling bag her notebook. Some minutes later, Amelia brought a tray with steaming black coffee and warm milk in a jug.

Marian sipped her coffee, savoured the silence, solitude, waited for her mind to settle.

But her mind did not settle. The public. She was thinking of the public.

The journey had been a time of self-examination. On deck during the Channel crossing, she had gone over it in her mind again. The last work she'd published was the long dramatic poem, *The Spanish Gypsy*. The public hadn't understood it, but if she was honest, she trusted herself less. Was she blind, half-sighted, like that old woman she'd glimpsed on the empty Munich train platform, feeling her way with that tap-tapping stick? Because when she contemplated her last works, *The Spanish Gypsy*, *Romola*, *Felix Holt*, she knew a thread of self-dissatisfaction.

She reached for her diary — she was sure she'd started the year in high spirits.

January 1. A bright frosty morning! she read. *And we are both well. I have set myself many tasks for the year — I wonder how many will be accomplished? A Novel called* Middlemarch, *a long poem on Timoleon, and several minor poems.*

Only four months ago, but it was like reading words written by someone else. A knock on the door and Amelia was back, wanting to discuss meals, laundry, and cleaning.

'It's the same as before,' said Marian, the colour rising in her cheeks.

Amelia said things might have changed.

'I assure you they have not,' said Marian, with a fraught half smile she couldn't control. She needed to know she would not be interrupted. In fact —

Lewes was in the drawing room, Ben the terrier snoozing beside him.

'George, I wanted to say —'

'What did you want to say?'

Cheerful man!

'I wanted to say,' said Marian, smiling in spite of herself, 'that it might be politic, not to to tell people we are back. I thought we could have a quiet Sunday this weekend.'

George agreed. Usually visitors crowded to the house on a Sunday afternoon.

Back in her study, Marian looked at the books, checked the side table. Letters, books, and the child's picture by Isaac she liked to display — sky, grass, tree. She opened her notebook to see what her jottings from the last year amounted to.

The first thing she read was this:

Timoleon. 'Took Epaminondas for his model.'

The aruspice, named according to some, Orthagoras; according to others, Satyrus. The brother-in-law named Aeschylus. Tragedies on the subject of the Fratricide by Alfieri, Chénier, La Harpe. 'Hoc praeclarissimum ejus facinus.'

C. Nepos

She flicked backwards. On page 5 — she numbered the pages — she had written:

Mean distance of the Earth from the Sun	*94,800,000 miles*
Greatest eccentricity may be	*102,256,873*
	87,503,039
making a difference of	*14,753,834*
Present eccentricity	*93,286,707*
	96,331,707
Cycle of precession	*25,686 years*

She suddenly felt tired. Why had she noted these giant distances down? Did she think this assemblage of facts could bring her closer to writing a novel? She could not even retrace the impulse. She gave up for the day.

$$\star \star \star$$

The following morning Marian opened her dark blue notebook again. Once more her neat, organised, black-inked handwriting, sloping to the right. This was what she read:

Welcker calculates the weight of Dante's brain from the data given by Nicolucci, & finds it very little above the average of mediocre men. Whereupon he remarks that such comparative deficiency of weight in gifted men he has observed to be present where there has been an inequality of skull owing to premature closing of the Sutures. He instances among other W. v. Humboldt, whose brain had a weight below the average.

The Sicilian (Syracusan) Dioklês, author of a new code, having inadvertently violated one of his own enactments, falls on his own sword to enforce the duty of obedience.

He does not creep along the coast but steers far out under the guidance of the stars.

The emblem of the triangle △ occurs on Punic basreliefs.

The leading authorities (modern) for the history of the Phoenicians are Gesenius, Monumenta.

Enough. She turns to her other notebook, in dark green. Her notes, in violet ink, on Lucretius. She lets her mind follow him. Drawing back and down into thought. And suddenly her mood changes. The sky outside moving pleasantly further away. At the edges, a moving object, almost in the visual field, yet just out of sight, configurations forming: the long tunnel-like corridor in the infirmary of Leeds, a coal-fire system of heating, Dr Allbutt's new clinical thermometer, six inches only.

Her hero a doctor. Dr Allbutt's interest, vigour constant, flattering to her, but genuine. His sense of her receptivity; and, encouraged, the funnel of confidences. Handling superiors with deference, never humility. Perhaps a spark of too much pride, necessary in a hero. Her heartbeat settles. Sitting there, at her desk, she is aware with her eyes, but without having even to move from her thoughts, of the magnolia tree at the trellis below, holding up its pearly crimson-slitted outsized buds; movement of the ash tree in the long right corner; singing, thrush, no, blackbird; sky moving with the wind; and a sensation of the purest pleasure filling her. There is possibility, of course there is. The great theme of history's form and meaning, and the deep pull of her idea: the ordinary heroic, the noble intentions that don't reach fulfilment; as tragic as the greater heroic. Why not?

She stayed in her study through the morning hours, and only at two o'clock did she find George. They ate bread and cheese, and as they strolled afterwards round Regent's Park, Marian was struck by the beauty of the cut paths, the combination of nature and man's organising hand. 'George,' she said, as they walked hand in hand, 'I would like to come to see your mother. I have been worrying that I was — brusque — yesterday.'

Lewes laughed. They'd see his mother for tea tomorrow.

He had known better than to ask her about *Middlemarch*. Everything about her, the interest lighting up her beautiful grey-blue eyes, the way she had stopped at the first rose they came across in the park, to try to identify it, told him she was feeling more hopeful.

She had a good morning the next day, then went with George to see his mother. On return, though, there was a bag in the hallway, a strange-looking trunk. It was a blistered dark red colour, weathered, beaten, straps, and a foreign-looking yellow and red label. A sound, and a young man in the doorway. A stranger. Sun-burned, with an emaciated face, skeletally thin arms, walking, — no, stumbling, but Lewes was catching him. Lewes was holding the man in his arms. Marian heard Lewes say, 'You're back.' With a lurch in her chest, Marian realised. It was Thornie. It *was* Thornie, she could see him in the smile that was faintly appearing.

She hadn't expected him for several weeks.

Thornie had made the journey back from Africa. He had injured his spine four years ago, after which pains had begun a year later, supposedly rheumatism. He had lost four stone. On that first night, Marian played the piano for him, at his request, Schubert's waltzes. 'Oh that's lovely,' said Thornie; but when she'd finished, and turned round, his features had fallen. Without cheer, his visage was again older-looking, hardly recognisable.

5

Dearest B.,

Thornie is come home in a very precarious state, and we are absorbed by cares about him. Come and see him — in the intervals of pain, he likes to be amused. Thanks for the flowers.

Yours ever, Marian.

Barbara arrived on Thursday with refreshments for the invalid: a basket of cooked chicken, fresh cream, and strawberries from the country. Just to see her, in her dress of royal blue, with her strong smiling face, made Marian feel more hopeful. Thornie was in the garden — Amelia and Grace had brought his bed out because the day was fine. Barbara took him his food on a tray. Thornie picked at the chicken. It was warm, they wore hats, then when Marian's eyes began to close — it was somehow so relaxing having Barbara here, taking charge — Barbara told her to go inside, leave her with Thornie.

Marian rested her head back on the sofa, closed her eyes. With the doors open, she could hear them: Barbara's tone playful, then speculative; they were both laughing. Barbara seemed to be talking with ease — about Algiers, where she lived for most of the year; how her husband was cultivating eucalyptus trees, though he still didn't speak a word of English (faint, watery-sounding chuckle from Thornie). For a moment, Marian was jealous: she sounded so natural! She couldn't help remembering how hard she'd found it to write to George's three boys when they were at school in Switzerland — to her stepsons, she corrected herself. She would tell them to work harder, or remind them to be good; she could never think of what to say.

Another gale of laughter — real belly laughter — reached her. What were they talking about, she wondered gloomily. She picked up Grote's *History of Greece*.

Thornie had always been difficult. Recently, she'd found an old letter from him, written from school, in which he described himself writing a story: *Getting on at an intense rate*, he'd written. *Steam is up; high pressure express; and away we go! Does your feeble imagination twig the metaphors?*

Does your feeble imagination twig the metaphors. Marian did not want to live with either Thornie or the youngest, Bertie. After school, Thornie had gone straight to Edinburgh to study, and then to South Africa, to shoot big game and make his fortune. Later, to Marian's intense relief, the youngest Bertie had followed him there.

Did she regret becoming a stepmother? The question was ludicrous. She'd had no choice. She was fond of Charles, the oldest, a dear boy, and biddable, too. When they were away, he became their secretary, in effect, dealing with and forwarding their copious post. And there were other advantages. She used to enjoy writing to friends about *our boys, our great tall boys*. Each time she penned the phrase, there was something curative in the words, as if she were magically drawing a new outline of herself.

'You were almost an hour with him!' she said, when Barbara reappeared.

'He's a delightful young man,' said Barbara, simply.

For a split second, Marian thought she was being ironic.

They left to stroll round Regent's Park, while Thornie was watched by Amelia. Feeling the warm air on their faces, Barbara thrust her arm companionably through Marian's, before asking about Thornie.

'We both think he will get well again, as does Dr Paget. But, my dear Barbara, what will he do? How can he earn a living? And I confess,' Marian added, with a twisted smile, 'when he is well, he will not be the most peaceful young man to have in the house.'

She hoped she did not sound unmotherly. She tried to make her face look tender.

'But,' said Barbara, more slowly, 'will it not be — a comfort? To have him, I mean? I would dearly like Dr Bodichon to have had children.'

'It is a question,' said Marian, thoughtfully. She was thinking now of *Silas Marner*, and all that she'd tried to express through the character of Nancy Lammeter, who wanted children so much and remained childless.

She couldn't have had children, living openly with Lewes. And they were already supporting not just Lewes' three boys, but Agnes' children by her lover Thornton Hunt. She, Marian, was by far the main earner.

'Do you not regret not having them?' cried Barbara, stopping, turning to face Marian.

'My position has never been — comparable to yours.'

'But do you not regret them?'

Marian did not know what to say. Thornie's arrival was — frightful.

'Not precisely. But you, my dearest Barbara, what of you?'

'No — no,' said Barbara, and she smoothed her reddish, golden hair, bright now in the sunlight, out of her eyes. She was biting her lip, saying quickly: 'I have to give up. I am forty-two. All that I feel,' — silently she gesticulated. Her eyes were glassy with tears.

'We are animals, as well as humans!' she burst out. 'Don't laugh, Marian. In my eyes, that takes nothing away from being human. It's a miracle of life — that we breed like animals, gestate like animals, but we're also capable of the finest feelings, the highest mental performance, artistic or scientific — have you read John Stuart Mill, by the way?' she said abruptly.

'I will. I will.'

'Do so. I would like to know what you think. But yes, I feel like a breeding animal that has had its chance snatched away by some freak of fortune. Two years ago, night after night, I became hot as an oven — like some terrible fireside stoking up its own fire. I know what it means. I have given up.'

Marian took Barbara's hand and pressed it. She knew how much Barbara had wanted children. The loss was profound. But Barbara's married life in

Algiers made it harder. So isolated she was! Barbara's husband would not even learn English — obstinate, odd character that he was! No wonder Barbara came to England when she could. Whereas, if she had had her own children to love and raise —

'I know you understand,' said Barbara in a low voice. 'I painted it, you know.'

Marian had seen the painting, a bleak landscape called 'Solitude', with a single stork flying overhead. As usual, she felt her own peculiarly self-tormenting brand of thinking lessened by another's trouble. Yet she did not relish her friend's unhappiness. 'But you have Dr Bodichon,' said Marian.

'I do. And he is a fine man. Not perhaps the easiest,' Barbara added, with a laugh.

Marian gave a deprecatory shrug. She did not want to say that she had heard odd stories about Dr Bodichon.

'Like most husbands,' joked Marian, to help Barbara feel happier with her lot. 'And Bessie? How is Bessie?'

'Bessie had a baby last summer,' said Barbara flatly.

Marian clicked her tongue at her own forgetting. Bessie Parkes was now Bessie Belloc.

'Ah — that was difficult. My oldest friend. I'd urged her not to get married, too. I felt it would be disastrous for her.'

As they walked, Marian felt, as she often did with even her close friends, that she understood more than she should: Barbara was perturbed for her friend Bessie marrying a Frenchman and living away from England, because she had herself found her own life in exile so trying. And this human tendency, to map the subjective experience outwardly, to see it elsewhere, interested Marian. This is how people are, she thought to herself. They do not know themselves, they see it in others instead.

'And has it been unhappy for Bessie, in France?'

Barbara didn't instantly answer. Then, with a rueful smile, she said she was remarkably well — much better than before her marriage.

'Her happiness ... when I heard about her baby, it was like a knife in my chest! I felt awful ...' laughed Barbara, shamefaced.

'Dearest,' said Marian, drawing her close for a moment. How she loved this friend! Who else was so honest?

'Yes, when she told me she was pregnant — it was agonising. And when she came to England, I couldn't stand to see her.'

'Of course you could not,' sympathised Marian. 'The contrast must have felt unbearable! This is life — this is one of the hardest things in life.'

'It's true,' said Barbara, heaving a great sigh. 'Please don't think I'm as selfish as this usually.'

Marian put out her arms and embraced her friend; with the slightly odd sensation of voluptuous softness, as she drew Barbara's form towards her. Her free-thinking friend, she could tell, was as usual uncorseted. How soft, yielding she felt.

They began walking back to the Priory.

'I know, too,' went on Marian, 'that you love Bessie.'

'I do,' said Barbara, hardly audible.

'And I know,' said Marian, 'that after she had her child — a girl?'

'A girl.'

'After she had her little girl, you did invite them both to your house, did you not?'

'I did,' said Barbara, again hardly audible. She was smiling, tremulously; Marian saw tears at the end of her lashes.

'Because you love her,' said Marian, now taking Barbara's arm in hers, and they moved on, walking in step. 'These are the challenges life throws at us. What would it be if we had nothing with which to compare ourselves? These points of comparison,' she added, thoughtfully, 'are the measures, and what power they have.'

Marian was thinking, a little, of her travels earlier this year, when they had stayed in Florence with Tom Trollope. Genial and delightful host that he was, with her own new novel still a tantalising figment, she couldn't help thinking of Anthony, his brother. Anthony was of course a dear friend, and in the last six months, his scope, his ability to handle the different threads of action on such a large scale, had impressed and worked as a reproach to her; an image of what she had not yet done, but felt she could do. Possibly better, she said to herself, more finely realised.

Leaving the park behind, they could see the high wall of the garden — but a cry was breaking through the afternoon air. The two women quickened their step, round the house to the garden. Thornie — what a sight — moving like a strange creature — breathlessly the two women ran. Barbara asked if they had morphine. Marian said they did.

'Where is it?'

'I'm not sure,' admitted Marian. Barbara flashed her a strange glance; Marian blushed.

Kneeling by the bed, Barbara was inserting a pillow under Thornie's head, asking, 'Where is it? Where is the pain?'

Thornie said between his gasps that it was everywhere.

'My dear boy,' said Barbara helplessly, but with feeling, 'we will do what we can as quickly as we can.'

'Indeed,' echoed Marian. Why, she was paralysed — she could not think. Where would George have left the morphine?

'Surely he would have left instructions with you or Amelia?' asked Barbara.

'Indeed, I would have thought,' said Marian, and it seemed that Barbara flashed her another strange glance. The calm May day — what a mockery it suddenly all seemed: this peaceful garden, the still sun and shadow, the Ceanothus, blue berry-like flowers blooming steadily.

Amelia was rushing towards them, no cap, saying she could search Mr Lewes' office.

'Excellent idea,' said Barbra, instantly.

'Yes,' echoed Marian.

While Amelia hurried off, Barbara knelt and stroked Thornie's hand.

What strength there was in her friend's face, with that firm chin, that tender look she aimed at Thornie — why, this woman never tired of working for others. Whereas she, even while Thornie was in agony — a most peculiar, most regrettably selfish sadness was rising and enveloping Marian, even bringing tears to her eyes!

'My dear Marian,' said generous Barbara, reaching out her one free hand to her.

Marian took Barbara's hand, but despair was turning inside her now like a twisting knife. Her tears were not for Thornie, they were for herself, her own hopelessness, her unwritten book most of all, her detestable self-concern that consumed her. Amelia came; Barbara administered the morphia. 'I know, I know, the pain will not go at once,' said Barbara to Thornie, who was keeping his eyes fixed on her, 'but very soon it will. Let us sing, Marian — what can we sing? Any distraction will be good.'

'My voice is very poor. I am better at the piano.'

'Come — sing with me,' — and Barbara launched upon 'Greensleeves', and Marian joined in, somewhat quaveringly, and Thornie, quiet, white-faced, was distracted for some seconds, before he turned his face to the side, his lips pinching to stop crying out.

'What is it? What has he got?' There was horror on Barbara's face.

Marian told Barbara all she knew. Dr Paget was not sure; Thornie had contracted an infection in Africa, and he thought Thornie's glands had hardened. It was likely he would recover. They had known about this at the end of last year, when Thornie had sent them a detailed letter.

'You never mentioned it to me,' said Barbara, turning to look at Marian with another strange glance. Marian muttered something. Why had she not mentioned it, she asked herself, after Barbara had gone. Perhaps because she hadn't wanted to. She hadn't wanted to. That was it.

Next morning, Marian took pen to paper:

Dearest B.,

I feared, after you were gone, that I had seemed to urge your coming in a selfish sort of way, and before your note came I was going to write to you to say, that you must only think of us as not the less glad to have you because there was an invalid in the house.

6

It's late February.

Coming home, I find the building tools in the same place as the day before. There is a thin brown film of builder dust everywhere. Upstairs it's the same: bathroom walls skeletal, just struts. The builder, a Romanian called Benny, hasn't shown up for two weeks. He doesn't take my calls.

I have an idea, and when Sal comes round, I borrow her phone and call Benny. Sure enough, he picks up from a number he doesn't recognise.

'Kate! Hi!' he says in a confidential voice, as if nothing strange has been happening.

Benny wears trousers that have a nineteenth-century actorly look, they narrow round his calves like breeches. He has an attractive, troubled face, and quite long hair, and likes to talk at length about the tragedy of his country, where he was an engineer. Now he says I must not worry, he will be back in two days.

Benny comes back.

The curtains and matting are removed, the floorboards are bare, the naked sash windows with their architraves are painted white. The Victorian bones of the house are showing. I pick up a sofa on the street, which Benny and his friend take up for me.

I'm still woken by the dogs each morning. Dale says the problem is the third dog. Before she came, they slept through the night. He has to look after the third dog for the next six months. I suspect he's being well paid for it.

★ ★ ★

I haven't been to Ann and Hans' place before. Inside the narrow hallway I can hear television, the bouncing, frenzied noise of a cartoon. The sitting room is two rooms knocked through. I've come to babysit, and I've brought Ann's chapters to finish in my bag.

Ann is kneeling beside her son, who is watching *Tom and Jerry*. 'PJs,' she is commanding. Her son, Ben, takes no notice. He sits erect, white towel at his waist, his bare back has an arch.

'I love *Tom and Jerry*!' I say. I want to smooth into these family surroundings. Ann snaps the television off, the arch in Ben's back grows as he rears, throws his head back, yells.

Footsteps, Hans enters. 'What the — hi, hi, this is so kind of you —' (to me).

Hans switches the television back on, scoops Ben up and into his lap, in the same second. Watching the television again, Ben automatically sticks out first one arm then the other, as Hans puts on his top; just as absently, he sticks out his legs, which Ann feeds into the pyjama trousers. 'He's ready,' says Hans, motioning his head upwards.

On the television, Tom is chasing Jerry into a tiny hole; a white star explodes and fills the screen as Tom bangs into the wall.

'He's ready,' repeats Hans.

'Have you done the bottle?'

'No.'

'I asked you to do it.'

There is an electric quality to Ann's face: motionless, the eyes lit.

'I'm happy to do it,' says Hans, without expression.

Hans gets up, he is a gawkily tall man. For once he is not in grey tracksuit trousers, he is in jeans. Leisurely, he goes out to the kitchen to make up the bottle. I wonder if his casual walk is for my benefit.

'I can't tell you how often I have to ask,' says Ann, in an undertone, before going upstairs to settle the baby. I stay on the sofa. Hans joins me with the bottle in his hands. We make departmental talk, then talk about the Eliot conference in Venice. We're both going, it turns out, and probably Ann too.

What's it going to be like teaching a class with this guy next term?

Hans shifts in his seat, absently elbowing two plastic cars aside to make room for himself on the sofa. The room is full of plastic, the floor a sea of toys.

* * *

After they leave, going to make tea, my foot budges a truck, a loud voice startles me, 'Way to go, Bob!' I pick the truck up and the voice stops. In the kitchen, I see framed black-and-white family photos above a shelf of books — and immediately I see three books on Eliot, familiar. Haight, Ashton, Hughes, three biographies. Rebecca Mead's *Road to Middlemarch*. So Ann disperses her books, she doesn't keep them all in one place. Or maybe she works in the kitchen? Above the table hangs a central lamp on a cord, low, spreading a pool of light. I look back at the books, and then at the bulging piles of paper in the shelf below, batches of A4 paper in elastic bands. I peek at the titles: *Fearful Caution: George Eliot and the Woman Question — 1st draft*. And another: *Fearful Caution: George Eliot and the Woman Question — 6th draft*. This is the book Ann is working on now. How many drafts is she doing?

In the sitting room, I take her chapters from my bag — and can't stop reading. After talking to Ann, I'd expected something antagonistic. But it's not that way at all. Ann suggests that Eliot is *like someone brought to a precipice, where the full landscape of women's possibilities, their possible lives, stretches out before her — but Eliot's adhesion to the real, to how life is being lived all around her, stops her from jumping.*

I think I understand what she's saying. The next chapter's more negative.

* * *

There are sounds at the front door.

'Hey! How's it been?' says Ann. She enters, cheeks red from the cold or alcohol or both. She is wearing a fur collar round her neck. They both look elated.

'Has it been okay?' asks Hans, also smiling.

'Not a peep. Nice drink?'

They say definitely.

'I should be making a move —'

They both protest loudly, and Hans reaches for the bottle of brandy. 'Isn't this Lewes' tipple?' he says, handing us glasses.

We sit back.

Hans says: 'So you're both writing books on Eliot, but you're doing a fiction book, right?'

'A novel,' I reply. 'A mix of fact and fiction.'

'But what does that make it?'

'All the letters and diary quotations are real.'

'Ah so. All of them. Without exception?'

'Yes.'

'You never said that to me,' says Ann.

'Hey!' I say. I tell her how much I like her chapters.

'Do you?'

'It's so good!' I say. 'Especially all that stuff about *Deronda*.'

Ann is smiling. 'So — like what?'

'Well ... as you say ... it's much darker than *Middlemarch*. The marriage market's kind of spooky — terrifying! But after that you're pretty down on Eliot, aren't you?'

'I don't like her,' sighs Ann, blowing a strand of hair out of her eyes. 'She saw it all so clearly, she still didn't want change. All right for her. She was the giant exception.'

I nod.

'But you liked it,' she says, with a grin, after a moment.

'Like I said,' I laugh. 'I do.'

'She won't believe you,' says Hans, with a smile.

A crackle, a squawk, a cry — the baby alarm. Ann goes upstairs and returns with Michael on her shoulder, his face hidden in her neck. She gently disengages him, adjusting his position so that he is lying in the crook of her left arm.

Discreetly she lifts her blouse, and then he is feeding. We are all quiet. Ann's face has that empty look I have observed when she breastfeeds. Every now and then one of the baby's feet lifts.

I feel I must say something. 'He looks happy.'

'It's downhill from here,' jokes Hans.

'He's not a bad rabbit,' says Ann, in her half-absent voice. 'Hello — yes, I'm talking about you —'

Michael has lifted his mouth off the breast, to look up at her. He is smiling. Ann has a small look on her face I have not seen before, a soft little encouraging look, her raised brows gently questioning. Abruptly I get to my feet, and go home, cutting their thanks short.

Back in my flat, I sit without moving on my sofa. I sit there for some time. Then I go to my laptop, and scroll through the Eliot letters that I've scanned in. Am I looking for a particular letter? I'm not sure. I do stop at this one though.

My dear Mrs Pattison,

I feared after you had left us that I had allowed myself an effusiveness beyond what was warranted by the short time we had known each other. But in proportion as I profoundly rejoice that I never brought a child into the world, I am conscious of having an unused stock of motherly tenderness, which sometimes overflows, but not without discrimination.

7

Lewes was hardly working now. He had hoped to be working on his magnum opus, *Problems of Life and Mind*, but he was occupied with nursing Thornie, too distressed to concentrate. He worried for Marian too. She had not, he knew, started the next novel, *Middlemarch*. It was not even clear she was going ahead with it. Last week, she had mentioned *Timoleon*, the long poem she was considering writing about the ancient hero of Sicily. Each time she mentioned it, his spirits inexplicably lowered.

But today at least was Sunday, they were having guests to lunch, and for the afternoon too. The prospect was cheering.

He liked to supervise these gatherings. Sometimes they drank a light German white wine, a Spät-Burgunder; Lewes himself had a weakness for the deep malt whisky, served in small crystal glasses, the kind favoured by Polly's Swiss friends, Monsieur and Madame d'Aubade: short glasses, sweetly curvaceous, engraved with a winding vine. At the same time — Amelia, to her credit, had become efficient at this — they served tea, in the two impressive Johnson silver teapots that Lewes had bought in Bermondsey.

But he was tired. Looking in the mirror as he shaved this morning, he had been shocked by his face. Cratered with anxiety; forehead rutted with lines; his chin — he had to laugh — more vanishing than ever. However, stroking his moustache, he enjoyed the smooth feeling of it, and his beard; lucky moustache, lucky beard; lucky with women. Agnes a beauty; Polly a genius; not bad, not bad.

He was tired because he'd been up and down the previous night four times to dose Thornie with morphine.

After the second time of giving Thornie drops, Lewes had found himself too agitated to sleep. What would settle him? Pickwick — *The Pickwick Papers*. He had gone in search of Dickens' novel, still the happiest book he'd ever read. But the book wasn't in the drawing room, nor in his own office, so he took his candle into Polly's study.

In he had gone, the house suddenly seeming very silent.

It must be said that he did not usually enter her study when she was not in it.

He lit the gas lamp, which flared unsteadily, throwing an uneven balance of light and shadow across the room. Then, holding a candle close, he searched in the shelves. No — no — he went through the three long shelves, but it wasn't there. What should he do? He couldn't possibly sleep — his heart was going too fast. He did not want to think about the boy.

Sitting at Polly's desk, his eyes fell on her dark blue notebook. How well he knew that cover, gleaming low in the candlelight. It had accompanied them to Trollope's villa in Florence, to Pompeii, to Assisi ... He had often glanced over her shoulder as she briefly wrote in it during their travels, yet never looked inside. Curious. He drew it towards him now. He hesitated. Then, feeling like a trespasser, he opened it. Polly's beloved handwriting: neat, consistent, something recognisably feminine about the graceful elegant control of that sloping hand, yet a determination, too, in its consistency, and what looked like, on first glance, the energetic compression of her entries.

An owl hooted. Lewes began to read. Then he began to read more slowly.

Why, how extensive were her researches.

Possibly his senses were distended by the silence and stillness of the deep small hours of the night: only the distant ticking of the clock from the hallway downstairs, and sporadic faint scuffling, mice, behind the skirting board. And perhaps he was affected by the late, lonely hour; the high, desperate agitation of fear and love for Thornie, in which he was swinging on a daily basis; and the fluctuating light from the candle and the gas. The first thing that struck him was the confident moving from language to language. A multitude of languages: jottings in Greek, Latin, German, French, Italian, Spanish — even, if he wasn't mistaken, some lines in Sanskrit. (What was that scent — verbena? And, perhaps, orris root? Could they be growing outside the window? The night breeze was bringing with it a soft but wild, exotic fragrance.) But it was her scope, the wideness of her searching eye, roving from ancient to modern, from historian to historian, that struck him with a flame-like clarity, then; that to understand history was her driving object — to understand, even, what might constitute history or progress. He read on: what was she chasing, with her reading? Was she meditating the idea that each perspective called history was in time superseded by another? Was no perspective, in short, the essential perspective? The drive, the eye, her remarkable eye, had a probing intention that was nothing short of majestic. In woman or man.

He continued turning the pages. But slowly he was aware of another realisation. She, novelist that she was, must incarnate her insights into human drama. No wonder she was dazzled by this challenge!

Or paralysed.

The owl hooted again. Lewes' feet were cold, in his thin socks. It was late; he was a taut combination of exhaustion and energy, his pulse still running hard.

He was scanning, reading, turning the pages. And then Lewes sat back. He had slid from apprehending the beauty of her aim — to something like horror.

This ambitiousness, this magnificent ambitiousness! It had occurred to him, in this candlelit room, that Polly was in the grip of such ambitiousness, she could not make her fictions carry the weight of them. Oh she could, of course she could, and had done so, she had managed to make *Romola* live — just — *just*. But with what difficulty. He thought of Mantegna's *Cult of Cybele in Rome*, where the grey figures were like statues, imperceptibly endowed with life, on the cusp. She had tried, like Mantegna, like the mythical Pygmalion, to bring her statue-like figures from an alien age to life. Her ambitiousness! This was why she had set *Romola* in that jewel-encrusted past of the highest painterly art, the time of Savonarola — the very setting had pomp, and, by being so distant, demanded an excruciating amount of historical research.

But who had set her off on this road? Who had fired her imagination and purpose? As the owl hooted again, Lewes had a second lurching moment. It was himself. The memory made his hands clammy. In Florence, reading about Savonarola in his guidebook, he, Lewes, had been struck by the idea that this period had excellent possibilities for a historical romance. He'd said so, and Polly had been receptive — instantly. Hadn't they gone the next day to San Marco? Where Polly had gazed and gazed at the Fra Angelico *Crucifixion*, her blue eyes narrowing with new interest; a new solemnity in her attention. A high solemnity. He, of course, had aided and abetted her, going alone to the monastery of San Marco (ladies not admitted) to take notes for her.

Lewes let his head fall at the memory. Why had he fired her up in this way? No — he remembered perfectly well why: the very removal to another time in history had seemed a balm — a potential release; hadn't she just suffered when writing about Maggie and Tom in *The Mill*, thinking so much about Isaac? Wasn't she suffering from the way they were living, unmarried — gossiped about, and the brutal rejection by Isaac and her family? More than anyone else, he knew what it had cost her to write *The Mill*, to re-enter that past with Isaac. Why, he had thought — he had thought — a historical romance was — a historical romance.

He had not anticipated the extent of her research.

When they had begun their next Italian trip to research *Romola*, she had written to John Blackwood, and Lewes had registered one sentence in particular. They were going abroad, she'd written, to Italy, *with grave purposes*. Grave purposes! It was his first inkling that his suggested subject might pull her down. Not only that: he had seen that steady, serious look on her brow — she, who'd just regaled the public with the exquisitely original, felt, lived *Silas Marner* — where she was, among numerous other things, damn funny! Like Mozart with his Papageno, Shakespeare with his Falstaffs, his Touchstones, his Bottom — she could enter and animate at all levels, high and low socially. But he had seen at once in that aloof, stern look —

Yes, the research.

Tennemann's *Manual of Philosophy*. Sismondi, *Vicissitudes of Florentine*

Government. Hélyot's *L'Histoire des ordres monastiques*, Machiavelli, Nardi; Buhle on Ficinus' philosophy; Savonarola's *Sermon* (fair enough); Lastri; Manni — ah — this was just the beginning. She'd acquired, on an ill-omened day, a reader's ticket for the British Museum. By this time, Lewes was beginning to suffer dyspepsia at her constant depression, her reiterated conviction that she couldn't write the book. She continued meanwhile to immerse herself in the biographies of Savonarola and Medici; naturally Vasari; histories of Italian literature — but then she began foraging in the original works of Sacchetti, Filelfo, Petrarch, Mach, Politian, Marullo, and others. She scoured old bookshops for stray volumes; read rare books on the state of Greece in the Middle Ages; and he could still remember the day she admitted she was occupied with a plan of rational mnemonics in history.

In these years, from early in the decade, both their health and spirits had suffered. 'I began it a young woman; I finished it an old woman,' she liked to say. Her spirits — and his — were tested.

Each day she would say to him, over supper, that she was 'utterly despondent' and on the verge of giving up the book; when she did eventually seem to be getting going, he spotted her poring through books of old Tuscan proverbs. He could only raise his eyebrows. Yes, she'd been buried in antiquities, which she then had to vivify. When would she start writing it? In a period of desperation, he had written to Blackwood, before the latter's visit in 1861: *Polly is still deep in her research. Your presence will I hope act like a stimulus to her to make her begin. At present she remains immoveable in the conviction that she can't write the romance because she has not knowledge enough. Now as a matter of fact I know that she has immensely more knowledge of the particular period than any other writer who has touched it: but her distressing diffidence paralyses her.*

This between ourselves. When you see her, mind you care to discountenance the idea of Romola being the product of an Encyclopaedia.

John Blackwood had risen superbly to the occasion, bringing with him, in his next visit, his wife, for the very first time — which went to the heart of things, as most wives avoided visiting Marian. Marian could not hide her pleasure.

Slowly, agonisingly, she wrote it.

When the book did come out, he was careful to shield her from reviews that were not favourable; but inevitably, the letter he didn't manage to stop in time was Sara Hennell's, who crept in with complimentary phrases, but managed to sneak a small sting in the tail, viz., that Romola was an idealised, rather than realistic portrait. Marian was plunged into self-doubt. Soon another letter came from Sara. He had begun reading it aloud; but glancing ahead, craftily pretended to lose it over toast, butter, hot coffee. He decided to take action.

My dear Miss Hennell,

Your letter to Marian was sent down to us with a batch to Littlehampton, where we are staying, and by good luck I had the reading of it aloud, and having seen the 'windup', was enabled to suppress that, and afterwards to 'mislay' your letter.

I have run up to town on business and will tell you why I 'mislaid' and suppressed that portion of your letter. After the publication of Adam Bede *Marian felt deeply the evil influences of talking and allowing others to talk to her about her writing. We resolved therefore to exclude everything as far as we could. No one speaks about her books to her, but me; she sees no criticisms. Besides this general conviction, there is a special reason in her case — it is that excessive diffidence which prevented her writing at all, for so many years, and would prevent her now, if I were not beside her to encourage her. A thousand eulogies would not give her the slightest confidence, but one objection would increase her doubts.*

He was doing his best.

The owl hooted again: Lewes went to the small gilt-edged mirror that hung near the door. Holding his candle up, his reflection startled him: his eyes looked sunken, his mouth leering, long hair receding further than he had realised (he put a hand up to touch it), his face was all light and shadow, a map of hills and dells. On impulse, he leaned forward and drew his lip up and back, like an animal baring its teeth. What a sight! He had a disturbing flicker of some other image.

His own work was exploring the connection between animal and human kind, the nervous system being the case in point. But when would he find the time, and the will, for that just now? Polly's was the weight. *Timoleon* was what she must avoid. An ancient topic spelled disaster. Leaving the room, he realised why that mirror image had shaken him. An echo of Thornie's newly sunken face. His son, prematurely aged.

He went and stood in the silent cool dark landing outside Thornie's bedroom, and listened. Silence. Thank God.

But now, today, Thornie out of pain, he'd had a couple of whiskies, and was on the way to recovery. He could smell roast beef rising from downstairs; the light chinks from the dining room suggested that Amelia was preparing the luncheon table, setting out wine-glasses; he'd better remind them to uncork the red; passing Amelia at the foot of the stairs, he said,

'Amelia, would you remind Grace that a bowl of horseradish would not go amiss?'

'Yessir.'

'Also — has Mrs Lewes mentioned that we have an addition coming to the household? A nurse, Amelia, a nurse. An extra pair of hands. To help us through these choppy waters! Charlotte Lee is the name.'

'Does she have experience, sir?' asked Amelia, in a prim voice.

'Plenty, Amelia; great shovelfuls of it,' — and he walked up the stairs. Amelia — good girl — could be tiresome — Marian too receptive to servants' moods —

Climbing the stairs, his mood continued to revive. After luncheon, the house would be filled with people: fine talk, laughter; cake; alcohol; tea. What a contrast to those quiet days in Wandsworth! He finished the stairs two at a time. Knocked on Polly's study door, went in.

Funny — nothing like last night.

'My dear — how are you? How's the masterwork-to-be?'

Marian had turned a drooping face to his, but then she began, in her elegant grey moiré dress, and the soft lace and velvet in her hair, reluctantly to smile. (It was part of her charm that although her moods sank deep, she did, usually, respond to him.)

'I'm researching.'

'Researching?'

'Grote on Ancient Greece,' she went on. 'For *Timoleon*.'

'Ah! Ah.'

Then: 'An important story.'

'Indeed,' said Marian, gravity returned.

The gravity was disturbing. Already he could feel his stomach react.

'But what about *Middlemarch*?' he said now, boldly.

'What about it?'

Her expression was strange, both imperious and hopeless. He asked her, was it set some time ago.

She laughed joylessly, even irritably, saying he knew very well when it was set, why was he asking her this?

'True, true,' said George, finding himself blushing, which was unusual for him. 'True! Thirty, nearly forty years ago. I do feel, Polly — that the more — recent — time — and close setting, viz., our provincial England, is perhaps,' — he was gesticulating in the air now, his old actorly ability renewing itself as he made expressive shapes with his hands — 'more fecund terrain, my dear Polly.'

He was babbling.

'More fecund? Than the Ancients?'

She was regarding him in genuine puzzlement.

George had to laugh.

'I'll tell you what, though, Polly; your *Middlemarch* is a genuinely ambitious idea!'

'Ambitious?'

He had forgotten. She often associated that word with a grosser kind of egotism.

'George — I want to move people, stir them to their best. Mr Huxley put it well. About *Silas Marner* —'

'Yes yes,' said George, hurriedly. 'A book to do great good to people.'

The doorbell had just rung.

8

By the afternoon the drawing room was full. Lewes noted Barbara's long dress approvingly: magnificent choice of colour, deep rose. Stanley, Mr and Mrs Howard, Alice Helps, Frederic Burton, Edward Burne-Jones. And Mrs Georgiana Burne-Jones, so neat and petite-looking. Though if gossip was correct, he could not help feeling sorry for her.

'Fine gathering.' Lewes recognised the terse tones of Herbert Spencer, turned to see his old friend's lofty forehead and beak-like nose. They shook hands.

'All the better for having you here,' said Lewes, rocking slightly on his heels. 'You'll have some claret?'

Amelia produced a glass of red. 'Remarkably good,' said the philosopher, in his curt tone.

'It's become a slight hobby of mine,' said Lewes, modestly. 'Wine, I mean.'

'Really. Really. Well — splendid.'

'You know everyone here, don't you? I don't think I need to ask you that!' laughed Lewes.

He liked supervising these gatherings. Their Sunday afternoons at home, with their swollen numbers, were famous across London, making the extra teapot and further cups and saucers essential. Often Lewes, a little the worse — or better, he liked to think — for the whisky, would look round at the artists and journalists and intellectuals, a ferociously well-known bunch of people, and feel like a successful theatre impresario, who each week pulled off an improbable yet delightful entertainment. And every Monday, like clockwork, Lewes noted in his diary the long list of agreeably illustrious individuals who had attended. And Marian in good spirits for at least two days afterwards. That was the point, of course.

'Yes, yes,' Spencer was saying. 'Oh — not perhaps everyone. Who's that?' he asked — rather rudely, thought Lewes.

'Burne-Jones. The painter, you know —'

Lewes couldn't suppress his pride in front of Spencer, whose circle of friends would include scientists and intellectuals and philosophers; but not those wilder, more sought-after flowers of the social field: artists and writers.

'I don't know,' responded Spencer, shortly.

'His wife is a great friend of Polly's. *The* Burne-Jones,' repeated Lewes, meaningfully. 'Edward Burne-Jones.' It was impossible Spencer hadn't heard of him! 'The group of artists, you know. Morris, Rossetti — a little incestuous,' he said, lowering his voice, and making insinuating movements with his eyebrows. Spencer's face relented, and as Lewes took him to see the wine below the stairs, it occurred to Lewes, contemplating the wine, that if Spencer had taken up with Polly when he could have done, all this could have been his! That is, of course, if he'd been able to cajole, encourage, praise. Unlikely.

'Most impressive,' Spencer was saying. He was on his knees, peering at the lowest bottles. 'Chateau Lafite ... Good lord! You've got a Chateau d'Yquem!'

'Yes, well ... you must know, Polly's books are rather remunerative.'

The understatement of the century, reflected Lewes, complacently. For *Romola* alone, she'd netted £5,000, and that was just English sales. And if she could only start this new provincial novel —

'One hundred times more so than anything yours truly could make!' he quipped in Spencer's ear, and was pleased to see Spencer's features once more relax.

* * *

Marian looked round her contentedly, she said to herself she was recovered.

She had found herself disturbed when Charles, Lewes' oldest son, had returned from holiday. Charles had fainted when he saw Thornie, so altered by sickness, and had tended him gently since. The contrast, in Marian's mind, with Isaac was excruciating: still no word after all these years. But now, seated with Barbara in the bow window, she had drunk a glass of wine, and more importantly, guests had come with reverential warm glances and extraordinarily admiring words, and she was transformed.

Barbara had asked after Thornie, and Marian had stated gravely that having a sick person in the house was necessarily to suffer change. 'We are thankful to have friends,' she finished earnestly, 'who can provide the happiest distraction.'

(How ponderous she sounded! She made herself sit up straighter.)

'Now,' said Marian, aiming for a more buoyant tone, 'I've finally been reading Mr Mill, and am as appreciative as you might have hoped.'

'Aha!' crowed Barbara, with a victorious smile. '*The Subjection of Women*! It's well argued, isn't it?'

Marian agreed. At the same time, she thought, Barbara must understand that when it comes to the position of women, *my own position is odd*, at the least. To change the subject, Marian asked Barbara what she'd been saying about Mozart, when they had earlier been interrupted.

'Oh!' said Barbara. 'It's Mozart's sister that intrigues me. Nannerl. No — my thesis is quite simple,' — and she summed up her point: that Nannerl had also been a musical prodigy, and in different circumstances, with the identical degree of cultivation and encouragement, doubtless she too would have been another Mozart, another Wolfgang Amadeus.

'Doubtless?' queried Marian. 'Ah — but Barbara — your statement begs so many questions.'

And this was neither the time nor the place, Marian reflected, to raise the fundamental questions of biology, as giving rise to those conditions of life, which were not to be transcended with lightning ease or speed. 'In what utopia,' said Marian gently, 'would Nannerl be raised? Who would be having and raising the children? Until we have a separate third race, of breeders' — why not indulge the fantastical! — 'this is an insurmountable part of most women's lives, is it not?'

Barbara was regarding her gravely, her jaw looking set. 'My dear Marian, this is surely no way to foster change. In this year of all years —'

'You have done so much!' cried Marian, impulsively reaching for her friend's hand. 'The first university college for women!'

'Girton will open later this year,' said Barbara, flushing with pride. 'I *am* accomplishing something. Along with Miss Davies.'

Marian hesitated before saying, 'You know Miss Davies came to see me last week.'

Barbara flinched, but said, 'She has been an indomitable force for good.'

Marian watched her friend as they sat on the ornate Biedermeier sofa. Marian knew all about Barbara's efforts, alongside Emily Davies, to rally people and money for Girton. But there were tensions between Emily and Barbara. As Barbara was known for her fiery support of the suffrage, Emily had excluded her from certain committees, so as not to put off potential backers.

'You know, the college is Anglican,' said Barbara abruptly.

Marian did know: Miss Davies was Anglican herself, and had fought to make the college so.

'It goes against the grain,' admitted Barbara. Every bit of money her family gave was to institutions undefined by religious allegiance. And they had lost support from Unitarian friends.

'It may be,' said Marian, 'that you and Miss Davies are a perfectly pragmatic coupling. I cannot think Miss Davies has your personal persuasive warmth, and — charisma. But she is tenacious, isn't she? Like one of those terrier dogs,' she added, smiling at her own comparison.

Barbara laughed out loud. 'I'm so glad to hear you say that! Between you and me, she hasn't an ounce of humour —'

'— dour as a grey day,' agreed Marian at once, twinkling.

The words were hardly out of her mouth, when Marian turned to look anxiously around the room.

'Still,' said Marian quickly, 'I find much to respect and like about her. I certainly don't want to be unduly dismissive —'

'My dear Marian,' cried Barbara, laughing and shaking her head, 'you'd think the Inquisition was on your path! No, what you say is true. Emily Davies is as dour as a grey day. *As a grey day,*' she repeated with relish.

Marian laughed thinly. She didn't like to hear her flippant words taken up so readily. She had the constant fear that any uncharitable remark would instantly live on outside her presence, like a live creature that could not be controlled. The floating live remark would then substitute for *her* in other peoples' minds. You could not rely on people to place a reported comment in a broader, more elastic, tolerant context. Fortunately, a couple had just entered the room, the Rector Mark Pattison and his wife, Emilia Pattison. Marian drew Barbara's attention to them.

The small-built, studious Mark Pattison had been endlessly at work on the renaissance scholar Casaubon. His wife, said Marian, was twenty-seven years younger.

'And I always have,' went on Marian in a low voice, leaning closer to Barbara, with her most secretly amused smile, 'the wicked but irresistible idea, when I am sitting with them, however fond I am of them both, that I am witnessing life wedded to death.'

* * *

Before the guests dispersed, Marian had a chance to exchange words with the diminutive Georgiana Burne-Jones. Knowing the wild stories about her husband's infidelity, she wished Georgiana, with her sad air, would confide in her. She saw a potential space for herself — to cleave closer to that friend, give succour, and so relieve that need.

What need? she wondered.

She wondered at its strength: what did she not innately possess, that she had such a need? It seemed to know no limit — to extend and extend. With this melancholy thought, she became aware of Barbara asking to see her study. She wanted to see where Marian did her wonderful work.

'My wonderful work!' sighed Marian, as she led the way up the stairs. 'I hardly think so.'

She opened the door. Barbara looked round appreciatively. 'I know you are working on something at the moment, as you are always busy, but I will not ask what it is.'

'I am completely unable to work.'

Her voice came out stark and cold. It was past six in the evening, and her study, which faced East and was unlit, was in gloom. Yet Marian was thankful for the gloom. She didn't want Barbara to register her face, could only imagine what she looked like in this kind of mood. Not just ugly, but vile — despairing.

'My dear!' said Barbara, who was, alas, looking at her, with peering, anxious, sympathetic eyes. 'Come, it's always difficult — work, I mean. Why — what's this?'

She was gazing in the gloom at the childish picture by Isaac: at the high line of blue sky, the low flat line of green grass, drawn in colouring pencil. 'Is this by you Marian?' she asked, in delight. 'From when you were small?'

'My brother. Age nine.'

'Nine! It looks younger.'

'He gave it to me. He was not a good artist.'

Marian's tone was flat.

'You are back in the fold,' said Barbara tenderly, and through the low light of the room Marian saw her friend's frank blue eyes.

'I am not back in the fold.'

Barbara stared.

'Why did you think that? What on earth made you think that? Have I said that to you?'

'Why,' stumbled Barbara, 'I assumed — since you had his picture.' Barbara stopped. 'I should not have assumed that,' she added, carefully.

'But beloved,' — and now Barbara came to her, opened her arms wide, and drew Marian to her. 'They don't deserve you,' said Barbara, passionately, holding her tight, speaking in her ear: indeed, Marian could feel the warmth of her friend's lips. 'You must detach yourself, dear Marian; if Isaac will not accept you, you must cut the bond,' she added pulling back, so she could see Marian's face.

The words sounded in Marian's ear as from a curious distance.

★ ★ ★

The morning after the gathering, Marian went to her study. No sound from Thornie, thank God.

She concentrated on her doctor hero, her brother and sister, Rosamund and Fred. Brothers and sisters: it was always hard not to think of herself and Isaac, as she tried to sketch out scenes.

No word from Isaac, all these years. Even with her fame.

A cry from the garden; she looked: Thornie on his garden bed, Charles tending him. Marian watched Charles' anxious, loving way of listening to Thornie, the head bent, glasses catching the light.

Marian shut the window.

She went back to her *Middlemarch* sketch, but soon after sank her head in her hands. What was it Barbara had said? She got up now, picked up that drawing by Isaac. It was, she thought resentfully, a constricted, empty, soulless little drawing, as bare as he was bare of human feelings. The branches of the spindly little tree bare, below that high strip of sky, above that sparse line of green. Why had she even kept it, reverenced it? In this false way? The detestable —

Her head pulsing violently, she left the room.

9

Entering Marian's study, Lewes stopped. The morning sun was streaming in, and through the dazzling light he thought he had mis-seen. Marian was crouched over in her chair, not facing her desk and the window, but half-turned from the window, so that he saw her in profile. She had a pair of scissors in her hand, cutting.

'Polly! What are you doing?'

She had in her hands the drawing by Isaac, yellow at the edges; but only half of it existed now; the rest had been cut away, shard by shard; on the floor were the slender fragments. And she was continuing.

'My dear Polly —'

That afternoon she went to bed, saying she had a headache, and for the two following days she was in bed. When, late morning each day, he came to bring her a cup of tea, she said she could never produce any good work again, this was the truth. He heard the litany. One, she must confront it and bear it; two, she had tried and failed. He spoke his usual encouraging words, but he didn't persevere. He was weakened by the strain of Thornie and broken nights.

Three days later, he woke to find the bed empty beside him. Polly was up. Not in the dining room either. After he had his own breakfast and coffee, he quietly mounted the stairs to the first floor landing, and saw a good sight: Marian's study door was shut.

With the lightest and quietest of steps, he went to his office. He said nothing at supper.

It was the same the following morning. But this time, before noon, he went upstairs. Her door still shut. He bent to listen. He thought — he thought — he could hear the scratching of her pen. Carefully, he turned the handle. At last! Seated at her desk, facing the window, writing. She had started her novel. She must have heard him at the door, but she was continuing to write. He stole close to her shoulder, peered over.

But it was not a novel.

Silently, without even turning her head, Marian handed him the first page:

> *I cannot choose but think upon the time,*
> *When our two lives grew like two buds that kiss*
> *At lightest thrill from the bee's swinging chime*
> *Because the one so near the other is.*

> *He was the elder and a little man*
> *Of forty inches, bound to show no dread,*
> *And I the girl that puppy-like now ran,*
> *Now lagged behind my brother's larger tread.*

'Why, Polly,' said Lewes. Silent still, she handed him a second page:

> *Long years have left their writing on my brow,*
> *But yet the freshness and the dew-fed beam*
> *Of those young mornings are about me now,*
> *When we two wandered toward the far-off stream*

> *With rod and line. Our basket held a store*
> *Baked for us only, and I thought with joy*
> *That I should have my share, though he had more,*
> *Because he was the elder and a boy.*

'My dear Polly,' said Lewes, softly.

By the third of July, Marian had finished her fifth sonnet. As she wrote, Barbara's words sounded in her mind: *You must detach yourself, dear Marian; if he will not accept you, you must not continue to be hurt; you must cut the bond.*

Barbara had meant well, but as Marian's pen moved across the page, as the thoughts and feelings came, she knew she was doing the opposite of what Barbara had urged. She was stepping in and down, back to that early happiness. She blew on the embers so that it was bright, lit once more. Why, the best of herself had its roots here.

> *Thus rambling we were schooled in deepest lore,*
> *And learned the meanings that give words a soul,*
> *The fear, the love, the primal passionate store,*
> *Those shaping impulses that make manhood whole.*

> *Those hours were seed to all my after good;*
> *My infant gladness, through eye, ear, and touch,*
> *Took easily as warmth a various food*
> *To nourish the sweet skill of loving much.*

There was deep, sweet relief in her coursing tears as she wrote these lines. She had pushed aside ugliness, hatred, to give her oldest feelings voice. Entering the past as one might enter a childhood house in a dream: found the garden, the familiar place of grass and lilac bush, tree stump and the strange sunless part where the grass hardly grew. And Isaac, whose love was like the sun. Nothing now could take it away. It had bright, permanent form in verse. *Ars longa, vita brevis.*

Over the days, as she wrote these sonnets, her headaches lifted. She slept better, she was restored in the morning. Her mind could move again.

In the following days she began to sketch out scenes. Lewes saw the shut door of the study, kept his counsel.

In the third week of July, she began writing *Middlemarch*.

10

Last summer Lewes had become acquainted with Clifford Allbutt at a meeting of the British Medical Association; following this, Lewes and Marian visited the young doctor at the Leeds Infirmary where he worked. Allbutt made an instant impression on Marian with his keenness, intelligence, ambition — the sense she had, in talking to him, that he desired to advance the medical field. Contemplating the notion of progress for her novel, as incarnated by an individual — even if the individual were eventually thwarted — she began to conceive Lydgate.

Marian was deep in her imagined provincial world, moving from ideas to the central theme to her characters' fine entanglements. Close after dawn, she arrived at her desk to sit in the complete quiet, aware of the garden outside, with its dense, particular early-morning quietness. She had been writing now for weeks. Today, as the light grew stronger, she deliberately put her mind back to that first meeting with Clifford Allbutt.

There was a commotion below: a muffled cry, Ben barking. She tried to turn Thornie's cries into mere sounds. She moved her attention back to what she had written today.

At present I have to make the new settler Lydgate better known ... For surely all must admit that a man may be puffed and belauded, envied, ridiculed, counted upon as a tool and fallen in love with, or at least selected as a future husband, and yet remain virtually unknown — known merely as a cluster of signs for his neighbours' false suppositions.

There. She had said what she wanted to say. People were usually guided by a 'cluster of signs' — picking out what they wanted to pick out, to fit their own 'suppositions'. But now Marian put her work down.

She had her own fears about how people saw her. It amounted, she thought, to a sickness. Just now she was distracted by Cara's visit last night. They had discussed Sara's annoying qualities. But what if her remarks were repeated to Sara? She could not work now. She must write to Cara. With a half groan she pulled her notepaper towards her.

My dear Cara,

I feel as if I had been indulging in cruel gossip last night, and I cannot rest without entreating you again not to let my needless mention of trivialities have any consequences that can reach our poor dear S. I shall always welcome her affectionately on her rare visits, for the old regard is much deeper than any new and transient irritations.

She was about to return to work again, but once more she hesitated, once more pulled out her notepaper.

She had begun corresponding with Clifford Allbutt, the man who had inspired Lydgate, on exactly this matter — the danger of unpremeditated talk. *My books*, she wrote now, *are a form of utterance that dissatisfies me less, because they are deliberately, carefully constructed on a basis which even in my doubting mind is never shaken by a doubt … my conviction as to the relative goodness and nobleness of human dispositions and motives.*

If Sara heard her remark, she thought, she would be as hurt as if it were Marian's total feeling for her. But it was not, it was a mere fragment of the whole. As an artist, this was her task, to move the reader to see people in the round.

⋆ ⋆ ⋆

The summer was going by. Thornie's presence made the house fraught, but Marian kept working on the book. Yet in August she began to stall, and welcome visitors. Towards the end of the month, Emily Davies, Barbara's Girton partner, came to see her. Marian was inevitably the focus of progressive women's attention — the way she lived and still lived with Lewes, the fiction she had produced. But as she said to Lewes, she didn't find it easy speaking her mind on the Woman Question.

'Doubtless,' he agreed. He was reading with his feet up, sipping a whisky.

'They want your scalp!' he added, irreverently.

'I beg your pardon?'

'They want your scalp,' he repeated, with relish.

'They want my opinion,' she sighed. 'Or rather, they think they do. In fact they want me to agree with them.'

Emily Davies arrived promptly at four. By the time they were talking in the drawing room, Marian had remembered why she always felt constrained in her presence: it was Miss Davies' doll-like air of immobility, combined with the small, sharp, determined movements of her head when she'd abruptly look up, to take Marian in. She'd come to quiz Marian on her views about the syllabus for Girton as the college was soon to open. Marian listened attentively. Emily wanted the syllabuses of men and women to be the same. Marian was careful to think before she spoke. She knew Barbara wanted a slightly different syllabus for women, with greater emphasis on physical wellbeing, and an allowance made for the fact that the young women would not have received schooling of the same standard.

'What,' asked Marian now, carefully, 'is at stake?'

'Parity,' was Emily Davies' instant reply.

There was passion in that quick response. Unexpected, in the composed face.

'In the sense that they learn the identical things?'

Emily Davies said yes, adding, in a rare flash of humour: 'We might have more novelists like yourself!'

Marian bowed her head to acknowledge the compliment.

'Ladies — ladies — can I ask Amelia to bring anything?'

It was George at his most jaunty, opening the French doors to the garden, to let in the sunny air, wearing his dandified floral waistcoat (an abberration, possibly; but Marian liked it). His hair, perhaps because of Emily Davies' gaze, looked unusually long and dishevelled just then. Marian wondered if Emily Davies might think she had broken up George's marriage. Many people still did. *Clusters of perceptions* died hard.

Emily declined refreshment, and after George had left the room, Marian, having watched Emily talk to George, came to certain conclusions about Emily. She did not have the look of a woman who would fall in love. Too wrought in her determination: the eyes too watchfully focused: like a bird looking for a snail. Nothing else could come in. An absence, went Marian's thoughts, of the feminine softness, or even susceptibility, or even the desire to play.

Marian admitted to herself that in Emily's presence, she felt proud, and even defiant, that she had Lewes, this creature of a different sex with his dandified waistcoat and lively mind, to love her.

How strange it all was. Feeling, thinking, the two sexes: could it all fit, neatly? How did this jigsaw puzzle work?

'Yes,' repeated Emily Davies, suddenly emboldened, 'we could have more novelists!'

Marian said a vague 'yes', while she tried to sort out her objections, which were rising in a tide.

'Although, my dear Miss Davies, I have a horror of mediocre literature — a horror of unnecessary books being written at all. I don't think it good to write a novel that adds to that pile of mediocrity. Indeed, I was late to begin, precisely because I did not want to add to that great pile —'

'But you did not,' said Miss Davies, succinctly.

The quiet four words, spoken in the warm afternoon air, formed a rebuke. For a moment, Marian thought she had underrated her interlocutor.

'I take it,' said Marian wryly, 'you are saying, if little or nothing is attempted, we cannot know what might have been.'

'Something along those lines.'

Was there a ghostly sense of humour in that face?

Marian tried to pick up her thread.

'In my view, fiction should only be written if the writer has talent. So much work is produced by people who should not produce — whether women or men. Oddly enough, my husband was just reading a rather outspoken piece I wrote many years ago for the *Westminster Review*, that set out this view.'

'What was the title of the piece?' enquired Miss Davies, politely.

Marian paused. Then she said, with a slight effort, 'Silly Novels by Lady Novelists.'

'Ah.'

There was a silence. Ben was barking — if only he'd run in, create a distraction.

'It was a provocative title,' said Marian, blushing. 'I was not attempting to pour mockery on our sex. What I objected to was this: because an author was a woman, bad work was indulged, even praised.'

To herself she thought: I will defend the integrity of art before politics.

To George later she relayed the conversation with Emily. She thought it was fine to have the same university syllabus for women as for men, but she didn't like the idea of the two sexes becoming the same.

She had been standing by the piano, leafing through music, but now two hands appeared, holding her breasts, gripping them. George right behind her.

'There's my answer,' he was murmuring, into her ear.

At which she turned round, kissed him; next they were kissing properly, forgetting for a moment about Amelia, Grace, Thornie — and for the first time in a long time, they made their way hand in hand up to the bedroom, intent only on each other.

★ ★ ★

The following morning, as usual, Marian was roving over her conversation with Emily. She was curious now to read the piece she'd written thirteen years ago. She found it in Lewes' study.

Silly Novels by Lady Novelists are a genus with many species, determined by the particular quality of silliness that predominates in them — the frothy, the prosy, the pious, or the pedantic. But it is a mixture of all these — a composite order of feminine fatuity — that produces the largest class of such novels, which we shall distinguish as the mind-and-millinery species.

The novels lacked realism, she said, and she quoted from *Rank and Beauty*, where the heroine first sets eyes on her love object, who happens to be the Prime Minister. *Perhaps,* warned Marian, *the words Prime Minister suggest to you a wrinkled or obese sexagenarian; but pray dismiss the image ...*

> "*The door opened again, and Lord Rupert Conway entered. Evelyn gave one glance. It was enough; she was not disappointed. His tall figure, the distinguished simplicity of his air — it was a living Van-dyke, a cavalier, one of his noble cavalier ancestors, or one to whom her fancy had always likened him, who long of yore had, with an Umfraville, fought the Paynim far beyond sea. Was this reality?*"

Very little like it, certainly.

The last dry remark was her own, and a spontaneous smile lit her face as she read it. What fun she had writing this piece! And really, she couldn't help admiring the skill with which she dissected pretensions. In *Compensation*:

> "*Oh, I am so happy, dear gran'mamma,*" *prattles a child of four and a half.* "*— I have seen — I have seen such a delightful person; he is like everything beautiful — like the smell of sweet flowers, and the view from Ben Lomond; ... and his forehead is like that distant sea ... there seems no end — no end; or like the clusters of stars I like best to look at on a warm fine night ...*"

The prodigy, says Marian, has a mother who is also a genius, extraordinarily learned and deep, who has *from her great facility in learning languages, read the Scriptures in their original tongues.*

Of course! cackles Marian (the emphasis is hers). *Greek and Hebrew are mere play to a heroine; Sanskrit is no more than abc to her; and she can talk with perfect correctness in any language except English. Poor men! There are so few of you who know even Hebrew ...*

Reading the piece now, all these years later, Marian felt as if she were in a cage, peering out at her old self. How free she had been! Now she was conscious of watchful eyes.

11

On the last day of August they took the train to Weybridge, to visit the Cross family. It was a relief to be getting out of London.

Having begun *Middlemarch*, and written forty pages, she was now stuck. Lewes and Marian sat in gloomy silence as the train rattled along. Each was absorbed. Marian was thinking of her own awkwardness as a stepmother.

Thornie was in and out of pain, the diagnoses unclear; she sat with him in the afternoons, brought him books to read.

'How was your night?' Marian had asked yesterday.

'It was excellent.'

For a second she thought Thornie was teasing her. She said, bending forward, and in a feeling voice: 'I hope it was.'

What a bore she was.

Lewes was also thinking about Thornie. They spent evenings in the drawing room, Thornie on pillows. Thornie often talked about Africa, last night he had described trekking for days, with the expectation that they would make their fortune — only to find that someone else had been there first, the deal already done. 'So what was your worst experience then?' said George, in an indulgent voice.

'Being hungry,' said Thornie, instantly.

'Ah. Aha,' said George, tone and face suddenly expressionless. He sucked on his cigar noisily.

At Weybridge they were met by a pony and trap. Inside the large white house, in the Cross family drawing room with its French doors open, they began to feel better. They were made at once so comfortable; at the same time Marian was noticing the pictures above the fireplace, the good taste visible everywhere, in the unpretentious armchairs, tables, the lamps with their silken shades. They were given glasses of champagne. And it was not long before Lewes and Marian were admitting the difficulty of life at the moment, with Thornie being ill, pouring it all out into the ears of their kind hostess. 'My dears,' said Mrs Cross, taking a hand of each (she was sitting between them on the sofa). 'I do sympathise so very much. We have our own fears just now. Zibbie is approaching her first confinement, and is exceptionally uneasy about it.'

And at that moment the beautiful Zibbie walked in, her dark-blonde hair curling, her face sweating slightly and flushed. Though walked was not quite the word, as, her stomach projecting before her, her walk appeared to be a slow, rolling, side-to-side kind of step. And in fact Marian had the mysterious sense that Zibbie's head had become smaller because of the distended body below.

At lunch Marian sat beside Zibbie's husband, Henry Bullock, war correspondent for the *Daily News*. He had a charming way of leaning back in his chair and taking time to think before he spoke; he talked un-self-consciously, modestly. He had advanced, liberal political views, partly as a result of what he had seen of the world. His literary interests (Turgenev was a personal friend) were genuine. He had reported in Mexico, Poland, even marched alongside Garibaldi into Naples.

For Marian, it was the splendid couple, Zibbie and Henry Bullock, who dominated the afternoon. She watched them closely, almost jealous of their new married life, this felicitous pairing of talent and beauty on each side, in a lucky family setting. And her half-jealous feeling made her penetratingly interested in both of their doings, as if she could fillet them, know them so completely that she would no longer be jealous, she would be inhabiting them instead. She ended up talking to Zibbie, absorbing her beauty, her swollen form, her apprehensiveness about giving birth. She made Marian think of a sailor on the brink of a momentous journey to an unknown place. Zibbie admitted to being frightened about her confinement; she laughed at herself, but had tears in her eyes when she laughed. Finally Zibbie mentioned her poems, as Marian guessed she would. Almost certainly Zibbie hoped, in the curious way people did, that by contact with Marian, Zibbie's own talent or genius might be helped to blossom, as if genius were a benign form of contagion.

The day became emotional when Zibbie performed at the piano, singing two verses from Marian's *Spanish Gypsy* that she had herself set to music. Marian cried as she embraced her. They had many things in common — had selected identical passages for their respective commonplace books, for instance. Zibbie even went to fetch hers, pale blue and frayed, to show Marian, *as proof.* For a moment Marian was sad: the younger woman presenting evidence of similar taste, as if this might indicate a similar artistic career for her — but she was about to have a child.

Marian had an image of the women she knew who had children, a shoal of fish travelling down the same stream.

Outside, Zibbie came to say goodbye, placing both her hands in Marian's.

'What a lovely family!' Lewes said when they left, as they were rattling home on the train. 'Perhaps we can borrow them.'

Less than a month later, a letter arrived from Mrs Cross. Marian had to read the letter three times. The last few sentences especially — she found it hard to read the words. Zibbie had had a fine baby boy, but had died four days after childbirth.

★ ★ ★

Upstairs at the Priory, at her desk, Marian plunged her mind down and into *Middlemarch* — and stopped. She had her idea, about a hero wanting to lead a life that counted, yet each time she went to her desk her neck stiffened, and as she tried to sink her mind into that fictional world, she was aware of half an entity in the corner of her vision, that she couldn't quite see.

12

It was a difficult autumn. Thornie became more sick. In October, he died. On Christmas Day they visited Thornie's grave in Highgate cemetery; the evening they spent quietly with Charles and Gertrude. The weather was cold, with a biting bright light that changed as the skies thickened and brought snow.

Neither Marian nor Lewes could work.

Lewes had headaches accompanied by ringing in the ears; he fainted; his hands and feet went numb. Trying to work on *Problems of Life and Mind*, in part an investigation of neurological illness, he wondered if he, ironically, was becoming neurologically ill.

The doctors prescribed change of scene. In the spring, they went abroad, meeting neurologists Reichert and Westphal in Berlin. They strolled down the wide Lindengarten Strasse, every building clothed in the brilliant blue-white light. Marian enjoyed using her rusty German again, and in afternoons they stopped at the Konzert House cafe for apple strudel and a glass of the fiery local liquor made from pears. Back in England, neither could work; Dr Reynolds recommended sea air. They went to Cromer, reading aloud on the beach — Trollope, Balzac, Mendelssohn's *Letters*, Rossetti's *Poems*, Morris' *Earthly Paradise*. They went to Harrogate in Yorkshire, where, walking the picturesque cobbled streets, they talked about the ominous new war between France and Prussia, and Dickens, who'd died last month. Lewes took the waters, Marian struggled with *Middlemarch*. But there were concerts, and one night they heard Grace Armytage sing, her rich contralto mesmerising the hall. During the second half, Marian found herself wondering what it was like singing to an audience — giving voice, literally. It seemed a magnificent idea. Returning to their rooms, the idea took on a dark twist: what if the singer lost her voice, just as she had lost hers? Here surely was an idea for a play — story — poem.

Travelling on to Whitby, they met up with Georgiana Burne-Jones and her children. Marian hoped that finally her friend would break her silence about her husband's infidelity, which she knew had caused so much suffering. Georgiana was composed, but her eyes showed fluctuations of feeling, and this combination of feeling and reserve intrigued Marian.

On their first morning they climbed up to the Abbey, from where they had a tremendous view of the shining sea below. There, in the light and the wind, Marian thought of the strange woman who had, against all pattern of expectation, become so important — the seventh-century Saint Hilda, female founding saint of the Abbey, whose advice kings and princes had sought; who ran her Benedictine monastery along strict lines, men and women living separately but worshipping together.

Later on the beach, while Lewes rested, Marian and Georgiana laid rugs beside a rock, so they were sheltered when the wind rose. While the children Margaret and Phil dug in the sand, Georgiana talked of her husband. She had been tidying Edward Burne-Jones' clothes, when she'd found a letter in his pocket. She never read his post, but an instinct, fatal, strong, compelled her. Opening the letter, she had instantly seen words of love. They were from the woman who had been posing for him, the Greek heiress Maria Zambaco. 'It was like a novel,' Georgiana cried then, her mouth pursing in woe.

Edward had agreed to give the woman up, but the heiress had threatened to kill herself, going with an overdose of laudanum to a canal in Little Venice. Edward intercepted her, the police were called, word spread round London.

Edward had given her up, but now Georgiana, watching his canvas, hated seeing Edward at work. Bit by bit, the face and form materialising was always Maria Zambaco, coming to life once more as a sorceress, or temptress. Georgiana had become haunted by the woman's lips, her fairy-tale face with its exquisitely pointed chin, the proud bewitching look of spoiled sensuality. 'She is like a dream made real,' confessed Georgiana; and, she cried, 'I can't control Edward's *mind!*'

'My dear Georgiana,' murmured Marian.

She felt pierced for her friend. To have to see the other woman's features, produced not by physical sight, but by the power of memory, and by Edward's artistry, too. Georgiana was leaning against the wall of the rock, a paradoxically beautiful spectacle of sorrow, features framed by the ascetically, medievally plain dress of dark grey, her habitual attire. Even the way she wore her hair — parted in the middle, braided at the back — had a beguiling simplicity to it. Marian ingested this image.

'It is hard for you, to feel so impotent,' said Marian, in a low voice, looking intently at her friend.

'It is! That face,' — and Georgiana shuddered.

'But you do not give up Edward,' said Marian tactfully. It was now her task gently to help Georgiana find her own strength, be clear about what she wanted to do.

Through all this, Edward Burne-Jones had kept coming to the Priory on Sundays. There he sat, often transparently absorbed by his own inner world, like a self-forgetful child and artist both. Marian admired that indifference to the world's opinion; yet self-absorption and selfishness: how close they must run, she thought.

Now Georgiana returned to the moment of revelation, when she had found the letter from Edward's pocket. Colouring, she had learned then that Edward was consumed by his need for this woman — which could not be healthy. He had become obsessed, lost to everything. Sometimes he couldn't even paint.

Marian knew the rumour that Georgiana and Edward did not have sex, to avoid having another child. She wanted to suggest forgoing abstinence, to practise birth control, to foster their intimacy, but feared intruding.

'An obsession like this,' said Marian instead, carefully, 'cannot survive in my view. It feeds on a hectic atmosphere, and cannot fit around the relatively contented doings of ordinary life.'

Georgiana's eyes were either bright, or had tears in them.

'I hope so,' she said, in a low voice. Georgiana's daughter Margaret had come to find them, sliding under Georgie's arm, to be tucked in, as under a bird's wing, absently, sweetly; Marian noted it all.

'Whereas you and Mr Lewes — your affection *does* fit around ordinary life.'

'It is the luck,' said Marian then, in a grave tone, 'of perfect compatibility.'

★ ★ ★

One afternoon, while Georgiana took the children back to her lodgings, Marian stayed on the beach on her own. She was still mulling over what Georgie had told her. But now, drawing her shawl closer, she thought over the last year: particularly the poignant sense she'd had last October, with Thornie dying, that life was at its fullest, was being most vividly lived, when she was helping him. All these months on, and it was still with her. The hole when he was gone — she had not been prepared for it. She wore, under her sleeve, the small African beaded bracelet he had given her; she wore it every day.

Thornie had changed before he died. He had become different. Or rather, it had become different between them. A strange thing had happened in the last six weeks of Thornie's life.

Usually, when Marian sat with him for an hour or two, he asked rote questions about her work, and she gave rote answers. But one day he asked as usual and she said: 'Going well, thank you.'

'Is it?' he said.

'Not really,' she said then. She was tired.

'Poor Mutter,' came the words, half under his breath. He still wasn't opening his eyes, but he stretched out a hand. For a moment she wasn't sure what to do — then she took it.

'I'm sure it will be alright,' he said, in his murmur.

'I'm not,' she said. His eyes looked closed, she detached her hand to leave.

'Don't go,' — came his voice.

She stayed another half an hour. This tiny exchange changed something — a small conduit had opened between them.

She began to sit longer with him.

The atmosphere changed. She was easy with him now; the old pressure to say things had gone. She began bringing him the peculiar dandelion concoctions Grace made for him in the kitchen, and taking a seat in the drawing room downstairs where his bed lived, to look for any sign of relief or pleasure in his face. When he was in pain she went as quickly as possible to find the dropper and the morphine, and waited to see the effect. She began sitting with him at eleven o'clock in the morning.

Late September, she didn't go to see him, she was in her own bed with an aching head. 'He's asking for Mutter,' said George, coming up to her room. She got out of bed. *Does your feeble imagination twig the metaphors?, Does your feeble imagination twig the metaphors?* she was repeating to herself, to remind herself of the impossible boy he was, she wanted to be strong. He was quieter day by day, thinner, and oddly wizened in the face.

He was sleeping for longer periods of the day. Her concern for her book dropped. At the beginning of October, Thornie gave her a present of beads, a bracelet.

'Why thank you Thornie. But maybe you should have it.'

He shook his head, and said it would give her good thoughts.

They sat in silence after that. 'You can tell me how it goes tomorrow,' he said, looking at her, with his tired, heavy-lidded smile. His eyes were closing, but they had told her everything — that he had always understood and forgiven her desire to leave him, to get on with her work, in the previous months.

She got to her feet. 'That's very kind of you Thornie,' she said, but her voice was not steady.

When he died, she wrote to Barbara:

Dearest Barbara,

Thanks for your tender words. It has cut deeper than I expected that he is gone and I can never make him feel my love any more. Just now all else seems trivial compared with the powers of delighting and soothing a heart that is in need.

13

It's hard to find Thornton Lewes' grave. Highgate Cemetery has unexpected slopes and byways, so many ivy-covered woody small hills and dells, 170,000 graves in total. Hans has gone to the cemetery office to see if they can help.

I see him minutes later walking through the trees, pushing aside the ivy, before stopping to light a cigarette. 'It's not going to happen,' he says. 'They don't know.'

We give up the search for Thornie, and begin our return to Eliot's grave, through the trees. 'Aren't you cold?' he asks.

It's April, and though there are small signs of new green, there's a chilly wind.

'I should've brought my coat,' I say.

'Here,' he says. 'No, please,' — silencing my protests, as he takes off his jacket and gives it to me.

'No really —'

'Please,' he says, in a matter-of-fact tone. Cautiously I take it. I can't really make Hans out. Still, as we continue walking I realise I'm enjoying it in a simple way — maybe just the pleasure of walking with a man beside me.

But periodically I'm still awkward in Hans' presence. I tell myself the reason is our different temperaments: he's one of those people who don't have to fill a silence, I'm one of those who do.

The three of us were meeting here, but Ann didn't come; when I ask him why, he says she changed her mind, she went to the British Library. He doesn't look at me as he says this.

We keep walking, by the slopes with their leaning graves, down the path. The wind is beginning to calm down. By the gate I say: 'I'm sending you that letter.'

'I'll expect it,' he replies, with a nod of acknowledgement. He stands quite straight, I notice.

At home, I click on my email, New Message.

Hans, I type, *here is the letter I want you to read. You may of course know it. It's when Thornie has died and 9 months later Eliot is still unable to work. It's to Lady Lytton, who is also bereaved.*

> *My dear Lady Lytton,*
>
> *I know now, from what your dear husband has told us, that your loss is very keenly felt by you — that it has first made you acquainted with acute grief, and this makes me think of you very much. For learning to love any one is like an increase of property, — it increases care, and brings many new fears lest precious things should come to harm.*
>
> *At present the thought of you is all the more with me, because your trouble has been brought by death; and for nearly a year death seems to me my most intimate daily companion.*
>
> *I try to delight in the sunshine that will be when I shall never see it any more. And I think it is possible for this sort of impersonal life to attain great intensity, — possible for us to gain much more independence, than is usually believed, of the small bundle of facts that make our own personality.*
>
> *We women are always in danger of living too exclusively in the affections; and though our affections are perhaps the best gifts we have, we ought also to have our share of the more independent life — some joy in things for their own sake. It is piteous to see the helplessness of some sweet women when their affections are disappointed — because all their teaching has been, that they can*

only delight in study of any kind for the sake of a personal love. They
have never contemplated an independent delight in ideas as an
experience which they could confess without being laughed at. Yet
surely women need this sort of defence against passionate affliction
even more than men.

Five minutes later, I receive an email back: *It's beautiful. Is that why you sent it?*
I type: *I think it's her first heartfelt feminist plea.*
I press send.
I email him again: *Coming directly from her own experience. ie not ideas.*
I press send again.
His email comes back: *Are you wanting to do a class on this?*
I reply: *Waiting to see what you think.*
His email comes: *Totally.*

I smile. It's typical of him. We don't always agree, but he is open. We've been teaching the class on personal writing for three weeks, and I've enjoyed it. That evening, I'm thinking about *Middlemarch* and Marian's delay in finding Dorothea, when looking at the Lytton letter, I suddenly think, surely this is the moment of change. Marian's own experience of loving and losing in a mother's way, and then being unable to work, has opened her to a new aspect of women's experience.

I open my laptop, click on New Message — then stop. I'm about to email Hans — again! Well, obviously, I say to myself. We're teaching a class together.

I realise why I like that letter. It's the first stepping stone to Dorothea. A feminist awakening??

Journey in the unconscious? from repressed self??

K.

I press send.

14

Marian did not know if she would ever write again. But at the end of the summer, she remembered her idea about a singer who lost her voice. Back at the Priory in September, she began it: *Today, under much depression*, she wrote in her diary, *I begin a little poem the subject of which engaged my interest in Harrogate.*

Lewes, when she gave him the poem Armgart to read, was curious: he did not love her poetry, but he was always intrigued by the way her poems expressed *her*. It was if he had, under his care, a rare iguana who might at any moment display new, strange, fascinating colours on her skin, or a combination of feelings and thoughts previously unseen.

But reading the first three lines, he felt his spirits sink. So, it was a verse drama.

GRAF:
Good evening, Fraülein!
WALPURGA:
What, so soon returned?

A parody of Shakespeare! He could feel his dyspepsia starting. The *Romola* problem again. In *Romola*, the people spoke a stagey English because they were Italian. Here they spoke a stagey English because they were German.

But he read on. And in spite of himself, began to enjoy it. In fact, he did enjoy it. At the end, he smiled. What a bald, peculiar little drama it was! Despite

the portentous language, it had a living core. And it was oddly, explicitly political too, on that matter on which she was usually so conservative — women. In
the poem, before the singer loses her gift, her suitor asks her to give up singing,
give up her *unwomanly ambition*, and marry him.

He found her in the drawing room, regarding him with that look he knew
well: proud but beseeching. It never failed to move him.

He thought it excellent — original — wonderful, in fact — etc. etc.

'Did you?'

He said he did.

'And?'

Lewes cleared his throat. He was thinking about her ambitiousness, wondering if she were shy about it, or ashamed of it.

He asked her why she had made the heroine Armgart a great artist, who
then lost her gift.

'Life,' was her reply.

He understood.

'Though not all women fail to achieve their ambitions,' Lewes said, point-
edly. He had a flashing intuition then of some complicated tension in Marian,
that existed between herself and her own sex.

'And yet,' went on Lewes (he could not resist), 'there is a fine description of
Armgart's, uh, ambitiousness, before her gift goes away.'

He had said it — launched the word on the air.

'True,' she said, examining her fingernails with great care.

Ah, Polly. Lewes had thought he read her soul when he read Armgart's
defence. Not only of the woman-as-artist, but of her, Polly's, determination to
have fame as her just reward for her gift. He turned back to the manuscript, and
read aloud, in the somewhat stagey voice of the poem, Armgart's plea:

> *Shall I turn aside*
> *From splendours which flash out the glow I make,*
> *And live to make, in all the chosen breasts*
> *Of half a Continent? No, may it come,*

That splendour! May the day be near when men
Think much to let my horses draw me home.
And new lands welcome me upon their beach
Loving me for my fame.

There it was, naked. Polly admitting she wanted fame as her reward — more, she loved it. She, woman artist that she was, guilty of her *unwomanly ambition* had finally put aside traditional feminine modesty.

That is the truth
Of what I wish, nay, yearn for. Shall I lie?
Pretend to seek obscurity — to sing
In hope of disregard? A vile pretence!
And blasphemy besides. For what is fame
But the benignant strength of One, transformed
To joy of Many? Tributes, plaudits come ...

Lewes was fascinated to note that somewhere in his dear Polly's consciousness, being a great artist ranked close to divinity. What else could that word blasphemy be doing? Fascinated, too, to read her fear of being just ordinary — *the millionth woman in superfluous herds.*

Herds, with perhaps a reference to breeding. No danger there.

In November, a month later, Marian began writing a story, one she'd always wanted to write. It was about a Miss Brooke, a woman who wanted to do something with her life, other than marrying and raising children. The lines came easily, and as she wrote, Marian knew that her opening sentence would take hold of the reader — it had such instant, kinetic charm.

Miss Brooke had that kind of beauty which seems to be thrown into relief by poor dress.

It took her three months, however, to realise that she had kept to her great theme of the ordinary heroic, the noble intentions that don't reach fufillment; that she had, in fact, found the missing part of *Middlemarch*. Now, although the fire was a little close, she had drawn the theme of ambition near, and stepped into it with her woman's feet. At last Lydgate had his great female counterpart, Dorothea.

Casaubon, James Chettam, Celia and Mr Brooke all quickly followed.

Part Three

1872

What do I think of Middlemarch? *What do I think of glory?*

Emily Dickinson, Amherst, USA

1

On a Sunday morning in November, Lewes was walking round Regent's Park. The day was cold but brilliantly clear, he went at a brisk pace. It was a triumph, he said to himself, a complete triumph.

From the moment *Middlemarch* had been published, it had been a sensation. For the whole of the last year it had come out in bi-monthly and monthly instalments.

He had his own theory about her success. She had given a picture of life so true that readers saw themselves there, but her narrative voice made the truth bearable. She sympathised, she understood; she seemed to say: if life is hard, and God uncertain, we can still help each other.

Still, it was, he admitted to himself, as he found himself out of breath, and the tall houses of Park Crescent came into view, almost odd. The tone was so reverential. It is *almost profane to speak of ordinary novels in the same breath with George Eliot's*, the *Telegraph* had said, and he did enjoy quoting that line. But there was an odour about it all the same.

The letters! He knew, because he opened the post each day himself. Letters and gifts poured in — not just from people in England, but from Europe and America too. The roar of her fame was sounding all over the world. Recently a letter had come from France, with no address on the envelope, simply:

George Eliot
the well-known authoress
Londres

Middlemarch had made them money, too. He was considering giving the investments to Johnny Cross. It had been Johnny's idea, a promising one in his view — Johnny was now such a trusted, close family friend, they'd started calling him 'Nephew'.

The Sundays had expanded even further. Browning, Darwin, Joachim ... on Monday mornings, Lewes enjoyed himself jotting down the names of all the distinguished people that had visited the day before — art collectors, aristocracy, artists, writers, philosophers, the younger Oxford and Cambridge intellectuals — very distinguished, there was no hiding it. Everyone bringing *their wives*. Marian sat in her usual place, he supervised carefully.

But in fact, he reflected, walking home, a reverence had been detectable before *Middlemarch*. He kept a folder of the most extravagantly praising letters. He treasured the one from the Pierce woman in America. *Dearest — You will not be bored by another love-letter — a little one? It is three whole years since I wrote to you before, and you sent me such a grave, kind, precious little answer. O how wise thou art! Where didst thou learn it all?*

The worshipful tone, the biblical language, had an excellent effect on Polly's mood. Except that on some days, nothing seemed to help. In this respect, not a great deal had changed.

2

Armgart, Marian thought, had been prophetic. Her fame had crescendoed. Everywhere they went, people wanted to know her, to shake her hand, kiss her cheek. Sometimes people cried. In conversation with Lewes, she humorously deprecated these incidents, but to herself she felt that the charged and grateful praise were her due. Yet why did she wake often filled with such suffusing sadness? Her years of isolation were over, she had done what she set out to do; why could she not remain happy? She had always thought if she achieved her ambition on this scale, her mood would be steady. But here she was — with a bitter-tasting mouth, in bed, the curtains half drawn.

Lewes came in. He had a review she might like to see, he said. The editor of the Academy had kindly sent him a proof.

Marian took it, but with a certain gloomy reluctance. No reviewer, she'd long ago realised, would understand what she had actually done.

She began reading, and then started to feel interested; paused at this sentence, and read it again.

Middlemarch *marks an epoch in the history of fiction in so far as its incidents are taken from the inner life, as the action is developed by the direct influence of mind on mind and character on character.*

It was, she had to admit, a genuinely penetrating remark.

To say that Middlemarch *is George Eliot's greatest work is to say that it has scarcely a superior and few equals in the whole wide range of English fiction.*

'Well!' laughed Marian, elation spreading through her like a drug. 'Well!

Who is he — this —'

'This *genius*, you mean?' laughed Lewes, excitedly. 'H. Lawrenny. I've read him before — always pithy, incisive. I might ask Appleton about him.'

Lewes sent a note of enquiry. A reply came the following day: the reviewer was a Miss Simcox. H. Lawrenny was a pseudonym.

'A woman,' said Marian, unable to conceal her surprise. It was unusual for a woman to write with such unforced intellectual assurance. Marian read it now in the manner of a detective. No, she couldn't immediately think of a single woman — herself excepted — who could write with such lucidity. Simcox went on to say that the conversations between Mary Garth and Rosamund, *will show to those curious in such matters, better than all Mr Trollope's voluminous works, how girls in the 19th century discuss the matters in which they are privately interested.*

Marian couldn't suppress a smile at this deprecatory remark about dear Anthony. And the final sentence was the clue to the writer's sex. What man would mention girls discussing matters in this century *in which they are privately interested*? Lewes put his head round just then. 'Reading it again, eh! I think,' he added, in a careless tone, 'I might ask her to drop by this week. Or maybe,' he added, thoughtfully, '*you* could write to her. Just a line or two.'

3

Three miles away, in No. 1 Douro Place, Kensington, upstairs in a bedroom, Miss Edith Jemima Simcox was staring at a note, in the handwriting of the great genius herself, asking if she would care to come to tea this Friday. She had re-read it and re-read it.

Edith Simcox was a diminutive figure, thriftily wrapped in a blanket as she sat at her desk. But at this moment, as she looked outside, even the great misshapen Sycamore tree, branches bare, bent as if a hand had twisted and pulled them in strange directions, looked not ugly, but wonderfully, beautifully interesting.

Writing under the pseudonym 'H. Lawrenny', Edith experienced a peculiar, delightful freedom. Authoritative, sweeping sentences issued from her pen, like those of an Oxford Don. And on this last occasion of reviewing *Middlemarch* she had worked harder than ever before. She had wanted to convey something of her own mind, Edith Simcox's mind. Age: twenty-eight years. State: spinster. Occupation: writer, housekeeper. Education: officially little (brothers, self; missed Girton by three years). Yet: considerable. Knows languages: Latin, German, French, some Italian. Interests: literature, philosophy, social justice.

Type of person: solitary.

The Academy was known to be one of the few journals Mr Lewes permitted his wife to see. Edith had seized her chance. Outside, the clouds were a thick dark grey, but they broke just then in the northwest. A portion of this light, like lacquered honey, lit her room. It was here, last summer, she'd begun reading

Middlemarch, and not wanted to move for eight hours. Sometimes she had tears in her eyes. Her most private wonderings had been given form.

After she had written her review, she found herself remembering a day in summer when she was a child. She played with her two brothers so often she was called the third boy. At one point she threw the ball high into the blue, and wondered where it would land.

* * *

Friday arrived: the morning seemed to go terribly slowly, and then too fast. It was noon now, and in some agitation, Edith tried on two pairs of boots. Usually she gave no thought to her footwear, but today she stared, then chose the brown ones: shabbier, but better quality.

At two-fifty she was standing in front of The Priory. So, this was what it looked like. A high wall, a wooden gate, two-storey house set back. She pulled the bell, the gate clicked open. Edith made her way forward, but she could hardly think, her heart seemed to be beating not just in her chest but in her ears.

From a dark hallway she was shown into the sitting room. A maid was lighting lamps, three figures stood up noisily as she walked in, two were advancing. She recognised the man with the red face and curly hair at once as the famous novelist Anthony Trollope, and guessed that the man with the moustache and lively voice was George Henry Lewes.

'So *you're* the mystery reviewer!' Lewes was exclaiming.

Lewes peered forward in surprise. Small, bespectacled, youngish, with a nervous pursed mouth: hair inefficiently pinned up, wisps everywhere. Holding herself upright as a doll. From behind the men, Marian also looked curiously at this new guest, her brilliant reviewer. She clearly gave no thought to her clothes: dress, worsted cotton it looked like; boots decidedly sturdy; lower part of her skirt dark with rain. Even her face was wet, spectacles covered in droplets.

Lewes, recalling Miss Simcox' remark about Anthony's 'voluminous works', took mischievous pleasure in introducing her to Trollope.

Marian was about to offer Miss Simcox a handkerchief, to wipe her face, when she noticed that Miss Simcox was using her sleeve as a towel, surreptitiously turning her face away.

In fact, Edith had turned away because of her colossal shyness. Her thoughts were flooding her so that she was confused. She was aware of a long, pretty room, books, prints, flowers tastefully arranged. Then she felt a touch on her arm. George Eliot was there, she saw a blur of pearls, lace, light brown hair. 'Miss Simcox, shall we sit down?' On the sofa they were only two feet apart. There was a scent, beguiling, soft. Edith found the courage to lift her head and look properly at Marian, and was surprised by her face, it was so kindly and tender. 'Tell me something about yourself, Miss Simcox,' the musical voice was saying. 'Have you — read anything of interest, lately?'

Edith mentioned Tennyson. It was the only name that came into her head. They talked for some time, then fell silent. Marian was looking at the rug, thinking, before facing her again.

'What — do you want to do?' asked Marian, hesitantly, with a look of real curiosity. She was beginning to feel better, something to do with her guest's difficulty and shyness — she wanted to put her at ease. 'Apart from writing reviews of a high order?'

How did Marian intuit her so accurately? She had asked the primary question — how she, a woman, should spend her life. In Marian's face, she saw now, there was not just kindness but sadness too, and that comforted her. Breathing more easily, Edith said she wanted to write books, not only reviews.

'And why should you not?'

'Why should I not ...' Edith repeated.

'You must do what you want to do.'

They were simple words. It was pleasant hearing them, though, from George Eliot, or Mrs Lewes.

Edith sat still, clasping her hands.

'I would also like to,' — she was encouraged by the other's simple directness — 'help.'

Watching her keenly now, Marian asked in what way.

Edith blushed. Complaints about social injustice had an obvious air. All she said was, 'I see much of London.'

She felt Marian absorbing her.

'But I do want to write. I know Latin,' went on Edith, suddenly feeling she could say almost anything. 'I know French, German, and I mean to learn Greek —'

Edith stopped, struck by the extraordinary beauty of her hostess' eyes. But then — the entire scene — how could she take it in? The smell of juniper from the fire, that rain drumming on the window, the snapping gently motoric activity of the fire and warmth, and the present famous company. How rich Mrs Lewes' life was! — full to the brim. How had she done it, earned her own heaven so perfectly? Her books, her lover, her hospitable home and admiring friends.

'You still look wet, Miss — ah —' said Anthony Trollope, in his loud, well-meaning way, standing up in his gloriously tasteless checked trousers.

'Simcox. The weather is inclement,' — nodding.

'Where did you come from?'

'Kensington.'

'What means of transport?' boomed the kindly Trollope.

'I walked.'

A hungry sparrow of a Dorothea, thought Marian, wanting to set the world to rights. She had given succour to the sparrow, she knew. And somehow to herself, too. Her gloom of the morning was gone.

Lewes walked Edith to the door to say goodbye, and said it had been a promising occasion.

Edith heard irony in his tone. 'He doesn't like me,' she thought, as she went down the steps. She was used to painful thoughts. Yet walking home, she was able to console herself. Before she left, Marian had held her cold hands in her warm ones, and said, 'You will come back, won't you?'

4

We are doing an experiment in the house. I take the mischievous third dog up to my flat at night, separating her from her companions, to see if the dawn chorus of barking will stop.

Her name is Billy, she is a mongrel, with a streak of chestnut spaniel. When I collect her, she speeds upstairs. In my flat she runs in circles, sniffing everywhere. I figure she's quite young, maybe two. We go up to the attic where my bed is, my desk, my work, George Eliot books, laptop, notebooks. I put a pillow down for her to sleep on, in front of the boarded-up fireplace. She takes a look, goes instead into the corner. After going round and round, clawing noisily with her paws at the floor, as if the boards are diggable earth, she stops, curls up. She's made the corner into her house, flanked on both sides by the walls. Her nose is wrapped into her tail, in a circle.

Lying there with the light off, I can hear her breathing.

She wakes at six-thirty, a big improvement. I put on boots, coat, take her out into the cold. It's light, the birds are noisy.

Dale has given me spare keys, when I leave for work I slip Billy through his door.

★ ★ ★

Next Thursday, Hans and I are preparing the class when Ann knocks on the door, and asks us to come to the canteen.

The canteen is cavernous with a high ceiling where the pipes of the building are exposed. As we queue with our trays, Ann glances at the photographs on the wall, in lurid colour, six feet high, of famous academics who have worked at QEC. 'So pleased with themselves', she mutters, frowning and shaking her head.

Ann is wearing a white long-sleeved blouse with a brooch at her throat. It's a warm day in April but the heating is on at full throttle.

'Listen,' she says, as we sit down. And now she turns to me. 'Are you free to go with Hans next Friday? To Coventry? To the Eliot museum?'

'Me?' I say in surprise.

The department is setting up an exhibition to accompany the conference, and Ann and Hans were going to Coventry to sign documents and check the exhibits. The plea in her eye resembles a young girl's. I look at Hans and then take a biscuit quickly. I don't like what I see. He looks so contemptuous.

'Why — do you — suggest this?' he asks, in a voice of extreme politeness.

'Because,' says Ann, 'I'm very behind, as you know. I'm behind on my book, I'm behind on everything, in fact.' Her voice is quavering. Hans looks away.

'Look,' I begin —

He says it's fine; if I am free, that would be great. I look down, I don't like my red skirt. It's agreed I'll go with Hans. I ring my sister Sal that night and try to describe the strange couple.

5

Spring came, and Marian admitted to herself that the germ of a new book was at last forming in her mind. She had begun researching Jewish culture — the theme, of a people seeking a home, stirred her. But going abroad in the summer, it was the sight of a woman in the grip of a compulsion, gambling, that caught her imagination.

She needed to find a quiet place for this germ to grow, away from socialising. They began to look more actively for a place in the country. So far nothing had been quite right, but Johnny Cross was looking for them. And they trusted him to get it right. Johnny, their Nephew as they called him, had invested their money into American railway stock with great success.

One autumn Sunday, when the guests had gone, Marian stretched herself out on the sofa. 'I hope I have not gone on too long,' Benjamin Jowett had said, before he left. On the contrary, she replied. Marian had touched his fingers. The touch would say much. The oil-lamps glowed and smelled faintly sulphurous. But now she was tired. She had begun every conversation with a gentle, careful enquiry, and with each guest she ended up witnessing her own effect. Her genius for seeing and understanding, compounded by her compelling need to give, gave her a taste in her own mouth of ecstasy. The candles burned brightly in her vision; she had a hot, wonderful sense of proof.

'Madonna, hello,' said Lewes. George's voice sounded odd, to her ear. He wanted to sit beside her, she could see, but lying there on the sofa she did not feel like moving.

'I had a letter from Bertie,' said Lewes.

Bertie, Africa. At once she felt bilious, the candles burned less brightly.

Bertie had followed Thornie out to Africa years before; his life so far had been a series of misfortunes. Illness, robberies, botched deals, loss, loneliness. He was married now with a child. Reluctantly, Marian shifted herself, sat up and took the letter. She read through, then more slowly:

I am still suffering from Neuralgia in my back and hips, and have got quite a skeleton. We have had a very long dry winter, and our oxen have been very poor, we lost three from poverty.

You did not tell me the name of your last Work. I have read a great deal latterly of a night, not being able to sleep through pain.

Love from Eliza and myself, to you and little Mutter.

Marian put the letter down. It was bad — very bad. It was a dread echo of Thornie. Briefly she closed her eyes. Bertie wanted them to suggest he came here. At the same time, it was clear he did not dare ask himself.

'It sounds like Thornie all over again,' said Lewes, at the mantelpiece. He was fingering his moustache repeatedly.

'If,' Marian said carefully, 'he comes home, his family will come with him.'

Lewes looked at her. 'It's a bad business,' he said. He moved away from the sofa where she was, to be near the window. He had glimpsed her now, her kind-looking face having acquired the massive, granite-like quality it sometimes did. They were both silent, the fire spat.

'They will all come,' she said, 'and where will they live?'

Lewes shrugged. He went back to the mantelpiece to light a cigar. But he could not stay still, he started pacing, smoking, his heart beating. He observed mechanically that Amelia had come in, and begun setting the empty glasses on a tray, bowing her shoulders as if to look invisible.

He knew he could not win this argument. If he was truthful, he, too, found the idea of Bertie and family coming here, extremely daunting. They were on a tight track, the way they lived. Yet to leave Bertie out there was to abandon him.

They came to no solution that night; they would send money, and talk again soon, when they had further news. Lewes slept downstairs alone in the study.

The next day, after leaving the London Library, he walked by the Thames. A boat was skimming fast, he could not help watching it. It was going diagonally, losing its course. He found himself descending the bank. 'Hey!' he shouted. He was in an incomprehensible welter of indignation mixed with fear. What was the fool of a skipper up to? Who was steering it? A man was at the helm in a black cap. At last the boat averted the shore, and began, wobbling, to regain its course.

Lewes patted his pocket. Bertie's letter was in there, he was aware of it as he walked. He had meant to read it again by the river. No, the sun was too bright.

He could smell burning leaves. He remembered the garden from his first year of marriage to diminutive, pretty Agnes, in Kensington. He had a nostalgic happy sensation, and his eyes were suddenly sticky.

Here we are all, by day; by night we're hurl'd
By dreams, each one, into a several world

He said this to himself, as he walked along Embankment. He and Thornton Hunt, his great friend, who became Agnes' lover, used to take night walks together by the river, just where he was walking now. Late, he would go home. Those babies, those toddlers. He sometimes sang to them in the dark.

6

Edith appeared occasionally on Sundays, sometimes with her brother, the classicist Augustus Simcox. More often she came alone. She was Marian's most intellectual woman friend. Edith's face was a mask of composure, tightly in place: but the same Edith had tears in her eyes on occasion, and would drop, abruptly, to the floor, and kneel at Marian's feet. These gestures, that were so without contrivance, touched Marian. Over time their correspondence became close, Marian felt herself to be nurturing and signed herself *Mother*.

Edith's courage grew. She began to demonstrate her affection, she began to give in to her own desire to kiss Marian's hands, cheeks. To her amazement her kisses were not rejected! Sometimes Marian would lean her cheek towards her to be kissed. She cannot dislike me, Edith said to herself, joy springing up in her heart. Her own sensations mounted in consequence. She knelt regularly now, on the Priory rug, and mostly, when she kissed Marian's hands, Lewes was there, giving surprising but definitely genial encouragement.

One day, when Edith was kneeling at Marian's feet, Marian felt the warm soft touch of Edith's lips on her foot, the upper part, where the shoe gave way to her stocking.

'Nay,' said Marian, softly.

'Oh, let her!' urged Lewes, good-naturedly, but impatiently.

Marian did so. Edith's homage was sweet. She blushed, her lip trembled, Marian read her emotions with dreadful ease. And she couldn't help it, her own dull mood lifted at the sight.

Yet Edith made her uneasy. The source of her unease lay in herself, she knew, but she could neither find, nor quite see it.

7

I am in the Herbert Gallery with Hans, in Coventry, looking at Eliot's kid gloves, her writing cabinet, a folding table. We come to the piano, her Broadwood grand. 'We certainly can't take *this* to London!' says Hans. I start talking about how musical she was, how the piano was a symbol of status. 'I know I know, she's really *your* George Eliot,' says Hans, half in my ear, joking as usual, in a mock-reassuring voice. I laugh; the day's been easier than I thought it would be.

After we've signed the insurance documents, we stand outside; neither of us speaks at first.

'Do you want to go for a walk?' he says, suddenly.

'Well —'

'You need to get home,' he says quickly.

'No ... no ... sure.'

We go to the War Memorial Park, and it feels like a holiday. The sun is out, we buy ice creams, find a bench near the pond. Children are feeding the ducks; I watch as Hans gives them a croissant: they suddenly freeze, almost comically, before snatching it and running back to the ducks. I'm more relaxed than I've been in a while.

At the station it's rush hour. Inside there are no two seats free next to each other.

The train starts moving. I'm seated beside a stranger, the aisle is on my left. Peering down, I can just see Hans' grey trainer and protruding knee on the other side. The train is noisy with its compressed, speedy rhythmic rattle, a high-pitched sound as we take a long bend. I take out my phone, put it down; take out my book, put that down too. I close my eyes.

After a while the train slows, we're coming to Milton Keynes. The doors are opening — there's a voice over the loudspeaker. Hans is standing, letting the person next to him out. I get up, pick up my bag, and take the empty seat.

'Hi — hi — I saw the seat —'

'Great.' He's taken his jacket off, rolled up his sleeves, and got his laptop out. I'm so near I notice the thin chain he wears round his neck. And I notice his arms. Why do I notice his arms and his hands? There's something capable about them.

'I've just sent you some letters,' he says. 'Eliot letters.'

Sitting next to him, I relax. I've always loved trains: the sprung motion and the sound of them. Outside it's light, the landscape is flat, the sun is just starting its descent, shadows to lengthen. Hans asks if I want tea. He returns with two polystyrene cups with lids.

'You were married, weren't you,' he says, out of the blue.

I say yes, to someone called Rob.

He hesitates; then: 'But you didn't want children?'

'Oh! No, I did.'

He looks at me. 'I don't mean to offend you, but —'

'He couldn't have them,' I cut in.

We are silent again. He is looking thoughtful. 'But you didn't want to, you know, go another route.'

'I did,' I say. I don't mind telling him. 'I did, he didn't. I sort of accepted it at the time — but when we broke up —'

I touch the polystyrene. The tea is still too hot to drink. 'It was too late then. I'm forty-six.'

'Difficult,' he says. He doesn't put too much sympathy in his voice; just a fragment.

'But you know,' he says, turning to me with a half-smile, 'it's not all skittles and roses.'

'Beer and skittles. No. I'm going to see Rob, actually.'

'Your ex?'

'Yes.'

'Why?' He is looking at me in complete surprise.

'We were together a long time. It's nice if we can be, I don't know, friendly.'

He is silent, before saying decisively — disapprovingly — 'I can't see the point of it at all. These things can rekindle.'

'There's no question of that; he's with someone else. His assistant.'

'Classic!' — contemptuously.

The ticket collector comes, we show our tickets, then settle back to watch the view go by. After a while:

'Ann says —' Hans, in a perfectly neutral tone '— that you don't see eye to eye about the conference.'

I think, then explain: Ann wants to grill Eliot politically on the first day. I worry this will set a negative tone for the whole thing.

We're silent; just the rumbling, comfortable rattle of the train. Eventually he says: 'The politically adventurous one is Simcox, right?'

I nod.

'Eliot and Simcox ...' he muses, as the telegraph poles flick by. 'That is one — odd — relationship! Why does Eliot let her kiss her feet?'

'I don't know.'

Eventually I say: 'I mean, I think they got on. And she liked the admiration, being loved. And, you know —' I shrug '— her self-esteem. It was good for it.'

After a bit, I can't resist adding, 'Not a problem for you, right?'

'No,' he says, non-committal.

Then he goes on: 'Well! Well — not all of the time! But ... sure ... everyone knows self-doubt.'

'Even Hans Meyerschwitz.'

He says, with a half smile, 'I must manage better than I think.'

'So when do you experience self-doubt?'

'When? Every time I give a bloody lecture! I'm nervous. Every time. Aren't you?'

He turns, the same instant I do, so that we're both looking at each other, and

I realise we're both smiling.

'I'm still sceptical,' I say. 'For me, it's a lot of the time. I sympathise with Eliot.'

'Ahhh ... haaaa ... I see. It's all personal is it?'

I say, very. I ask him which part of Germany he's from. He grew up in Hamburg. He goes back; his mother lives there still. She brought them up, he and his brother, on her own. His father left when they were young.

The train is speeding up, and the countryside is beginning to take on a richer, deeper hue. The sun is in the west. The low rays stream across us. 'So you had a ring here did you?' he says as, to my surprise, he takes my hand and runs his fingers along my fourth finger as if feeling for an indentation. 'Yes,' I'm saying, half blushing, when the train careers round a sharp bend, we are thrown to the left, and I rescue my hand. And as the train steadies, I can feel my heart beating, and it feels suddenly very sweet, the view, the passing hedges, houses; the sky has turned pinkish.

'Where exactly are we?' I say.

'I've no idea,' he says. I look out of the window again. What I see are two long wide flat fields, a church spire, low modern houses, a cluster of dark trees. We could be anywhere. Somewhere in France, going south, with weeks ahead.

The train is slowing. We're nearly at Euston.

Downstairs, I take Billy in my arms, which I haven't done before. She's only a small spaniel, but she's heavier than I expect. In my flat she scampers everywhere, racing in her usual circles. I have a cooker now, a bath; Benny has exposed the fireplace.

With the window open, and my peculiar restiveness, I drag the bag of coal over, cut it open, put the coal in the grate. I break up firelighters, add kindling from a plastic bag, light it. I wait, then add a log. The fire is burning, and seems to draw.

When it's down to its embers, I check my email. There is one from Hans. *That was a good day. I enjoyed it very much.*

Here's the diary entry I wanted to send you. What do you make of that sentence about 'mental efficiency'?

I thought it might amuse you.

Talk over coffee? Thursday?

H

George Eliot's diary:

Jan 1874

The happy old year in which we have had constant enjoyment of life notwith-standing much bodily malaise, is gone from us forever. More than in any former year of my life, love has been poured forth to me from distant hearts, and in our own home we have had that finish to domestic comfort which only faithful, kind servants can give. Our children are prosperous and happy — Charles evidently growing in mental efficiency; we have abundant wealth for more than our actual needs; and our unspeakable joy in each other has no other alloy than the sense that it must one day end in parting.

A second email comes.

Here's another letter, in case you haven't seen it — a sad one, from Bertie.

H

Unfinished posthumous letter from Bertie Lewes to George Henry Lewes, June 1874, arriving after Bertie's death:

Dearest Pater,

I was obliged to draw upon you for £50. I have been here a month and my own money has been down some time. I am better than when I last wrote. All my glands are swollen. My ankels and feet have been swollen so that I could not get my boots on. The Doctor attends me about every other day. He says I progress too slowly so has changed Medecines.

I forgot to thank you in my last for — It has been touch and go with me. I feel it will take some time to get back my old strengtht. I have been expecting a letter from you every mail. Did you get mine of last month?

1878

8

On a cold day in March, Marian and Lewes were climbing St George's Hill in Weybridge. They kept thinking they were nearing the top, when they weren't. Each wore a heavy coat, their breaths smoked. From where they were, it was hard to see the exact shape of the land because of the fir trees. Finally it became level, the trees cleared. They were at the summit. All around — below — were hills, fields, a small wood, copses. They had a full, glorious, 360-degree view.

On the bench, Marian put her arm through Lewes'. The silence seemed to be imperceptibly deepening. She could see everything — the pattern of the fields, even the defining patchwork lines of the hedgerows.

She took a long, satisfying breath. It was a splendid view. But in fact, she thought, with a touch of complacency, it was no better than their own. They finally had their own country house. They had found it fourteen months ago. Or rather, Johnny had. The Heights, at Witley. It was perfect: with a garden, fields, even a wood.

They had gone there from London this morning to check the progress of the new cottage for the coachman, and then had travelled on to see the Cross family at Weybridge.

Marian looked again at those clear patterns below. The last few years had been fruitful. *Deronda* had come out to critical acclaim, confirming her status, if she was honest with herself, as England's reigning novelist, even though it was a more demanding book than *Middlemarch*. Now she was embarked on *Theophrastus Such*: a strange endeavour, but it cost her less to write, that was for sure.

Lewes took his arm from Polly's, thrust his hands into his coat pockets.

Freezing air was sneaking under his scarf to his neck, and he drew it tighter. Polly was exclaiming about the splendid view, and it was, it was; but he could not stop thinking of the letter he had come across last night. He had been going through his post before preparing for the trip today, and glimpsed, deep in his drawer, an old envelope, with different rich-coloured African stamps, and many postal markings, and before he quite knew what he was doing, he pulled the letter out. It was from the Sandersons, the couple who had looked after Bertie when he was dying.

Lewes tried not to think about it now. He tried to take in the view. Even that seemed oppressive: everywhere he looked were fir trees, great massed regiments of them, with their straight dark trunks. Inside his coat pockets he made fists of his hands to try to warm them. Bertie was dead. But it was past, nearly three years ago.

As they sat, the silence seemed still to be deepening. Then Lewes saw a snowflake, and another. He watched as they came down in threes and fours. He drew his coat tighter around him. Snow began to come in a slow silent constant fall, from the pale sky above. The silence was total, the view partially obscured.

They began walking down carefully, holding on to each other.

They were welcomed back at the Cross family house, though the mood was quieter than usual, because of Anna Cross being ill. Eleanor and Florence showed them in. The rich, warm light of the dining room contrasted with the snowy light outside. Willie Cross was there, Johnny's oldest brother. Kippers, ham, toast, gingerbread cake too, and tea were served. Johnny finally appeared, from his mother's sickbed. 'Ah, difficult,' he said at first, gesturing in the direction of his mother's bedroom. But he was pleased to see his guests. He had pressed them to stay.

★ ★ ★

'Are you wrapped up, Nephew?' said Lewes, as they left the house next day. They had stepped into the freezing morning.

Snow had fallen again overnight, but the sky was clear; the world was brilliant white and blue. Lewes, with a shaky, red hand, lit a match, lighting first Johnny's cigar, then his own.

'I have a particular fondness,' said Lewes, 'for the cigar in the open air.' Willie had produced a box of Havanas. 'Ahhh!' breathed out Lewes, watching the smoke rise, though the exhalation nipped him in the stomach. Lewes wore an enormous amount of scarves; Johnny wore a single scarf looped more elegantly around his throat, and a good overcoat (not for the first time, Lewes wondered where Johnny bought his clothes). They walked, the snow new, crisp yet soft underfoot in the dazzling light. Gradually they left the house behind, going over stiff, frosty stiles into new terrain of fields and more fields, stray trees offering long dark shadows on the glittering white. They left the fields to go down a winding lane, surrounded by smooth-capped hedges. Lewes paused to smoke.

'Damn good.'

'Willie has good taste, and cigars are his passion,' said Johnny. 'But how is Mrs Lewes?'

'For *her*,' Lewes confided, 'she is well, yet there are melancholy moments. But she really has no reason! Do you know, Nephew,' — he derived pleasure from addressing the noticeably tall, well-built, younger man this way — 'I have come to the conclusion that only the queen is more celebrated than her. The extra-orrrrrrrdinary tributes she receives! You know Mrs Elma Stuart who sent her the wood carvings? She has kept a handkerchief as a relic ever since Marian wet it with her tears! It's the truth, Nephew, it's the truth.' He paused and added, thoughtfully, 'She always wants more, that's the problem.'

Johnny listened to Lewes' gleeful, boastful, loving voice, the sound carrying in the thin quiet air of the morning. And he heard the rhythmic sound of their feet, that precise fluttering sound of the snow compacting underfoot, that reminded him of cards shuffling through the air. The softness, the beauty of the snow, were ravishing. He was in the mood for Lewes' voice, relieved to forget his mother's illness for two hours. (How small were Lewes' footprints, compared to his.) His business, with offices in Cornhill in the city, was going well. And the Lewes' portfolio was splendid, with railway investments yielding twenty-six per cent.

And this morning, walking with Lewes, he was reminded that it was only he, of his family, who knew the stellar friends intimately. Life with the Leweses felt like an enhanced existence, somehow, where the quantity of pleasure per hour was squared or cubed: similar, all things being equal, to joy. (Was it Lewes' quick-fire vivacity, generosity, his endless anecdotes? Or her quieter richness of thought? Or the half-conscious idea that he was with people who would be remembered? His closeness to them, certifiable proof of his — his —)

As they walked, the fluttering crunching sound of the snow was beginning to remind him, if he paid really close attention, of a cat purring, or was it the sound of a million wings? The greatest genius of the country — or rather, her spouse, as it were — confiding in him.

'She is an exception to the rule,' said Johnny, boldly.

At the stile, Johnny waited for Lewes to go first. Lewes gave him a little push in the back, as he said, no, go ahead. The younger man's tone had annoyed him. They were walking on the flat now, and he suggested to Johnny to go on, he would follow directly. He wanted just to idle and reflect, he said, for a minute or so.

Alone, Lewes walked the last stretch more slowly. He needed to complete *Problems* this year, he said to himself.

Blackwood had been keen to publish it. In their correspondence, the Scottish publisher developed a flattering habit of referring to Lewes' 'Great Work'. Lewes wrote self-deprecatingly in return of his *Key to all Psychologies*; even joking that 'his Dorothea' would finish it after his death. The affectionate correspondence continued until, as it was going to press, Blackwood just turned round and said he didn't like it. In fact, he couldn't publish it — he found it gratingly atheist.

Trübners took it instead.

Blackwood remained their friend, of course, and Lewes was in constant correspondence with him about Polly's work, but the episode had stung him.

★ ★ ★

In the drawing room they played cribbage, then roasted chestnuts. From her armchair Marian regarded Johnny fondly. When Bertie had died, he was the one person she had written to in full about it. Lewes, fearing condolences, hadn't wanted to tell anyone.

Johnny was eating chestnuts, one and then another. He was just dreamily splitting the warm outer skin with his thumb, to find the soft nut within, when he realised he was being spoken to.

'I said,' Lewes was saying, 'when are you getting spliced, Nephew? We were wondering about Miss Simcox. We know you buy your shirts at Hamiltons.'

An unfair joke, thought Johnny. He only bought his shirts there because the Leweses had suggested it to him, as they did to all their free-thinking friends. Hamiltons was the all-women shirtmaking cooperative set up by Miss Simcox, in Soho.

Johnny was not sure what to make of Miss Simcox. He could not like her, he had to admit. She was consistently rude to him.

He remembered the time when, entering the Priory, he had thought there was a cat on Marian's lap. With a shock, he realised it was a woman's dark head — Miss Simcox, in fact. She was kneeling, her head resting against the upper part of Marian's thigh. Then she had shuffled round on her knees, taken Marian's hand and kissed it, repeatedly. Lewes had laughed away, like a depraved monkey!

Johnny had heard stories about how debauched Lewes had been in his youth, a follower of Shelley, hanging round older debauchees like Leigh Hunt. Apparently he had espoused the principles of Free Love, condoning his wife and his best friend. Johnny had heard tales of more than two in a bed.

He picked up another chestnut, but instantly put it down, as it was rather too hot.

9

Upstairs in No. 1 Douro Place, Edith Simcox was doing her accounts. But she kept stopping, picking up her pen to turn it round in her hands. She was wondering about visiting Marian. Should she? She looked out of the window. After some minutes, she pushed the accounts away — she had seen two magpies, that was enough. 'One for sorrow, two for joy,' she said aloud, as she began to get ready.

She took her reticule, and another larger, more serviceable bag. In the corner of the hallway she found the flowers she had bought this morning, and inspected them. The last pansies of the season, they were already wilting, yet the grey tint in the violet-blue was just right. They were, she judged, the colour of Marian's eyes.

She walked up Gloucester Road, crossed into Kensington Gardens; proceeded in a northeast direction through the park, heading north on Gloucester Place. Regent's Park appeared on her right, she quickened her speed. At the Priory, she pulled the bell. The gate clicked open, then the front door was opening and there was Brett, the new parlour maid.

'Is Mrs Lewes in?'

Edith had just noticed that the drawing room shutters were closed. She held her breath.

Brett said that Mr and Mrs Lewes were in Oxford for the weekend.

Edith stayed standing.

'Is there anything I can do, Ma'am?' asked Brett, after a moment.

'Can I leave these for her?'

Brett, regarding the flowers, said she did not know if they would last.

'Do please give them to her,' said Edith, matter-of-factly. Edith said goodbye, but near the gate she turned. 'You will say who they are from?'

'Yes Ma'am.'

Edith walked back towards Kensington. Her spectacles were misting up, blank white clouds were covering the sky with amazing speed, the light was chilly. The walk home was slow. In her room, from her drawer, she pulled out a teak box and took out the bundle of letters. They were from Marian. She read one, then another, then another. Then she put them down.

Each note expressed intense, fond, careful care for her. At one moment the tone was anxious, the next humorous. No one else wrote to Edith like that. At the end of each letter, Marian signed herself, *Your Loving Mother*.

Perhaps it was the fact that Marian had been out, or that Edith had just re-read those sweetly worded enquiries — asking in one about Edith's earache, in another, years before, about negotiations for premises in Dean Street — but Edith's spectacles were misting up again. She kissed each envelope in turn. She had smudged the ink with her tears. Hers — she, who had written her first book; who lectured at working men's clubs, walked the poorest streets in London, managed her cooperative, translated German for Max Müller, attended Trades Union meetings, yes, she was crying. She washed and dried her face.

Some time later, she took a book from the drawer of her desk. It was bound in green Moroccan leather, with a brass lock. She felt for the tiny key that lived in the far right corner of the drawer and unlocked the book.

It contained her handwriting, on the right-hand page: very small, compressed, blue-ink handwriting. She wrote mostly about Marian, which meant her own experience of Marian, in great detail. This was her secret diary. In it, she was free to write whatever she liked. No one would ever see it.

She closed it with a snap. She would not write today.

★ ★ ★

Two days later, outside Smithfield Market, Edith bought sweet pea flowers. The seller couldn't have been more than twelve, she wore a tattered, bruised once-elegant lady's hat, that was slipping off. After which Edith made her way to Paternoster Row and Trübners. Climbing the stairs rapidly, she bumped straight into Lewes.

'Miss Simcox! What are you doing here?'

'Trübners are my publishers.'

'Of course they are. I probably suggested them.'

'You did.'

He waited while she collected a cheque for a disappointing sum, and they left together. As they walked he said he hoped she was coming to see them soon.

'I am intending to.' She was shy of admitting she had even hoped to come today; they knew well she had called two days before.

But Lewes said, 'Why not now? Madonna is a little low in spirits.' He would not take no for an answer. Who was she to go against Mr Lewes! He began to hail a hansom.

Did he not want to walk, she asked.

A smile of disbelief appeared. 'My body is a ragged thing these days, Miss Simcox. On no account.'

The hansom went at a good trot, but on Farringdon Road there had been an accident, and a ghoulish crowd had gathered.

'That reliable human instinct,' sighed Lewes, as an injured man and what could be a corpse were taken up from the road. 'You should hear Mrs Lewes on the subject.'

'Of accidents?' said Edith, curious.

'No no,' laughed Lewes. 'Biographers! She hates the idea of people writing about her.'

Edith looked out of the window.

The cabman apologised for the horrible sight. 'No matter,' said Lewes, waving his hand.

It was clear the journey was going to be slow. Lewes lit a cigar. Edith was thinking. How strange it was, that she was not jealous of Mr Lewes. She coveted

Marian, yet she adored them as a couple. It did not make sense. Lewes was talking to her, asking about reviewing.

'I beg your pardon?'

He put his question again. Edith admitted she didn't use a pseudonym any more.

'Do you miss it?' asked Lewes. He was thinking not just of Marian but of Charlotte Brontë and the name Currer Bell, whom he had championed decades before.

'I think I have a man's brain,' said Edith. She cracked her knuckles, a habit she had recently acquired.

'What makes you say that?'

'I won't bore you,' said Edith, stiffly.

'I like people to tell me things,' Lewes announced, puffing on his cigar.

Edith regarded him. She would tell him a little.

'It is nothing interesting.' She used to think she was a boy — that the doctors would diagnose her as a boy. It wasn't so unusual, in her view. The hansom was beginning to pick up speed.

'Physiognomy, psychology, the question is certainly begged,' murmured George Henry Lewes, whose work was on body and mind.

They were approaching the Priory.

But on arrival, Marian's headache was worse — George was sorry for having dragged Edith here. He offered the carriage to take her home. Edith refused.

* * *

In her room, Edith lay on the bed, her eyes shut, in rigor mortis position. She put her hands together like the brass knights in church floors. She would let time pass. Five minutes later she sprang up, pulled out her green book from her desk, put the key in (why did she bother to lock it?). She had an urge to look over herself, to understand herself, this was why she wrote this diary, she said to the room.

Yesterday I had a few lines bidding me come on Wednesday at 3.30 ... Oh! how sweet to sit by her alone, to be folded in her arms. My darling, my darling!

Very good. Marian did sometimes fold her in her arms. She flicked back further.

I have been looking over my journal — acta diurna amoris — and counting the days till I may hope to see her again. I do not hope for anything else.

The same as now. What progress was she making?

... in the rest I have written finis on my tombstone and in sanguine moments force myself to mutter 'Sat est vixisse' — I have lived for a few seconds now and then. I love her just as much as ever and a touch would bring me back to unconsciousness of everything but the love.

The struggle for existence is an infernal process.

Really, in all these five years of loving Marian, what had changed?

She read some more, but her left temple was beginning to ache, so she fetched water from downstairs to drink. Another entry:

Dearest, Dearest. Day by day let me begin and end by looking to Her for guidance and rebuke ... make a dread rule to myself out of the vow that every night what has been done ill or left undone shall be confessed on my knees to my Darling and my God.

She did want Marian's advice, in the deepest sense, on everything. She wanted absolution from her too. She read on.

On Friday I went with fresh patterns of silk; Johnny was there and she — asked me to come some other day, Sunday or Monday or Tuesday. Returning home through Kensington Gardens, if the truth must be told I sat down under a spreading tree and cried.

Ah, she was too vulnerable, too easily upset.

She did dislike Johnny Cross though. She had once caught a look between Johnny and Marian as he bid her goodbye, where they both seemed to be unconsciously smiling.

After this she could not be polite to Johnny. Marian and Mr Lewes often reproached her for being rude to him. But they also teased her for her jealousy.

She said they had laughed at the fatality of my crossing with Johnny last week: I said I knew I should poison his shirts some day, and she hoped I would not, he saved

them a great deal of trouble about money affairs, besides being the best of sons and
brothers — I said of course, that was just why; I was jealous.

Johnny was conniving, she was sure.

I had just begun to despair of reaching more interesting topics when the fatal
Johnny came in, he had missed his train yesterday and had a book to return by way
of pretext. I stayed about half an hour, all told, and left the field for Johnny.

★ ★ ★

'Talk of the devil,' said Lewes, genially, when Edith appeared. She had taken her
courage in her hands and come.

'Don't look like that, child,' said Marian, mildly and kindly.

Edith said, 'Mother, I am happy to see you,' — dropping her eyes, then her
knees. Then she took Marian's hand close to her cheek.

They discussed Hamiltons, Goethe, Goethe's treatment of love, marriage.
The mother of her friend, Edith said, wanted her daughter to be married.

'What about you?' said Marian suddenly. 'Don't you want to be married?'

Edith let go of Marian's hand.

'Marriages,' went on Marian, briskly, 'are happening later and later. People
who go on developing have a much better chance of marriage after thirty than at
twenty; and you, Edith, have never been so ready to marry as now.'

'That is not saying much,' said Edith, in a scarcely audible voice. She had
started rubbing at a hole in her stocking.

Lewes unaccountably added his voice to the chorus, saying it would be good
for Edith, and make her less 'anti-men'.

They both laughed and agreed heartily. Together, they often accused her of
being prejudiced against men.

'Did you have an opinion about *Natural Law*?' said Edith, desperately. She
had given Marian a copy of her book, about ethics, with a riskily personal message inscribed. For several months Marian had said nothing about it. Now she
met Marian's eyes full on. Marian hesitated, then said she did like it. 'Nothing
jarred.'

On the way home Edith stumbled at a pothole. The author of *Middlemarch* had suggested she get married. She could not understand it.

But within days she was thinking, what does all that matter? The month was June; any moment Marian and Lewes would disappear for a hideous amount of time, to their summer house in the country, at Witley.

The following morning, Edith pulled out her green diary, picked up her pen:

June 16, 1878

Last night came one of those sweet envelopes — bidding me come tomorrow for the dreaded farewell: after which life becomes a blank for alas! nearly 5 months.

10

On the longest day of the year, Marian and Lewes arrived at Witley. Everything was as they hoped. The pictures were tastefully hung, the new William Morris wallpaper was in the drawing room. The cottage was ready for the coachman. Outside, Lewes walked to the end of the terrace and threw his arms open to the view: the garden, the fields, the hills in the distance and the wood. The sun was not too hot; Marian removed her shawl, felt the air on her arms. They spent the evening outside in a replete, quiet mood, drinking wine, absorbing the small sounds, with a sense of release and peace after London.

Marian woke some time in the night, in the confusion of sleep and a dream, in which there was a crying child, a boy, and an arrival of some kind of animal, a badger, possibly — and then she was waking properly, the room was in fact dimly illuminated, and she saw Lewes out of bed, seated by the wall. At the sight of his face, her stomach contracted. She got up to help him. Slowly, his pain eased, and he made his way back to bed.

Lewes was cheerful at breakfast, he wanted to walk round 'the property', all nine acres of it. He said the phrase with relish, which made her smile. But while dressing she could not forget his face in the night: when the silent countryside around them, that had seemed so glorious only hours before, had become frightening.

Doctors had come and gone in London; Sir James Paget had seen him, but nothing was clear.

★ ★ ★

In the summerhouse they made themselves comfortable, the new matting pleasant underfoot: Marian was reading *Theophrastus Such* aloud. Privately, Lewes wearied of the ironic pedantic narrator — Casaubon, he thought, without the fun.

But soon the cramps of the night returned. He stood up — said sorry — went out. The sensation in his lower stomach and bowels was as if a thread had been run through him, and was now being tightened. Walking, though, seemed to ease him. He began getting up at dawn and going out to walk, and Polly came with him, a woollen shawl over her nightdress. They went together on these anxious dawn walks. There was great beauty in the silent fields.

He was better, he was worse, then he was better. The pain was intermittent, but he could not read as he used to. At the back of his mind he was afraid of not finishing *Problems*. They continued to socialise, and sometimes, even if they wanted solitude, a garrulous neighbour, Mrs Greville, from up the hill, stopped by unasked. Lewes suggested inviting Edith for two days, Marian said one would be enough: Edith's recent rudeness to Johnny bothered her more and more. Edith came for the day. Mrs Greville visited, leaving the newest novel by Mr James, *The Europeans*.

★ ★ ★

In October, the weather changed, the pains were back in force. Lewes was often out of bed at dawn, but now it was cold and dark. At the start of November, the rains came in earnest. The rain fell on the roof, the house was noisy with it. They sat in the drawing room. No fire was lit, water had come down the fireplace.

Unexpectedly, the doorbell chimed, and Brett announced Mrs Richard Greville and Mr Henry James. Marian and Lewes glanced at each other, in a moment they had read each other's faces.

They greeted the guests without enthusiasm, and resumed their seats. Talk was halting. They did not offer tea. This visit, thought Marian, is perhaps the most undesirable of my life.

The night before, the bleakest realisation had been dawning on both sides. Sitting in an armchair close by, Mr James was making efforts at small talk.

Marian glanced at him: his heavy-lidded eyes were half smiling, and, she could see, registering everything. Yet — perhaps not. Could he sense anything of what was going on, this fellow author? She had glimpsed, on the table next door, his volumes. James wore a complicated expression of tension knit with goodwill; as he had taken his seat, it seemed to her that he moved with particular deliberation, possibly, she speculated, the product of an intense self-consciousness. Then his manner had become more urbane.

Just as they were leaving, Lewes rushed to find *The Europeans*, catching James as he entered the carriage. 'Ah,' cried Lewes, 'take them away, please, away, away!' — and he thrust the volumes into James' hands.

It was good to return those books — they were going to London soon. Then he remembered he had enjoyed talking to Henry James, not so long ago, in April. It was the birthday Johnny had hosted for Lewes, in the Devonshire Club. So, things were like that, he thought; they changed without warning.

11

It's the beginning of June. In the soiled warm air of Bloomsbury people walk without their jackets and coats. Students camp out with their lunch in Russell Square Gardens; traffic stalls in Southampton Row, there are sirens, but tables are on the pavement, people linger outside pubs, cafes, restaurants. Talk drifts on the air as it gets dark.

At home the packing cases are emptied and gone. Light comes in at the western and southern windows, stronger now.

The main hall is ready for the conference, chairs in rows; the room next door has tables up for caterers. The conference will begin as Ann wants it to, with a sprightly attack on Eliot's conservative remarks about women. Posters have sprung up, with Eliot's face, and the words: *Saint or Hypocrite?* And below:

She recommended

SUBLIME RESIGNATION

Tickets sell out for the Saint or Hypocrite day. Marcus, the chair, waltzes Ann round his office at the news.

★ ★ ★

At the start of the year, I don't remember seeing Hans often at work. But now most days I glimpse him, as if chance is constantly placing him in my orbit, and the days have a lightness they didn't before. There he is, walking along the corridor, abstracted usually, then we spot each other, slow, stop, talk, talk just a bit more; go our separate ways. Sometimes we exchange a text. We know we will meet for our hour on Thursdays, preparing the class; and then there's the class itself. If I go into the canteen, my eyes — as if they have a will of their own — are scanning for that figure, with the slightly bowed shoulders as he reads alone, the light-coloured hair falling forward.

I print out my air ticket to Venice.

Three days before the QEC conference, Ann asks me to come round.

She is in the study upstairs, in the armchair, feeding Michael. Ben is standing near, begging for a story. 'A very, very little one,' Ben is saying wisely. 'This big,' — and he holds out his third finger and thumb.

She tells Ben to go to bed, and asks if I can wait — Michael is about to fall asleep.

I take the chair opposite her.

Michael is in a white towelling garment. I can just make out his cheeks going minutely in and out as he sucks. His eyes are beginning to close. On the floor are his Moses basket, and two soft animals, a floppy cow with a pink nose, and a caramel-coloured dog with black nose and ears. The lamp is shining its light on the walls. His sucking is getting slower.

My eyes are drawn to the cork board: pieces of paper with big words on them. *The day is short and the work is great* is printed out in bold, across three pieces of A4, above the capitals, *EDITH SIMCOX\TALMUD*. Below it is another large-printed sentence: *I say, Philo! how is it that most people's lives somehow don't seem to come to much?* And below that, in the same red scrawl — it looks like it's been done in a permanent marker — *EDITH SIMCOX*.

The baby is sleeping. Even from where I am, I can see under his small pink eyelids the REM moving pattern.

Ann is wearing a black dress, I notice, and black tights. She tells me she wants to give a paper on Simcox rather than Eliot at the conference, and maybe also at Venice.

'Simcox!'

'I wrote it in two days. It's the easiest thing I've done.'

'That's a very interesting idea,' I say, slowly.

I've also become rather obsessed with Simcox. I look at Ann, her complacent mouth, and suddenly feel tired. As usual she's jumped ahead of me.

'In many ways Simcox is *like* Eliot,' she is saying, looking at me intently. 'She's gifted, not on the same level, obviously, but gifted. They're both intellectual and ambitious, they both want to make the world a better place. Eliot wants to do it by changing the way people understand others; but Simcox faces what she sees right under her nose — squalor of London, these terrifying children not going to school.'

'Why have you got candles as well as lamps?'

'The power-cut. You must have had it too, three days ago. No?'

I did.

'Hans wanted to go and collect candles from you. He was sure you had a good supply. I said, don't bother her.'

'Right. Right. Why are you wearing black?'

'I feel like it. I get sick of white. And I think I'm at a kind of crossroads,' she adds, with an enigmatic look. 'My whole soul is a longing question — Simcox on Eliot! Isn't that great? Her passion.' She smiles, as if thinking about something else.

I ask if she's writing about Simcox and Eliot together.

'Odette and Odile,' she says, at once. 'Eliot so good, Simcox so desperate. Simcox the outsider. So ambitious, but she doesn't know what to do! She's like a twentieth-century ghost in the wrong century. Questioning everything — the family, society, capitalism, gender. She's the first female delegate at the Trades Union Congress. Did you know that?'

'Along with Emma Paterson,' I say, automatically. I'm thinking how conservative Eliot's going to look, put next to Simcox.

'Yes, questioning everything. She even asks, what would wives really say about sex with their husbands, if they could speak? In Victorian England, she's asking this! So free in her thinking.'

I drop my eyes. 'But it's an Eliot conference,' I say faintly, looking at my knees. 'Why Simcox?'

'Because I can relate to her,' says Ann bluntly.

She starts to speak, then closes her mouth.

'What?' I say.

After a moment, Ann says: 'She's struggling to *be* something, and I know what that's like. Simcox moves me. She's like all the women who never got their voices out there, voices in the dark. You may say this is a cliché but it's true. The only reason she was *found* was because she kept her obsessive diary, documenting every crevice of her feeling — and later, in 1951, someone listening to a Woman's Hour programme on Eliot realises she's got this book lying around her house, with references to Eliot in it, and sends it to the BBC — it's Simcox's diary! I mean, who can honestly relate to Eliot? Eliot was like a god.

'And to be honest,' Ann continues, depressively, like a balloon losing air, 'I think she half despised mothers.'

I look questioning.

'Oh, it's all in *Armgart*,' she sighs. 'You know, Eliot can't bear to be an ordinary person. The millionth woman in superfluous herds.'

There is the sound of the front door, footsteps. And then Hans is coming in, holding Ben's hand. Oh it's good to see him. 'I thought I heard voices,' he is saying.

I say I'm going, and hurriedly walk downstairs, out into the open air. It's raining.

12

While the Leweses were in Witley, the summer was very long for Edith. A single day she had seen them, on that one visit to Witley. Since then she had walked to the Priory in September, again in October. In November she received news of the impending return.

The time draws near — I cannot express the passion of glad longing that possesses me. There is only Sunday and Monday! I mean to be so good and make the time fly by translating furiously. I dream of all sorts of new ways of wooing her — if I could feel that she was learning to know and love me more! — after all I have never given myself a chance with her.

She would see them, she guessed, in about a week. Her old enthusiasm returned — she was planning a history of ancient property ownership, inspired by socialist theory.

The days went by, she was ringing the Priory bell at last. She entered, with a quick step. There! — there they were — but — and she stopped. In a terrible few seconds she registered the change. She saw Lewes' altered face, and Marian's expression, and felt the sadness of the room. The doctor came. She saw it all. She was moved. At the same time, rolling through her, was her own sickening, overwhelming disappointment. For months she had looked forward to this day.

Back in Douro Place she sat in her chair, then took out her diary. Each time she saw Marian, the visit remained in her mind, but as she wrote about it, she saw it better still. In her diary she was telling her story, and fusing her story with Marian's:

Monday came at last, but hardly the greeting I had dreamt of: the first thing I saw was Lewes stretched upon the sofa, and in concern for him I lost something of the sight of her. He was affectionate and when I said I wanted to kiss her feet he said he would let me do it as much as I liked — or — correcting himself — as much as she liked. He could enter into the desire though she couldn't. I did in spite of her protests lie down before the fire and for one short moment gave the passionate kisses that filled my eyes with tears; — and for the rest of the evening her feet avoided the footstool where I had found them then. She was unhappy about him, I cried all the way back — at the intense pain of her anxiety — which I was tempted to share. I was sorry for myself too: all one's gladness turned to pain.

***

Sir James Paget came, old friend and doctor. He examined Lewes, described the problem as a thickening of the mucous membrane. Marian asked if it would pass. 'The actual trouble will soon be allayed,' said Sir Paget. After he had gone Marian went over and over his words. Everything bewildered and frightened her now — the extent of George's pain, the impossible future. 'You must look after yourself,' he said to her. She could not reply. Paget came each day early. Lewes' bed had moved into a different room. Their lovely house — it was like a picture of a lovely house now — nothing more.

***

Edith kept calling. She could think about little else. Marian's life was the centre of hers, she felt.

Today I went in the morning and the answer was the same. In the afternoon I went again, trying to hope she would let me be with him in the night. I sent up a written line with the prayer. It came down I think unread in the servant's hand — she could not attend to anything. 'Mr Charles' would write to me! I could not expect anything else, and yet her intense excitement and distress — the servant said she could do nothing but cry and fret — make it cruelly unfit for her to be alone. God forgive me! I feel as if I would give my mother's life for his! There is nothing left but tears — and duty.

★ ★ ★

Marian sent a note to Johnny, asking him to come. His own mother was on her deathbed, but he appeared.

'Give my cigars to Willie,' said Lewes, holding out his hand to Johnny, from his bed; before discussing finance.

Edith came on November 30.

I reached the house about half past three, a private cab was driving up and down slowly before it, I waited till that was gone and then rang at the gate. Brett with a white face and dark eyes answered me: 'He is very ill —' then 'there are no hopes' — I stood stupefied, without word or sign, without feeling, and so turned away. It was as if something quite different from my fears had come.

I could not leave the place and walked up and down, and almost immediately a carriage like a doctor's drove up fast and two men got out. I hastened after them and they entered the gate: the other carriages followed and the two, with 4 sleek horses stood a few paces back. The coachmen talked and laughed, cabs and coal carts and men and women on foot passed by as I stood behind the carriages, watching the gate down the fog-bound road.

Then — in about 20 minutes, the 2 figures came in sight. I strode towards them and as they stood speaking together, I asked was there no hope. A tall man — probably Sir James Paget answered kindly: None: he is dying — dying quickly. Then again I could not speak, but the tears rushed up — shading my face with a hand I cried hard with this worst of griefs. She cannot bear it: there have been unendurable sorrows, but I do not see how any can equal hers — who can feel as she does, who could have so much to love? But whether she lives or dies — there is no comfort for her left on earth but this, to know that their love and life have not been in vain for others.

At five forty-five, on November 30, George Henry Lewes died.

Part Four

1

After George died, Marian stayed in her room for seven days. She didn't go to his funeral, she stayed within those four walls, on the bed or the floor or in a chair. But wherever she was in that room, whichever wall she faced, whether she was prone or upright, there was no relief to be had.

She couldn't eat, and for a day she couldn't cry; then tears came, as if a physical flap had opened: she heard her own noises, but the pain in her chest seemed only to grow, moving her into a new darkness. And then on again.

It was possible she was having a fit.

Charles and Brett were both holding her and moving her to the bed. Each on one side, they stayed with her until she was quiet.

On the fifth day, Marian allowed Brett to help change her clothes. Like a doll, a very old doll, thought Marian, she sat inert on the edge of the bed, as, with Brett's help, the dress she had worn for four days was removed. Across the room, rain was falling outside the window. After Brett left, the fact that she was in clean clothes didn't comfort her. She'd hoped it might. She began to weep.

Downstairs, Charles heard the cries and shook his head. Letters had been pouring in. He was dealing with them, answering and saying that Marian was unable to communicate but would do so at some point. Brett said, 'The lady's been again: Miss Simcox.'

'Again,' said Charles.

On December 6, Marian went for the first time down the stairs. She held tight to the banister. Step by step. Her legs were trembling. Crossing the hallway, peering around her like a stranger, in fear, at the door, walls, floor, all now without George, she entered George's office. His things, they were all here: the picture of the small girl in red, his books, his pen. She knelt in front of the bookcase, found, on the lowest shelf, two piles of manuscript. She took the larger pile — his handwriting cruelly dear and distinctive — to the desk. The first ten pages were notes from an asylum in Florence. Dimly, she registered surprise that he had made so many notes on that visit. Below that — yes — the unfinished manuscript, with crossings-out, additions in the margins. It was what he had been working on when he died, the last two parts of *Problems*.

She made herself read the first paragraph. It was an effort to try to let her mind receive a thought, an idea. She continued, pushing herself. The tightness in her chest continued too.

For the rest of December, from when she woke to when she slept, she sat in her room, one curtain gaping open to let in light on the desk, dragging her dishevelled mind to George's words, focusing as clearly as she could. This is what she would do for him, it was her act of love. She would finish his work. She read and corrected and amplified. She had an aching head, pains in her upper back and side. She pushed her mind to the matter. Increasingly, with practise, she could stay in the line of his thought. Yes, she had her capacity.

Parallel, too, was the sensation in her chest.

Snow was falling.

In early January, for the first time since his death, she stepped outside, into the garden. It was covered in white frost, in the pale sunshine. The grass crunched under her feet. She walked like an ill person, slowly, carefully. She blinked in the daylight. She was very thin, she realised. But she had now read through Lewes' manuscript twice.

She had written in her diary: *Here I and Sorrow sit*, from Shakespeare's *King John*.

She quoted Heine:

Einst ich wollte fast verzagen
Und ich dacht'ich trug es nie,
Und ich hab'es doch ertragen,
Aber frag'mich nur nicht wie.

At first I was almost in despair, and I thought I could never bear it, and yet I
have borne it — only do not ask me how.

And she copied out these lines from *King John*:

Kneeling before this ruin of sweet life,
And breathing to his breathless excellence
The incense of a vow, a holy vow,
Never to taste the pleasures of the world,
Never to be infected with delight,
Nor conversant with ease and idleness ...

She would keep working until she had his manuscript fit for publication.

Of the mountain of letters that had come, she had read none. She began
to read a select few. Two days after going outside, she wrote her first letter, to
Barbara.

Dearest Barbara,

I bless you for all your goodness to me, but I am a bruised creature, and shrink
even from the tenderest touch. As soon as I feel able to see anybody I will see you.

Your loving but half dead

Marian

The idea of seeing anyone was painful. Bessie Belloc, Johnny, Georgiana Burne-
Jones had all called, Edith incessantly, but she had refused to see them. She
would dedicate herself to *Problems of Life and Mind* until it was finished, as a

memorial to him; she was reading and re-reading Tennyson's *In Memoriam*, and writing out verses from it; no other poem expressed so fully what she felt.

2

A letter had come, from Dr Foster, a Cambridge physiologist — offering Marian help in finishing Lewes' book should she need it — that had given her a memorial idea. She could found a studentship in his name, enabling young scientists to get the kind of training that Lewes had lacked.

But now she had another source of bitterness: all her securities, which amounted to more than £30,000 — the money in her bank account, the shares, and the two houses, were in Lewes' name. She needed access and control of her money. That month she went through the exquisitely sad process of changing her name by deed-poll to Mary Ann Evans Lewes, with George dead.

Yet gradually her seclusion was being broken down. Matters demanded her attention: besides George's book, there was her own — *Theophrastus Such*, completed the previous summer, which had arrived in proof five days before George died. She needed to correct and return the proofs.

It was a bitter winter. When the snow began to melt, she wrote to Georgiana: *The world's winter is going, I hope, but my ever-lasting winter has set in. You know that, and will be patient with me.*

I can trust to your understanding of a sorrow that has broken my life, she wrote to John Blackwood.

★ ★ ★

Edith Simcox had gone to Lewes' grave in Highgate, and lain down behind the bushes to cry. She had cried for Marian's grief, and for the dead Lewes' understanding.

Charles Lewes said in his letter, that she would never be able to endure any caress — I knew that — and so was not specially hurt by his saying it — though I cried behind my veil all the way across the Park yesterday.

Outside the Priory:

I was looking vacantly eastward when I saw a tall reddish bearded man coming up, I stared without moving and when he had come within two or three paces he made some sign of recognition and I knew it was Johnny. I had thought we should never meet so again. It was an intensely painful moment; there is nothing much more pathetic than a look of set gravity on a habitually cheerful face. I was faintly pleased at the strange chance which brought us there together, because I thought, servant-like, Brett would tell her of the fact and I hoped it would please her to think of our meeting as friends.

Edith knew that Johnny's sombre face was not on account of Lewes, but his mother, who had died just recently, too.

★ ★ ★

Marian corresponded with publishers, and began to deal with financial matters alongside Charles and to realise all that Lewes had done for her, in a practical way. She had to monitor the payments still being made to Agnes Lewes in Kensington, and Bertie's widow Eliza in Natal, for instance; she had to make sure cheques were banked.

It was reassuring to remember Johnny, who had handled their money matters so efficiently for years. In emergency she could turn to him.

Brett, Charles, Sir Paget, and Dr Clarke all told her that she must start receiving visitors. A note arrived from Johnny, saying he looked forward to the end of her isolation. She must not stay isolated forever; it would be fatal for her. She wrote back:

Dearest Nephew,

Some time, if I live, I shall be able to see you — perhaps sooner than any one else. But not yet. Life seems to get harder instead of easier.

She read articles written by George, early in his career, and late, too. She spent a day writing out remembrances of herself and Lewes — the time in Jersey, the first months in Weimar and Berlin. *Wrote memories,* she jotted in her diary, *and lived with him all day. Read in his diary 1874 — Wrote verses to Polly — Wrote verses on Polly.*

It was agony to be reminded of him; she wept. She wanted to sleep, to empty herself and her mind.

Late February, Charles came upstairs to tell her that Johnny was below. She said she could not see him.

She took pen to paper:

Dearest Nephew,

When I said 'some time' I meant still a distant time. I want to live a little while that I may do certain things for his sake. So I take care of my diet, and try to keep up my strength, and I work as much as I can to save my mind from imbecility. But that is all at present. I can go through anything that is mere business. But what used to be a joy is joy no longer, and what is pain is easier because he has not to bear it.

Then, in a sudden mood of contrition:

I bless my friends for all their goodness to me. You will not mention to anyone that I wrote about seeing you. I know your thoughtful care.

Was that enough? She added:

But if you feel prompted to say anything, write it to me.

Always your affectionately and gratefully

M.E.L.

Barbara was also urging her to come out. *Dearest Barbara*, she replied,

Bless you for your loving thought. But for all reasons, bodily and mental, I am unable to move. I am entirely occupied with his manuscripts and must be on this spot among all the books. Then, I am in a very ailing condition of body ... have never yet been outside the gate. Even if I were otherwise able, I could not bear to go out of sight of the things he used and looked on. Bless you once more. If I could go away with anybody I could go away with <u>you</u>*.*

Your ever loving

Marian

3

The morning after she wrote to Barbara, she had the usual waking — a slow coming of consciousness, embalmed at first, and then all over again, as if it were new, the piercing fact of George being dead. She closed her eyes. It was hardly light. He would not be here, he would not be here to speak to. The door was opening, she kept her eyes shut, it would be Brett, and there were the usual sounds of the fireplace being swept, freshly stocked, and then lit, all the while the sounds of Brett's exertions and breathing.

Some time later, she was dressed — this morning, she had let Brett help her put on the warm woollen stockings, as her left hand seemed thick-fingered and stiff. Going down the staircase, the odour hit her nostrils again, a return of the noisome smell that had been there since the day the pipes froze. In the dining room she ate half a piece of toast, and part of a watery egg. Charles came in with the post, and pushed a letter her way. It was from Johnny, a reply to her weary letter of some days before. He had perfectly understood her desire to stay alone — was sorry for importuning her — and he referred to the strangeness of grief, the difficulty of imagining that anything could ever be joyful again. And in the same letter, he said that they talked of her every day — he and his sisters.

She had a flicker of relief at this. The idea of Johnny, Eleanor, Florence, Mary, Emily and Anna, all the Cross siblings, talking about her every day — did suddenly give her a tiny burst of something like pleasure. And at the back of her mind she was worried about the studentship and the finances. Quickly she wrote:

Dearest Nephew,

I do need your affection. Every sign of care for me from the beings I respect and love is a help to me. And I did not mean that I should prefer you or my dear nieces not to call. Only I fear it takes up valuable time to make this out of the way round.

In a week or two I think I shall want to see you. Sometimes even now I have a longing, but it is immediately counteracted by a fear. The perpetual mourner — the grief that can never be healed — is innocently enough felt to be wearisome by the rest of the world. And my sense of desolation increases. Each day seems a new beginning — a new acquaintance with grief.

I have written this just on receiving your kind answer. Love to them all at home.

Your affectionate Aunt

★ ★ ★

The next day, she ordered the carriage. She wanted to go out.

It was strange indeed, walking out of the house onto the drive, on her own. The horse shaking his head in that dipping frantic way, larger than she remembered. Strange having Robert open the door for her, hand her in to the carriage — and go inside, alone. It was as if she had never seen the interior before. Never noticed the wadding on the ceiling, the criss-cross pattern of lines. The door clicked shut. The carriage jolted but the ride became smoother and automatically she reached, just as she used to, for the fur rug, and put it over her lap. They went along the Kilburn Road, past the new houses with their squalid fronts, and then they were in country. The carriage stopped.

Peering out of the window, she saw grass, denuded trees, boughs black; she wrapped her shawl around her more tightly. Robert helped her out.

It was cold, but better than a month ago. She walked down the lane. How tremendously pointless it all was, this cold air, this lane, the trees. But she continued. After a while the motion of walking, and the sensation of air on her face, and the birds, although there weren't many, faintly roused her — it was like a dim waking, and she became a little glad that she had come out. Four hundred yards down the lane, she turned round. On the way home she began to feel queasy.

Turning in at the Priory. What a sight — the empty silent building, windows blank.

But she was able to eat more of her supper that night, and she read in Lewes' study, in his chair, the first article he had written on Goethe, the very beginning of his long interest.

★ ★ ★

Each day was difficult. The third part of George's manuscript was flummoxing her. But again she went out in the carriage, again she walked. She repeated the outing, walking farther. A letter arrived with a Nuneaton postmark. She tore it open quickly. It was a letter of condolence, but only from Isaac's wife, Sarah. There was no mention at all of Isaac. Marian wrote back, rather slowly, to Sarah, ending:

> *Give my love to my Brother and believe me always —*
> *Your affectionate Sister M.E. Lewes.*

The following day, a letter arrived from Natal. Just setting eyes on the postmark, she knew a ripple of disturbance. It was a bill of accounts from Bertie's widow, Eliza. A little panicked, she wrote to Johnny, saying, *If you happen to be at liberty tomorrow, or the following Friday, or tomorrow week, I hope I shall be well enough to see you. Let me know which day.*

4

Johnny came the next day. At the sight of him, as he entered the drawing room, Marian's stomach contracted: the sheer familiarity of his tall figure, his face, was associated so much with George. She could not rise to the occasion — couldn't smile, stand, speak. It was all dreadfully familiar — his jacket of navy wool — his regular, slightly immobile cast of features forming an instant, lacerating contrast with George's beloved features, George's animation.

Johnny was the first friend to visit her. She had only seen Brett and Charles and the doctors.

A minute later, and she realised he had seated himself, he had not come to kiss her hand, it was as if he understood. He was speaking to her now, asking how she was, saying how pleased he was to see her. She was noticing his face: he was thinner, his face more angular — gaunt. His air of restraint was not, she realised then, because of her; he had his own grief.

Anna Cross had died nine days after George.

As Brett set out the tea, they began to speak more easily. He told her of Eleanor's and Florence's grief, his brother's and Mary's. It was easier for Emily and Anna, because they were married.

'Whoever knew your mother, loved her,' said Marian. He nodded without speaking. His eyes were shining. He cleared his throat as he said, she was a wonderful mother — and then he looked away, towards the window.

Yes, you are grieving too, thought Marian.

'I am glad you said I could come,' he said then. 'We have been all of us worried about you. We thought you might die.'

His voice was level, he didn't meet her eyes as he said this.

'I haven't much to live for.'

She would finish Lewes' work as best as she could; then correct her own *Theophrastus Such* proofs. Aside from that —

'— this house!' she sighed.

She gestured to the room, which used on Sundays to be so crowded with people.

Johnny said he feared for her, subject to painful reminders all the time.

'Would it not be better for you to go away? My dear Aunt — so difficult to be beholding this,' — and his gesture echoed hers, towards the room.

She followed his gaze. Every part of the room had its association with George. She turned to Johnny, but nausea rose in her like gall. This man in George's seat.

'Ah,' she said, bleakly. No, it was too soon to see anyone. She was not fit.

'You have not been out. But when you do feel — feel that it would be beneficial, I hope you will come to see us. No one would be more welcome.'

His tone faintly pleased her — though her pleasure was as shallow as the surface indentations made by a duck-and-drake stone across the pond.

'Why do you not come and live at Weybridge?' he said suddenly. 'There is space. It would be a comfort to you.'

'At Weybridge,' she repeated, slowly.

She thought of that house she knew so well, where they had so often stayed. There would be associations, but it would be mercifully different to this, where every inch was saturated: there was the rug they chose for Wandsworth; there the little clay statue of a dog they found in Florence. She wondered if it would be rude now to mention her financial worries, the whole problem of managing it all, and Eliza's bill. She didn't trust Eliza's letters, which she considered conniving. 'That is a very kind thought,' she said, slowly.

'There is no one we would rather have stay with us.'

'That is very kind,' she repeated.

After Johnny left, she went upstairs to her room. She could do this. She could stay at Weybridge.

The doorbell went. She heard Charles coming up the stairs.

'Mr Spencer would like to see you,' said Charles. She heard hope in his tone. He was a kind boy.

'No thank you dear,' she said. 'I don't want to see him. I don't really,' she added, 'want to see anyone.'

The next morning, she wrote to Johnny:

A transient absence of mind yesterday made me speak as if it were possible for me to entertain your thoughtful, kind proposal that I should move to Weybridge for a short time. But I cannot leave this house for the next two months — if for no other reason, I should be chained here by the need of having all the books I want to refer to.

* * *

In March, Henry Sidgwick came to discuss the possible studentship; a few days later, so did Dr Foster. At a meeting it was decided: it would be called the George Henry Lewes Studentship in Physiology, and the Trustees were selected: Francis Balfour, W. T. T. Dyer, Pye Smith, Huxley, Sidgwick. After, she was aware that she had gone through the list of concerns efficiently, directed the conversation, discussed the issues with clarity, and written her cheque for £5,000. She had begun dressing as she used to, with a degree of care, though in black; she wore a black velvet ribbon in her hair, and her black widow's cap. She used a small amount of paste on her face, very discreetly, under her eyes, because the circles were so dark — one morning, in the glass, they seemed the colour of pitch.

She arranged to have supper with Charles.

'I want to ask your advice,' said Marian, as Brett ladled the pea soup into the bowls. She had corrected the proofs of her book, *Theophrastus Such*, and Blackwood wanted to publish it in May.

'Excellent!'

'Yes ... yes. But I am concerned,' went on Marian, suddenly contemplating her napkin, 'that I do not injure my influence. I finished the book before George died, as you know. But if it comes out ... so soon, in May — it might, ah, seem as if I wrote my book ... in my grieving state.'

'You are concerned you will seem callous.'

'Well,' smiled Marian thinly, trying to hide her displeasure at this bald description, 'I suppose you could put it that way.'

'You want people to understand the extent of your grief,' went on Charles, warmly. 'But if the book comes out in May, people will naturally assume you wrote it before the Pater died.'

'I will have to urge Blackwood to delay publication,' she said abruptly. 'You have more trust in the reaction of the public than I do. It is my view that people do not readily arrive at sympathetic interpretations of others. The pleasure to be had,' she said sardonically, 'lies elsewhere.'

'But Mutter!'

His face was wreathed with good-natured pity.

'I have seen you suffer ...' he began; and he swallowed. Marian had a strange idea that he might be about to cry. 'The love between you and the Pater was —'

He was unable to speak.

'Thank you Charles,' murmured Marian. She closed her eyes.

★ ★ ★

Maria Congreve was the first woman friend she saw after Lewes' death. 'My dear Marian,' Maria was murmuring, in her soft voice, as she held Marian close. 'So much for you to bear. I have been feeling for you — every day. But so many feel for you. I have heard concern expressed, as to whether you will be able to go on living, without him.'

It was comforting to hold Maria's hand, see again her intelligent eyes, under those arched brows, and those small attentions to dress that made Marian wish to look at Maria more — Maria's crocheted shawl, woven in soft-looking pale wool, which Marian had found herself stroking half unconsciously.

Georgiana came three days later, in her medieval-looking grey cloak, her simply parted hair braided at the back of her head. 'I would not have wished,' Georgiana whispered in Marian's ear, as they embraced, 'this separation on any two people who love each other. But most of all, you two.'

For the first time since George's death, she walked into the bedroom they had shared. She had asked Brett to clean it and put down fresh bedding. One by one, she put George's periodicals and books into the bookroom closet; stored his dusty microscope; removed his photographs and prints. She was back in their bedroom, alone. *Felt beaten with sadness,* she wrote in her diary.

And now, in the dining room, she drew out the boxes of letters, assiduously sorted by Charles. All those that evoked George particularly, or paid special tribute to him and to their life together, she put to one side.

Spencer came. They embraced, though Spencer rather quickly detached himself. It was Spencer who had introduced her to George all those years ago. Having sat down, Spencer hitched up his trousers and said: 'My dear Mrs Lewes, I have certain matters to discuss at the moment, which are really rather pressing: my autobiography.'

Marian listened to him. She could imagine George's jokes.

Shortly after that she had an unexpected visitor: Vivian Lewes, George's nephew, asking her for £100. Marian stared. For twenty-five years now she had been supporting Agnes Lewes and her family, and was continuing to do so. Yet this ruddy-faced young man, though he had requested the money with an apologetic smile, sat there with an air of simple confidence. Marian got up, walked around — what would George have done? She wrote a cheque for £50. 'Here, to start with,' she said helplessly, as she handed it to him.

The next day, a letter arrived from Vivyan, returning the cheque and apologising. Marian read it with relief. Going through the rest of the post, she recognised Bessie Belloc's handwriting; eagerly she opened it. After she read it, she put it down.

'An egg, Ma'am,' Brett was saying.

Marian said she wasn't hungry. Bessie, her old friend, had asked her to lend her £500. So this was the start. Upstairs in the bedroom, her headache mounted. She must calm down. She must face the fact that she was a woman on her own, she would be targeted with demands like this. She was a widow, and rich. This was the future.

She got up, called out over the banister: 'Charles — Charles!'

Her voice echoed in the hallway. There was only silence. 'He's gone out, Ma'am,' said Brett, appearing downstairs.

She went back into the bedroom, sat down, and had a shooting pain in her shoulder.

'Brett,' she called out over the banister, louder this time. 'Did Mr Charles say what time he would be back?'

Charles was out the whole day.

She wrote to Bessie then, describing her own confusion. When she read through what she had written, it sounded accusing. She had another spasm in her shoulder.

She took up another piece of paper. Who could she turn to?

Dearest N.,

I am in dreadful need of your counsel. Pray come to me when you can — morning, afternoon, or evening. I shall dismiss anyone else.

Your very much worried Aunt

5

Johnny arrived that evening.

She was in the drawing room, cold in spite of the fire, in a thunderous depression. She had been writing out a list of her dependants, including the relatives of Agnes Lewes, and the charitable donations she made.

Johnny walked in swiftly, sat down beside her. 'What is it?'

She heard full concern in his voice.

'Money,' she said, with a faint smile, yet she knew she was radiating sadness. She felt cold, her hands freezing yet damp.

'My dear Aunt,' he said, taking her hand. His hand was large, warm and dry. 'You must let me help you.'

She told him about Vivian and the cheque, and Bessie's request; tried to explain how exposed she felt. 'She is my great friend — it bothered me that she should ask me this just now.'

'I understand why it bothers you.'

He thought for a moment.

'She should not have asked you, certainly not now. Refuse her immediately. Write the letter tonight, and banish it from your mind.'

He had conviction. She took his advice. As he left, he said he would call tomorrow to make sure she was easy in her mind.

She slept a little better that night. She had written to Bessie and said no. And somehow it was no surprise when Johnny appeared before noon the next day.

'Last night,' said Marian, as they had tea in the drawing room, 'you helped me greatly. I was so distressed — and I want you to know that I feel better.'

'Are you eating?' he asked suddenly.

'Yes — yes.' It seemed an odd question, so personal, so practical. But she wasn't displeased. 'Not perhaps quite enough —'

'It is important. I meant to give this, by the way, to Brett —'

He took out a brown-paper package, small, about three inches square. 'Tea,' he said. 'From Ceylon. Held in some estimation, I'm told. There is an excellent little shop at the bottom of Cornhill. If you drink enough of this, you might be strong enough for visitors.'

'Thank you. Thank you! But what of you?' said Marian. 'How have you been faring?'

'Ah,' he sighed, and gloom returned to his face. 'With Mother gone, it has not been — marvellous. What can I say? I was very close to her, my life was very bound up with hers. I think I can safely say that I did everything for her.'

'I can believe it.'

'And with her death — I can say it now! — at first I couldn't even say those words. But with "her death" — there has been ...' He stopped. 'I have time on my hands.'

'Is that not a good thing?'

'I sink into gloom! But I've started reading Dante,' he said with a slightly self-deprecating laugh. He was a modest kind of man. 'I've never read the *Divine Comedy* before.'

'What a good idea ... what a good idea. I've also been reading for distraction. Homer.'

She paused to sip her tea. Then she said slowly, 'But Dante is an even better idea. In the original?'

'Good heavens, no! I have my translation with me all the time. It's here, in fact,' he said, patting his pocket; and he drew it out.

Longfellow's translation. Marian read a few lines, then put it down. Longfellow — what a choice. Still, the idea of reading Dante stirred her — Dante, who went to the heart of everything.

'I could read it with you,' she said suddenly.

Once the words were out, she half regretted them; she knew Johnny's obliging nature.

'Please do!' he said, at once.

She smiled sadly.

'My dear Nephew ... you are ... good-natured to a fault. Do not let me take advantage of you. You might, understandably, prefer to read it alone.'

She was looking at him in a pleading way. It was, in fact, a glance of the utmost seriousness. Almost, she wanted him to say no. She could not have said why.

'I would love nothing better,' he said, and his face had mysteriously cleared. 'When shall we start?'

6

The conference in London is a success, especially Ann's paper on Simcox; and then it's all over. The classes resume. Except that on Thursday I wait in my office for Hans to come, and he doesn't show.

I sit there. It's five past two, he's usually dead on time. Then it's two thirty, and he's still not here. He's clearly not coming. But there's no text from him either.

It's just a class, I say to myself. I must get on. I click on email, the emails multiply and replace, but after staring I grab my purse and head down to the canteen. I can't think why I want to go there, really, except that I want to leave my office. Just then there's a bleep from my phone. 'Ann broke her leg. Be in touch about class, H.'

In the corridor, the department secretary confirms it: Ann slipped down Staircase E, on the lower ground floor. She's at UCH hospital.

Marcus is in a frenzy about liability, as the stairs are in our department.

The secretary sends Ann a bunch of flowers, and a small posse go to visit her the next day.

I don't. In my flat, I attempt to understand myself like a forensic investigator. I peel an orange, digging my nails in — scrap by scrap, the peel comes away. I remember what I felt when Hans didn't come to my office. I separate the parts of the orange, segment by segment, put them out on the plate. I pick up the bangle that Ann left a good two months ago, contemplate twisting it out of shape, quickly put it down. The white walls of my flat, in the open afternoon light, look terrifically boring. I haven't put up pictures, I realise.

Later that day I collect Billy, but her scampering irritates me. Yes, cancel Venice, I think. Next day at work, I have a headache, speak sharply to the student who's late with her essay.

A text comes from Ann, asking me to visit her at the hospital.

Arriving in the lobby, I ring her to ask what she wants. A coffee, she says — flat white, please, not a cappuccino.

'Anything to eat?'

'No thanks.'

'You must need something.'

'I don't,' — crisply.

My eyes feel dusty; there's a smell of disinfectant. At the florist, I buy a miniature rose in a pot; as soon as I've paid for it, the pink looks sickly. In the loo, checking myself in the mirror, I catch, with a lightning shock, a saccharine, over-tender smile on my face. So this is what I am! Up on the fourth floor the corridor is warm, with a smell I recognise — enclosed yet clean, attractive yet faintly repellent. I press the button; I'm buzzed into the ward.

Ann is in a room on my left. 'Kate! Hi!' she says, when she sees me. The sight of her gives me a slight pain. I think I'm jealous. It's an awful feeling. Her leg is suspended in a pulley-contraption, cased in plaster, the outline smooth as snow. She wears a pale-blue hospital gown.

'I'm not bad,' she says, in answer to my question. Her face looks rested. 'Now Kate, I've emailed Venice to let them know what's happened. Because obviously I can't come.'

'What about crutches?'

'What, with those bridges?'

She is tired, almost glad to be in bed, she declares.

'But I am wondering,' she goes on, 'and this is a big ask, if you could possibly read my Simcox paper for me at Venice.'

'Me —'

The ironies are rising.

'Hans should read it.

'Why?'

'Why? He's your husband.'

She takes a breath, neatly laces her two hands together, looks intently at them. 'First, I want a woman to read it. Second, I haven't found Hans,' — she hesitates — 'he doesn't get my way of thinking. He's not supportive. He didn't want me to apply to Venice.'

'Didn't he?'

'He's very critical. He puts me down, that's the truth of it.'

The hospital lights are hot, my hands are damp. I have the tumbling sense that everything is becoming clear. I'm wondering, in fact, if I know Hans. He's married, but interested elsewhere. What does that tell me about him? How did it go bad between them? Perhaps with neglect of Ann. Perhaps he's undermined her for years.

He blocked Jo Devlin: spectacularly petty. I look round the hospital room: the walls are square with no give.

Ann, regarding me narrowly, picks up a cracker from her bedside tray; breaks it, piece by piece; drops the bits with an airy gesture back on the tray.

'I wasn't going to go,' I say.

'Please, Kate. I'm asking you.'

The pale-blue hospital gown is large on her slim shoulders. I'm torn. I say I'll think about it.

7

Two days after deciding to read together, Marian and Johnny Cross were seated in the dining room at the Priory, side by side, with a copy of Dante's *Commedia* in front of them on the table. Marian shifted in her seat, cleared her throat. She had a cold and she couldn't help making this noise. But with Johnny so close, she was embarrassed.

She had felt constricted, too, when he had arrived. She suggested they read in the dining room, even as, painfully, she was regretting her original suggestion they read together in the first place. It suddenly seemed odd. She was fond of Johnny, who had been a pleasant, even treasured part of their life for so long, but she had never, she realised, spent time alone in his company. She had straight away noticed the formal cut of his jacket, and the way his grey suit drained his face of colour. And as they went together to sit in the dining room, she had a moment of shamed awkwardness she didn't understand.

In the first hour, it wasn't clear how to proceed. Marian asked questions. It was soon evident Johnny understood nothing of the background to the poem, though he had a struggling grasp of the Italian.

Haltingly, woodenly, Johnny was reading:

> *Allor fu la paura un poco queta,*
> *che nel lago del cor m'era durata*
> *la notte ch'i' passai con tanta pietà.*

He turned to look at Marian, questioningly.

She said: 'Will you translate?'

Johnny nodded.

'So ... was the fear ... made ... soft — no, quiet, *che*, that —'

'Which,' put in Marian.

'which, *nel lago*, in the lake, *del cor. del cor.*'

Johnny stopped.

'Of the heart,' said Marian.

Johnny cleared his throat. 'Had lasted ... the night ... that I passed, *con tanta pietà.*' He turned to look at her. 'That I passed with — much pity.'

'*Pietà*,' said Marian, 'A beautiful word. And meaning, too'.

It was April, there was green outside the window: Easter time, the time of *pietà*. The small birch tree had its new leaves, but cold rain was falling.

Then Marian read aloud in her mellifluous voice the three lines that Johnny had said, but her tone rode with the rhythms. She began to feel easier as she did so.

'You say it well.'

'But you will get better,' she said gently, and she was pleased to be able to offer him kind words. 'So ... Then quieted a little was the fear, which in the lake-depths of my heart, had lasted throughout the night I passed so piteously.'

They were silent. Now Marian lost sight of all her earlier embarrassments with Johnny. She was feeling the weight of the words, her dark months without George. The lake-depths of her heart. Johnny was looking straight ahead of him, with that slightly wooden expression. She understood. He was self-conscious. And he probably found it strange to be sitting near her, in this house that was now so queerly empty, without George's vivacious presence.

But she sensed that the words moved him also, his eyes were dark with feeling.

He said: 'I fear the relevance of these words for you.'

'It does feel relevant,' she said, simply.

Neither spoke.

'Perhaps —' began Marian.

'You have had enough,' said Johnny, quickly.

She said she thought she had. He rose, his chair scraping noisily, at which he grimaced.

'I hope we can try again. I will be a better student —'

'You will be. You are,' she added. It suddenly seemed important that they did not immediately abandon what they had begun, and when he suggested returning in two days she agreed.

This will occupy me, at least, she said to herself, once he had gone.

When he returned, three days later, she had again the feeling that an over-large man was coming strangely close, in this dining room. As they turned the pages of the book, she noted his large hands, and the clean, groomed fingernails. She remembered George's dark-yellow cigar-stained and bitten fingers, his hopeless habit of biting his fingernails. She half smiled; it was painful to think of this. She must marshall her will, help them both.

'I will read,' said Marian. Her sadness was growing; she fought it. She would do what she could to make this interesting. She read, with the gentle, easy authority of the teacher:

Tant'è amara, che poco è più morte;
ma per trattar del ben ch'i' vi trovai,
dirò de l'altre cose ch'i' v'ho scorte.
Io non so ben ridir com' i' v'intrai.

'Now,' she went on, 'do you want to try?'

'Do I dare!' sighed Johnny, with a slight smile. The smile pleased Marian. He was not bored, he was not disgusted by being so close to her older, lined face, he did not resent her atmosphere of nearly undiluted sadness. 'Do not expect, Aunt, that I can do like you.'

'I do not expect that.'

He looked hard at the Italian verse in front of him. He was biting his lip. Then: 'It is ... so — bitter, but to treat of the good that I found — for you — I will speak of things ... I have learned for you.'

'Imperfect, I'm afraid,' he muttered.

'It isn't quite right,' said Marian. How glad she was to be able to put her mind to this. Now it was she who couldn't help, even from her sadness, giving a faint smile. 'I think you are confused about the word *vi*, and the V apostrophe. Without wishing to be pedantic,' she went on, in a tactful, light voice, 'the word *vi* can be a pronoun "to you", but in this context it is the adverb "there". He is talking about the good he found there, and what else he discovered there.'

As he left, Johnny stammered his thanks, and said something about having something to live for. It was half a joke, but it felt real, too.

Johnny began coming regularly. To teach, Marian found, was helpfully distracting. To help ease another's sorrow — even to be aware of another's sorrow — was good. She found the emptiness of her days slightly leavened by this regular appointment; in its small way, it was something to look forward to.

8

Some weeks later, Marian drove to Highgate Cemetery, dismounted, walked to the Dissenter's Area. A granite slab had been laid: *George Henry Lewes, Born 18th April 1817, Died 30th November 1878.* Scrubby grass had begun to grow around it, weeds were green and fresh and proliferating. Marian placed her copy of *The Times* on the ground, knelt on it, then began to uproot the weeds, pulling gently so that they would not snap, but would bring up their thin trailing roots. The roots reminded her of George's tadpoles, when he had started training himself to become a biologist. Once she had pulled them up, she laid her own posies of violets and pansies on the grave.

Pitifully small. Why had she not brought larger flowers? How neglected it looked, the stone garishly new, the untended lumpy grassy earth. Next day, she took the carriage to Covent Garden market. Robert warned her to be careful. The air was full of dust and bits of straw, the street was stinking, strewn with rotting vegetables.

'Did you buy the whole shop, Ma'am?' asked Robert, when Marian came back, carrying a big basket of flowers; behind her walked a boy, arms wide with three great bouquets of roses. Robert drove her back to the cemetery, the gardener helped lay out the flowers. When she left, his grave was now the most flowery part of the cemetery, a small oblong of clustering pale roses.

Back home she went to bed. Her forehead was damp, Brett said she had a fever.

It was beyond comprehension.

For weeks now she had been reading Dante with Johnny. The last time had been three days ago. But how could she describe it? A day of such extremes. Only that morning she had read three letters from George from the month just before they left for Weimar, in their first year together. She was full of George then. When Brett announced that Mr Cross was here, in the dining room, she experienced a sudden lurch of dislike, almost repulsion, at the younger man waiting for her there, with the Dante on the table — and a stab of self-loathing, also. He had looked at her and then begun reading, with a high colour. In that second, she knew he had detected her repulsion.

But after she had sat down, she noted the flicker in his cheek she had seen before, a tiny spasmodic muscle, and she was swept by pity for him. It would offend him if they stopped this reading altogether. They read the twelfth canto, and it was beautiful to enter the regions of the poem, away from herself, and to have Johnny's attention so fastened on her explanations, and to see him lighten as he listened.

'*Cotanto maestro,*' murmured Johnny, after she had talked of Dante's own life.

'Flatterer.'

'Not at all. I mean it. It is a great pleasure for me ... to learn like this.'

He had turned to face her. His smile was gone; he seemed to be probing her own expression, with a pleading look, too.

She dropped her eyes, but she too was smiling, in the strange, sudden joy she was feeling.

'I hope we will meet soon,' she said formally, when he went.

'We will.'

And how was it that, for an hour that day, she felt as if, in a small way, she had company? She liked his large, quiet masculine presence, even his well-cut City clothes pleased her in a way she didn't understand.

She had an image of her insides: as if a tiny being, perhaps the size of Tom Thumb, had been placed there. A good little seed had been planted. And some absolutely diabolical oppression lifted.

It felt like salvation.

She wrote to Blackwood that day: *I am much stronger than I was, and am again finding interest in this wonderful life of ours.*

And that afternoon, looking into the garden, she was glad they hadn't chopped down the ash tree as planned. Then she thought of going to Witley later this month. The thought of Witley, the slanting meadows — open under the sky — was suddenly attractive. In the drawing room, she found Charles.

'My dear Charles, you have done so much for me,' she said, in a voice of sudden, moved happiness. 'I don't know how I can thank you.'

Yes, she would go soon to Witley.

Since then, Johnny had come twice more. And she, sitting beside this much less educated man, found it pleasurable to try to make what she saw and experienced in the poem available to him. In so doing, she experienced the poem more richly than ever before. Periodically, she drew on her extensive knowledge of the political and theological background. Johnny would get up, at times, and walk around, talking about what he understood and saw, and how he was beginning to appreciate the Italian sounds (he did his best to imitate her more idiomatic rendering); she watched his reactions smiling. 'You are a good student,' she said to him then. He had crossed the dining room in a purposeful motion that had surprised her, to kiss her hand. She caught her breath.

'You will come quite soon,' she said, with a faint smile, as he was leaving.

'I will.'

Lying in her bed, she was flooded with terror. In her diary, she wrote the word *Crisis.*

9

By the time she left for the countryside, for Witley, in late May, she had had several days in bed with renal pain; Dr Paget had come and prescribed her a pint of champagne a day. 'A whole pint,' he had repeated severely.

'I will,' she replied, meekly.

Days earlier, Blackwood had published *Theophrastus Such*, with a Notice inserted inside: *The Manuscript of this Work was put into our hands towards the close of last year, but the publication has been delayed owing to the domestic affliction of the Author.*

Arriving at Witley, the cab took her down the familiar road from the station. When they reached the Heights, she half shut her eyes. The clipped large yew bush on the right; the house, wide, gabled, red brick, hanging tiles, like small flags, below the roof. All the same as it was.

She tipped the driver, asked him to leave the bags in the porch; walked round to the back terrace overlooking not just the gardens below but the whole valley: meadows, fields, small trees.

When they had first seen it, it was Johnny who had taken her and George round. He'd shown them the rooms, the grounds, talked of Tennyson living just near. It had been a day like this, in golden November. Except that today the earth was at the opposite end of its circuit — it was May and the world was unfolding and opening. Looking across the fields she could hear a faint humming in the misty light everywhere. The air was soft and had the soapy, intoxicating atmosphere of late spring. She could hear the servants inside: what sounded like boxes being dragged — a bang, a clamorous noise like cutlery being dropped, a cry. They had come down before her. Now Brett was singing the song she sang when she thought no one else was listening.

Marian walked down to the lime tree, to the bench where she'd often sat with George. As she sat, she could remember George, putting his shoulders back, resting his forearms on the low back edge of the bench, in an attitude of the greatest freedom and relaxation. How he enjoyed things, relished things! He would have liked that cloudless sky — would have been funny, possibly sorrowful, reflective, all in the same ten minutes. Only weeks ago, she had finished re-reading his biography of Goethe — the words full of his spiced, lively mind. She closed her eyes. Her mind was sliding.

The sun was slowly moving round the sky as she sat. Her eyes were still shut. She could hear the birds, a sound in the distance she couldn't identify, a shout from the house, a smaller cry, servants. She was weeping.

Her mood had tipped down, the tightness in her chest, the old ache. Where could she go, with this grief, this love for George? There was no George to give it to.

Twenty minutes later her tears had gone. She was dry and empty. She stayed sitting until the air began to cool, and the sun was orange on the horizon. The birds were singing their twilight song, madly.

At supper, the trout tasted wrong: bland yet unpleasant. She ate some of it to please Mrs Dowling, but it was an effort.

The lamp had been lit in her bedroom. Coming in, she noticed a worn, flat, very familiar box, which she at once raised to her nose: George's cigar case.

Sleep was coming when she heard a sound. It was at the window, a bird tapping. But how strange: something was happening to her body. Heat was stealing over her, beginning at her feet, moving up her legs, her stomach, up to her face. She was hot, sweating. The next second, cold was passing above as if spread by a giant hand moving back and forth over her. The cold air so chilly. She sat up. The whole room was freezing. A pressure on her shoulder, like a touch, a hand, and then a sound in her ear, quite distinct: Polly, it's me. As if by magic, she smelled the aromatic, crackling burning smell of cigar — as strong as autumn leaves.

She was looking round the room: by the wardrobe a new density. She lit the lamp. Nobody. She swung her head round, could still feel the pressure on her shoulder.

'George?' she said then. 'George?'

She took her shawl, sat in the chair. She waited an hour, a second hour. She woke in her chair.

Three days later, she felt him again in her room. It was nearly June. In her diary, she wrote: *His presence came again.*

★ ★ ★

Johnny visited. Brett placed a jug of homemade lemonade on the cloth-lined table on the terrace.

'Is it all as you expected it to be?' asked Johnny.

'All?'

'The house — The Heights,' said Johnny, looking confused, and colouring.

'Very much. I had low expectations, as you might imagine. I thought that I might find it intolerable.'

He bowed his head respectfully, took out his cigarette box, extracted a cigarette, tapped it absently on his leg. 'Florence and Eleanor are hoping they might see you soon. Have you had — company?'

'Charles was here for three days. We went for a drive.'

'You enjoyed yourself, I hope, Aunt?'

'In a manner of speaking.'

'Would you — like to walk?'

They went down the wide shallow steps beside the sloping lawn, down past the small willow and pond, and then there was a gate, and they were in the lane, leafy and shaded, pooling dark green and dappled with moving dots of light, bordered by high grass and cow-parsley pressing up on every side, and bushes of May, sour-smelling in the earthy air of the lane.

'Do you recall the way?' asked Marian, as they rounded the bend, and the shadowing trees gave way to the open sky, the view of low hills.

'I do.'

They continued in some silence, until they came to the stile.

'Please,' said Johnny, promptly opening it for her. She went through.

He caught up with her. 'I hope we will meet, now you are so close to Weybridge.'

'What is the distance?'

'Fifteen miles. Negligible.'

'I would say it is a considerable distance.'

They were both silent as they returned to the house.

Two days later, to her surprise, she heard the sound of wheels and horses, and saw, from the upstairs window, the tall form of Johnny bending forward as he dismounted. As she signed the forms he'd brought — acceptance forms for her investments — she thought to herself, it would be better if he went.

'I was hoping,' he remarked, 'that we might be able to read Dante. That you might be — unoccupied — this afternoon.'

His mood looked gloomy — mouth truculent.

Marian asked Brett for tea, adding, 'and some of Mrs Dowling's biscuits.'

After Brett went, Johnny said, 'What are Mrs Dowling's biscuits?'

The simple solemnity and darkness of his manner, made her slightly smile.

'They are made, I believe, of almond and sugar and butter.'

'Ah.'

Marian asked after Eleanor and Florence.

'Florence has had a cold; Eleanor is quite well.'

But the silence was so oppressive that Johnny finally got up and walked around, stopping at the piano. He ran his fingers over the lid. 'The piano is so well placed here — just in the light of the window. I assume it does not receive direct sun? You would not want it to.'

'It does not.'

After a moment he said, 'Will you play?'

Marian hesitated.

'Why don't you try? You are, after all, alive.'

Marian looked up — the remark was practically impertinent. But Johnny looked only grave, and she sat at the familiar seat, lifted the lid. She hadn't played since George had died, and now the dense smell of the piano was suddenly released: woody, resinous. She played Schumann, the last movement of the *Fantasie in C*, with its slow rising arpeggios, its dreamlike rising currents. Just to feel the smooth cool keys under her fingers again, and to fill the room with sound, felt bewitching. All the time Johnny was watching her, leaning on the piano, three feet away.

★ ★ ★

He was back three days later.

It was a fine day; they positioned themselves on the terrace table, but the breeze would nick the pages, making them flap violently, as if in a slick of sea-wind. Marian, roving the fields with her eyes, noticed the summer house.

'If it is swept,' she said, 'we might do well to try there. It is a pity to be in the house.'

A solitary octagonal affair, with a timber and glass roof, long windows all round, down on the second lower lawn, close to the great oak tree, but exposed to the sun. The summer house had flaking, white-painted dried wood sidings. The room smelled strongly — of being closed up, sun-saturated yet warm, as if damp had recently dried out. It was a queer pungent smell, but not unpleasant. There was a table and four chairs. The top windows were hung with muslin to filter the light.

Johnny began reading the eleventh canto of the *Inferno*. Marian regarded his thick-lashed eyes, the brutish handsome whole of him subordinated to the single mental effort — of reading and enunciating the Italian correctly.

'How much,' said Johnny abruptly, putting the book down, 'does Dante pass judgement on those sinners — those very ordinary sinners?'

'A good question,' admitted Marian, flashing him a glance of surprise. 'To my mind, he finds the perfect balance in Canto V. The famous one. Between judgement and compassion — I'm sure you remember,' — she was already flicking the pages, until she reached the story of the adulterous couple, Paulo and Francesca, who were spotted by Dante gliding so lightly on the winds in hell.

'Tell me more,' said Johnny, with a faint smile. She smiled, too. She was always explaining to him how events in the poem related to Dante's life. In life, the adulterous woman was Francesca, married to the crippled son of the lord of Rimini. She became the lover of the son's brother, the gallant captain Paulo.

'Eternal suffering, for falling in love!' said Marian. 'But Dante feels for them at the same time.'

Francesca and Paulo were innocent friends reading Lancelot alone, and while they were reading, they had no suspicion that anything was going to happen between them; even though their eyes kept meeting, and they kept blushing. But one particular event mastered them.

Marian herself was blushing now. She was not sure she wanted to go on.

'Continue,' said Johnny.

She hesitated, then, in slow Italian:

> *Quando leggemmo il disïato riso*
> *esser basciato da cotanto amante*

— and she tailed away.

'Translate, please,' Johnny said. The way he was looking at her made her colour rise further.

Her heart was making great beats inside her, her insides were like jelly. She spoke slowly, the trembling inside herself did not stop. 'When we read, that the smile — the longed-for smile — was kissed by the great lover —'

> *questi, che mai da me non fia diviso*
> *la bocca mi baciò tutto tremante*

She paused.

'He who — never shall be parted from me, all trembling — kissed my mouth.'

A bird sounded outside; the light in the white-clothed summer house was milk-coloured.

Marian continued:

quel giorno più non vi leggemmo avante.

'That day,' she added, scarcely audibly, 'we read no further.'

'What do you think?' said Johnny.

'What do I think?' she replied, mechanically, her limbs still watery and strange. 'There is judgement, you see. For putting reason aside. They are carried by desire, like the wind. That's why they glide so lightly on the wind.'

She had looked down at her hands — she did not dare look up. When she did, Johnny was moving his chair towards her, his arms were reaching for her, and he was leaning forward to kiss her. They kissed, fully, mouth on mouth.

10

While she was at Witley, she was ill, then she was well. She would grieve for George one moment, but in a tipping second she might be feeling the air of a June summer day, looking over the fields at the elms with their pools of shadow: aware that Johnny would be here this day or the next or at worst the next. Weybridge was only fifteen miles away.

In the milky light of the summer house, warm on a sunny day, even after the sky had become cloudy, Marian and Johnny read more of the *Divine Comedy*, Marian speaking the words aloud in her soft, musical voice. In the evenings, they drank champagne.

When she was ill she took to her bed, and when she was better she made intermittent resolutions. She wrote a note to Johnny saying she needed solitude for the next week; but the same day, when Mrs Dowling asked her about groceries, she hesitated. Because now her mind, like some rogue creature with a will of its own, was bent on calculations, such as how many soles and oysters to order for Johnny's forthcoming visit, these being foods he liked. She would name various items to the cook, and then say she was expecting Mr Charles and probably Mr Cross on Thursday. Was she? She had to admit she was.

Charles was helpful as ever, dealing with the river of post that came to the Priory at Witley, and bringing down to Witley the post that he thought she might like to see.

'I'm awfully sorry,' said Charles on his next visit, his whole face distorted, 'the holiday will be for at least two weeks.'

He was referring to his family vacation.

'My dear Charles,' she said, confidently, 'any business at the bank or with Mr Warren, Mr Cross will easily attend to, and he will order anything for me from town.'

She wrote to Georgiana: *No one is permanently here except my servants, but Sir James Paget has been down to see me, I have a very comfortable country practitioner to watch over me from day to day, and there is a devoted friend who is backwards and forwards continually to see that I lack nothing.*

And when Barbara had come, early in the month, she had exclaimed, 'Ah, Marian, too thin!', tugging at Marian's clothes; but then she had stepped close, gazing at her face like a doctor performing a forensic examination. 'My dear Marian — you look much better than I expected!'

'I surprise myself,' admitted Marian. 'The world is so intensely interesting. So much to live for —!'

The words had come out, as almost a cry. Barbara had hugged her — uncorseted as ever. After she had gone, Marian thought, yes, the world was interesting. Life was interesting. Emotions were interesting. In fact they were impossible. How was it that only months after George's death, after twenty-five years of being with him, she had found herself enjoying the company of this man twenty years younger, their Nephew; how was it possible that a romantic intimacy had sprung up between herself and Johnny?

Hard to describe. His face animated as soon as he saw her, and her mood lifted too. He would sit close; he wanted to find out how her day had been. Even his moments of uncertainty — he had a habit of putting his hand in front of his mouth if he was not sure of what he was saying — endeared him to her.

He seemed to want to look at her for pleasure.

Her!

She looked in the mirror.

It was not good.

Her face was lined: there were lines on her forehead, around her mouth. The size of her head — she had no illusions about it, it was large. But his attention, so fastened on her, was life-kindling. He waited for each word she said — as if she were dropping jewels on the air. He bought her lavender, eau de cologne, strawberries, poppies he had picked himself. When they were in the same room, she could feel that he was riveted to her, even with others in the room. They had, for several weeks now, taken it for granted that his visits were for the purpose of being together, rather than financial consultation or business of some sort.

In August, in the milky light of the summer house, he said he wanted to marry her.

In her diary Marian wrote: *Decisive conversation.* For some weeks after that she referred to him not as Johnny, but as Mr Cross.

11

At the end of September Marian received a letter from Barbara. Barbara wanted to come and see her, to ask her advice about one of her protégées, Hertha Marks. Barbara arrived on a warm September day, and everything about her, the vigorous way in which she flung her arms around Marian, and then insisted on carrying her own bag, made Marian feel that Barbara carried life with her, in a healthy way, in contrast to herself. Barbara's cheeks were ruddy and sunburnt and freckled from painting outside.

On their first walk, Barbara explained in more detail about Hertha. Hertha's sister had had a nervous breakdown, Hertha wanted to give up her studies to go and nurse her.

'But my dear Barbara,' said Marian, 'she wishes to be a — curative — presence to her sister.'

'It is the kind of self-sacrifice I loathe.'

'To do what is right ... is not always easy,' said Marian.

'*You* do what is right —!' said Barbara, in her usual easy way.

Marian half-shuddered, as they walked through a part of the lane that was in shade from overhanging trees. 'No,' said Marian, aware that she was blushing. 'The one who always did what was right, and without calling attention to it, was George. He brought me always to my better self. He had the surest instinct.' With tears starting to her eyes, she went on: 'Barbara, you knew him so well! He encouraged me —'

'He did a great deal for you,' admitted Barbara, as they began walking back to the house.

'My whole day is taken up with letter-writing now. He did it all —'

'So you could do your work.'

'Exactly,' — a tremulous smile.

'He was a wife, really,' said Barbara, thoughtfully.

' — No-o-o!'

'No?'

Marian tried to smile. Where was her strength? Barbara meant no harm. She must hold it in perspective —

grief was gone. Starlings rising in a sudden cloud, with their massing cries, up, up, and into the lime tree, the peculiar unity of movement.

'How did you find this wonderful house?' asked Barbara. 'It has everything one could wish for.'

'Mr Cross.'

'Mr Cross. Johnny.'

'As you say,' said Marian, flicking a fly off her sleeve. 'He'd been looking for several years. It had the advantage of being close to where he lives. In Weybridge.'

'And why is that an advantage?'

'Why! Because we — I — am a close friend of the entire household; and Mr Cross manages my financial affairs.'

Barbara looked slowly up. 'My dear Marian, you must forgive me my questioning. I sometimes think my memory suffered.'

Marian took Barbara's hand. She kept forgetting about Barbara's stroke.

Inside, in the east-facing drawing room, they were served tea and pie by Brett. Barbara lit the fire, there was a quick blaze, the room began to be filled with ruddy light, Barbara exclaiming how delicious the pie was. And everything that Barbara did conveyed health to Marian, and seemed indirectly to point to her as someone caught in her own sadness.

Over tea, Barbara said, 'Now, tell me about The World. How is Mr Spencer?'

Marian couldn't help smiling. Barbara, who hadn't an ill-natured bone in her body, always enjoyed hearing about Spencer. Marian said he was as self-absorbed as ever. He, who once said that biography was the most stupid use of a person's brain, was now embarked on a giant autobiography! 'No other subject, I believe, will compel the same level of interest,' remarked Marian, her eyelids lowering.

They laughed.

'Of course, the person people will want to write about is *you*.'

'I hope you are wrong. All one's private concerns subjected to the cold, hard curiosity — the eye of a stranger ... to whom one's struggles, deepest yearnings — are nothing. No — no.'

As Marian spoke, an enormous dark melancholy was descending softly and taking whole possession of her.

'I understand your feelings. Why should you be inspected, poked at, *torn apart*, and held up for judgement!'

Marian smiled thinly. That terrible phrase — poked at, torn apart — she changed the subject. The fire was snapping and burning strongly.

★ ★ ★

When Brett came to brush her hair early evening before supper, Marian was impatient, saying sharply, it's enough — it's fine — so that Brett stopped, helped her instead into her black silk dress. Brett said, 'It's guests you are having tonight, ma'am.'

'Yes Brett, Miss Cross and her brother are coming to dine.'

Marian embraced Eleanor Cross, not wishing to look at Johnny, but she was aware of his taller presence behind, lifting her head she caught his eyes, enough to see that their expression was open and directed at her. They sat down with drinks, Barbara talking about Girton College, saying, 'I am in a dilemma.'

'Please tell us, Madame Bodichon,' said Johnny respectfully. Marian kept glancing at him; he was sitting forward towards Barbara, as if nothing else in the world interested him.

I can't believe he is really so intrigued, Marian was thinking. But he's certainly very expert at presenting that kind of façade. And she found herself disapproving of Johnny, condemning him as a cunning social performer.

Barbara talked about Hertha Marks. Her real name was Sarah, she was the daughter of a Jewish refugee from Poland. '*Maestro* here,' said Barbara, indicating Marian, 'has been a kind support to Hertha, and found her, I hope, an aid when writing *Deronda*.'

'True,' said Marian, and she listened while Barbara explained about Hertha wanting to give up her studies to nurse her sister, even though Barbara was prepared to *pay someone else* to nurse the sister.

'There is surely no question,' said Johnny, warmly. 'If you're willing to *do that* — why shouldn't Miss Marks continue her studies?'

'I agree with you!' said Barbara.

For some reason, both Barbara's remark and the glad glance she flashed at Johnny, and Johnny's own remark, so certain, acted on Marian like an irritant. 'It seems to me, Mr Cross, that you are disposing of this sister's needs in a cavalier way.'

'But as I understand it, Miss Marks' education has been struggled for —'

'But you can't just *cut out* this segment of the larger reality, bending life to fit your view,' said Marian, with a sinking sense that she had somehow spoken with unnecessary harshness.

Brett announced supper.

* * *

The guests had gone, Barbara lay stretched full length on the sofa opposite the fire, looking up to the ceiling, one arm dangling down. For a minute or two, no one spoke. Then Barbara lifted herself onto an elbow, to look at Marian.

'Isn't Mr Cross a close friend? I recall Mr Lewes being intensely fond of him. I had the impression tonight that you actively disliked him.'

'He's very ignorant,' said Marian, aware of her own almost sly, mysterious half-smile.

'Why should you mind *that*? I have never seen you so cold. Has he lost you money?'

'He lost his mother,' murmured Marian, and her own view of the room, in the firelight, began to slide, everything condensing, as if between the squeezing handles of an organ grinder. Compressed, elongated, now spreading wide again.

'Did he lose you money? He's a fine talker. I liked what he said about Tennyson.'

'He has his favourite poems.'

A small, dry, unpleasant smile began to play about Marian's mouth.

'If I talk about Kant, he thinks I am saying *cant* — the bibles, both bibles, were written originally in *Latin* ...' Marian rolled her eyes.

But a moment later, her tone changed. 'My dear Barbara, when one is grieving, everyone is a disenchantment. Myself,' she said, with a sudden curious smile, 'most of all.'

12

Marian had an impression of sliding shifts, of awarenesses that were vague and then piercing. When marriage had been raised by Johnny, a pleasant dream had been interrupted. The sense of interruption didn't go, either — it morphed into something much, much larger, like an indescribably frightening plant that was growing in front of her.

The next morning she was woken by Brett's knocking — Brett had heard cries, apparently. Staring at Brett, all Marian could think of was her dream. She had been walking down a street like a river, Johnny at her side; strangers applauding, then Benjamin Jowett — Master of Balliol and translator of Thucydides — had drawn up close. She was too near for comfort, seeing all of him: receding hair, hair tufting fluffily at the sides; colour in his cheeks, stray broken vessels; his usual wise, penetrative, sympathetic look; tears of laughter on his cheeks.

Through the morning and the day, the thoughts pursued her. What had she been doing? — what had she been doing with Johnny, 'Nephew', stand-in son, this banker twenty years her junior? She, George's widow, known everywhere for her moral vision, and her love for him — that once despised, illegal social atrocity, which had then, like a broken bird, been mended and become beautiful in the eyes of others, as the best example of love.

She had seen again and again the look on friends' faces when they visited. It was pity, but with a kind of reverence. *Love has happened*, their eyes seemed to say, we are thankful to have seen it in you and Mr Lewes. We feel for you, but we honour you.

Opening her folder of letters upstairs, she recognised Turgenev's handwriting. *I don't dare to trouble the very deep grief you must feel ... May you find in your own great mind the necessary fortitude to sustain such a loss! All your friends, all learned Europe mourn with you.*

All learned Europe mourn with you.

She put it down, picked up others. Everyone talked of the dreariness and isolation she had to face. Yet ... she had found a way to live.

The two realities didn't belong together. She loved and grieved for George; she also loved this man. There was no other way to think about it. And yet, did she quite believe her own account of things?

She was ill again. From her sick bed she could see the splendid dark-yellow lilies Johnny had brought, on the table in front of the window. They spread a drifting, thick sweet smell. Lying on the bed, the lilies, in their stately, undulating beauty, blocked the view; she could see nothing beyond those dark yellow petals, with their serpentine outline. She asked Brett to throw them out. Brett protested they were still good. 'Please discard them.' Those flowers with their diabolical yellow stamens, that stained where they touched.

* * *

Barbara and Marian took the carriage to Thursley. Rain had made the road more uneven than usual, but the day was sunny with a low breeze. Barbara was talking again about Hertha. By the time they reached the churchyard, Marian was giving Barbara her verdict.

'She must do what is right,' said Marian, as they walked past the railing, behind which were the mossy tilting gravestones, and she was gripping Barbara's arm. To herself, she said, if I go ahead, my legacy will be nothing. They were entering the shadowed interior of the church, with its dense cold and smell of incense. Through the gloom — there were only two windows at the end of the aisle — they could see the massive black timber beams, and Marian led Barbara to the slender timber-framed bell-tower, rising out of the centre of the nave floor. They walked up and down, Marian feeling the smoothness of the thick great oak arches with her hand. Emerging into the light, she was suddenly aware of the warm air on her face. '*Non fiere li occhi suoi lo dolce lume?*' she murmured, smiling. Just like that, her troubles had slid away. She was thinking of Dante, when the father in hell, seeing the visiting poet, asks him about his son in the world. *Does he not still live? Doesn't the sweet light strike his eyes?*

'*Non fiere li occhi suoi lo dolce lume?*' Marian was saying again, liking the words in her soft voice. The sweet light of the world. How green it was, she thought, on this late September day — and she blinked. How green it was.

13

Rain came, heavily. The house smelled of wood smoke and damp. Drops fell singly, loudly, from the eaves — The Heights was designed with gables in all directions.

Always a long gap, somehow, in the afternoons before supper. Fires were laid, it was October, dusk was falling earlier, the twilights had a different smell — wet, earthy, the land so brown. Under the lamp, Marian read: Plato, Sainte-Beuve, Xenophon, Hercules choosing between pleasure and virtue. She thought about the separation between the two. There was strength, and then again, there was strength. It depended on the point of view.

On this morning it was raining again. She was irritable when Brett helped her dress, annoyed at herself for not having replied to Johnny's note from the day before. He needed to talk to her about the Baltimore investments, and in a postscript had mentioned that a copy of the deed to the Priory was missing and he had to find it. Brett was visibly nervous at doing up her stays.

Downstairs, it was dreary, the light flat, white, chill. And what did she have to look forward to? Herself. It was almost comic. What a prospect.

There was no fire — the fireplace had not even been cleaned from the night before, she knew another spasm of irritation, before remembering that Brock was away. She must reply to Mr Cross, as she tried now to call him; everything was a great effort. She rang the bell, asked Mrs Dowling to bring coffee quickly.

Johnny came the following day, and she signed the papers without once meeting his eyes. Then he was gone.

Walking round the rooms, she was aware of her own footsteps. The rooms were large. The house was not designed for one person.

During the days that went by, she read, wrote letters.

Johnny wrote again, saying he needed to see her about the gas and coke shares, which had fallen in value. But she knew, if she knew anything, that it was better he did not visit her at all. She did not reply, but guessed he would come. Before he did so, she positioned her black widow's lace cap prominently on her head. When he appeared — it was a gusty, rainy morning — he passed her the form, she read it without taking in a word, and signed it automatically.

That was the last time she saw him for seven days.

★ ★ ★

Her sense of him grew, in proportion to his absence. She could think of nothing else. She was caught. Time would deal with it, she said to herself. But the mornings in the house seemed extraordinarily long. She read Plato again; she read again Sainte-Beuve.

The rains were back, the drops from the eaves loud. Then she realised they were not just from the eaves. She had seen the darker bits of the wall and realised they were wet; she looked upwards, saw the ceiling, went upstairs, found the source, the hole in the roof of her bedroom. Brett put a bucket under the drip. The rain dropped loudly into the bucket. Brock was still away.

She wrote to Johnny, asking if perhaps his coachman or servant could help. The rain continued. The night before, she could hardly sleep because of the drops falling into the bucket.

In the early evening she heard a sound that gave her a start. It lifted her feelings instantly — the noise of carriage wheels. She got up. Yes, the carriage, it was stopping, the doorbell.

Brett was opening the door: 'Mr Cross, ma'am.'

He stood in the doorway with his look of arrogance, as if savouring his height, chin raised — an illusion, a misleading prelude to the modest person he was. (Was this a fragment of an earlier Johnny?)

He asked her where the leak was, he went upstairs. She heard him come downstairs, then the front door was opening. Then she heard sounds that seemed to come from one of the outhouses. Those footsteps, purposeful, even the rhythmic intake of breath, as he was going upstairs again. There was the sound of the hammer. She sat quite still, in the wing-back chair. She concentrated on preserving her composure. The door was opening, Johnny had come in. He was saying he had fixed the roof, it was a temporary job only, but it would do for now. He would check in a few days that it was still in place.

'Thank you very much,' she said.

'But why,' he was saying, 'are you crying?'

He was taking both her hands. Still her tears fell.

'I miss seeing you so much,' she heard him say. 'The last month has been the most difficult of my life. Please,' — he was taking her to the sofa.

He was looking intently into her face, handing her his handkerchief. She wiped her eyes and face.

He stayed for a late supper.

* * *

He was an innocent, he was modest and kind. He had said: we are not hurting anyone; she heard the truth. Again, she kissed his hands, and life seemed possible. Now she could tell him freely, truthfully, how her days had been. The relief was tremendous. He came the next day and the next. He called her his Beatrice. He brought her the *New Quarterly* journal, which featured a review of George's book. When he went to London, she missed him. She had a cold, her head ached. She wanted to write to him.

She used the nearest paper to hand — mourning paper. She wrote within those stark black borders.

Best loved and loving one — the sun it shines so cold, so cold, when there are no eyes to look love on me. I cannot bear to sadden one moment when we are together, but wenn Du bist nicht da I have often a bad time. It is a solemn time, dearest. And why should I complain if it is a painful time? What I call my pain is almost a joy seen in the wide array of the world's cruel suffering. Thou seest I am grumbling today — got a chill yesterday and have a headache. All which, as a wise doctor would say, is not of the least consequence, my dear Madam.

Through everything else, dear tender one, there is the blessing of trusting in thy goodness. Thou dost not know anything of verbs in Hiphil and Hophal or the history of metaphysics or the position of Kepler in science, but thou knowest best things of another sort, such as belong to the manly heart — secrets of lovingness and rectitude. O I am flattering. Consider what thou wast a little time ago in pantaloons and back hair.

Triumph over me. After all, I have <u>not</u> the second copy of the deed. What I took for it was only Foster's original draft and my copy of it. The article by Sully in the New Quarterly is very well done.

I shall think of thee this afternoon getting health at Lawn Tennis, and I shall reckon on having a letter by tomorrow's post.

Why should I compliment myself at the end of my letter and say that I am faithful, loving, more anxious for thy life than mine? I will run no risks of being 'inexact' — so I will only say 'varium et mutabile semper' but at this particular moment thy tender —

Beatrice

14

From the aeroplane window I can see banks of white and gold cloud, soft as cotton-wool, as if for some godly child to play in. We are crossing the Alps, and land an hour later. From Treviso, I take a coach to Piazzale Roma. By the time I am on the ferry it is dusk, and raining. Because of the rain, the seats at the front of the *vaporetto* are empty. I have my raincoat, and manoeuvre my suitcase and sit in the open. The boat enters the Grand Canal, I am sitting out there, in the dark and the rain at the front.

The boat is making its way steadily through the water: we round the first corner, the dome and front of the San Simeone Piccolo church appear, white-bright, brilliantly lit, strange, lovely. The church is actually rising from the water. Within the hour we reach my stop. I wheel my suitcase in and around streets, across a bridge — carrying it over the wide, shallow steps — to the Pensione Accademia.

At the hotel reception, I bump into Professor Gruber, he introduces me to his wife. I go on upstairs. I have a shower, then slip between the tightly stretched clean white sheets of the bed. Now I take out my phone. Hans has texted, asking if I've arrived. I consider before replying.

Hans has come out a day early to see his closest friend, Bruno Seabright, who's running the conference.

I think, and finally text: *Going straight to sleep — exhausted! K*

Now I feel nauseous. I get up and eat crackers from the plane.

In the dawn I don't remember where I am. Water noises, a splash, a motor churning, silence, splash, a distant shout. And then I remember. And again that small text I sent to Hans comes into my head. I turn at once onto my other side, and try to go back to sleep. After a hurried breakfast I make my way to the Ca' Foscari, also on the Dorsoduro, where the conference is being held. It is not far; I have to weave round corners in the secretive streets and cross three bridges.

The Ca'Foscari, once a palace, is now a university.

It is still raining, but there is a strong, warm wind. Inside, the conference room is on the first floor, with a grandly decorated ceiling, magnificent tall windows overlooking the canal. Gilt chairs are in rows, enough for a hundred. About twenty are sitting, the rest are milling around. I introduce myself to Bruno Seabright. 'Katie Boyd! I've heard quite a bit about you,' he says, in an easy, friendly way. He is tanned, has a spectacularly healthy American look. He tells me where to get coffee, on the long dais. Cup in hand, I turn to find Hans beside me.

'Hi.'

I get a sort of shock. I've forgotten how much I like to be near him. He's wearing a short-sleeved shirt, I see his forearms, mechanically notice the light hairs on them. His sandals make me smile. They look like something a European explorer might wear circa 1940.

'Have you had a nice time?' I say.

'Where are you staying?'

'Accademia.'

I drink my coffee quickly, then ask where he is staying, though I know. 'Pensione Wilder. Don't hurry,' says Hans, seriously. 'You'll spill your coffee.'

Talks follow in quick succession. By some process about which I'm not clear, I am standing beside Hans in the small break, and I ask automatically how he is. 'To be honest with you,' he says, doing that funnelling movement with his lips, 'I feel like a smoke. I've seen the inside of too many conference rooms in the last two months. Is it still raining?'

I can't tell. Through the windows, I seem to see some sun.

* * *

The talks are less than thirty minutes long. I put on my jacket, the air conditioning is cold and dry. But the schedule is merciful, stopping at two o'clock, allowing time for sight-seeing in the afternoon. A group of us convene at the front of the building. The Chair and Hans' friend, Bruno; two English academics I don't know, from Nottingham and Sussex; a Swiss woman called Cornelia; an American called Marcia. We are blinking in the powerful sunlight. The sky has cleared completely. It is blue — sheer — hot, everyone clamps on sunglasses. We go to find lunch, heading not as I expect into the Dorsoduro, but east: round the back of the Accademia Gallery, over humped bridges, the dome of Santa Maria della Salute hoving into sight, suddenly above us. Then we are standing at the edge of the promontory. The heat has leapt up twenty degrees. In the newly clear sun, the lagoon is glittering, open before us, the Adriatic sea.

'It's something,' says Hans. Everyone is exclaiming, getting out phones to take photos. Professor Gruber is using an old-fashioned camera, bending down in front of it, turning the lens, squinting and clicking.

We retrace our steps in search of lunch. Hans and I, going slower, follow Bruno and the group down the second turning; after a hundred yards we arrive at a small campo, with five different streets leading off it. It's empty. Hans calls Bruno, no reply. We give up, sit at one of the restaurants with outside shade; order salad, pasta.

Waiting for the wine and water, we chat about Ann's paper on Simcox. 'I do think it's very good,' I say, meaningfully. It seems to me he half shuts his eyes, and winces. Though he could have been shutting his eyes from the sunlight. There is a curious layer of mist in the air above the paving stones of the campo, as if moisture is still being burned off.

'It's been days of rain,' says Hans mechanically.

The wine arrives. 'I'm not very good with drink in the middle of the day,' I say. It is an automatic remark. I shift in my seat.

'So, tell me,' he says. He moves his chair to sit in the sunshine, and he suddenly looks happy. His shirt is open at the neck. 'Apart from Ann's paper, how do you like Simcox?'

'She's great, she's like a camera in the room!'

'Go on,' he says, 'unless this is a gem going into your book that has to be secret.' I smile. It's a relief to hear him joke and look half sarcastic.

'Ha ha. No — there are tons of moments that only Simcox's beady eye catches. For instance, she's visiting them, talking to Lewes, and Marian is just walking by in the drawing room, when Lewes seizes Marian's hand to kiss it quickly. Simcox records it all.'

Hans looks expectant.

'It's unusual in a marriage,' I say, blushing for some reason. 'To have that degree of sustained, ardent admiration and love —'

Hans doesn't reply. He drains the rest of his glass, asks if I mind if he smokes, reaching for the cigarettes before I say yes.

'I don't like to drink without a smoke.'

He drinks, lights, inhales. I drink some more wine.

'Better?'

'Much.'

We sit in silence. The campo is golden. At the end is a church of white-blackened stone. Now we start talking about Simcox's diary again. And again, Ann's paper comes up, and in an absent way, Hans remarks on how it's great that the paper was accepted at Venice, because he was worried Ann wasn't going to pull it all together in time.

I say: 'Well she did.'

After the pasta plates arrive, Hans says to me, his colour a little raised, 'I don't mean to — cause offence — but why do you — make that remark in that tone?'

I wind spaghetti slowly round my fork.

'I think it's been difficult for Ann.'

'That is true.'

I put my fork down, and begin to fold my napkin into a neat rectangle.

'I just — gathered from her — that you, you know, didn't encourage her to apply for Venice.'

'True. At a certain point.'

He stubs out his cigarette, shrugs. 'Her first piece for Venice was on Eliot.

I thought it needed more work. I wasn't saying, don't send it ever. Just, she needed to work at it. I thought it might be rejected as it was.'

He adds: 'Her Simcox piece was good from the start.'

After a while, I say, driven by I don't know what — I feel like a gardener digging in the earth, searching with a spade for a stone somewhere — 'But couldn't you have encouraged, helped her on the Eliot piece?'

'And you think I didn't?'

We walk after lunch over the Accademia bridge, then eastwards. The heat is now stupendous, even through my sandals I feel it. We go along the Riva degli Schiavoni, the lagoon on our right. Hans is sweating, hair damp where it meets his neck. I am thinking about what he said. As we walk back, I have my old sense of constriction. Finally I say, I imagine I jumped to assumptions.

'I imagine you did.'

1880

15

In early March Marian took the carriage, accompanied by Johnny Cross and his sister Eleanor to the South Kensington Museum. As they went through Hyde Park — trees still bare — she waited to catch sight of the Serpentine. The carriage swerved, all three thrust to the right, Eleanor crying, 'I beg your pardon!', and laughing breathily. Eleanor's head had tumbled right across her and Marian could smell her scent, a light musk rose.

'It is no one's fault,' said Marian, when they had steadied.

Her voice was magisterial. The road becoming cobbles, now they were jogging up and down in undignified movement, Eleanor beginning to giggle, before laughing hysterically.

'Nelly,' Johnny was saying, on her right.

Marian couldn't help smiling.

Inside, the room was crowded with stands, on which hung paintings, alabasters, bas-reliefs. Lost stray columns stood here and there, reminding Marian of a cemetery. 'What do you make of this strange crowd?' she asked Eleanor softly. Eleanor said it was remarkable.

Marian wished Eleanor would brave an opinion.

In the North Room, Marian asked to have a moment by herself. Now she was alone in front of this altar. It had been ripped from the Church of Santa Chiara in Florence. Two columns left and right, saints below, and above, two angels with buoyant knees raised in the air. Bending close, she thought she could smell the odour of incense. It had to be an illusion. She stood and waited. What was she waiting for? She had the lunatic idea that the insoluble muddle of her life could resolve itself into a clear shape, in front of this displaced altar. She could laugh at herself, if she weren't so terrified.

★ ★ ★

Since returning from Witley in November, Johnny had visited her at the Priory several evenings each week. Brett tacitly understood the situation. They took drives together, walked, visited the British Museum, the Grosvenor Gallery, The National Gallery, the Dulwich Gallery. Johnny was the family business manager, old family friend, his presence excited no comment at all.

The last day of November had been the anniversary of George's death. Marian took Lewes' letters to the room she had lived in after his death, again disused, with a papery shut-up smell of wood, or linseed oil. She put her hands on the wall: here she had endured it all.

She could not catch it as it was, though. It was a bit frightening.

Lewes' letters to her were utterly bittersweet. Then there were letters from him to other people, less familiar, sent to her after he died.

If I cannot seduce Polly from her beloved Theocritus, I ramble among the fields, glens, or over the moors musing 'on lovely things that conquer death'. If I can seduce her we both ramble and talk of the said lovely things. To be with her is a perpetual Banquet to which that of Plato would present but a flat rival.

Momentarily she reeled. His light-depth, his love — there was no one to match him. What was she doing? She picked up another — to Barbara, when Barbara had detected her as author of *Adam Bede*.

You're a darling, and I have always said so! I don't know that I ever said it to you — but I say it now. You are the person on whose sympathy we both counted ...

What was it her niece had said, about never having met anyone so full of life?

'What is it, Mutter? Can I help you in any way?'

It was Charles.

'I would like — his letters — to be buried with me.'

Charles was taking her hand, leading her into the drawing room. 'My dear Mutter, you are not well, you are entirely unwell, in fact. Come, sit. I will ask Brett to bring you tea. You are brave, you — *are* — *surviving*.'

At Christmas she was alone except for the servants. She sat by the fire in her study, where she had moved the enlarged photograph of Lewes.

Before leaving Witley, she had heard that John Blackwood, friend and publisher of so many years, had died. Now she received his nephew, William Blackwood, and in a faint echo of those Sundays before, had begun receiving guests. One by one, like so many supplicants. Herbert Spencer, Charles Pigott, Georgie and Edward Burne-Jones, Sir James Paget, Lady Bowen, the Darwins, Leslie Stephen, Mr and Mrs Beesly, Florence Hill, Frederick Myers ... on and on they came. Half-shutting her eyes, imagining the stream of visitors, there followed like steps in an illness the knock-knock-knock of depression.

On that Christmas Day, she had copied Emily Brontë's poem into her diary:

> *Cold in the earth — and the deep snow piled above thee*
> *Far, far removed, cold in the dreary grave!*
> *Have I forgot, my only Love, to love thee,*
> *Severed at last by Time's all-severing wave?*

$$\star \star \star$$

But now it was the next year, it was March, and Johnny had proposed to her for the third time. She could be open, she could be honest if only she dared. After the day spent in South Kensington Gallery, Marian had sat alone in her study. This was the room where she had written *Middlemarch* — at that desk, in front of the window, above the garden. What should she do? Neither way seemed possible. She remembered the dread emptiness of those days at Witley, without Johnny.

And she remembered *Mill on the Floss*, Maggie Tulliver stuck. Now she was stuck, strange.

What did she fear? She was not ambivalent about Johnny. No. She feared how she would be seen. She feared what people would think and say. Those Dodsons, those Gleggs. But not just! Those ordinary people, friends, close loving friends — she feared they would no longer recognise, and love her. She would drop in their regard. Even, a little, in her own.

The following morning she wrote a note to Dr Paget.

16

Waiting for Dr Paget's arrival, Marian could not stay seated. Should they be in the drawing room, full of George and their life together, or go to her study, where the enlarged photograph of George would look down at them as they talked?

She led him to the study. They sat in chairs by the fire.

'My dear Mrs Lewes,' said Dr Paget. He had a long lean and sallow face, with a projecting forehead, and bushy eyebrows. 'I am honoured to be contacted by you, on what you describe as — a private, and, yes, delicate matter.'

How could she say it? Hopelessness flooded her. This was the beginning. She had told no one at all so far.

She opened her mouth: 'It is kind of you to come —'

She must push on. Colouring, she said, 'As you say, it is a private communication.'

Dr Paget would say nothing to anyone.

Was there, however, a flicker of unholy interest in those eyes?

And if there was, so what, she thought next. It's human nature to be curious.

Still, she knew a creeping dismay inside herself.

'I do not know,' she began slowly, 'if you are acquainted with a Mr John Cross. The family resides at Weybridge.'

'I think ... is he a tall fellow?'

'He is.'

'Is it possible I have met him on a Sunday?'

'He was a regular visitor.'

'In that case, I think I have met him.'

A conscious look between them.

'An agreeable, sensible man, I thought.'

'I am glad you find him so.'

She gave a sudden gaseous, utterly nervous smile.

'Sir Paget, what I am about to say, might come — assuredly *will come* — as a surprise. Mr Cross has asked me to marry him.'

Marian tried to see. His face. His face. She strained forward, as far as it was seemly. A fluctuating colour — small upward motion of surprise — reined in — superbly — and now, a look of goodwill.

'For the third time,' she added.

He cleared his throat.

'Are you disposed to accept him?'

Silence.

'I have rejected him twice. If I do marry him, all my monies and property will go as previously to Mr Lewes' children and relatives. But now — after an interminable struggle,' — and she could not help giving a very deep sigh — 'I am inclined to accept him. He is a decent man. He is independently wealthy. He proposes to dedicate the rest of his life to mine, now that I am alone.'

Disconcertingly, she was hearing herself. The high seriousness of her tone, and the great primness of it, too.

'He wishes to care for me.'

'And why should he not fulfil that office?' said Sir James, kindly, at once.

Marian shot him a grateful look.

'I understand your hesitation. But it is not necessary.'

'My concern ... is my legacy. My influence.'

She turned a questioning look at him.

'Your work, Mrs Lewes, will endure. You have much to say to people. What you say will not be lessened — or — or —'

'Contaminated,' she said.

'Contaminated! — certainly not.'

'You do not think.'

'I do not think.'

They sat in silence for some moments. Marian said: 'I have a further question. I have passed my sixtieth birthday. Where — conjugal relations — are concerned —'

'You are perfectly fit for them.' (Briskly.) 'There is nothing to suggest an unfitness. Mr Cross is —'

'He just turned forty this month.'

Did she note a flicker of surprise in his face?

'He is in the prime of life. And you are not so far from the prime of life, my dear Mrs Lewes. It is my considered opinion that conjugal relations assist in the happiness of most unions. — Menstruation is — long past —'

'Oh! — Yes.'

'I wish you the very best, Mrs Lewes.'

After Dr Paget's visit, Marian stayed sitting. The fire glowed molten gold, crackled and spat. Everything was changing. Dr Paget had thought it a reasonable, a good thing to do, if she read his face right. He had dismissed the idea that her influence would be ruined. She got up, held on to the mantelpiece, it was strong, solid. Sir James was of the world, an intelligent, educated, canny, as well as humane man. She would go ahead. She would tell Johnny today. But she would have to hold her courage. There would be no going back. Even the thought of telling him — and now the line from *Macbeth* was running through her head, about screwing her courage to the sticking place, as if she were on the brink of murder ... murdering — who? What?

She took one of the sugar-plums from the bowl on the mantelpiece, a leftover from Christmas, and ate it. And why should she not have a happy life? Without loneliness, with Johnny near, and she *Mrs Cross*, a truly legal wife at last?

The fire was burning her it was so hot. She stepped back. A fierce, new, happy sensation had her in its grip. The marriage would be small, secret. It would be in a proper church. Only Charles and Johnny's family present, and then they would be *out*. Out of England. No one would know until they were gone.

They would marry in three weeks' time, on May 6. The very next day she went with Johnny to look for a house. It would be no good to stay in the Priory, so associated with her life with Lewes. They found exactly what they liked: 4 Cheyne Walk, a tall, gracious four-storey house, overlooking the Thames. Johnny had been surprised when he learned that she wanted to be married in a church, and a traditional Anglican one, but she explained she wanted the proprieties to be fully observed. They would leave the day of the marriage, spend the night in Dover, and honeymoon abroad. Johnny listened and took note. He would tell Robert the next day — the sooner he knew of the impending absence the better.

'Robert?'

Johnny smiled. Marian was liable to forget his work existed. Robert Benson was his business partner in Cornhill.

'You cannot possibly tell him,' said Marian, looking pale. 'I am sorry — very sorry — if I did not make myself understood — but obviously, my dear Johnny! — *No one*, except for your family, and Charles, can be allowed to know of this event.'

Her hand was clutching his arm.

Marian's emotions commanded his respect, in their intensity and strangeness, as the necessary accoutrements of a great writer. At the same time, sensations, like colours in the air, were passing, just out of view.

Marian was soon busy going for fittings at Madame Victorine's, close to Bond Street, commissioning a large lace mantilla as well as two hats; fittings at Mrs Garfields, for her wedding dress, of satin, muslin, and tulle, in a cream colour, suitable for her age. She ordered two travelling outfits. She wanted to buy an attractive nightgown, too; but would she be able to raise this with Mrs Herbert? Or would that small lady, from underneath her fringe of curls, give her a faux-sympathetic look, to hide secret mockery? And afterwards, would she gossip, to other favoured customers, in a private tone, about her famous client?

The solution came to her. Edith. A silk night-shift from Hamilton's. Perfect. Not that she would enlighten Edith as to her plans. A simple silk shift: she wanted to avoid at all costs something fussy, engineered, as it were, for the purpose of seduction.

Johnny obtained the special licence, so they could dispense with the Banns. He was working long hours, resigned to leaving a letter behind for his partner, Robert Benson, once they were gone. Marian was thinking of her trousseau, and consulting both Baedekers and memory for places to see.

Johnny told his family. The reaction was just what she had hoped. Eleanor felt like a natural confidante. To her, she began to admit her fears. *I quail a little*, she wrote, *in facing what has to be gone through — the hurting of many I care for.*

She must tell Maria, Georgiana, Barbara, Elma Stuart, Edith, Cara, and above all, immediately, Charles. So far she hadn't.

Serendipity — the doorbell went, it was Charles! He had news. He had been promoted to Principal Clerk at the Post Office. She congratulated him, then grew serious. Now she must give him *her* news.

Observing her peculiar expression, he said, 'You are thinking how pleased the Pater would be if he were here. I know.'

'I — yes.'

'I know.'

He pressed her hand feelingly.

She had the darting suspicion that her stepson achieved exalted states of mind in her presence. And this horrid suspicion, like a twinkling little mocking star, seemed somehow linked to other horrid, mocking, twinkling little stars.

She had failed again. Talking to Johnny, she had a sudden idea.

'Could *you* tell Charles?'

'I?'

Johnny hesitated. 'I am happy to. But — Charles is almost my age — do you not think it would be better ...'

Her expression was so distressed, he gave up.

'I will tell Charles,' he said, good-naturedly.

Charles came the following evening straight after seeing Johnny. He had wanted to see Marian immediately. He was happy for her. The Pater wouldn't have minded, either — he didn't have a jealous bone in his body. Marian had never been so fond of Charles. She in turn tried to explain herself to him. 'I couldn't have written my books,' she said, 'if I hadn't been human.'

Marian asked Maria Congreve to come and see her. She arrived with her husband.

Richard kissed her hand reverently, and as he bowed Marian noticed the bald spot on top of his head. 'We are all expecting something from you, my dear Mrs Lewes,' he said heavily at once. 'You know that I have declared my independence from Harrison. My conception of Positivism is more — spiritual, though I say so myself. But you — you. In our sect, we feel that no one living is so fit to write the creed. Do you think you might be able to — write something?'

'I beg your pardon?'

'Do not look like that,' said Mr Congreve, with an unexpectedly deep, kindly laugh. 'Without a doubt, *you have written it*. In your books, and in your life. You anticipated the Positivist creed. Your marriage, the love you shared together, did not need the sanction of the church.'

The ironies were grotesque.

Marian went to see Georgiana; looked for, and failed to find the right words. Every single sentence that arose, seemed a strange contradiction of what had passed between them previously. Painfully, she remembered the honest way Georgiana had told her in such detail about Edward and his lover Maria Zambaco. Marian stayed on, trying to summon the words.

Finally she rose to leave. She stumbled towards honesty. 'I am so tired,' she said, as she put on her coat, 'of being put on a pedestal, and expected to vent wisdom.'

18

The marriage preparations were underway. A note arrived from Edith: the silk shift was ready; the following day, Edith delivered it.

Entering the drawing room, the fire was blazing, Marian was framed in a peninsula of light. Edith took her seat opposite Marian, they talked of how the Hamiltons business was doing, of Gladstone's folly.

Edith said, suddenly, 'Did you by any chance read that piece in the *Cornhill*, comparing Tennyson with Chertbury?'

'Ah,' said Marian, shutting her eyes for a moment. She knew very well what Edith was referring to. Then, with perfect deliberation: 'You mean the piece by Collins, comparing Chertbury's *Ode upon A Question Moved, Whether Love Should Continue For Ever*, with stanzas of *In Memoriam*?'

'I do.'

'I did read it. I cannot say I know what to make of it. Men's characters are as mixed as the origins of mythology.'

'Which is to say —?'

Marian now properly opened her eyes. 'It's the question of principle.'

Edith's eyes were lynx-bright, with small pupils: for a moment Marian wondered if Edith ever wrote down what she said — then dismissed the idea as fanciful.

But Edith had come to the needle-point. How, Marian did not know. There was some way in which Edith seemed to shadow her. To distract Edith from this topic, she said, 'Come, sit by me.'

Edith at once did so.

But now, seated, Edith stopped. She was thinking about her newest attempt at writing. She had searched and searched for a way of writing about the dominant passion of her life, outside the arena of her diary. She had developed a hybrid, a partly autobiographical kind of fiction, with thinly disguised references to Marian, called *Episodes in the Lives of Men, Women and Lovers*. She wondered if she could mention it to Marian. Marian, who had said to her that she had the moral matter in herself; enough to write. Then she was kissing Marian's cheek, and her thoughts flew to pieces. She was saying she loved Marian. She said it again.

'Nay, do not exaggerate.'

Marian's voice was guttural. For a moment, Edith was disturbed. But she was a resourceful lover. She knelt instead, and began kissing Marian's feet.

With sharp suddenness, the feet withdrew.

Edith fell back on her heels. And now she was embarrassed. Worse, she was blinking away tears; which soon were running unchecked down her cheeks.

'I thought you believed me at least veracious —'

'Veracious!' cried Marian.

'Yes,' said Edith. 'Veracious.'

Marian and Edith looked directly at one another.

Marian said, evenly, 'It is a hard thing to say of anyone. It is nearly impossible to attain perfect truth.' She found herself colouring, though, as she said this.

'What is more,' went on Marian, with her hot cheeks, becoming sidetracked, 'it can easily be an overdone virtue. On the whole I would rather scold you, Edith, for imperfect veiling of unpleasant truths, *as when you don't like someone*.'

They were both silent, each regrouping. Marian was thinking of Edith's rudeness to Johnny.

'I like,' said Edith, 'for you to tell me the truth.'

'Would you really like that?'

Marian's words came like a cold challenge. Edith nodded.

Marian narrowed her eyes, she was trying to penetrate into Edith's mind, to see how Edith saw *her*, to feel the shape Edith had made for her.

Marian said: 'The love of men and women for each other must always be more and better than any other.'

Marian wanted to penetrate Edith's atmosphere, cut into her, break and shatter her delusion.

'I have never, all my life, cared very much for women.'

'I have always known it,' Edith said, quickly.

'I care for the womanly ideal. I sympathise with women, I like to be their confidante. They are close to me in one way, but not in the essential intimate way. I hope I make myself clear.'

'You do.'

Marian sat still: the sensation of violence — or was it rage? — had vanished already.

'Edith, it has probably been my fault. I have a painful susceptibility to encourage a certain — approach in others. — As a person I need — these things,' — and she gestured vaguely. What she really meant was love. 'But that mood might not last; in fact, it does *not* last,' she added, in a surge of strange hopelessness: it was as if she had stepped towards a grief, and was now in danger of getting lost. Then Marian saw beyond herself to Edith, shoulders hunched. 'My dear Edith, I have so much respect and admiration for you — so much more than I used to —'

Edith was nodding dumbly, and Marian caught her own words. Surely they were implying something hurtful all over again.

★ ★ ★

A week before the wedding took place, Marian was writing to Elma Stuart. She had looked at all the wooden objects Elma had carved for her. Could she tell Elma? The best she could do was warn her. She had already mentioned that she was going away, and now she added: *I hope to see you before I go away. What I would ask of you is, whether your love and trust in me will suffice to satisfy you that, when I act in a way which is thoroughly unexpected there are reasons which justify my action, though the reasons may not be evident to you.*

* * *

It was the day before the wedding. The trunk was packed and ready in her bed-room, her wedding dress hung in the corner: deep cream with a garment of lace that would be worn on top; small, satin-covered buttons on the sleeves, wrist to elbow. Taking a last look at this dress, her first wedding dress, she went to her study, lit the oil lamps, and sat at her desk, where she had written *Middlemarch*, and *Daniel Deronda*.

It was familiar. She was about to write letters to leave behind, and she was about to go away. Her movements to her close friends were a perfect secret. It was uncanny what she was doing. She was repeating what had taken place, twenty-five years ago, when she had planned to leave England with Lewes.

Except it was the opposite.

It was strange to think that this step into respectability would be scandalous. She had an image of shapes morphing into new shapes, thesis to antithesis. And *then* she had that moral certitude. No certitude now. Almost the converse.

Barbara first. *I am going to do*, she wrote, *what not very long ago I should myself have pronounced impossible for me, and therefore I should not wonder at anyone else who found my action incomprehensible.*

To Georgiana: *A great momentous change is taking place in my life — a sort of miracle in which I could never have believed, and under which I still sit amazed. If it alters your conception of me so thoroughly that you must from henceforth regard me as a new person, a stranger to you, I shall not take it hardly, for I myself a little while ago should have said that this thing could not be.*

She did feel sad — becoming a stranger to Georgie was an awful idea. But it was what she feared. People had such set ideas about other people. *Explanations of these crises, which seem sudden though they are slowly dimly prepared, are impos-sible. I can only ask you and your husband to imagine and interpret according to your deep experience and loving kindness.*

She sealed the letter.

Charles had agreed to speak to Edith, Elma, and Maria Congreve. But she would send an advance warning to Maria.

A great, momentous change is going to take place in my life ... With your permission Charles will call on you and tell you what he can on Saturday.

Ever with unchanging love —

* * *

On May 6, at St George's Church in Hanover Square, Marian walked, with a careful but measured step, on Charles Lewes' arm, up the aisle. It was a small gathering: Charles and the Cross family were present, and Henry Bullock-Hall. After, they returned to the Priory to sign their wills.

As Charles Lewes waved goodbye to the carriage leaving for Dover, he remembered what she had said to him a week ago. 'I couldn't have written my books, if I hadn't been human.'

Charles thought of the words now, and he would think about them many more times in his life. The human machinery was imperfect — was that what she meant?

19

It is the last full day of the conference. Our papers are read, Hans', Ann's, mine, and after dinner three of us, Bruno, Hans, and I, ride in a gondola. The lagoon is like open sea, the sky is reflected everywhere. Swiftly, in his purple bolero and hat, the gondolier plunges the oar down and draws us into the city. It is dusk, the stone walls and buildings are illuminated a rich amber as the blue sky deepens. Down the long canals, this way and that. I have no idea where we are. The gondola drops off Hans first at St Marco; then drops Bruno and me at the Accademia, where we are both staying.

Entering the lobby, Bruno says, 'I won't be able to go straight to sleep after that gondola, and that's a fact. How about a drink?'

We drink Cent'herbe in two comfortable armchairs by the bar — small, strange-looking green drinks that Bruno orders. After sipping it, I start the conversation. 'You're Hans' great friend,' I say.

'He was my best man,' says Bruno, at once. They met years ago, at Columbia University in New York. Bruno says he liked what Hans read today, and what I read today. We go over everyone's paper in brief. Then I mention the fact that Jo Devlin didn't come.

To my surprise, Bruno grins.

'I did a wicked thing,' admits Bruno. 'I put him off. At the last minute.'

'Really!' I add that Devlin didn't come to our conference either.

'I know,' he says, promptly — eagerly. For a moment, he looks doubtful. Then: 'If we're going to have this conversation, I'm going to have to order another.'

He does so.

'Kate Boyd. Boyd. Where's that name from?'

'Scotland and New Zealand.'

He pauses, he's frowning and thinking.

'Hans — I mean I don't know how to say this. He's a — how can I say —'

He stops again. Then says: 'He hasn't talked about Devlin to you, has he?'

'No.'

Bruno holds up his drink to the light. 'They make 'em stronger here. No — I mean, the fact is, I know he hasn't talked to you about Devlin. He's a very strange man Hans, I have to tell you.'

I swallow.

'Bruno, I don't understand what you're saying.'

'You like Hans.'

'Well —'

'Don't worry, don't worry. I'm saying this very badly. Listen, Ann has been having an affair with him for a good while. Devlin, I mean. A really very good while. And I have to say — I have said to him, he should tell you, so you get the lie of the land.'

'No,' I say. 'No.'

But in the next minute, as I sip my green drink, which tastes bitter but also strangely pleasant, I'm thinking, yes. That makes a lot of sense.

'She's always getting him out the way,' Bruno continues, as he regards me. He sticks up his arm, waves to the barman. '*Due ancora!*'

I sit back in my chair; I am still trying to take it in.

'You know, as his friend, I haven't enjoyed this. But he made a stand, about the conference. He told your Chair. He wouldn't have Devlin there. That's how it happened.'

He mutters about vaping, pulls out a blue vape, moves his chair so that he's partly concealed by the large plant, vapes, and then says, 'How do you feel?'

I say, 'But why didn't he mention it to me? I mean, not that it changes so much, but — I don't know.'

He explains. When Hans told the Chair, Ann thought it grotesque of him.

And her bargain was, he must tell no one else. No one. 'And she ... she's quite freaked about the department, if you hadn't noticed.'

'Why doesn't he leave her?' I have a sensation, a little like terror, as I say this.

'It's coming,' he says. 'He's slow to break up his family. But he's absolutely going to.'

Hans was brought up without a father, he adds. I'm silent, looking at the plant: the complex threads and weaves of these great dark green leaves.

'There's another reason he didn't. Apart from some fucked-up German sense of honour, I mean. He was convinced it would seem like bargaining with you.'

'Bargaining.'

I go up to my room, open the window. So, nothing is clear — nothing is clear at all — but still — I put my head out into the air. I try to work out where Hans' hotel is. Tomorrow we go back to London.

Part Five

I think you are quite right to look over your old letters and papers and decide for yourself what should be burnt. Burning is the most reverential destination one can give to relics ... I hate the thought that what we have looked at with eyes full of living memory should be tossed about and made lumber of, or (if it be writing) read with hard curiosity. I am continually considering whether I have saved as much as possible from this desecrating fate.

Marian Evans, letter to Cara Bray, 1880

What does it all mean, and after the state of desolation she was in after poor Lewes' death it is to me almost unaccountable. What would my uncle [John Blackwood] have said, and does it not take away all the romance of her connection with Lewes?

William Blackwood, writing to his London manager Joseph Langford, 1880

I am still thrrrrrilling over a conversation I had yesterday with Charles Lewes. Lionel Tennyson was here; he declared that his hair stood on end as he listened. Charles Lewes said he wished to tell me all about the wedding. He gave her away, and looks upon Mr. Cross as an elder brother.

I asked him if she had consulted him and he said no, not consulted, but that she had told him a few weeks ago. She confided in Paget who approved and told her that it wouldn't make any difference in her influence. Here I couldn't stand it, and said of course it would, but it was better to be genuine than to have influence ...

Anne Thackeray Ritchie to Richmond Ritchie, May 1880

1

A man of business, a son, a brother, but he had never believed he would become a husband, yet he had done it, and she was his.

They had rattled on the train to Dover, seated on the westerly side as it snaked southeastwards from St Pancras. Beside her, he could now take her hand in public. Through half-open eyes he registered the Kent Downs, green in the afternoon May light. The scenes were passing fast.

With the soporific rhythm of the train, his deep exhaustion was rising. He could at last admit the strain of the previous weeks.

Why else was he so tired? He had had four hours' sleep each night, scarcely more. There had been so much to take care of. The new Chelsea house, the lease, endless meetings with Mr Armitage about decorating it; the ceremony, the travel, the files he had had to leave for his business partner Robert, the dreadful letter he had had to write to Robert, the way he had to lie to Robert. What would Robert think when he read his letter? But he could not deal with that now, and he would not. It was over. This was the start. And then he had a sense in the train of floating, of release. Yet feeling for his watch, his waistcoat was loose. 'I have lost weight,' he said, as, with a screech and a roar, they arrived at Dover.

She had observed it, she replied.

Waiting for a hansom, he ventured, 'My dear, I've heard it said that the King's Head is much more out of the way. Would that not suit us — you — better than the Warden?'

He spoke with respect. The Lord Warden was where she had stayed with Lewes, but she was damnably exercised about watching eyes, so she took up the suggestion. He enquired, came out to tell her they had rooms, he had inspected them, they were clean as a whistle. They registered, unpacked, went out again. The day was fine, it was past five, the sea air pinchingly brisk yet not cold, pleasant, and half gold, and those high spaced cries from the gulls were sounding and sounding. They walked on the shore, holding hands, the air in their faces. 'I cannot believe,' said Marian, turning to him, the light catching her beautiful grey-blue eyes, 'that we have managed this.'

Nor could he. He really could not. '*Mia donna,*' he said. His heart was in his chest. 'How you are,' he said, 'is everything to me.'

It was no more than the truth. His senses were trained to her. He tightened his hold on her hand, raised it to his lips. They were face to face in the gaping open light of the sea, the lines of her face pitilessly revealed. He scanned her greedily for them, before kissing her. He liked to see her dear lines, her flaws, he was daily thankful for them, as sparing to him, and they embraced. He had a swooning, indecent excitement. 'We should turn back,' he said. He wanted to rein in his indecent sensations, and Marian so frail, too. It was all very queer.

Walking back, Johnny was going over Marian's face just then, her eyelids lowering, and the sense he had of her growing elation during the kiss. Perhaps this was indicative of the night to come. His ignorance was something. Lewes came into his mind, with all his experience. Lewes was dead. He was here now. Again the sheer arc of the horizon, a long ultramarine, becalmed, nearly, on this late afternoon, and then again the strange freedom he could feel they both had, like a present. The breeze was on their faces, whipping up the dusky gold-pale light. Over supper Johnny insisted on two bottles of champagne. 'Is that expensive?' she asked.

'Yes,' he said, with authority. 'I want the best, because I have the best. I am married to the best.'

It was a boast, but he knew the truth of it.

They drank the champagne quickly. Drunkenly, they made their way to the rooms. In between the sea's thirsty roar, he heard the sounds of Marian changing

next door, small clicks, rustling. He did not turn when she entered, only realising, in a half stupor, that he had not yet undressed. Impossible to take off his
clothes in front of her. He extinguished the lamp. In the dark, he realised from
the warm heaviness of his own half-numb hands and his head that he was very
intoxicated; it was hard undoing the garters of his socks. He was in under the
covers beside her, heart thumping. She did not move and he wondered if she was
already asleep. Even while wondering this, sleep was literally claiming him, the
long, long exhaustion of the last few weeks was mounting.

He was dreaming. He was in the Sussex coast where they went as children,
and he was feeling with hands along the rocks for the secret cave, encountering
only hard unyielding rocks, except the cave was close, he was sure of it; his hands
were now finding, both of them, the long flat wide aperture, his hands were
gripping inside and what they were gripping was soft and powerfully sucking; he
was in the cave, and moving towards the light, his fingers locked perfectly into
the aperture, and he was through, in an extraordinary moment. Seawater was at
his thigh.

The softness beneath him was Marian, bearing his full six-foot weight. 'I
hope ... I hope ...' he was whispering, in the darkness, as he levered himself up
and off her, fear growing; 'I hope ... I have not hurt you.' A soft laugh sounded.
He was glad of the darkness, glad of her.

They crossed the channel the next day in the Calais-Douvre, with a luxurious private cabin on deck. There was scarcely wind, and the sky was cloudless.
Wedding days were maligned, they joked. By late afternoon, they had reached
the Hotel du Rhin in Amiens. 'You are spoiling me,' Marian murmured. She had
not wanted the honeymoon suite, which would potentially draw attention to
them as a couple. Their rooms were palatial, with a charming sofa and table in
the window.

'You must sleep where you please,' said Johnny, in a gentle tone to her, as
they strolled round the two rooms. He still had a notion that he might have in
some way damaged her the previous night. Yet he also had a wild, golden thrill
when he reimagined the night, his stomach tumbling.

Early evening, they stood before Amiens cathedral in the late sun. 'The architect had the stone cut before it was built,' said Marian.

'Stone cut?' repeated Johnny. He felt stupid.

'Cut to its final size. It is built in the Gothic Lanceolate style,' went on his wife.

She was looking at it keenly, a complex look of assimilation in her narrowed eyes. She was reading aloud from the guide, but Johnny suspected she knew it all anyway; even if she didn't, their meaning was percolating in her in a way that was beyond him. But after looking awhile, he felt a small shimmer of rapture up his spine. So he had it in him. He walked back to the hotel with a buoyant step. Over supper in their room, he told Marian about the moment of rapture. 'Oh I am pleased for you,' she said, with passion.

Supper was over, the waiter took the tray away. It was all so comfortable, with a fire going. 'Dare I suggest a little Dante?' she said.

'Dare away,' said Johnny cheerfully. Tired, he smiled. He had a memory of his sister Eleanor, Nelly. He had confided in her that he was having a set of his wife's works bound, in a small edition of calf leather and vellum, as a wedding present, which he would give to her in Venice.

'You don't want to lug too many books on your travel,' Nelly had pointed out. He said they were taking so many books anyway it would make no difference.

'I hope you don't mind having supper brought to our room,' said Marian, anxiously, 'only I do not like to be recognised.'

'I quite understand,' said Johnny. 'It is the curse of being famous.' He looked at her with pride. He was married to England's most famous novelist. Famous all over the world. Some moments he thought he was ill or dreaming. He could not believe it. He laughed.

'Dearest, what is funny?'

He told her, they both laughed, she said she was so thankful, he was too. 'It is almost too perfect,' agreed Johnny. He prayed nothing would spoil it. They spent a nostalgic hour alternately reading and translating the Dante; then they had reached the end of the canto. Johnny's eyes were closing.

'Shall we try a little *Eugénie Grandet*?' she suggested.

'Why yes,' he said. Except he was fearfully tired. He knew *Eugénie Grandet* was by Balzac, and he hoped it would be in English, but he had an unfortunate memory of the volume on its side at the bottom of a trunk, a French word on the bottom of its spine.

She was kneeling now to pull it out. 'This will exercise our French,' she cried. 'You begin!'

It was more amusing than he could have predicted, though his great tiredness, like a potentially smothering and sucking ocean wave, kept swelling up. They were nurturing their minds as other people watered gardens, straining for Balzac's meaning through the prism of another language, and he shot an admiring glance at Marian when it was her turn to read, her energy so utterly undimmed. He had the sensation he used to have with Lewes and Marian, that life with them was lived at no ordinary level.

In Paris, they rented rooms at the Hotel Vouillement. 'I remember it well,' said Marian sadly, as they entered it. She had stayed here with Lewes.

Johnny did not feel even a flicker of jealousy. To show her this, he asked politely, 'When did you and George stay here?'

'Five, no, six years ago,' she said absently. 'Before we dine, shall we walk to the Arc des Etoiles? Also, I'm hoping we will be able to hear the glorious singing that I once heard at the Russian church tomorrow. I have set my heart,' she went on, 'on you enjoying it as I did.'

'I hope so too. You look blooming.'

It would have been impolite to say what he really thought, which was that she looked much younger: the healthy colour coming in and out of her cheeks. The chestnut trees were in early leaf as they strolled down the Arc des Etoiles; later, they went for a drive in the Bois de Boulogne.

'I keep thinking of that small dear group in the church, wishing us well,' said Marian, as the driver went with sudden swiftness under a cedar tree, the lowest branch of which Johnny could reach up and touch. 'There is only one cloud on the horizon, and that is the missing brooch,' she said. It had been lost just before they left. It was the most valuable jewellery she owned.

'It's only a brooch,' mused Marian, 'but I can't stop thinking about it. I hope it is found before we get to Venice.'

'Why then?'

'No reason at all! Only that it bothers me,' she admitted. She laughed because she had a superstitious feeling about it — if it were found, the darkness, the dark thing, would lift.

'Don't let it worry you too much,' said Johnny, shooting her a concerned look. She saw new signs of his kindness every day; he had a naturally courteous, generous nature.

They visited the Sainte Chapelle. 'Your response to art is growing,' she said, when they left.

'I am beginning to see it with your eyes,' he joked.

They saw Notre Dame, lunched at the Cafe Corazza. Marian loved Johnny, this modest man whose beauty — she had glimpsed him naked for the first time two mornings ago — had shocked her, so different to Lewes. They were an odd couple, she sixty, he forty; at a stroke, she had deprived him of the chance to have his own children, or a bride his own age. Yet like some strange chemical combination, as if the gap in his circle of electrons were filled exactly by her extra ones, she thought, they were right together.

But London was on her mind.

The day of the wedding, the news would have been out. She had no illusions. It was a thrilling moment when someone in public showed feet of clay — the higher the fall the better. How the judgements would rain! Of those who loved her, a few might defend her. Letters had never been as important as now. Each time they reached a new city, Johnny, in his correct jacket, which he put on every day with an absent air of duty, looking every inch the Englishman, went off to collect the letters post restante. When he returned, it was an effort not to snatch them from him.

Edith had written, sensitively. Barbara's letter outshone the others.

My dear I hope and I think you will be happy.

Tell Johnny Cross I should have done exactly what he has done if you would have let me and I had been a man.

You see I know all love is so different that I do not see it unnatural to love in new ways — not to be unfaithful to any memory.

If I knew Mr Lewes he would be glad as I am that you have a new friend.

What a woman, what a friend. Cara and Sara sent kind notes. She still had no word, though, from Maria Congreve, or Georgiana. And Charles was strangely silent on that matter. They had received a kind note of congratulations from Mr James, Mr Henry James. She had heard from Elma Stuart.

Johnny decided to write to Elma. Picking up his pen, he remembered her wooden gifts. What painstaking labour! He had a guilty sense he had stolen the prize.

But the great event, he wrote, *that has happened in my life seems to have taken away from me all power of doing, or thinking of, anything except how marvellously blessed is my lot — to be united for life with her who has for so long been my ideal. It is almost too great a happiness to have got the best.*

He was not exaggerating. In the Bois, the blossoms flamed in his vision, the colours in the stained-glass windows of La Sainte Chapelle had burned unnaturally, making his heart beat faster. They were travelling southwards to the sun.

Marian liked to write her letters just after breakfast. She wrote that Johnny had elected to dedicate his life to the remaining fragment of hers. She liked this picture of the robust man helping her, the frail one, walk and live; no whiff of unseemly, hasty, lusty romance. Johnny, *much loved and trusted by Mr Lewes*, now that she was alone, *sees his only longed-for happiness in dedicating his life to me*. Johnny was caretaker, really. There was even a religious ring about the word dedicate. Yet — it was a Sisyphean job, this attempt to control it all. What was she doing? She was like Canute, really, trying to push back the waves.

2

After the sunny days, the storms came at Lyons. From their hotel apartment they watched the sheet lightning after supper, the curtains drawn. The Fouviere Hills in near darkness transformed in livid instants into a different picture — white-filled, strange, and ghostly. Then Johnny lit the oil lamp. He had his jacket off, and Marian reached to touch the scarf round his neck, which felt icy-smooth in her fingers. 'It's silk,' he remarked. Marian went on feeling it. She was slightly jealous, in fact, of Johnny and his siblings' easy loving unity. The scarf was his wedding present from them. He used their nicknames with careless fondness. Mary was Marly; Emily, Emmy; Eleanor, Nelly; Willie, Will. Marian kissed his hand in penance for her inward jealousy; pushed away thoughts of Isaac. She was joining the family anyway. Johnny was tap-tapping the sofa arm, still watching for the ghostly lightning. She did hope he would sleep in her room tonight. She would not suggest it. Strange, sweet man! Each time they were together in the night, he had woken in the morning with a banging headache at the base of his skull. But would he come to her room tonight? As he had grown thinner, his face had grown in beauty. She had not known *this* pleasure with George.

But where was that brooch? Brett still had sent no word.

★ ★ ★

In Verona, in his own room, Johnny woke before it was light. A mosquito had disturbed his sleep. He opened the french doors to the balcony, and sat. The sky was deepest blue, beginning to lighten. Below him spread the russet corrugated rooves at all angles. The bell tower of the Basilica was outlined against the horizon. His thoughts were already mounting; in a funny way, they were like the rooves, pitted against each other at all angles, they kept coming. He had never read so much in his life before, as in the last month; nor seen so much art, nor looked so hard, and he was rising, he could feel it, he was becoming knowledgeable, with her incomparable mind to help him. They never dined out, always in the hotel apartment, so she would not be recognised. It made absolute sense. But he had been glad, two nights ago in Milan, to see Rossi in *Hamlet*. He had been determined to see Rossi. She despised Rossi's performance, but he had a secret sympathy for the troubled prince. At the same time, he had listened with her ears and eyes, seen Rossi's crudity. He was split, he had held on to his view. The molten sun was rising, the morning silence over the sleeping city was dreamlike. His knowledge filling his head to bursting. The days were getting hotter, but his summer clothes did not fit him, he had lost too much weight.

Later, as the day began to grow hot, and the insinuating waiter had taken away the breakfast things, Marian took out her paper and pen. I am happy, I am full of vigour, she thought defiantly. Against all the odds. It doesn't matter what the world thinks — and she threw a crust to the cheeky pigeon that was swaying forwards and backwards, with an insecure grasp, on the balcony's edge. With a greedy, gobbling coo, the pigeon descended to eat the crust. She wrote to Florence Cross: *What can I say to give your affectionate hearts a sense of our happiness? Only that we seem to love each other better than we did when we set out, which seemed then hardly possible, and we often talk of our Sisters, oftener think of them. You are our children, you know.*

Has she had achieved the impossible? Found a happy life with George dead? The hope made her want to cry aloud with joy. *You know that you are a very celebrated person,* Benjamin Jowett had written, *and therefore the world will talk a little about you, but they will not talk long and what they say does not much signify. It would be foolish to give up actual affection for the sake of what people say.*

She folded this letter into two, then four, then eight, inserted it into her reticule. It would live there with the letter from her brother. Isaac had written to

congratulate her on her marriage, breaking twenty-five years of silence.
The next step was Venice.

3

There is a last morning of talks, then it's over, and there's a final lunch in the Ca'Foscari before everyone goes to the airport. Hans is at the other end of the table. 'Looking forward to London?' says Bruno. He looks hung-over.

'No,' I say, as I sip my fizzy water.

On the wall hang black-and-white photographs of Venice, in a neat row. They remind me of a scanty row of pansies in a flowerbed. I'd like to rearrange them, mess them up. 'Katie Boyd, you look very distracted,' says Bruno. I reach for the wine.

'*In vino veritas,*' he adds, approvingly.

Talk picks up at our end about the conference, and then about Eliot herself. Marcia, who's wearing a crocheted cream-coloured vest, so airily stitched that I can see her bra, says, 'Oh! I have a problem with her, I really do.'

'Do you,' I say, with interest.

'I do! She's insufferable.' Marcia looks exhilarated as she speaks. 'Takes herself too seriously — and greedy. Too much appetite.'

'That's my feeling too,' says Bruno. 'There's something off about her.'

I drink my white. 'No, no, she was so brave. She was terrified of what people would think. But first she lives with Lewes, then she married Cross.'

'But Cross was gay!' cries Marcia.

The talk continues, but I'm not listening. I'm thinking about Eliot, doing something that she knew would make people dislike her, or feel disillusioned with her. But she did want to enjoy life; and it did take courage. At the other end of the table is Hans. I'm looking at him and considering.

I think it's then that I decide. The seat is empty beside Hans just now; someone has perhaps only temporarily left it — but without more ado, I walk over, sit beside him.

'Well, hello,' he says.

'Hi,' I say. 'So I'll see you in London.' My voice isn't very steady. I think I can read his face.

'You will,' he says.

★ ★ ★

It's time to go. Hands are shaken, cheeks kissed, goodbyes said. Everyone is going to catch a plane later. Hans and I step out of the Ca'Foscari. It has been raining all morning, and it is still raining.

'It's flooding,' says Hans, calmly.

He is right. The sky is a thick, pale grey, the rain steady, the wind warm. And I can see, below the steps of the entrance, on the pavement between here and the canal, water — about two inches. Hans looks down dubiously at his tennis shoes. Boards have been erected on the nearby quayside.

I say goodbye to Hans quickly, we hug for a moment. I will see him at the airport later today. But before then there's something I want to do. There is a Carpaccio Eliot wanted to look at, for which the painter Bunney arranged a special viewing, which she didn't get to see; but there's also a second one she did see, vaunted by Ruskin, a *St George and the Dragon*. I want to look at it myself.

I walk fast — as fast as I can. But arriving at St Mark's, the entire square is now covered with an inch of water. I walk to the northeast corner of it, hardly looking at the fairy palace. My feet in their shoes are sloshing through water, the air is weirdly warm yet rainy.

I spend time in the church, dark, cool, smelling of incense, looking at the *St George and the Dragon*, the moment of confrontation. I try to see what Ruskin was talking about, which is what Eliot would have been seeking, I think.

Coming outside back into the light, I turn left, but the street is a cul de sac, and I am obliged to go back. After that I try to head south, but soon stop for an espresso, to look again at Google Maps, as I realise I'm lost. I can see the hovering little blue shimmer indicating where I am, but it makes no sense. I turn my phone upside down, squint at it. Outside it is still raining, the sky still soft, pale grey, but the air has a noticeably cooler tinge. I determine to use the phone as a compass, go southwest. But each time I try to go in that direction, the canals seem to be thwarting me — suddenly there is no street in the direction I want, only a canal, with a bridge further up, and after that I can't work out the best route. The flood water, I realise, is rising. People are erecting more boards on metal scaffolding. The boards are about two feet high, I calculate. I hit dry streets where I can walk fast again. Then, drawing closer to the lagoon, it is back to wading. The water is even higher.

So Venice is flooding. Everywhere shops are closing, I look in as I pass, and see surreal spectacles: shops, with water nearly two feet high, people rapidly removing goods from lower shelves, transferring them to higher shelves.

I remember now the remarks of the waiter at breakfast about flooding. I had taken no notice, as the receptionist dismissed it as a rumour, saying not in June. Now water has splashed up my dress, the bottom half of my dress is in fact soaked, and the wading is increasingly slow. There is a smell everywhere that is new. I know the Venice smell but this is concentrated, more obvious. By the time I am back at St Mark's, the water has risen from two inches, to knee height.

St Mark's is a swimming pool. People queuing for the Doge's Palace are being corralled into lines in the water. How strange. Everywhere now people are wearing turquoise galoshes over shoes, a cord fastening under the knee. Magically, black wellingtons also appear. Then I see the vendors.

Slowly I go west, get to the bridge. Approaching my hotel, I take out my phone: missed calls and messages from Hans. I need, he says, to book a flight the next day, there is a room at his hotel, Pensione Wildner. What is he talking about?

The lobby is packed with people and their bags. A crowd has gathered around the reception desk, there is no queue. I tap the woman in front of me, she turns round. 'There are no more rooms,' she says. Everyone is trying to speak to the receptionist. A baby is crying. I ring Hans. The *vaporettos* are not running, he says, the water is too high. You can't get a water taxi now, they're gone. There is no way you will make the flight. He has booked a room in his pensione, but they are going fast. He would bet the Accademia doesn't have anything now, and of course he is right.

★ ★ ★

I have nothing to wear for these flooded streets. I put on my soaked, wet sandals again, ignoring the smell. I pay, leave, and as soon as I'm outside, see that I can't possibly wheel my suitcase. I will have to hold it up. The water is everywhere; only the bridges are exempt.

Hans is waiting for me in the colonnades at the west end of St Mark's Square, a tall figure with straw fair hair plastered to his head. 'Look at your feet!' he says.

'It's extraordinary —'

'It *is* extraordinary,' he says. 'It's happened so fast.' He takes my case.

The police are moving people out of St Mark's, cordoning it off. Their costumes and boots are immaculate. We walk away from the square, down towards the lagoon by a back street that is also two feet high in water. Everyone is holding their suitcases as best they can, some above their heads. Gradually, we come to the quayside in front of the doge's palace. The lagoon — I stop for a moment to look at it. It looks strange and wild, choppy and out of control. There is nothing to mark the point at which it ends and the quayside begins — the Adriatic sea is flowing right over the city, straight over St Mark's.

Hans' trousers are dark up past his knees, soaked by the water. We wade, pushing our legs through the knee-high water, in which I can feel the current of the sea. The wind is stronger than before, all the awnings are flapping. It's the north African wind, Hans says in a loud voice so I can hear him. I am glad to be with him. People are thinning out now. 'That's it,' he says, indicating the Pensione. It is small, with a glass-cased restaurant at the front, but as we draw near I see chairs on tables, everything is stacked on tables and counters, there is two feet of water inside it, people are busy with buckets and wellingtons. The entrance is next to the restaurant. The reception area is flooded like the restaurant, so is the kitchen, the calm receptionist wears high waders, water covers even the first stair. I follow Hans up the narrow staircase. I am soaked and tired. It is modestly decorated, for a hotel that's right on the lagoon. We leave the water behind, yet the stairs are filled with the peculiar sour-sweetish smell of the water of Venice. Up we go, four flights. We are breathless at the top. Hans opens the door, switches on the lights. The room is not large, but it has two windows directly onto the lagoon. Hans opens the shutters and the windows, immediately there is a violent rattling from the wind. But the colours. The colours are extraordinary: the air blue under the grey sky: the lagoon churned up, the magical aqua-tinted water flecked with white. Right across the water is San Georgio. 'It's something,' says Hans, coming to stand beside me. Then he turns and begins unzipping my rainjacket. 'Hans,' I say, he shakes his head and continues. I peel it off myself, my face is still damp from the rain. I put my arms round his neck and kiss him. This is the beginning of the end of the most confusing and beautiful day. And this I will not forget.

★ ★ ★

It is dusk when I wake. Hans is closing the shutters; he switches on the lamp at the far side of the room. He asks me what I want to do, then he comes and sits beside me. I reach and touch his cheek with the back of my index finger. He kisses my finger. He says, doing a down-turning with his mouth, more peculiar things with his mouth, 'I want to be with you.' I see a stricken look on his face. 'It doesn't make sense otherwise. I've thought about it, over and over.'

We go out to get supper, or rather, we go downstairs. The hotel manager shakes his head. '*Non e permesso*', he says. It is not safe. Their own restaurant is officially closed, but the cook is managing to make a simple meal for three rooms now — a pasta — he can do the same for us. We say we want to go out. We ask the kitchen for bin bags, and we put one each round each leg, clumsily try to hold the bags tight.

We step from the safe hotel, out into the wind. Outside it is eerie. There are hardly any people. It is dark, the awnings are whipping and flapping noisily in the great wind. We are wading through a low, windy sea at night, the water shining black here and there in the lamps. We go on wading. We will have supper together, somewhere will be open.

4

She could not pretend to understand it all.

They were here in Venice, the city of water and light, and their adjoining rooms at the Hotel Europa, the Palazzo Giustinian, on the Grand Canal, were magnificent. The floors were of polished stone, a tapestry hung on Marian's wall, the painted ceilings showing cherubs and gods. Johnny marvelled at the cunningly painted pottery rendition of St Mark's Square that was beside his bed. Through the French doors, on the balcony, he saw light glitter.

'Shall we try dining out, *mia donna*?'

'I might be recognised.'

By early evening, the waiter had laid the table in the apartment with the white cloth for dining, and a splendid supper of a barbarous-looking fish in a gleaming oily orange sauce was served. When it was cleared away, Johnny read Alfieri's autobiography aloud in slow Italian, while Marian corrected him. They turned next to Ruskin's *Stones of Venice*. The evening was darkening, a light wind was crossing the lagoon. Gently, Johnny said, 'Dearest, would you prefer to be alone?'

'Entirely as you please,' she said. The idea of Johnny feeling conjugally obligated did not bear contemplation. She smiled. The man who would have been funny about this, of course, was George.

Johnny said, 'I will be alone, I think. My tiredness,' — and he gestured. But in the night she became aware of being kissed and caressed, and she woke fully when Johnny pushed himself into her. In the morning, Johnny looked exhausted.

Over breakfast he asked her, 'I didn't hurt you?'

'You must rid yourself of this idea completely.' She enquired after him with the same solicitousness.

'The usual spot at the back of my head,' he said, almost rudely. He retired for another hour to his own room, unusually shutting the double doors completely.

Venice was splendid, the queen of cities. Ruskin was Marian's guide, she had made it his, too. Over morning coffee, when Johnny had risen again, they watched as the sun struck the dome of Santa Maria della Salute opposite. The heat was already rising, a vaporous mist was on the water, a magical acquatint under the hot sky. They saw pictures in the Accademia: Mantegnas, Bellinis, Carpaccios. To travel anywhere was easy: waiting for them, always, was their gondolier, Corradini. Johnny had remarked to Marian on Corradini, whose smile was unreadable, and who had no top teeth. She had been surprised at the remark. 'I have become too used to being your eyes,' she joked. In reply, Johnny said that life through her eyes was a poem.

The morning's freshness was gone by noon. The sun was a white metallic pulse in the sky, the street reflected heat back into his face. Johnny was caught between sky and street. He had disloyal thoughts of an English summer day at Weybridge: temperate, shady cedars and small willows, the lawn mown, sweet to the spirit. Marian had quoted Homer's anvil of the sun, and now he understood: the sky so louring, so actively productive of heat, as if a Vulcan lived above.

'Shall we take the gondola?' Johnny asked, polite. They had left the Accademia. He wanted so much to be on the water, his impatience felt desperate. But in the Piazza, Marian was reading the Ruskin pamphlet Johnny had got for her yesterday, and with that complete concentration, with which he was now so familiar, she nodded in his direction but did not lift her eyes. He must wait. The heat was making him faint, he could feel his heart speeding up, he put two discreet fingers to his pulse, he knew his own tendency. But it was in this blinding white heat that it occurred to Johnny that Marian was not all she seemed. He had heard her last night, a cry from the depths. He regretted going into her room, and his impulse to do so was now a mystery to him. Sweat was pooling under his arms and on his back. He would wash himself when they returned to the hotel. She said they needed refreshment, particularly Johnny. But she seemed not to have heard his suggestion of going on the water. 'I would like to go on the gondola,' he said again, in a slightly strangled voice. The effort involved, to control his sense of urgency, was excruciating. But they stayed in the piazza and had ice cream.

Finally, they were on the water, Corradini steering them out onto the pale swell. 'To feel the breeze is ecstasy,' said Johnny. He put his hand to the back of his neck, then his palms out to feel the breeze. The breeze was taking the pain in his neck away. They were on the open lagoon. A wonderful, wide space of water under the sun: but it was marvellous! He was here, and she was Mrs Cross.

'Where did you get the Ruskin guide from?' she asked.

'The man's name is Bunney.'

★ ★ ★

Later, Johnny went alone in search once more of John Wharlton Bunney, whom he had met the day before. He walked along the Zattere. St Mark's Square on his left — *St Mark's Square*, only one of the world's glories! That was not a bad way of putting it. Dear God, on his right, the water of the lagoon, he had never seen such a colour. Riva degli Schiavone, keep going, *diritto, perfetto*. Per-fay-to, he enunciated. He put his hand to the back of his neck. Castello ahead. He tried to remember the night, but there was nothing where there should be a memory. Gone. He found the house. Mr Bunney, a painter, acted as an agent for Ruskin's books and pamphlets, a sideline. Johnny would be curious to see him without a hat. Hats were sometimes worn for purposes of concealment.

He hadn't bargained for children. A maid and a child admitted him. The child, a red-head, or orange head, a gap between two teeth, stamped up the stairs ahead, lifting each sturdy-looking leg as it were burdensome, before, stamp! — 'Are you a stranger?'

'I am,' said Johnny. You never could fool children. The gap between the child's teeth looked dreadfully quaint.

'Mr Cross.'

'Mr Bunney.'

He had forgotten how close-set Bunney's eyes were, and the way his eyebrows slanted downwards above the asiatic eyes. He spoke like an Englishman. 'You look like a regular painter,' said Johnny, indicating Bunney's overalls.

'I am a regular painter.'

The overall was pocked with colours: blue, yellow, red, every colour under the sun.

'The sun is extraordinarily hot,' said Johnny aloud. His shirt was sticking to his back. A baby was crying. 'Mrs Bunney is out with Jack and Em,' said Mr Bunney.

'It's not really a problem,' said Johnny, meaning to be kind.

Mr Bunney was walking down the corridor. They were up on the second floor, the large room had three great windows, and easels. 'Good God! you do a lot of painting.'

He was crass. He was making Mr Bunney smile. Johnny spent an hour looking at the canvases. He thought they were subtle and atmospheric, and said so. 'But really,' added Johnny, 'I am after Ruskin. I understand you have more pamphlets.'

By the time he left he had pamphlets safe in his cotton bag. 'Ruskin has been very good to me,' confided the painter. 'He is a fine, thoughtful man — a genius, in my view.'

The word prompted Johnny to smile before he could stop himself. 'Might I bring a lady-friend with me, to admire your pictures? Would that be possible?'

'Certainly.'

'I am sure she will be interested,' said Johnny. He couldn't damp down his own smirk, unfortunately. Not that he wanted to seem mysterious, or secretive. But what would Mr Bunney have said, if he knew that the lady in question was England's greatest novelist? It was audacious, being in Venice incognito. No one had the smallest idea that she, *his wife*, was here; no idea at all. They took all their meals in their rooms; they did not go to St Mark's Square to a cafe — she would be spotted before you had time to blink. They went to galleries, churches, or into silent green-water roads and alleys, navigating impossibly hairpin bends in the long black boat with velvet smoothness. Silent, between high walls, the dark water, the sun and shadow; the discreet sound of the long oar breaking the water's surface, as round-shouldered Corradini pulled up and then pushed down, drawing them deeper and deeper into the secret Venice. It was hard to unite the two — the ravishments of the open lagoon and these secret, hot, silent alleys.

* * *

Two days later, Johnny strolled with Marian along the Zattere, listening to the familiar sounds: the cries, the splashes, the birds, the low broad churning noise of the large ferry, that made a furrow in the water; the begging children that appeared in your gaze, looked directly into your eyes. It was only twenty minutes' walk before they had reached the quayside Bunney home in Castello. 'My wife, Mrs Cross,' introduced Johnny. 'Dear, this is Mr Bunney.'

The morning was a success.

'I understand why you have Mr Ruskin's approval,' commented Marian. 'The sky and the sea, in these subtly varying lights — a rhapsody, Mr Bunney.'

Water and air, vaporous mists, changing colour, poetry of mood: did the changes seem infinite in their possibility? Infinite, as human variety is infinite, no two people being in personality identical?

Marian spoke without self-consciousness. At once, Mr Bunney was intrigued. They were talking now as if they had known each other a long time.

'But is this what Ruskin thinks?' demanded Johnny, interrupting.

'We were not talking of Ruskin,' said Marian, in mild surprise, smiling.

'But he is very sure of himself,' cried Johnny. Johnny wanted to press this important point home. Marian's hat was on the point of falling — he adjusted it, she turned round, again looking surprised.

'We are on the second floor,' said Johnny. 'As heat rises, it is bound to be hot.'

Mrs Bunney entered with a tray. It was while he was drinking the white wine that Johnny noticed the smell from outside, the power of it. He went to the window and looked out. This was a dismaying fact to absorb. All this beauty, and the smell.

★ ★ ★

Opening the shutters in the morning, it was hot, humid, but it was raining. Good heavens, he said aloud. The lagoon's pretty pale green was now darkish and unlovely. Even the rain here was hot. But the foulest smell was present. He had heard that the rains in Venice made the smell worse. Standing in his room, he realised then that he had already put on his jacket, but he was too hot, he took it off, tearing the lining as he did so. It did not matter. None of his clothes fit him now. In Marian's larger room, the white tablecloth was laid. He had a heart-breaking sensation that the deliciously appointed breakfast table, with the fragrant coffee in the pot, the bread rolls, hams, was, poignantly, a façade. Marian was asking how he was. 'I am exhausted, to say the truth,' he said. It was true. Far from rested, the night had left him feeling hollowed out, half broken with tiredness.

'The rain is stopping,' she said. She was right. The clouds were breaking, bits of light and sunshine were coming through. A servant announced that the Bunneys had arrived, and Johnny's heart lifted. They stopped for some minutes to admire the rooms, Mr Wharlton Bunney picked up the small clay figure of St Mark's, he too was charmed. 'It is the colour, the painting, that is so intricate,' he marvelled.

'Did you have a successful day yesterday?' Johnny asked Mr Bunney.

'So-so,' smiled Mr Bunney, a touch melancholy. He was not a complacent man. Johnny warmed to him again.

'Having seen your work,' Johnny said, 'I suspect you are more successful than you allow.'

'Kind words,' said Mr Bunney.

The clouds were gone, the sky was blue — regal, without peer. And what was he, John Walter Cross, so distressed about? It was a storm in a teacup, after all. He was childishly glad Mr Bunney seemed to like him. He was himself again. 'Good god, the weather changes in a heartbeat!' he said, cheerfully, and the ladies, Marian in her straw hat, Mrs Elizabeth Bunney, glanced at him. Profound relief made him yawn. Corradini was waiting, chewing something which he spat out of his mouth recklessly, in front of them. '*Al-lora!*' On the lagoon, the rising warm breeze was pleasant, and the buoyant swell. The women chatted, thought Johnny cynically, as if they had known each other all their life. He realised Mr Bunney was asking him about their journey. 'We had a marvellous time, to say the truth,' confided Johnny in an undertone. 'I became in a small way an art expert. All through the eyes of Mrs Cross, of course. But I felt as if I understood the forces that produced Mantegna, and I can vouch for Kugler — though it is my wife who reads him in the German. But no doubt you have read him. Though I fear he is a little dry?'

'I cannot say I have read Kugler,' said Mr Bunney, with a puzzled expression. 'But you would recommend him?'

'Oh, heartily. Though you might do better to talk to Mrs Cross about him. She is very wise,' he added, sadly. 'We have been reading Alfieri.'

'Now you've lost me!' laughed Mr Bunney.

'His autobiography, And my Italian improves apace. Does it not, *mia donna?*'

Still melancholy, he appealed to Marian, who turned to look at him in the penetrating way he disliked. Blushing, Johnny turned away. The water had been churned by a larger tugboat at some distance; a loud slap of sea on the gondola. Johnny stood up, nervous.

'*Non — non,*' said Corradini. '*E meglio sedersi.*'

Mr Bunney, smiling, was helping him to sit. Marian looked pale.

They returned to have lunch, the four of them, at the hotel; then resumed their seats in the gondola, for further sight-seeing.

'I have a confession to make, and that is, I do not like Tintoretto. His colours — they fog the eye and bring the soul down,' cried Marian. 'Especially the red.' She shuddered. Johnny was alert to the note of suffering, from his own increasing darkness. Looking at Marian, a vestige of tenderness stirred. At the same time — how she drew attention to herself. His slow repulsion returned. My soul is in revolt, said Johnny to himself.

With joy, meanwhile, Mr Bunney had gone into the fray, arguing that

Tintoretto was the giant of Venetian art, the one who brought movement and life to Venice, with his death-defying energy.

(Corradini was slily guiding them in the still, silent back-waters of Venice. The heat, incredibly, was intensifying.)

Johnny was exhausted just listening to Mr Bunney, even if he did like him. It was tiring, being able to see the posturing so clearly. Mr Bunney, he said to himself, wants to show Mrs Cross that he is interesting.

He preferred Mrs Bunney, suddenly. Her silence was admirable.

Out of the blue, he remembered that cry the other night, in the middle of the night, from Marian. It was depraved. At the same time, he had grown, he could not fail to notice, excited at this idea. He shifted in his seat, sunk in new self-loathing.

'Are you all right, my dear?' said Marian softly, under the preposterously large hat, the brim of which was wide as a platter.

'I am hot.' He forced a smile, and pulled out his handkerchief and applied it to his forehead. The little girl was correct. He was a stranger. Stranger. His misery was bottomless. The water was a soft green, secretly still, and what was it? Good heavens. Effluvia — human waste, doubtless. The heat was making him faint.

'I say,' came Mr Bunney's voice, and Johnny became aware that Mr Bunney was passing him his hat. 'You'd better put this on, before you get sunstroke.'

Johnny recalled his manners. 'What about yourself?'

It was painful. He had put on his old self like a jacket, in the moment of courtesy, and it reminded him of everything he had lost. It was going so fast, his self. He glanced at Marian. Alas, it was possible. Then he glanced at the water. He did not know how deep these secretive silent waters were, but the lagoon was deep.

But they were still talking! Was there never an end? Mr Bunney on Tintoret, as he called him, with a knowing air of familiarity. Was everyone a braggart? Was it all about power and posturing? Madonna speaking now, in her most musical voice, about Ruskin.

'Ruskin,' Johnny announced, interrupting them, 'is altogether too sure of himself. He thinks he is the only one to see Carpaccio's merit. He is a schoolboy showing off.'

No one spoke. Corradini, round shoulder bent in his goblin-like way, was drawing them swiftly out of the high-walled water alleys, with the concentrated stench — out, out, and in a last bolt southwards, they were released into the lagoon, the open light. A gust of fresh air, the boat lifted.

5

They went to the Accademia again the next day, with a plan to meet the Bunneys later. By now, the Bunneys had discovered that Marian was in fact George Eliot, but they had promised to keep it secret. Johnny said: 'What would you say to lunch *al fresco*, or perhaps at the little place Mr Bunney mentioned?'

Courteously voiced, the answer was no, as Johnny had guessed it would be. It was a rotten test. Yet he had wanted to avoid eating in their apartment again. But they returned to the hotel, the Palazzo, where the obsequious flunkeys waited on them instantly. Johnny had given Corradini an outsize tip: he had no idea why. In their rooms he saw the bed, and some memory, some terrible intimate memory, was pushing its way through his mental membranes. Yesterday, he remembered again, the Bunneys had found out that Mrs Cross was also George Eliot.

'I will not,' said Johnny, aloud.

'You will not *what*?'

Johnny said, 'You are angry.' His tone was outright sullen. In truth, he was defeated. 'What?' he now demanded. His eyes took her in. It was not her physical blemishes he minded.

'You are not yourself.'

The jury was out. He walked through the double doors to his room, lay down on the bed. Jury out. She was sincere, he supposed. Now she came to his room to talk to him. He was all ears.

'Mr Bunney is making a special effort, so that we can see the Carpaccio.'

'We've seen the Carpaccios.' His voice was unclothed now. Brutal. Looking at her, he saw a woman, not much more. Not so much between them, if God was on his side.

'I am talking about *Due Cortigiane*, at the Correr, that is not publicly on view. Ruskin describes it as the finest picture in the world. Mr Bunney has put himself out, and arranged a private viewing.'

'I care this much for it,' sighed Johnny. He had sat up in bed and he put his thumb and index finger together to indicate zero space. He was insolent. Then he saw beside him the exquisite painted clay object, St Mark's with its strange tower. He picked it up, held it out, dropped it. It smashed into pieces.

Marian started to cry. 'My dear Johnny,' she was saying, fearfully, looking at him. She had turned pale.

'I want to sleep.' He motioned her out with his head. She had consumed him. Well, she could see what it *was* she had consumed. She might not like it.

'I have made you angry,' she said, still fearful.

He saw tears in her eyes, but he was not moved a jot. 'I am so tired of pretense, of lies,' he said.

He was disgraceful, he sank lower. He closed the shutters, shut the double doors. Hours later, a maidservant tiptoed in, and swept up the broken pieces. It was all cleared away. No affect, he would be better dead. Towards midnight, she came to sit by him. She looked appallingly sad.

★ ★ ★

'How are you?' she asked, the next morning, as she sat beside him.

'It is intolerable,' he said, thoughtfully. It was already suffocatingly hot, the sun slanting in, potent. 'I did not sleep all night, and my head is light and heavy at once. It is better if you leave me alone. *Altogether* better,' he added, meaningfully.

First, she looked at him; then she opened the shutters on to the balcony. 'This is one of the loveliest views in the world,' she said, sorrowfully. She wore her emotions like clothes. He shut his eyes and waited. The back of his head hurt as usual, he put the pillows behind him, sat up. Even from here he could smell it, the tang of urine in the air. He had never been more homesick in his life. The modest green gardens of home. Good God. Already he was sweating: his brow, under his arms, his back. She sat by him, touched his arm, he pulled it away quickly. 'You are my husband,' she was saying, wonderingly. She was reminding him that he belonged to her, he thought, in sickness and in health. He shut his eyes, tears squeezing stickily out from behind his lids.

Some time later, he woke, and he heard a strange man's voice in the next room. '*Ma che cos'è*? To what ... do you ...'

'Madness,' came Marian's voice, clear, from the same room. He heard the tone of knowledge. 'He has a mad brother.' Johnny got out of bed, the doctor was speaking. He no longer cared. He went out of the French doors, he was on the balcony, in the sun. Facing the sky and the Santa Maggiore: the glittering splendour of Venice and the lagoon, radiant in the heat. As quietly as possible, he moved the table to the stone balustrade; mounted the chair to mount the table; registered two — no — three gondolas below; then stepped on to the balcony edge, and with sudden stupendous energy, from a simian crouch he leapt — over the gondolas, into the waters of the Grand Canal.

6

Back in London, my flat looks different. It is both better and worse, smaller and bigger: every single aspect of my existence has been bent out of shape. In my retina's scope, there are images to be pushed away, then pulled back, then pushed away. I say to Hans, it will be impossible with me, you will have to cope with infinite demands, and chronic jealousy. He says it will be fine. I say the reality will not be fine. He says it will. I like him in every way. I think he and Ann are a bad fit.

Hans talks about Jo Devlin, but mainly his marriage. I don't believe every atom of Hans' representation — in any case he is careful to find fault with himself — but his account feels true. That it's grey, inflected with other, wilder colours, of which I can't possibly have knowledge, I take for granted.

And writing this book, I have been fascinated when Eliot finds herself sprouting feelings and sensations, like some impossible plant, growing from her own chest, arms, hands for Cross. But just now I have half an eye on myself. I think what will happen if I stay with Hans and his marriage breaks up. What will the department think? What will Ann feel? And the bomb for the kids, with its long, long emotional fuse. 'It's easy to judge,' I say to Hans, when he comes to my flat. 'Here.' I pass him my *Mill on the Floss*.

We agree that the ending, Maggie and Tom reunited in the flood, is incredible. She's written herself into a corner, Hans says. Where can she go? Who doesn't want Stephen Guest and Maggie to be together? Impossible to part two people who love each other, push the love away. There is no good way out of it.

Eliot kills Maggie off, but not before pointing her finger at the most dangerous emotion — righteous indignation.

It is lovely to talk to Hans about her. We are lying in bed and I read aloud this section:

To have taken Maggie by the hand and said, 'I will not believe unproved evil of you ... I, too, am an erring mortal, liable to stumble, apt to come short of my most earnest efforts; your lot has been harder than mine, your temptation greater; let us help each other to stand and walk without more falling,' — to have done this would have demanded courage, deep pity, self-knowledge, generous trust; would have demanded a mind that tasted no piquancy in evil-speaking, that felt no self-exaltation in condemning ...

'Isn't it superb?' I say. 'Isn't it needed more than ever in our personal, public, political life?'

(I suppose Eliot, who kept a figure of the crucified Christ on her desk while she translated a text that would help unravel Christianity in her own century, could have said, 'Let he who is without sin cast the first stone.')

I say to Hans, that part of *Mill* is my favourite bit of Eliot's soul. He likes it too, we kiss some more.

I meet Ann for a coffee at work. After a few minutes, she tells me she is pregnant. My coffee cup rattles loudly as I put it down. She is explaining: they had done her bloods because she complained in hospital of being tired, and found her HCG was sky high. She only heard at the end of yesterday. I say slowly, congratulations.

She says, thank you. 'At first I was hysterical with fear and loathing. I am not exaggerating. I was going straight for an abortion. But now —'

She looks around her with a puzzled, almost dreamy air.

'I'm kind of pleased. I just am.'

'I can understand that,' I say, haltingly.

'Are you all right?' she says, looking at me suddenly. 'You just — your colour.'

I say I'm fine. And then I ask: 'And work? What about your book?'

'It will be set back a little,' she admits, cautiously.

'What do you mean, a little?'

'Work, life,' she says. 'It's hard to get the balance right. Everyone finds that hard.'

I am silent.

'I was wondering, in fact, if you'd like to be a godparent.'

'No.'

Ann looks at me in surprise.

'No.' I get up, but I knock my tea as I reach for my bag. The tea goes flying. There is tea pooling under the table, and around the chair. I kneel on the floor, mop it up with napkins; then I need more napkins, to soak it all up. It takes several minutes, by which time I have a pile of tea-stained, crumpled napkins which I put in the bin. Then I say I have to go; I begin walking, and find my way out of the building. I walk down Southampton Row, and then east. I do not know where I am walking to. I think I recognise the Inns of Court.

I suddenly need to sit down. There is no bench, but there are steps.

I sit on them.

I sit for a long while. I can see the sky, the trees, the houses. No — I want to go on for the moment. I get up and start walking again. And I keep walking, until I reach the river. It's a grand width. My eyes aren't dry and I reach in my pocket. It's a crumpled napkin, I realise. I hold it up, and then I see, in scrolling letters, *Cafe Tomaso, Venezia.*

The Thames is not like the grand canal. But still.

A text comes. It's Hans.

You are not to worry. Meet at 9?

I will be there.

Because, what a lovely man. What a lovely man he is.

7

He couldn't put them together: not this couple, with the couple he'd seen a month before. Willie Cross had received a telegram from Marian, and had come to Venice the next day. Apparently Johnny had jumped into the Grand Canal, and Corradini and a couple of waiters from the hotel had rescued him. He had heard privately that Johnny begged them not to rescue him.

Johnny stirred, half opened his mouth, licked his lips.

'You need a drink, old fellow,' said Willie.

Willie waited while Johnny moved to a better position. Johnny sipped, then lay back, before asking what day it was. Willie said it was Friday.

'Good to see you,' said Johnny. A bleak look came into his eyes, which grew. Johnny moaned and shook his head. Willie took his hand. 'Stop, stop —'

'Does he need chloral?'

At the sound of Marian's voice, Johnny held on to Willie's hand more tightly. 'What's going to happen to me?' he whispered.

'Nothing's going to happen to you, old fellow. See here,' — Willie pulled out from his pocket a packet of cigars, selected one, reached into his pocket for clippers, cut it; lit it — 'Just bought these round in St Mark's. A very well-appointed shop — how's the head?'

'Banging a bit.'

'Where?'

Johnny indicated the base of his skull.

'Willie,' said Johnny in a voice close to a whisper, 'don't go.'

'I won't.'

Willie puffed away. Marian came in to the room, asking how the patient was. A look of distress appeared on Johnny's face. Willie ignored Johnny's appeals, and let Marian sit in his place. 'Are you feeling better?' she asked.

'Please don't look at me in that way.'

'I am — waiting for you, to be — to come back.'

Johnny had averted his eyes, was examining his arm. Marian begged him to look at her again, and he asked, 'Why?' She said she loved him. But if she were not mistaken, his lip was curling. In a sort of sneer.

'I don't know why you look like that,' she cried.

'I still find you intolerable,' he said, in the same thoughtful voice. He tapped the wood of the side table. 'The words are as real as this wood.' His face was gaunt and sombre.

Willie appeared, Marian left. 'Thank God,' said Johnny, as Willie shut the door behind him.

'Now look, J, you've got to do better. She says you say unspeakable things to her.'

Johnny was making two fists with his hands, raised in front of him, the knuckles bleaching white, and staring at them. 'I broke through.'

'I don't know what you mean.'

The room was filling with Willie's blue cigar smoke. Johnny was reminded of Lewes. He noted his brother's face. Willie had always been a scamp. In fact, it did Johnny good to see him. Even now, Willie was tut-tutting but he had a lightness, there was a shred of amusement in his eyes. 'Can't you see?' said Willie, in an undertone. 'You're putting her in a very difficult position. You can't just say you don't like the woman. You're just married. You've lost a lot of weight,' he added.

'See here Willie — what can I do?'

Johnny had no desire to live.

'You don't have a choice,' said Willie. 'Come on, J. I'm pouring out money into these many-fingered hands for people to keep their mouths shut. It's all good at home. Chelsea's coming along. Armitage is a rum character, but he'll do something fine.'

Willie looked at his brother with asperity. When he had arrived, Johnny had been out from the chloral: an almost unrecognisably sunburnt face, gaunt, mouth hanging open; within ten minutes Johnny had said the words 'foul' and 'desecration'. Amateurishly, Willie was contemplating these words as if they were pieces in a jigsaw, whose completion would yield understanding.

A day later, they were seated outside the Hotel Europa at a table, drinking *spremuta di limone*, though Willie had ordered a mezzo of white wine. Marian asked Johnny if his head were better.

Johnny closed his eyes.

'Answer, J, for pity's sake,' urged Willie, as he dipped his head deftly in the sunlight to light his cigar. His eye was half on Johnny and half on the waiter. He kept hoping the waiter would materialise with a plate of salty ham and piquant anchovies, as he had when he first arrived. Johnny said in a cold voice that nothing had changed and it was better the pretence was ended.

'The pretence?' queried Willie.

Johnny motioned his head callously in Marian's direction.

'My dear fellow, you can't be like this,' protested Willie in an undertone that was perfectly audible to Marian. Willie left, Johnny's face was sombre and cold.

'I can't understand you,' said Marian, tremblingly. 'What has happened to you?'

Johnny picked up his cream linen napkin, monogrammed with a curling *HE*, and dropped it on the ground, like a naughty child. At the sight of a spark of anger in Marian's face he smiled. 'The pretense is at an end, Mrs Cross,' he said, bowing his head. It was all so terrible he might as well scrape amusement where he could. She went away. Johnny was on his own. It was the first time in seventy-two hours that he had been left unsupervised.

8

Willie had agreed with Marian that it was a bad business. Privately he thought the marriage was finished. Marian did not cry. 'We had hopes,' she admitted at lunch, when it just the two of them. She pursed her lips together tight, and looked grimly ahead of her. He had persuaded her to have a glass of the white. Johnny was now safely knocked out with chloral.

'It is a strain for you,' said Willie. He was not especially given to sympathy, and he found himself mildly alienated by her daily, frantic enquiries about the activity of the press. He knew for a fact that it had been written up in at least three local papers, but he had been liberal with the lire, especially to Corradini, who had helped fish poor Johnny out, and whom he didn't trust an inch. 'Please tell me the truth. How many times has Johnny — how — prone is he to being —'

She did not know how to describe it. He seemed not like a human being. He was cruel. It was clear that it was hateful for him to look at her, be near her, listen to her, or touch her. What sense was left?

Willie, whose heart was buoyant and rather closed, considered what to say. 'He has had one episode before, with the Jay girl. Not like this, but not easy. I think ... was he under strain with the wedding preparations?' He spoke carefully. His sisters, especially Nelly and Flo, in the awful flurry of the news of Johnny, in England before Willie left, were adamant Johnny had been pushed too hard, having to keep everything secret, while also having to get everything done. Willie sipped his wine, tried to enjoy the sound of the birds, of water slapping gently against the gondolas moored some feet away.

At the same time he was worried about the cost of staying too long at this excruciatingly expensive hotel, with its pink stone veneer and gothic-eastern pediments. He was constantly hungry. Johnny had no appetite at all, Marian little. Willie had a pronounced taste for Italian food, and he found himself wondering if he couldn't stay somewhere more modest, where he could slip out to the odd restaurant for luncheon; tantalising smells of roasting meat, garlic, tomatoes were in the air intensely from noon onwards. Each time he descended the stairs, the uniformed servants were looking at him as if they expected a large tip, for nothing. It was costing the earth to stay here, time was moving on.

Johnny was awake. Willie came down to see Marian, and suggested they all three venture out. Marian said it would be good to walk, there was even a freshness in the air. But Johnny would not want to see the inside of a church.

Willie did not understand quite what this had to do with it. Confused, he said: 'He does not want to see churches?'

'I think not.' (Crisp.)

'But you do.'

'Yes.'

'Let's bring him along,' said Willie. 'Safest plan.'

They ventured along the Zattere, avoiding St Mark's, as too public; along the Riva degli Schiavoni, in the direction of the Bunneys' apartment; then turned northwards into the city. After going up and down several small bridges, led by Marian, they continued along a high walled street, narrow as an alley, arriving at a tiny piazzetta, and a stone white church. Away from the lagoon, Willie realised that it was in fact spectacularly hot. The air was mist-thin and motionless. The city felt as if it had no skin, it lay unpeeled to the elements. Marian turned to speak in a low voice to Willie. This was the Dalmatian church favoured by Ruskin (the last part sunk to a total whisper). 'Do you not want J. to come in?' replied Willie, under his breath, frowning and sweating. He didn't quite understand what the problem was, but it was too hot standing out here. 'He might dislike the idea,' said Marian, her set face unmoving. She opened her scarlet fan, the colour of which matched her face as she used it. Willie found the fan's movement compelling.

Johnny had sat down on the step.

'Would it be simpler if we just all walked on?' asked Willie, polite. The business of visiting a church was obviously a problem.

It was strange, though. In a crisis you got to know someone in a new way. Willie had seen Marian effortfully moulding herself to circumstances she had never anticipated, even her face was altered, as if this new blow delivered by life had made her jaw larger and more set. Willie, never prone to sentiment, the brusque, canny, spry maverick of the family, was beginning to be slightly moved by her. She stepped closer to him. 'Ruskin values the Carpaccio here highly,' she said, in a low, deliberate tone. *'You shall not find another piece of work quite the like of that little piece of work, for supreme, serene, unassuming, unfaltering sweetness of painter's perfect art.'*

Her voice and lips were trembling now, Willie had a dim notion she was clinging to a raft. 'I will take Johnny on, we will return this way,' said Willie hastily. He did so, unable to resist glancing back at Marian, who had followed her purpose — he saw the back of her linen skirt billow briefly as the church door closed. He walked on with Johnny over yet another small bridge, up, down, through the alley, and into a small triangular opening where there was a place to have refreshment in the shade outside. Their faces were wet with sweat. Willie thought of the tremendous expense of each day at the Hotel Europa; of how much richer these two poor devils were than he.

It was a bad situation. They must pack and leave as soon as possible.

They left the next morning. They went to Verona. Then they travelled northwards into the mountains, the Alps. The heat was less, the air fresher. Having had breakfast with Willie, Marian returned to her room, shortly there was a knock on her door. It was Johnny. He had a puzzled look. 'I wanted to say good morning,' he said. Marian stood where she was. His arms were by his side. She had little hope left for him. In the last days, she had made herself try to imagine their future life together; the prospect was frightful. They stood there, the silence went on between them. 'It has been terrible,' he said. He looked dazed. She examined him with her eyes, she had become hard and suspicious. He came in, sat on the chair that was near the door. 'I have said terrible things,' he admitted, but in bewilderment. He sat in silence, staring ahead, as if absorbed by what was in his mind. One or two silent tears had begun to go down his cheeks. Soberly, she got up, and sat by him. Her own tears were beginning to go down her own cheeks, also scarce and silent. The sadness and terror of the last days were stirred up by the fragment of hope she couldn't help feeling, at his face, where the eyes were no longer cold. She could bear it no longer, and she sobbed, her heart too full, putting her face in her hands.

9

The journey home was made in stages. The first two days in Innsbruck it rained and they could not see the mountains: the town was clothed in mist. The sky cleared on the third day; the sight was a tonic, hot fresh sunshine, coolness coming fast in the evening, and the high Austrian Alps in view. 'Venice was a hell,' announced Willie, lighting a cigar. Johnny was eating better; to Willie's satisfaction, they were all eating better. He noted the quiet, careful affection between the couple. Curious, he thought to himself. In Munich, they went to the Glyptothek and the Alte Pinakothek.

The train was going noisily northwards. Marian thought of her last meeting with Mr Bunney. A kind man. She had admitted to him that in the previous week she had had to put out efforts and powers she had never been accustomed to use before and did not think she possessed. She trusted Mr Bunney. Now, on the train, she reflected how queer it was that she had told so much to a man she hardly knew. In a small way, it was so with Willie, and with Dr Ricchetti. Dr Ricchetti had said that any resumption of what he called conjugal relations was dangerous to Johnny, who had a 'delicate nervous system'.

In England, they went straight to Witley. The sight of the English country-side, the copses, low hedges, the small enclosed fields in the mild English sun, was dear. Gradually their life resumed. She had written to friends that Johnny had become ill in Venice owing to the heat and the unhealthy air and drains.

They went to stay at Weybridge, with Johnny's family. They dined with Florence and Eleanor. Sometimes Johnny saw his episode, as he called it, as a lost part of his life, as other people viewed blackouts when they had been drinking. The memory made him afraid. Marian watched his health carefully. He quickly became tired.

They saw all his extended family, including Henry Bullock-Hall in his large estate at Six Mile Bottom in Cambridgeshire. Marian and Johnny went to stay. Gently, they were reviving their social life. As Henry showed them the library he had built for the tenants on his estate — he had long ago remarried since Zibbie's death — Marian found herself wondering what he had heard of Johnny's illness. She wondered if the truth in any form had reached him. Assuredly it would leak out, this she knew. It always did.

They were staying until Monday, and on Sunday night they gathered with guests in the great drawing room, under the beams. It was a gracious setting: through the windows in the early September evening light, she could see the smooth green lawn, in which was a small weeping tree, surrounded by a circle of uncut grass. Marian talked to Henry Sidgwick, one of the trustees of the Lewes scholarship, they discussed the current scholar. Their chat was broken by the arrival of Richard Claverhouse Jebb, the classicist. Some time after that she was approached by Mrs Jebb, whose slender elegance had already caught Marian's eye. She knew something of Mrs Jebb's interesting history. 'It's an honour to meet you,' Mrs Jebb was saying, smiling.

'You are from America, are you not?' enquired Marian. 'I am a little acquainted with your husband.'

Mrs Jebb was, she knew, married for the second time, having been widowed at the age of twenty-eight. Marian's sympathetic eye was already alerted.

'It is one of my most significant memories from before we were wed,' cried Caroline Jebb, warmly. She was pretty and shapely in deep grey satin; neck encircled by pearls. 'He always remembers talking about Sophocles with you; it is a pleasure now to meet you in person.'

'Thank you,' Marian said, earnestly. 'It was, in fact, an essay by your husband that woke me to Sophocles —'

'The delineation of the first primitive emotions,' said Caroline Jebb, smiling.

'You remember the phrase,' said Marian, also smiling.

'The moment stayed in the memory,' said Caroline Jebb, simply.

They dined in the great hall, around the long oak table, which would not have been out of place in a monk's refectory. Later, in the bedroom, unlacing her stays, Marian remembered Mrs Jebb with quiet pleasure.

She must have slept for an hour, when she woke with a ferocious thirst. Sir Paget had said that with her complaint, she could expect to be thirsty. The drinking jug was empty. In the other bed, Johnny was sleeping. She lit her candle, it was not long after midnight; she would take her cup to the new bathing room Henry had installed. Stepping out of the bedroom, it was completely dark: she held out her candle — it shed a small circle of light. Walking carefully down the dark corridor she noticed low sounds from the room on her right; thought nothing of them; but suddenly she stopped, a soft uneasy thrill passing through her. A voice was rising clearly from the blur of sound, that sounded like Caroline Jebb.

'... felt sad for her! ... has done everything to look young ...'

There followed the low tone of a man, presumably Richard Jebb. Marian held her breath. Then the woman, sounding irritated, or sad, but strangely emphatic: ' ... will suffer for what she has done ... not a person in the room, Mr Cross included, whose mother she might not have been.'

Silence, the indistinct low sound of the man. Caroline Jebb again, wise: '... obviously hurt her to have him talk so much to me ... has never heartily liked a pretty woman, everyone knows ...'

Marian didn't move for some seconds. She was suddenly very cold.

She returned the way she came, noiselessly. Her entry, or her absence, seemed to have woken Johnny. 'Are you all right?' came his voice, soft in the dark.

Saying she was, she blew out the candle, which was shaky in her hand. In bed, her heart was beating. The words kept coming, repeating, penetrating her like needles. She lay, breathing quickly. No, she could not sleep. After some time she got up, drew a curtain. The moon was silver: the garden faintly illuminated, unearthly, still-looking, the weeping tree visible in the circle of long grass. She sat, finally returned to bed.

Lying there, she tried to settle herself. It was only what she knew, after all. She had had a small glimpse, outside her purview. It was not afforded to most people. She was awake for more than an hour, then her thoughts began sliding and weaving into dream, and then strangely, *The Mill on the Floss*. She hadn't thought of it for a long time. She would find that passage tomorrow.

The following day, back home, Johnny was pacing around, notebook in hand, planning the removal of books and furniture to Cheyne Walk. Watching him, Caroline Jebb's words echoed in Marian's mind. *Not a person in the room, Mr Cross included, whose mother she might not have been ...* Of course she was seen like this. She was her own great puzzle. She had known this when she married him.

Johnny turned. 'I wanted to suggest,' he said, with his old innocent good humour, 'that we walk. The sun has come out.'

Her thoughts dropped away. She said it was a lovely idea, and rose to join him.

Epilogue

This day stands alone. I am not afraid of forgetting, but as heretofore I record her teaching while the sound is still fresh in my soul's ear. This morning at 10 when the wreath I had ordered — white flowers bordered with laurel leaves — came, I drove with it to Cheyne Walk, giving it silently to the silent cook. Then, instinct guiding — it seemed to guide one right all day — I went to Highgate — stopping on the way to get some violets — I was not sure for what purpose ... Then I laid my violets at the head of Mr Lewes' solitary grave and left the already gathering crowd to ask which way the entrance would be. Then I drifted towards the chapel — standing first for a while under the colonnade where a child asked me 'Was it the late George Eliot's wife was going to be buried?' — I think I said Yes ... Then someone claimed a passage through the thickening crowd and I followed in his wake and found myself without effort in a sort of vestibule past the door which kept back the crowd ... then the solemn procession passed me. The coffin bearers paused in the very doorway, I pressed a kiss upon the pall and trembled violently as I stood motionless else, in the still silence with nothing to mar the realization of that intense moment's awe. Then — it was hard to tell the invited mourners from the other waiting friends — men many of whose faces I knew — and so I passed among them into the chapel — entering a forward pew ... I saw her husband's face, pale and still; he forced himself aloof from the unbearable world in sight ... but what moved me most was the passage — in the Church Service lesson — it moved me like the voice of God — of Her.

Awe thrilled me. As at the presence of God. In the memory of her life bare grain — oh God, my God. My love what fruit should such seed bring forth in us — I will force myself to remember your crushing prophesy — that I was to do better work than you had — that cannot be, my Best! and all mine is always yours, but oh! Dearest! Dearest! it shall not be less unworthy of you than it must ... The grave was deep and narrow — the flowers filled all the level space. I turned away with the first — Charles Lewes pressed my hand as we gave the last look. Then I turned up the hill and walked through the rain by a road unknown before to Hampstead and a station. Then through the twilight I cried and moaned aloud.

Edith Simcox's diary, 29 December 1880

Only three weeks after moving in to Cheyne Walk, Johnny Cross was alone in the tall fine home overlooking the Thames. He was a widower. Before that, exhausted by moving, just before entering the house, they stayed in Bailey's Hotel in Kensington for two days, reading Tennyson, Goethe, Comte. He had the strange feeling of one who had spent much time getting tremendously prepared for an event — that never happened.

She wanted to be buried in Westminster Abbey, he said. This was the least he could do. Spencer, Sidgwick collected signatures; but they were warned off. An atheist who had lived unwed with a man for a quarter of a century, to be buried in the Abbey! Johnny gave way.

But he was certain it was what she had wanted. He was sure he could remember where she first mentioned it, the Bridge of Sighs in Venice.

Yet it was not all over. Though something had broken with her death, he had to admit to himself that some great project still hung mistily, rainbow-coloured, in the air.

The wine he was sipping began to taste sour as he took stock. Almost certainly, the burden of writing her Life must fall on him. Who else could he trust with this sacred office? He knew exactly who was going to come knocking at the door, with maniacal plans. He would, he must, thwart Edith Simcox. Often Marian had talked about hard, prying, greedy eyes. Who would understand her yearning and complicated, loving and driven soul? With trepidation, he opened the teak chest with the worn metal corners containing her diaries and letters.

He shut himself up to read. He opened at random the first one. Geneva. Baldly confessional, wistful, self-critical. He read on. — Good heavens! He hesitated, then made himself rip the page, as one might rip off a plaster — quickly.

Brett brought him coffee, and apple pie — 'No — No' — he waved Brett away. He had the extracted page in his hand, he crumpled it, threw it like an absurdly light tennis ball into the fire. Gone. She would be pleased. He continued reading. No — there was nothing for it — he tore out, then tore out again.

In the new year, Willie came to stay. 'Thought I'd better keep you company in the palatial.' Palatial was Willie's short-hand term for the tall house overlooking the Thames. 'Ah, Johnny. You sad old thing. After all that —'

They went for silent walks, under the leafless trees, in the cold, by the Thames.

★ ★ ★

Upstairs in Finsbury Park, I am writing the last pages of the book. The sun is slanting in and getting in my eyes. I close the laptop.

'Kate?'

It's Hans, slightly out of breath. His shirt is outside his trousers and he asks if I want to see where he's put the desk. We go downstairs. The black desk — it's just been delivered — is next to the fireplace where Billy now likes to curl up. I say it looks great.

'What's wrong with it?'

'Nothing.'

'Come on, come on ...'

He's smiling with that percipient gleam.

'No — I just — you know what? It's fine. I mean, maybe it's a bit close to the fireplace —'

We move it to the other wall, then briefly embrace, as we haven't been living together long; and it's still a half surprise to find ourselves near each other, for the evening, and the night, and the next day.

Ann is having her baby, and the father is Jo Devlin.

Letting go of Hans, I see a postcard on the floor, where the desk was. Highgate Cemetery, Eliot's grave. 'Ah!' he says. 'That's where it all started.'

'Really?'

'For sure!'

'Maybe.' I can't resist being dubious. Hans laughs, shakes his head. We are, I think, perfectly imperfect together.

Upstairs I shut the door, and return to my desk to write the final paragraphs.

$$\star\ \star\ \star$$

Marian is gone, Marian has died, but the impulses and emotions she generated continue. So although Johnny will never go near an altar again — he lives unmarried till 1924 — in the immediate aftermath the old rivalry continues. Edith goes to Coventry three days after Marian's funeral to gather material for the Life she wants to write. Johnny visits her, puts her straight. She steps aside.

Herbert Spencer hears that Johnny is writing the Life, and makes sure to tell him that it was a fabrication about a romance between himself and Marian. The world must know, in spite of his great regard for her, that he never found her physically attractive.

Henry James visits Johnny. Over lunch, Johnny modestly jokes that he was a cart-horse yoked to a racer. Henry James demurs, but smiles into his beard. *My private impression*, he writes to his sister, *is that if she had not died, she would have killed him. He couldn't keep up the intellectual pace — all Dante and Goethe, Cervantes and the Greek tragedians.*

Edith Simcox's hungry love continues. She becomes friends with Barbara and Maria Congreve, and discovers, in an odd way to her delight, that Maria Congreve loved her darling 'lover-wise', also.

Edith publishes her strange, fictional hybrid book, *Episodes.*

Are you jealous, sweetheart, of my amours with the spirits of the waves and flowers? And besides, what was there to tell? It is a long story, and yet it comes to very little.

I was ill and went to the seaside, and the waves broke, sweet wild flowers grew, and the changing sky was overhead. I saw visions and dreamed dreams, but rash mortals fare ill who would woo the very gods. The island imps teased me, they hid when my heart was aching; but I think, darling, they meant it kindly, for after every trick they played me came back the memory of a sweet, fair face, with grave brown eyes that could not tease or trifle; and but for their mischievous bright magic I had despaired at once of life and love, and — Marian — you.

Author's Note and Selected Bibliography

This book is heavily indebted to other books. Perhaps most of all, to *George Eliot: A Biography* by Gordon Haight, with its special wealth of detail and insight; Rosemary Ashton's fine *George Eliot: A Life* and *G. H. Lewes: An Unconventional Victorian*; Kathryn Hughes' briskly excellent *George Eliot: The Last Victorian*; and Edith Simcox's *Autobiography of a Shirtmaker*, ed. Constance Fulmer and Margaret Barfield.

Other books that have informed this one include: Rosemary Bodenheimer's *The Real Life of Mary Ann Evans*; and her equally penetrating essay 'Autobiography in Fragments: The Elusive life of Edith Simcox'. Also: Rebecca Mead's illuminating *The Road to Middlemarch*; Nancy Henry's *The Life of George Eliot*; Ina Taylor's *George Eliot: Woman of Contradictions*; *George Eliot* by Jennifer Uglow; *George Eliot: The Emergent Self* by Ruby V. Redinger; Gordon Haight's *George Eliot and John Chapman, with John Chapman's Diaries*; Rosemary Ashton's *142 Strand*; *George Eliot: Interviews and Recollections* edited by K. K. Collins; *A George Eliot Chronology* by Timothy Hands; *George Eliot: Novelist, Lover, Wife* by Brenda Maddox. Henry James' *Autobiography*; *Herbert Spencer and The Invention of Modern Life* by Mark Francis; *Johnnie Cross: The Intriguing Story Behind George Eliot's Mysterious Last Year* by Terence de Vere White; *Trollope* by Victoria Glendinning; *Edith Simcox and George Eliot* by Keith McKenzie; *A Circle of Sisters* by Judith Flanders; *Memorials of Edward Burne-Jones* by Georgiana Burne-Jones; *Barbara Leigh Smith Bodichon: Feminist, Artist and Rebel* by Pam Hirsch; *Emily Davies and the Liberation of Women* by

Daphne Bennett; Gillian Beer's dazzling *Knowing A Life: Edith Simcox — Sat est Vixisse? George Eliot's English Travels* by Kathleen McCormack; *George Eliot's Feminism* by June Szirotny; *Memoirs and Letters of Sir James Paget*; *Letters of Anne Thackeray Ritchie*; *George Eliot and Herbert Spencer* by Nancy Paxton; *Recollections and Impressions* by Eleanor Mary Sellar.

I have drawn throughout on Gordon Haight's edition of *George Eliot Letters*, as well as *The Journals of George Eliot*, ed. Harris and Johnston; and also *George Eliot's Life, as Related in Her Letters and Journals*, put together by Johnny Cross. I have also had recourse to *George Eliot's Middlemarch Notebooks*, ed. Pratt and Neufeldt; and Jerome Beaty's *Middlemarch: From Notebook to Novel*. For the original Dante text I have used the Princeton University Press edition.

Events in the novel are closely based on events as they happened in real life, and it has been my intention to try to imagine my way, as faithfully as possible, in to Eliot's experience as it might have been. On occasion I have tampered with real-life events. The most significant instance of this is when Johnny Cross and Henry James meet in my book at the Priory.

In real life, Henry James did visit George Eliot in May 1869, only to find Thornie — days after Thornie's return from Africa — on the floor in agony; and he did rush off to try to find Dr Paget for morphine, but Johnny Cross was not present.

Henry James wrote up this experience in his *Autobiography*, and I have drawn on his account for dialogue.

Throughout, I have drawn on Eliot's letters for text and dialogue, and Edith Simcox's diary, her *Autobiography of a Shirtmaker*, for the same.

I am grateful to Rosemary Ashton for talking to me about George Eliot over tea; to Ina Taylor for her hospitality in Shropshire, and conversation about Eliot's relationship with Johnny Cross, about which she made such intriguing claims in her biography; and also to Felicia Richardson, descendant of Johnny Cross, who did her best to pass on glimmers of family folklore concerning her elusive ancestor. I am grateful to Felicia for her hospitality, and for her kindness, too, in driving me to see Lincoln cathedral. Thanks also to Rebecca Lancaster for patiently sifting through Terence de Vere White's files in the Howard Gottlieb Library in Boston for me.

Thanks to Kate Summerscale for her encouragement, critical counsel and interesting talk; to Denise Bigio, for her perceptive reading; to my mother, Edna O'Shaughnessy, for her consistent belief and encouragement; to my husband, William Fitzgerald, for the same, and for reading a variety of texts; to my son, Patrick, for his close careful reading of this manuscript. Thanks to Henry Sutton. Thanks above all to my wonderful agent Rebecca Carter, whose judgement is so sure, and who has guided me so patiently through drafts; and to my editor Philip Gwyn Jones, for his vision and brilliant suggestions. Thank you to Molly Slight for such sensitive and careful editing. Thank you finally to my family, William, Patrick, Tom, and Beatrice, who have, I feel, lived long enough with George Eliot hovering around the house.